THE TREASURE HOUSE OF
MARTIN HEWS

THE
TREASURE HOUSE OF
MARTIN HEWS

By

E. PHILLIPS OPPENHEIM

Wildside Press

THE TREASURE HOUSE OF
MARTIN HEWS

CHAPTER I

In a fit of utter dejection, I stopped in the middle of
the long cinder path and looked miserably around me.
It was, perhaps without exception, the ugliest landscape
upon which I had ever gazed—a flat and swampy region,
ignored, apparently, by the agriculturist and scorned by
even the most optimistic of builders. There were evidences
here and there of calamitous speculative enterprise—a
deserted brickyard, overrun with weedy grass, a one-
storied factory which showed no signs of ever having
been occupied, and every window of which was broken. For
the most part, however, the land was a wilderness, with
here and there an isolated and squalid-looking cottage.
The fields, the grass of which seemed to lack any shade
of colour or breath of vitality, were separated by dykes
in which black, unwholesome water stood stagnant. A
few cows seemed oppressed by ruminating gloom. There
were no trees, no birds save occasional flocks of inflying
seagulls, great patches of sedgy, irreclaimable land
stretching to the river banks. In the far distance, upon
the other side of the unseen waterway, were factory
chimneys, gaunt and stark, looming through the misty
sky. For sound, in this dreary waste, there was only the
screech of a passing locomotive from the branch line by
which I had completed my journey, the distant hooting
of a steamer, or the melancholy call of the drifting gulls.
There came upon me, as I lingered there, a strong inclination to turn around, retrace my steps to the station, with its draughty shed for a booking office, sit down
upon that solitary, decrepit bench, and, abandoning my

enterprise, wait for the train which would take me back to the warmth and humanity of a great city. Then my hand stole into my trousers pocket, the coins jingled through my fingers—ninepence-halfpenny, and an oblong piece of cardboard—my return third-class ticket to London. I remembered that this completed the total of my worldly possessions, and off I started again down that hideous cinder track, facing what had seemed to me from the first moment it had loomed up before me, the grimmest, the ugliest, the most fearsome building I had ever seen or conceived. It reminded me of one of those unnatural nightmares, the earliest sign of incipient lunacy, when one's brain fails, and the ordinary buildings of some fancied city suddenly assume gigantic unnatural proportions, a hundred times the size of any possible effort of human hands. There was no doubt, however, as to the reality of this architectural abortion, and, as I stepped over the stile into the road and caught a fuller view of it rising from perfectly flat lands, arrogant, overmastering in its bare, assertive ugliness, an unpleasant conviction stole in upon me. I stopped the only human being I had seen since I had left the station—a road-mender, plodding slowly through the mud.

"Can you tell me what that building or institution is?" I asked him.

He turned a rheumaticky neck, and followed my pointing finger.

"That be Breezeley Mansion, sir," he replied.

With that he had had enough of me and went on his way, and I, struggling with my fit of nervous aversion, pushed on until I stood almost under the shadow of this monstrosity of brick and stone. There was no lodge, no wall to protect it from the road, no garden. There it stood, a great building which age seemed only to have rendered more hideous, straight-fronted, with rows of uninviting windows, and at the two ends round towers, with huge windows. It was big enough for a prison or an asylum, and unpleasing enough for either. That it should be the dwelling place of any sane man seemed to me incredible, and yet in my pocket reposed a letter addressed to "Martin Hews, Esq., Breezeley Mansion," and that letter, together with ninepence-halfpenny, was my last resource against starvation.

I trod the granite avenue, pressed the electric bell, and received my first shock. The door was opened even before my finger had released the knob. A butler, who would not have disgraced a Grosvenor Square mansion, opened it and leaned forward with an air of benevolent enquiry.

"I have come down from London to see Mr. Hews," I explained. "I have a letter of introduction to him."

The man smiled at me reassuringly.

"That is quite all right, sir. Will you come this way?"

He led me across a hall which, in those confused moments, seemed to me like the anteroom of a palace, motioned me to enter a small, automatic lift, followed me in and closed the gates. We shot up some three storeys, after which he again took charge of me, ushered me down a corridor where my feet fell soundlessly upon the thickly piled carpet, and at its further end touched the knob of a bell. We heard its gentle tinkling in the room, and almost immediately, without any visible agency, the door of an apartment almost as spacious as a museum swung open.

"The gentleman you were expecting, sir," the butler announced, leading the way towards a distant corner—and forthwith took his leave.

I advanced a few steps farther and stood staring like the clumsiest of rustics. Before me, seated at a large rosewood writing table, upon which were several telephone receivers, a row of ivory push bells, and various

other unusual-looking instruments, was the man whom I
had come to visit. My first impression of him was that
he was seated—but at that moment I could not be sure of
anything definite as regards his posture. He was enclosed
in what seemed to be an amazing sort of Bathchair, the
front of which was hidden in the knee hole of the desk,
so that only the upper part of his body was visible. The
effect he produced upon me, during those first few minutes,
remains to this day an indescribable thing. One would
have expected, from an afflicted person, a certain delicacy
of expression and outline, the pallor which is nearly always associated with every sort of suffering. The man
before me was of an entirely different type. His face was
inclined to be round in shape. He had colour upon his
cheeks which at first seemed to me as though it must be
unnatural. His brown eyes were curiously prominent, almost beady. He had carefully trimmed, bushy eyebrows of
a lighter shade, and a mass of brown hair, arranged with
such absolute perfection that from the first I suspected
it to be a wig. His mouth was by far his most attractive
feature. It had a delicacy of its own, and a sensitiveness
almost childish. He was dressed with meticulous care in
dark clothes, his folded satin tie of deep purple fastened
by a pin with a quaint foreign stone. When I tried afterwards to reconstruct in my mind his personality, from
amongst a haze of tangled impressions, I could think of
nothing but the curving mouth and prominent eyes which
seemed never to leave my face.

"You are Major Owston?" he asked, looking across
at me.

"That is my name, sir," I answered.

"What sort of employment do you want?"

"Any sort in the world which will keep me from starvation."

He scrutinised me thoughtfully, raised his hand and

pointed to a chair. I sat down, and would have moved it a little nearer to his desk, but found to my amazement that it was screwed to the floor, and that underneath the seat was a maze of wire and tubes. I found also that it faced the great window through which the light was streaming in.

"You will forgive the peculiarity of the chair," my host begged. "I have visitors of many sorts, and I like sometimes to know exactly how far they are away from me. It would perhaps amuse you—"

He broke off, and touched one of a line of ivory knobs on the right-hand side of his desk. I felt a sudden tingling in my arms and legs. If the room had been on fire, I could not have moved from my place. He chuckled softly, touched another knob, and everything was again normal. He rubbed his hands together with positively childish delight.

"One of my little devices," he explained, with a curious touch of vanity in his tone. "I am a helpless person, you see, and I must defend myself. . . . So you want any sort of employment, Henry Owston? Are there any limitations to that somewhat daring statement?"

"None that I can think of," I assured him.

He eyed me critically.

"You are not overscrupulous, then?"

"Not in a general way. I don't want to get into trouble. I have been in prison once. That was quite enough for me."

"In England?"

"No, in France."

"Ah, I remember," he murmured, nodding his head reflectively. "It was at Marseilles, was it not? That affair with a French Artillery Officer. You have a violent temper, I imagine."

I looked at him in astonishment. Not even Leonard

Joyce, my friend who had given me the letter of introduction, knew of that episode in my life to which Martin Hews had alluded.

"If I have," I told him, after a moment's deliberation, "it is very seldom roused, and there is generally sufficient provocation."

He eyed me appraisingly.

"You are how tall, Major Owston?" he enquired.

I was a little surprised, but I answered him at once.

"Six feet three and a half, sir."

"Magnificently developed around the shoulders," he went on, moving his head a little sideways. "A trifle underfed, I should say, by the look of you. I have need of strong men, Major Owston, both for my own protection, and to carry on my business."

"I am not a weakling," I assured him.

"Apparently not," he assented. "Let me see. Shall I tell you a little more about yourself? In the Inter-Varsity Sports eighteen years ago, you won all the prizes which were worth taking. Later you have thrown the hammer as only the Americans can throw it. You were in the semi-finals of the Amateur Boxing Championship twelve years ago. There was a rumour that it was a gesture of chivalry which prevented your winning. You were supposed to be good enough for county cricket, even for Yorkshire, but the war came, and you developed into a keen soldier. You did a little more than average well—twice mentioned, I believe, and the D.S.O. Afterwards you had the usual bad luck of a man who had not settled upon his profession definitely when the war broke out. You left your regiment and tried soldiering in Morocco with the Spaniards. Then, of course, there was that French affair—rather an unfortunate episode just then. Anything I have forgotten, Major Owston?"

I was speechless. I could think of no living person who

could have told me as much as this stranger had done. He watched my surprise with that same smile of absolutely childish gratification.

"Ah, well," he went on, "if I take you into my employ you will realise that it is my business sometimes to know everything. Directly Joyce mentioned your name, I began to set enquiries on foot. By-the-by, did he prepare you for the fact that I was an invalid?"

"He gave me to understand," I admitted diffidently, "that you were—that you had lost the use of your legs."

He frowned as though, for some reason, my answer annoyed him.

"I never had any legs," he explained abruptly. "I am a human freak, Major Owston. I was born without legs. You can see very nearly all there is of me. That is why I sit in the most amazing motor chair that has ever been designed. My own invention, Major—entirely my own invention."

I muttered a word of sympathy, which he acknowledged gravely.

"I wonder," he speculated, "whether I really lose much through not having legs. You shall judge. Sit still. I will give you an exhibition."

There followed the most extraordinary performance I had ever seen in my life. With the touch of a finger upon the steering wheel of his chair, an engine began to throb, and he glided from behind the desk in a graceful backward curve. He came to a standstill, and then suddenly seemed to flash away from before my eyes. He was across at the other side of the room before I could realise that he had moved, threading his course amongst chairs and tables, skirting the edge of various articles of furniture with the most amazing precision, now and then revolving, running backwards with only a careless turn of the head over his shoulder, never losing that curiously conceited smile, and glancing more than once quickly across at me as though for my approbation. Finally he passed me like a streak and before I could thoroughly collect myself he was seated again opposite to me behind the table. The motor ceased to throb. His eyes sought mine triumphantly. He was evidently wrapped in deep enjoyment of my stupefaction.

"Have you ever seen anything like that?" he demanded.

"Never in my life," I assured him, as soon as I could find words. "I can't even now understand how such delicate steering can ever be learned. It's—it's miraculous!"

His smile was like the smile of a child whose dolls have been praised, or a mother whose infant has been flattered. It transformed his whole appearance, and it helped me to appreciate the persistence of those small vanities which were woven like a thread through the man's whole being. Incidentally it gave me confidence. I had no longer any fear about that ninepence-halfpenny in my trousers pocket. He pointed to the window—the great, uncurtained window in the full light of which I sat.

"Go over there," he ordered. "Follow the road back to London. Tell me if you see anything."

I obeyed him and looked searchingly along that soggy, ill-made, muddy thoroughfare, stretching across the marshes bordered by the threadbare hedges and yawning dykes, to where a lowering mass of mingled mist and smoke hung over the approaches to the city.

"I see the road until it disappears," I reported. "It is empty."

He glanced at an electric clock upon the table and frowned. Then he lifted from its stand one of the telephone receivers by which he was surrounded and spoke into it so softly that I failed to hear a word he said. Again he turned towards me.

"Your eyes appear to be strong," he remarked. "How far can you follow the road backwards?"

"Past the station," I told him, "past what seems to be a sewerage farm, across a wooden bridge to what might be a main road beyond."

"Look again," he enjoined. "Watch."

There ensued a brief silence—a silence of perhaps three minutes—during which no sign of human life appeared upon the miserable plain across which I looked. At last, at the far end of the road, there was a speck. I scrutinised it narrowly.

"There is a vehicle—a motor car—coming," I announced.

"Describe it to me."

I waited until it came nearer. It was being driven at a great speed, rocking from side to side upon the road, sending up little fountains of water from the holes across which it sped. I turned my head.

"It is a very big car—I should say a Rolls-Royce. It is being driven apparently by a chauffeur. There is another man inside, and I think a girl."

My new employer—already I felt that I was in his service—nodded shortly.

"Come here," he directed. "Turn around. Look at that wall."

He pointed to a strip of oak panelling, not far from the door, and before my eyes, without any visible agency, it parted and slid gently open. Afterwards I knew that he had touched a button under his desk.

"Go in there," he ordered. "You can listen to all that is said by means of the instrument standing on a bracket upon your right-hand side. There is a lookout hole there too. If I should strike the desk with the flat of my hand twice, I need help. The door will open by means of a button underneath the bracket."

"I understand," I assured him.

I moved towards the recess. As I was crossing the threshold, he called after me.

"With the flat of my hand twice," he repeated, "but do not be disappointed if nothing happens, Henry Owston. Others have been before you, and waited in vain. I run my risks as does every man who has enemies, but never yet, poor cripple though I am, have I had to call for help. To-night, however—it may be different. It depends in what spirit my visitor comes. . . . Take your place, please. Adjust the microphone to your ears. You can open the door, remember, if I give the signal, by pressing the button just below the instrument."

After which instructions, he dismissed me with a little wave of the hand, and I passed into my hiding place.

CHAPTER II

I FOUND my temporary refuge larger than I had expected, with some sort of ventilation from overhead, and lit by an electric bulb which flashed out with the closing of the door. I fitted the microphone to my head, and established myself in a not uncomfortable chair before the spy-hole. Then I suddenly received an unexpected shock. Exactly opposite to the opening through which I had entered there flashed, through a chink in the wall, a thin line of light. Noiselessly the panels rolled back and a woman stood framed in the aperture—a woman whom I judged at first, notwithstanding the youthfulness of her figure, to be elderly. Then, as she lowered her head a little, I saw that what I had taken for grey hair was in reality a very beautiful shade of ash-coloured blonde, fine as silk, and glimmering almost to gold as she stooped to enter the closet and stood for a moment under the electric bulb. She held up her finger, and I checked my first exclamation of surprise.

"Pay attention, please, to what I have to say, and answer me in as low a tone as possible," she begged.

"But who are you?" I enquired.

"I will explain directly. Put on your microphone again, and listen for the opening of the door. Your mission, which I suppose is to guard Martin Hews, does not commence until then."

I obeyed her, almost unconsciously. Her voice, soft and pleasant though it was, had in it some curiously compelling quality. With the instrument fixed to my ears, my sense of hearing became at once more acute. I could hear the scratching of a pen upon note-paper, the hissing of a log in the grate; otherwise there was silence in the room.

"You are poor," she continued. "You came down here on a desperate chance. You may not know it, but you have failed. Martin Hews has decided not to employ you. The car is already ordered to take you back to the station."

It was like a sentence of fate, and my heart sank.

"How do you know that?" I demanded.

"It is my business. I am Martin Hews' niece. I know most of the secrets even of this house."

"Well," I sighed, "I hope you are making a mistake. Unless you have been listening—"

"I have been listening," she interrupted, "and I know my uncle."

"He was pretty well my last chance," I confided gloomily.

"Then you have lost it. You are, I think you said, in straightened means. You can earn this, if you care to."

She handed me a folded slip of paper. I opened it out and found that it was a twenty-pound Bank of England note.

"Who am I to serve for this?" I asked. "Your uncle or you?"

"Me," she answered calmly. "Hush!"

I, too, had heard the click of the motor chair. I looked through my peephole. Its occupant had simply changed his position in order to reach a box of cigarettes. He lit one and recommenced his writing. The room was still empty. I turned back to the girl. Her eyes were fixed upon me—grey eyes with a glint of green in them, indifferent, almost inhuman, as it seemed to me at that moment, yet curiously impressive under her strange-coloured hair. For the first time I realised that in her own fashion—and a very distinctive one it was—she was beautiful.

"You can earn this twenty pounds," she whispered, "by leaving your place here and catching the train for London which starts in twenty minutes. I will show you the way to where the car is waiting. All that you will have to do is to deliver a letter in Berkeley Square, and never come near this house again."

We looked at one another for a few seconds in silence. Her eyes never left mine, but it would have taken a cleverer man than I to have guessed what was passing in her brain.

"If your uncle will not engage me," I said, "that is my misfortune. I have accepted the task of watching here until his visitor has gone, and I must carry it out."

"Take my advice," she begged. "Don't waste your time. You owe nothing to Martin Hews. Soon he will dismiss you with a cynical word of farewell. There is not a soul in this house who does not hate him. Those of us who live here and obey his orders do it because we must. As yet you are free. Take my offer and hurry away."

"And leave him without a protector in case there is trouble," I reminded her.

She laughed very softly, but with a scorn which was almost malicious.

"My uncle can look after himself," she assured me. "Besides, if his time has come, you would be of very little help to him. It would be all over before you could get halfway across the room. Will you come?"

I looked at her once more, and my decision, if anything, was strengthened by what I saw in her eyes, but failed wholly to read.

"I will not," I decided, turning my back upon her, and peering through my spy-hole. . . . "There is some one coming into the room. Please go away."

Apparently she was convinced of my obduracy, and, in a measure, reconciled to it, for I heard the door roll smoothly back and the click of its fastening. I had no time to indulge in speculations as to this strange happening, for it was obvious that the expected visitors had arrived. I heard the opening of the door and the butler's sonorous voice. I saw Martin Hews' eyebrows go up, saw him lean a little forward in his strange chair. Then the other two figures came into view—a fair, sturdily built man, commonplace enough in appearance, but with a bulldog type of feature and keen blue eyes. There was a look of suffering in his face as though he were ill, and he leaned upon a stick. He was dressed in reasonable clothing, but his hair was unkempt, his collar crumpled, one of his shoe laces undone. I judged that he had come from some adventure, for there was an air of exhaustion about him, and in his eyes there was fear. Holding on to his arm was a girl—a little Jewess she seemed to me—small, with an exquisite cameo-like face, dark brown eyes and hair, and brilliantly red lips. She looked defiantly at Martin Hews.

"I was expecting you, Jim Donkin—but the young lady?"

The man sank into the fixed chair with a little groan of relief.

"You'll have to look after her, Guv'nor," he declared. "If she can't come with me, you'll have to keep her safe. You know what happened last night?"

"I know that you committed a murder," Martin Hews observed calmly. "You are trying me very high, Donkin. You were on your own last night, you must remember, and it is not an easy thing to protect a murderer. Tell me about the girl."

"You know who she is. This is Rachel. 'Tain't her fault, but it was because of her the row began last night. The newspapers haven't got half of it yet. There were a hundred of us fighting down in the Mews, back of the Bethnal

Green Road, and Phil Abrahams wasn't the only one who got his. We were obeying orders too, you know, Guv'nor. The cops were getting too inquisitive about what we were really out for. You wanted a real hooligan fight, and we b——y well had it."

"There isn't a great deal of time to waste if I am to get you away," Martin Hews warned him. "Why have you brought the girl with you? It is quite true that I am willing to undertake the task of looking after her, but I did not intend to have her here."

"Where in hell could I leave her in London?" the man demanded. "Abrahams took her from me, as he had sworn to Joseph that he would, but he was a dying man before he could hand her over, bleeding to death in Aldgate Passage. We're pretty well wiped out now, though. They'll get her if I leave her in London."

"Half a dozen of 'em," the girl intervened, "half a dozen of 'em who reckon I never ought to have left Joseph, and who mean to get me back if they can. Mind you, they'll soon forget it," she went on, "and I don't know that I'm so scared as it is. Joseph would have something to say if they turned ugly, but Jim here, he's all for me lying low. You're afraid Joseph will get me again, ain't you, Jim?" she asked, with a mocking laugh.

"I'd come back from the dead, blast you, if you went back to him," the man growled. "What about me, Chief?" he went on, looking anxiously across the desk. "It wasn't exactly your work we were on last night, but you wanted a row—a real, ordinary row—to put the cops off the scent. Yesterday's began on the race course, went on in the train from Newmarket, and finished—my Gawd, what a finish!—down Bethnal Green Road way."

Martin Hews leaned forward in his chair and contemplated the two. His face was unclouded, his smile almost benevolent. He might have been the head of some great charitable organisation, evolving his plans for the protection of this outcast.

"I grasp the position," he said at last. "Everything is arranged so far as you are concerned, Donkin. You must be prepared to leave here in five minutes. A car is waiting for you now. As for the young lady, I shall offer her at any rate temporary shelter."

"What, here?" she demanded, with a grimace.

"Certainly. You will be safer under this roof than anywhere. The housekeeper will look after you. As for you, Donkin, please follow my servant downstairs now. I shall keep my word and get you out of this, but you have disappointed me. I wanted Joseph's gang crushed. I wanted Joseph himself removed. You have failed me."

"If I get over this," Donkin muttered, a spasm of pain suddenly contorting his face, "I'll get Joseph as soon as I can sneak back to the country."

"That is your own affair," Martin Hews said equably. "I shall probably have settled with him myself before that can happen. In the meantime, kindly follow my servant downstairs. You will be provided with ample funds, and I wish you well; at the same time, in the struggle between you and Joseph, you are up to now the loser, and I have no use for the second best."

He dismissed them with an imperative little wave of the hand, and they disappeared, ushered out by the butler who had entered without any visible or audible means of summons. The panels glided open in front of me, and I stepped out. Martin Hews looked at me thoughtfully.

"You can drive a car?" he asked.

"I can," I answered, with a sudden return of hope.

"You can fight, I know," he continued. "Do your best to get Donkin away. If you come up against the police, you had better offer no resistance and be sure that my name is not mentioned. If any members of Joseph's gang try to intercept you, that will be a different matter. Fight if you have any chance at all. They will kill Donkin if they get him . . . Here!"

He opened the drawer and handed me a flat-handled automatic, of the latest type, fully charged. Behind me was standing once more that ubiquitous butler, waiting to show me downstairs.

"Don't use the gun if you can help it," Martin Hews enjoined. "Those things are for show more than for use, but remember they'll kill Donkin if they get him. You may report here later if all goes well. . . ."

Five minutes afterwards we were swinging down the straight, muddy road leading towards the river, in a large, open touring car, built apparently for speed. Donkin was by my side, muffled up in an overcoat and groaning every now and then in pain. A dark-complexioned chauffeur in the front crouched over his wheel. One glance I threw behind as we started off, and curiously enough I looked, as though by instinct, at one particular window. Leaning out of it was the girl who had offered me the twenty-pound note and assured me that Martin Hews had decided to turn me down. She stood like a statue, watching us. I shook my fist at her. She turned away.

CHAPTER III

WE drew up, after a ghastly six-mile drive across the wilderness of my destination, at the end of what was little better than a rough cart track leading down to the river. My companion, with a final groan, stepped heavily out, and looked with anxious eyes first along the road by which we had come, and afterwards at the motor launch moored a score of yards out in the sluggish stream. He stepped into the dinghy which was waiting under the bank, and for the first time the strained look of apprehension seemed to pass from his face.

"He's a rum little devil, but he's kept his word," he muttered, as I helped him in. "I knew if any one could get me away, he could. Tell Rachel I'm safe."

There was no other word of farewell. He clambered on to the motor launch, the dinghy was drawn up, and the former swung round and started off seaward, the spray already breaking over her as she crept into speed. I watched her for several moments, until she disappeared into the grey, drifting mist. Then, just as I was turning around, the chauffeur touched me on the shoulder. He pointed along the road by which we had come, and I saw a motor car approaching, furiously driven.

"This road don't lead anywhere, sir," he confided. "There's no room to pass, and the dykes are full. I am thinking it means a bit of trouble for us."

"Anyhow, we've done our job," I remarked, peering forward. "We've got our man away, according to orders."

"Yes, and they'll never catch him now," the chauffeur agreed. "There aren't any boats round here, and not a launch that could touch that one nearer than Rother-hithe."

"I wonder if it's the police?" I suggested.

"I don't think!" he rejoined grimly. "It's my belief it's some of the gang he's been scrapping with. Ugly fellows they are, too."

The car rushed towards us, swaying from side to side, splashing the water lying in the sunken pools of the road high into the air, more than once only just avoiding a dangerous skid. When at last, with grinding of brakes and tearing of gears, the vehicle came to a standstill about a dozen yards away from us, we were completely ignored by its occupants for several moments. An apparently young man, wearing a long motoring coat of fashionable cut, a cap pulled down over his forehead, and unusually large spectacles, slipped from his seat by the driver and strolled to the edge of the muddy bank beneath which lapped the waters of the river. His eyes followed the trail left by the disappearing motor boat, and he seemed to be doing his best to peer through the gathering gloom to her possible destination. Whilst he watched, his hand as though mechanically sought his pocket, and mine immediately followed suit. He pulled out a cigarette case, lit a cigarette, and, with a last look down the river, turned away and swung round towards us. He glanced at the chauffeur cursorily and addressed himself to me. He kept at least half a dozen paces away, and his features were completely hidden.

"To whom have I the pleasure of speaking?" he asked, a faint note of truculence lurking in his tone.

"My name is Owston—Major Owston—at your service," I answered.

"I have to thank Martin Hews for this, I suppose?" he demanded, pointing down the river.

"I am not here to answer questions," I told him.

"Mine was only a matter of form," he assured me. "You have spent, I trust, a pleasant afternoon assisting in the escape of a cowardly murderer. Present my compliments to Mr. Martin Hews and my congratulations upon his organisation. You, I imagine, are one of his new mercenaries."

I made no reply. It was an extraordinarily silent stretch of country, and there was no sound whatever, except the gentle gurgling of the water against the river bank. Curiously enough, the memory of those few seconds remained in my mind for long afterwards—the car, splashed with mud, steam rising from its bonnet, drawn up by the side of the road, its three very formidable-looking occupants staring menacingly across at us, the young man facing me, so thoroughly disguised by his coat and hat and spectacles, yet with strangely subtle suggestions of something sinister and threatening in his bitter words.

"I wonder," he speculated at last, and his tone seemed to grow in insolence, "whether you are likely to be any trouble to me in the future? Why not a life for a life, eh? It's a sound doctrine, a lonely spot, and the river's deep just here."

I answered him, I hope, with equal coolness. At all events, I know that the hand which gripped the butt end of my automatic was firm and steady.

"Your car leaves tracks," I reminded him. "Your presence here was expected. There is no part of that river so deep but that it gives up its secrets with the flow of the tide."

Perhaps he saw the dull glitter of metal raised an inch or two from my pocket. He waved his hand contemptuously towards it.

"We kill when the need comes," he said, "without fear or scruple, but we are not butchers. Add this to my message. Tell Mr. Martin Hews that I hear his gewgaw castle has become the asylum for damsels in distress. Nevertheless, when the fancy takes me to recover Rachel, I shall come and fetch her."

He touched his hat and mounted again to his place by the side of the chauffeur. The car, with its evil-looking load, moved slowly back in the reverse until it reached a turning place, when it was driven off at such a reckless pace that it was speedily out of sight. My first enterprise in the service of Martin Hews was over. Not a blow had been struck. The afternoon had ended, in fact, a little tamely, but I could very well guess what would have happened if the young man who had accosted me—and his friends—had arrived before Donkin had boarded the motor boat.

Again I sat in the fixed chair of audience and made my report to the master of Breezeley Mansion. He listened to me with a changeless, sardonic smile. It was almost as though he found food for humorous reflection in the tardy arrival of Joseph and his friends.

"So we are in the position," he remarked, when I had finished, "of holding an unwilling Helen, with Hector flying for his life and Joseph advancing to the assault. Dear me, what troubles our good nature may lead us into. Come Major Owston, do you feel inclined to help in the defence of this eagerly sought-for young woman?"

"At your bidding, sir," I replied. "May I take it from the suggestion that I am engaged?"

"You are engaged," he told me calmly. "Your salary will be a thousand a year, and if you fail to give me satisfaction I shall ask you to walk out at a moment's notice."

"What about my duties?" I queried.

"Your first and principal one is to guard my person. I

have enemies. The man Joseph, whom you probably saw to-day, is one of them. So long as Donkin's gang was in existence, I was comparatively safe. Now that they are wiped out, Joseph will look this way. I have treasures, bought and paid for, which he thinks should have gone to him. He is a fool. He was outwitted. He will always be outwitted."

"The man with whom I spoke to-day," I ventured, "seemed to me anything but a fool."

My new employer scowled. The effect upon his features was singular. His lips were withdrawn, showing his white teeth, and his beady eyes seemed to recede a little into his head. He rather resembled the statuette of some malevolent oriental deity.

"You are right," he acknowledged. "Joseph is not a fool. He has a cunning brain, he has genius, he is a great opponent. He has moments of weakness, though. He smarts always under the sense of fancied wrongs. He permits himself to hate—he hates me. Passion of that sort disturbs judgment. Feeling for my throat, he will some day thrust his neck into the noose."

One of the telephones upon Martin Hews' desk tinkled gently. He listened and spoke into it a nearly inaudible word. Almost before he had replaced the receiver, the white light above the door flashed. He touched a button upon his desk, the door swung open, and the girl who had intruded upon my hiding place with her singular offer entered the room. I watched her as she walked with measured footsteps towards an easy-chair set behind a small, Chippendale desk. Of me she took not the slightest notice, nor did any gesture or word of greeting pass between her and Martin Hews.

"Since you are joining my establishment, Major Owston," the latter said, with a little wave of his hand, "let me introduce you to my niece—my lay-secretary, if I may call her so, for she does nothing except act as intermediary between myself and my bureau of information, into whose secrets you shall be one day initiated. My dear," he went on, turning to her, "a young Goliath who has guaranteed to protect me against the assassins of Shoreditch—Major Owston—Miss Essiter."

I rose to my feet. Her eyes met mine, expressionless and vacant. She inclined her head very slightly and took no further notice of me.

"Where are you staying in London?" Martin Hews enquired.

"At Rowton House last night," I told him. "I imagine it would have been the Embankment to-night."

"Your clothes?"

"Mostly pawned. I have nothing except what I stand in."

He studied me thoughtfully—a pudgy little finger played with the end of his chin.

"I am, as a rule," he admitted, "suspicious of such destitution. In your case, however, you will receive the benefit of the doubt. Beatrice, my dear, fifty pounds from your coffer, if you please."

The young woman leaned forward, opened a wonderful ivory box with clasps which seemed to me of solid gold, and counted out fifty pounds from what appeared to be an inexhaustible supply. She took the notes across and laid them on her uncle's desk. He passed them over to me. I had to hold them very tightly in my hand to be sure that I was not dreaming.

"I will take it for granted," he continued, "that you are not on speaking terms with your tailor, and I will telephone to mine. You must have some clothes. Most other things we can provide you with. For the present, you will sleep here, until I have decided what to do with this fair Helen of Shoreditch. Before the week is over, I shall probably have other work for you in the West End. That must wait, however, until you have your clothes, and until your rooms are engaged. Do you happen to belong to any clubs in town?"

"I am still a member of the Rag, sir," I told him—"rather a matter of kindly sufferance, I am afraid, but I am supposed to be out of England."

"Service clubs are not the slightest use," he snapped. "What about Ciro's, the Embassy, the Blue Skies, and that sort of thing?"

"I know them, of course," I admitted. "If I had been able to pay their subscriptions, I should have spent the money on food before now."

He made a note upon some tablets by his side. A bell rang softly. The white light flashed out, the door opened. My employer's expression became almost benevolent.

"Come in, Minchin," he invited—"come in."

A man entered and approached the table respectfully. He was dressed in sober black, and there were many points about him which seemed to indicate the well-trained gentleman's servant. He was a person of curiously nondescript appearance, with small features, bald head, and slanting eyes set rather wide apart. Suitably attired, he could have passed anywhere for a Chinaman. On the spot I took an instinctive but violent dislike to him.

"Minchin," his master announced, "this gentleman, Major Owston, has accepted a post of responsibility in the household. He will sleep here to-night. You will give him the laurel suite on the ground floor. He will need a great many articles for his toilet, most of which you will doubtless be able to provide."

"Certainly, sir."

"In five minutes," Martin Hews concluded, "return and show Major Owston to his rooms."

The man departed. My new employer turned towards

me, and the indifferent note left his tone. His expression had become almost ferocious. He looked at me intensely, his eyes seeking mine, holding them with an almost portentous concentration. I was as nearly afraid of him as I have ever been of any man in my life.

"Owston," he said, "from now on, until we part, you are my man. Don't question my orders. If you fail to carry them out or neglect to obey them, scuttle away as fast as you can, but I warn you now, as I warned you before, that my enterprises in life are not undertaken for purposes of philanthropy. Sometimes it may happen that I am actually aiding and abetting criminals. Often I am against the law. I alone plan; you, my servants, obey. You may refuse to carry out my instructions and quit my service, but if a breath of my doings reaches the outside world or a confidence of mine is betrayed, you pay—you pay to a very ugly limit. Is that understood?"

"Perfectly," I assured him. "I have my own principles left, such as they are, and nothing will make me swerve from them, but the world has treated me badly, and I am not squeamish."

With that, he touched a button under his desk, Minchin reappeared, and I became an inmate of Breezeley Mansion.

CHAPTER IV

THE apartments to which my new employer's peculiar manservant in due course conducted me were, after the hard time through which I had recently passed, a revelation in comfort and luxury. There was a pleasantly furnished sitting-room, with a bedroom and large bathroom communicating, all on the ground floor, and the windows of all three protected by iron bars. With a suit of clothes it was impossible to provide me, but linen, sponges, and all manner of toilet articles seemed to have appeared by magic. Minchin, at his master's wish, reappeared, after I had had my bath and made as much of a toilet as I could, and he told me strange things in a curiously matter-of-fact fashion.

"Mr. Hews thought, sir," he confided, "that you had better become acquainted with the constitution of the household. In addition to the ordinary domestic staff we have five footmen in the house."

"What on earth for?" I asked.

"For purposes of defence. Mr. Hews is very nervous about burglars. Then there are three electricians."

"Also fighters?"

"They are generally too busy to think about anything but their work," he said. "The house, as you may have noticed, is full of electric devices. Even the master's carriage runs up or downstairs in grooves connected with an electric dynamo. Then there is a complete set of burglar alarms indoors and out, and the secret doors are all worked in the same manner. We have a huge searchlight in the tower, and some other smaller contrivances which

Mr. Hews will probably tell you about himself. So far as I have been able to observe, sir—and I have been here for eleven years—I should say that the electricians are the hardest worked members of the staff."

"Well, it all sounds odd to me, of course, Minchin," I acknowledged, "but I daresay I shall get used to it."

"Life here usually has plenty of variety, sir," the man continued. "Your meals can be served in your sitting-room at any hour you order them, and there is a car at your disposal whenever you require it. Across the passage there is a library. There is also a billiard room. The master wishes you to keep for the present the automatic you have, and there are other weapons and ammunition in the cupboard."

"Who actually lives in the house beside the servants?" I asked.

"Miss Essiter, Mr. Hews and yourself, sir."

"Why, there must be forty empty rooms!" I exclaimed.

"There are a great many," he admitted. "Still, there are visitors—foreign chiefly—coming and going all the time, and the whole of the north wing has been converted into a museum for pictures and suchlike. The master often spends several hours a day locked in there."

"What on earth made Mr. Hews choose this singular neighbourhood?" I asked.

"It has its advantages, sir," Minchin explained. "You saw one of them to-day when we were able to get Donkin away by means of the river. Years ago," the man added reflectively, "we used to have a great many callers drop off from the steamers. The police became a little inquisitive, though. There was an accident on the road between here and the river one night. A Chinaman was shot with some very valuable precious stones upon him. I am afraid the police since that time have been a trifle suspicious of this house and our doings."

It occurred to me that I was perhaps becoming too curious concerning matters which were not exactly my affair. I endeavoured to change the subject.

"Talking of the police," I remarked, "don't you think they'll get Donkin? There must be a warrant out against him, and they can telephone and wireless down the river."

"We are not afraid of the police, sir," Minchin assured me. "The only trouble was getting Donkin on to the motor boat before any of Joseph's lot arrived. The police are all very well in their way, but they are much slower. The motor boat did the trick for us. By this time, Donkin is on a tanker. He leaves that to-night for a coasting steamer, and so on. The master is a great organiser. It gives him pleasure to arrange these things. His agents in London are almost as clever. . . . At what time will you take your dinner, sir?"

"At any time that is convenient," I told him, trying, by adopting a casual tone about the matter, to conceal the fact that I had had no luncheon.

"It will be served about eight o'clock then, sir," he announced.

He laid upon the table the evening paper which he had been carrying, and respectfully took his leave. I looked after him for a moment or two, wondering why the man had inspired me with such a profound sense of distrust. His manner was quiet and civil, almost impressive. There was nothing in the least furtive about him. He looked one in the face, and he was certainly an excellent servant. He was of a secretive type, without a doubt, but as likely as not it was his master's secret he guarded. I mixed myself a whisky and soda and stretched myself out in an easy-chair to reflect upon this amazing household of which I had become a member. Exactly what was Martin Hews' object in life? What were the thoughts and schemes with which that strange brain of his was occupied? Why

had it become a point of honour with him to secure the
escape of a desperate criminal and give shelter to his
mistress? That he should keep his house closely guarded
was not an unreasonable thing, especially if that other
wing, of which Minchin had spoken, was filled with as
many priceless treasures as was the library in which he
usually sat. On the other hand, I was not at all convinced
that his energies were purely defensive. His organisation
outside must exist for some purpose or other. Was he, I
speculated, the head of a band of criminals of his own, of
which I was already a member, or was he simply a receiver of stolen goods on a huge scale, a financier of robberies and fraudulent exploits? After all, my interest in
the matter was really little more than academic. After
years of bitter hardship, I had adopted the vagabond's
philosophy. There was to be a roof over my head to-night,
food to eat, wine to drink, tobacco to smoke. Questions of
ethics could go hang. I was content to wait for the first
problem to present itself. . . .

My room became a little close, and presently I took advantage of a cleverly concealed door, and, finding the
fastening with some difficulty, opened it and stepped out
into the night. A slight drizzling rain was falling, which
cooled my cheeks, as I strolled down the flinty path
towards the road. There was scarcely a sound to be heard
except the melancholy hooting of steamers crawling up
the river, and the prospect all around was as dreary as
ever. Suddenly I was aware that my solitude was about
to be disturbed. A motor car or taxicab had stopped in
the road some two hundred yards away, and a man was
proceeding on foot towards me. The incident in itself was
ordinary enough, but the singular part of it was that,
although it was a dark night, the vehicle had approached
without lights and the footsteps which every moment I
could hear more distinctly seemed to be the footsteps of

a man seeking as far as possible to avoid attention. Even
when he came in sight—a large, bulky figure, wearing a
bowler hat and a long mackintosh—his progress was furtive, and at his first glimpse of the light of my cigarette
he appeared to hesitate. In a moment or two, however, he
came on, and paused as he reached my side. I recognised
him at once. It was Miles, the butler, who had admitted
me. He had lost his manner, however. He was no longer
the dignified but affable major-domo of a large household;
he gave one the impression of a man skulking in from an
errand of which he was ashamed.

"Good evening," I greeted him. "You have had a wet
walk, I am afraid."

He lifted his hat with an effort at politeness.

"A miserable walk, sir," he confided. "A shocking neighbourhood this. You'll find it dull, I'm afraid, if you're
staying with us long."

My immediate reply was interrupted in a singular
fashion. I felt suddenly blinded, bathed in a great sheet
of light. I shielded my eyes with my hand and swung
around. A brilliant shaft of electric illumination from
the further tower had caught us both, played on us for
a moment, and travelled over the mud-soaked wilderness to the road beyond. The water in the dykes glistened,
the wizened trees stood out one by one. About halfway to
the station, the vehicle in which Miles had arrived was
clearly visible—a motor car or taxicab perhaps—being
driven very slowly, and still without lights. Then as suddenly as it had appeared, the searchlight was shut off,
and the darkness around us seemed more intense than
ever. I realised to my surprise that the man by my side
was trembling violently.

"God bless my soul, sir, what was that?" he gasped.

"A searchlight," I explained. "Minchin told me that
they had one in the tower."

"Curse their spying ways!" he exclaimed, with an abrupt vehemence which astonished me. "As though a man couldn't take a little jaunt to see a friend without their wanting to know all about it! It's a strange household, sir. I shall not be able to stand their ways. I'm used to something very different. I shall give notice to-morrow."

"It's an unusual household, at any rate," I admitted. "I daresay they heard our voices and wanted to see who was about."

He lifted his hat once more, mumbled something which I did not catch, and hurried back towards the house. Presently I followed his example and returned to my room. Here I found a surprise in store for me. Seated in the easy-chair which I had drawn up to the fire was the young lady who had travelled down with Donkin from London that afternoon. She was still wearing the dark red gown and tam-o'-shanter in which she had arrived. Her feet were upon the high fender, and she was smoking a cigarette from the opened box which I had left. She started at my unexpected appearance.

"Gawd, how you scared me!" she exclaimed. "Is this house all secret doors and passages? Don't any one walk about like a Christian being?"

"I believe they generally do," I assured her. "I haven't seen much of the place myself yet. Making yourself comfortable, I hope?"

She turned her head and looked at me for a moment through her dark velvety eyes.

"Oh, I'm O. K., thanks," she remarked, sinking a little lower in the chair. "Gives me the creeps, this place does, though. Tell me about Jim? You got him off all right?"

"With about five minutes to spare," I answered, drawing up another and smaller chair to the other side of the hearthrug. "Mr. Joseph himself, I believe it was, arrived with a small band of desperadoes before the motor boat was out of sight."

She nodded thoughtfully.

"I expect it was Jo. I can't think why he's so bitter. One of those two was bound to get his before they'd done, and I always reckoned it would be Jim. He's pretty well all in, poor chap. I don't know as he'll be able to stand a sea voyage."

"In any case, I'm afraid you'll have to make up your mind to wait some time before you see him again," I warned her. "It may have been a fair fight, but he killed his man—there's no doubt about that—and a knife's an ugly thing to explain away."

She stretched out her hand for another cigarette.

"The Wolves all carry knives," she confided. "Phil Abrahams had his—they found it on him—but he couldn't get at it. Jim had his gun as well, but he didn't use it. I don't see much to choose between 'em myself."

"If Joseph wanted you so much, why didn't he come after you himself, instead of sending another man?" I asked.

"Oh, he wants me all right," she replied, lighting the cigarette which she had selected. "He's been after me, too, more than once, only the luck was our way and we managed to dodge him. He and Jim would have been at one another's throats pretty soon, anyhow, but it happened to be Phil we met first, coming out of a pub in Aldgate. Jim never used his knife till he was down, and Phil had his halfway out, so they couldn't make it anything but manslaughter. I say, what do you and the old gentleman upstairs expect me to do if Joseph comes down here after me?"

"Lie low, I should think," I answered. "Martin Hews promised to keep you safe, and I fancy when he says a thing he means it."

She looked thoughtfully into the fire, and I found myself studying her. Her frock was of the sort which had probably come from Shaftesbury Avenue—daring but in its way well fashioned. It disclosed the lines of her exquisite little figure with purposeful artistry. Her silk-clad legs, beautifully shaped, were both extended upon the fender. Her dark, glossy eyebrows were gathered together in a little frown, and her brilliantly coloured lips were distinctly pouting. She turned at last towards me, and there was a gleam of laughter in her eyes.

"Nice thing for me to be cooped up here like this, ain't it?" she complained. "I don't know that I wouldn't just as lief have been left to go my own way. Jo, he wants me back again bad, but he wouldn't dare touch me unless I were willing. There's no man breathing would. Do you know what I'd do to him?"

"I imagine you would make yourself remarkably unpleasant," I ventured.

She thrust her hand unashamedly up the side of her leg and produced a little poniard in a small sheath. She removed the latter and sprung the steel with her finger—a streak of wonderful blue metal.

"I'd stab him," she confided, "if it was the wrong man. The right man—well, that's a different thing. I've chosen all my life, and I shall choose to the end. No one will have me against my will."

"All your life?" I repeated, smiling at her. "Why, how old are you then?"

"I'm all but twenty," she answered. "I began young. What do they reckon they're going to do, these fellows of Joseph's, if they come along? Bash you all on the head, I suppose, and carry me away. Seems to me I'm giving a bit of trouble."

"That was what your famous prototype discovered many years ago." I told her.

She stared at me suspiciously.

"Who are you getting at?" she demanded. "What I mean is, that if Jim were to hear I'd gone back to Joseph, he'd come after me from South America or wherever he was. Why can't they leave me alone, that's what I want to know? I can make up my own mind. I'll have to have some sort of a man. If I fancy Jo, well, it will be him. I don't know as I do, though. Jim's a good sort, he'd stick to me, although he's a bit rougher. What do you think about it all, Mister? I expect you're wondering why any two men should go kind of wild about me."

She showed all her beautiful white teeth as she smiled, and her soft, dark eyes coquetted for mine. She was the London type, without a doubt, the child of the East End streets, but she had her charm just as surely as the peasants of Naples, or the pleasure children of Marseilles. I had wandered about Southern Europe a good deal in my younger days, but I could remember, at the moment, no one of the type who had seemed to me so devilishly beautiful.

"Well, I really don't know what to think," I told her. "As a matter of fact, I don't fancy that girls are much in my line."

"I'm a good looker, ain't I?" she persisted. "They all say so. I can make 'em all crazy when I try—the whole gang. They would have fought about me every night—but Donkin's lads all knew that I belonged to him."

I laughed, and something in the quality of my mirth apparently annoyed her. She frowned angrily.

"I'm not your sort, I suppose, eh?" she demanded.

"You're good looking enough to turn any one's head," I assured her hastily, "but you must remember that I'm a great deal older; besides, I'm rather a dull person with your sex anyhow."

She surveyed me appraisingly.

"You're not so very old," she said, "but I dare say you're kind of set in your ways. Jim, now, he was always up to some devilment or other to keep things merry, and Joseph—he was the cleverest man at tricks I ever knew. We used to have wonderful nights before he and Jim quarrelled, and the gang split up—mostly about me that was too. You ain't so bad, though. You're a good looker, and my, you're strong, I should think! Why, I could sit on your knee, and you wouldn't feel me."

"I might," I warned her quickly. "I was wounded in my leg during the war."

"Well, that's better than having none at all, like the poor gent upstairs," she observed. "I say, do you think they'll let me out of here now and then? It seems kind of dead and lonesome without the electric cars and lights and horns tooting."

"I am rather afraid," I told her, "from what I know of Mr. Martin Hews' methods, that you won't be allowed a great deal of liberty."

She yawned.

"I ain't sure that the air of this neighbourhood's going to suit me," she decided. "I like a cinema and a bit of a dance at nights."

A footman, in very correct striped waistcoat and dark livery, entered the room, attended to the fire, and brushed up the grate. Rachel watched him quizzically.

"Will it be convenient for me to lay the cloth for dinner now, sir?" he enquired.

I nodded assent, and he disappeared. The girl looked after him.

"Gee!" she exclaimed. "Are they going to do that sort of thing to me?"

"I don't know," I answered. "Perhaps you'd better run along to your quarters now and see. It must be getting on towards dinner-time."

She swung herself on to her feet and indulged in a little grimance.

"Nice sociable sort of a fellow, you are!" she grumbled. "You ain't going to put on airs with me all the time, I hope?"

"It appears to me, my child," I said evasively, "that my job is going to be to fight for you if that gang comes along."

"Well, there's many as have done that," she confided, pausing and boldly linking her arm through mine as we moved towards the door. "I don't mind it. There's always a kiss for the winner—sometimes for the other chap, if I fancy him. . . . My, have you come all this way just to open the door for me."

"Why not?"

"Want anything for it?" she asked mischievously.

"I am too frightened of your knife," I replied.

She stood upon tiptoe, smacked my cheek lightly with her hand, and darted away with a little mocking laugh. For a moment I lingered there, I must confess half angry. Then I forgot all about it. From somewhere in the upper regions of the house came the most appalling shriek of terror I had ever heard in my life.

CHAPTER V

I NEVER doubted but that this was a job for me in my new capacity as protector of the household, and I sprinted off down the corridor towards the hall, meaning to ascend at once to my employer's room. I had scarcely gone half a dozen paces, however, before Miss Essiter appeared round the corner, coming towards me. There was no sign of alarm in her face. She was calm indeed and unruffled.

"Didn't you hear that cry?" I exclaimed. "There is something wrong in your uncle's room."

"There's nothing wrong which need concern you, Major Owston," she assured me coldly. "When you are wanted, you will be summoned."

Her demeanour seemed to me, with the echoes of that cry in my ears, stupefying. There was a supercilious turn to her lips as she stood there, barring my progress. It flashed into my mind that she had probably seen Rachel run laughing to her room.

"But surely," I protested, "something must be wrong up there? Some one must be in distress of some sort?"

"Nothing that is happening is any concern of yours," she insisted. "When your services are needed, you will be sent for. I was on my way to speak to you."

"Will you come into my room?" I invited, turning back reluctantly.

She followed me. I lingered upon the threshold, listening, and, reassured to some extent by the silence which now reigned in the house, I closed the door. She stood for a moment looking around the room. Then she walked to the window and drew the curtain a little closer. Afterwards she tried the catch of the outer door and finally made her way to my easy-chair, into which she sank with a slight gesture of relief, and sat gazing at me with almost disconcerting intentness. She had changed her dress, but she was still wearing black—a gown of cunningly devised simplicity which seemed to fall in one line from her neck to the hem of her skirt. She wore no ornaments, and her strangely coloured hair was arranged in unfashionable and severely simple coils. Nevertheless, I was beginning to realise that notwithstanding her apparent indifference to the fact, she was really an unusually beautiful young woman. Although her voice, her eyes, her changeless poise seemed to bespeak a curious lack of human sensibility, she had the air of living in a world of her own from which she emerged upon necessity with a certain amount of resentment. I seated myself in another chair and waited, a little obstinate in my silence. She had sought me out. It should be for her, I decided, to explain her errand. This she did, after a somewhat prolonged interval.

"You are wondering, of course, Major Owston," she remarked, "why I tried to persuade you to go away."

"It was scarcely a kind action," I complained, with some trace of indignation still in my tone, "and, if you will forgive my reminding you of the fact, what you told me was not the truth. I have been looking for a job so long that I think if I had failed with your uncle I should have given up hope."

"You must acquit me of any personal malevolence," she said. "I simply followed out exactly my uncle's instructions. He wished to test your tenacity of purpose and your intelligence. A mean action, of course. My uncle is a Jesuit, however. He believes that the end justifies the means, and we who live with him have to think as he does."

"Yet," I ventured, "you seem to me to have a will of your own."

"I have," she admitted dryly, "but it is in subjection to a much stronger one."

There was a brief silence. Then my companion, who had been looking steadily into the fire, turned towards me and disclosed the reason of her visit.

"My uncle," she confided, "does not wish you to look upon yourself only as a mercenary in connection with your engagement here. In other words, he does not want you to be forced into a desperate position without some idea of what you are fighting for. You must have questions which you wish to ask."

"I certainly have," I confessed. "I really have only the vaguest idea as to what it is all about. Are we expecting a raid upon the place with the object of rescuing this young woman, and what do they exist for, anyhow, these bands of criminals? How does Mr. Martin Hews happen to be connected with them?"

"That is one of the things which I must explain," she said. "You have probably read in the newspapers of rival gangs of hooligans who are supposed to frequent race courses and carry on feuds connected with racing affairs, bogus bookmaking and that sort of thing."

"Certainly I have read of them," I acknowledged.

"Well, that is newspaper bluff to a great extent," she continued. "The gangs exist all right, and the fierce fights take place. Very much more serious they are, too, than anything reported in the newspapers. The truth is, however, that these gangs are composed not of mere desperadoes and pickpockets, but of really organised criminals, who are a serious menace to the police. Their race-course activities are mostly bluff. From their head-quarters have been planned all the great burglaries of recent days, the counterfeit money exploits, the holding up of banks, and even murders, both here and on the Continent. Donkin was the nominal head of one band; Joseph of the other. My uncle's sympathies and interests have always lain with Donkin—unfortunately, as it seems at present. Donkin was under my uncle's protection—for services rendered, you might say—which accounts for this afternoon's exploit. He was holding his own against Joseph, but as usual these men must complicate everything by their ridiculous love affairs. Are you a susceptible person, Major Owston?" she asked, looking across at me with an insolent little droop of her eyelids.

"I don't think so," I rejoined. "I have had very little time for women in my lifetime, even as playthings."

She bit her lip for a moment, but remained otherwise unmoved.

"That is so much to the good," she said. "Owing to his ridiculous infatuation, Donkin has become a fugitive —his gang of course would be useless without him—and Joseph, we understand, at some time or other during the near future, means to risk his security and the security of his adherents, by an attack upon this house for the purpose of recovering the girl. You have a vague idea of the situation now?"

"A vague idea," I admitted. "What I should like to understand, though, is this. What is the precise *quid pro quo* which your uncle has received as a return for his support to Donkin's gang of criminals?"

"Yes, I imagined you would ask that," she observed thoughtfully. "I am not sure that I can entirely satisfy your curiosity. I might tell you as much as this, though. My uncle is one of the most famous collectors of art treasures in the world. There are many which are not for sale. Sometimes they come into the hands of thieves by illegal methods. They have to be sold to some one. My uncle buys them through an agent, without asking inconvenient questions. There are pictures, for instance, in his gallery, for which he has paid—not their value, perhaps, but a great deal—which would never have been parted with by their owners voluntarily. That is all I can tell you for the moment, Major Owston."

I nodded assent. It was quite as much as I wanted to know; perhaps a little more.

"At any rate," she went on, the disagreeable note creeping once more into her tone, "your first enterprise in defence of the household will be one of chivalry. You can picture yourself, if you will, a Sir Galahad, or any other hero of romance. Your task will be to aid in the protection of that most enslaving young woman from Shoreditch whom I saw fluttering out of this room a few minutes ago."

I ignored the subject of Rachel's visit. My conscience was quite clear on that account anyhow.

"Very well," I said, "I am quite ready to take that on. I want to ask you another question, though. Don't look upon it as a sign of cowardice. It is simply a matter of common sense. If your uncle knows that there is going to be an attack upon the house for the purpose of carrying off that young woman, why doesn't he inform the police?"

"You're terribly logical," she remarked. "The police will be summoned if it becomes absolutely necessary, but only as a last resource. It has been a matter of etiquette between both gangs to fight their quarrels out without reference to the common enemy. I suppose my uncle is obeying a precedent. There have been many fights," she added, after a moment's pause, "between these men, and the plans of the attacking party have often leaked out, but neither side yet has ever appealed to the police. It is slightly different now, of course, and at the proper moment the authorities will be summoned."

I must have seemed to her almost stupidly obstinate, but I felt that she was not giving me her whole confidence.

"I can't see," I persisted, "why we shouldn't just ring up the police station and give them an idea of what is likely to happen."

She half closed her eyes. She had the air of a patient school-mistress dealing with a backward child.

"I should have thought," she pointed out, "that after what I have told you, you would have understood why my uncle does not care for a police visitation in this house except in a matter of emergency."

A footman entered the room for the second time, to lay the cloth for my evening meal. She waved him impatiently away, but rose to her feet.

"There is another very important matter which I have to explain to you," she said. "Come over here, please."

She produced a small, stubby key of complicated pattern and unlocked a desk which stood against the wall. It contained all the ordinary writing materials and three telephone instruments, the receivers of which, and the uprights, were painted different colours—yellow, white and red. She touched the first.

"This," she explained, "is the one most in use. It communicates with my uncle's room. He will speak to you upon it, or you can speak to him. The white telephone is used merely for domestic purposes. That will bring you a servant for orders, or if the staff have anything to ask you that is the telephone they will use."

"And the red one?" I asked, as she paused.

Perhaps it was my fancy, but I had an idea that she shivered slightly before she answered.

"The red one means danger," she warned me. "Just at present you are scarcely likely to use it yourself—you are not sufficiently involved in any of my uncle's enterprises. It is only used, at any time, as a last resource. If my uncle had news to communicate to you, even serious news of impending danger, he would still use the yellow telephone. You understand?"

"I think so," I assented.

She pointed to three bulbs projecting from the wainscotting. One was yellow, one was white, one was red.

"Directly the telephone rings," she continued, "the light will flash out there from the one in use. They are duplicated in your bedroom, with a bell under each. Remember the red telephone is only used in cases of direct extremity. Its ringing for you will mean the greatest danger which could happen to the household—danger to my uncle. You are quick on your feet?"

"Moderately," I admitted. "No, I won't be modest. I think that I am quicker than most men in getting off the mark."

"Then, if that summons should come, take your gun— you should always have it ready—and hurry by the way I am going to show you to my uncle's room. Come with me now, please, and afterwards I shall leave you to your dinner."

She led me to the wainscotting of the farther wall, and for a minute her fingers played with the scrolled design of the woodwork. There was a little burr, like the muffled ringing of a telephone, and a panel rolled back.

"Follow me," she enjoined.

I obeyed in silence. The thrill of adventure was creeping once more into my senses, and the depression of months was passing. We were almost in the darkness, and so close together that once her hand swinging back touched mine. There was a curiously indistinguishable perfume about her hair or clothing which reminded me of some of the byways of the bazaars at Constantinople, where nameless essences are brewed. Presently she came to a standstill. Her fingers rested upon my arm.

"We mount the stairs here," she whispered. "Not many, because, as you realise, we have been walking on an incline all the time."

I followed her, and we faced a ruby lamp. There she stopped.

"All that you have to do," she continued, "is to place your hand upon that lamp and push forward. You will find yourself in the recess where my uncle sent you when Donkin and the girl arrived. You know your way out of that into the room?"

"Perfectly," I assured her.

She led me back to my sitting-room, where my table was now prepared.

"I am afraid," she said, "that a portion of your dinner will be spoilt. It was necessary, however, that you should understand these things. Joseph is a man of very quick action, and there is no telling how soon he may strike."

"We ought to have some scheme of defence," I suggested to her, "and I should like some other weapon besides a gun—a heavy stick or a life preserver. I am not very fond of shooting in a scrap of this sort."

"I will tell my uncle what you say," she promised. "He will very likely send Minchin to talk to you."

She was moving towards the door, sphinxlike and cold as ever, when a sudden instinct of the hostess seemed to possess her. She covered over one of my dishes and jerked my cocktail shaker gently, as though to be sure that the ice had not all melted.

"I hope you will find everything all right," she said. "Please don't hesitate to tell Miles if you have any special wishes."

"I am sure that I shall not find it necessary," I told her. "You wouldn't let me—shake you a cocktail, I suppose?"

She demurred for a moment.

"That is very nice of you," she said. "Please do."

We drank together, and for a moment she seemed more human.

"I am afraid your fish will be cold," she regretted.

"Miss Essiter," I confided, "I told your uncle the truth, as I didn't wish to come here under false pretences. My last meal was yesterday at five o'clock, when I had two cups of tea, and two slices of thick bread and butter, for which I paid fourpence. I had a cup of coffee this morning, before I came down to see your uncle, and that is all. You don't seem to realise that you are feeding a starving man."

Then indeed for a moment she changed from a cold and lifeless being into a creature of sympathies and kindness.

"But, my dear man!" she expostulated. "Why didn't you ask for something before? Now that I look at you —why, I believe you're half starved!"

I felt a sudden weakness. I had told her the truth, and more than once during the day the dizziness had come. She hurried to the door, but the farewell glance that she sent me was sufficient to turn any man's head.

"Not another word," she ordered. "Sit down this instant."

She waved me away from the door, and with her departure I abandoned the struggle for appearances. The perfect cooking and the delicate sauces were half wasted on me. I sat down and ate as only a ravenous man can.

Unforgettable, that moment when, some five hours later, wakened out of a profound sleep, I sat up amidst the cool sheets I had found so delicious, striving for realisation. The room was unfamiliar to me. The silk pyjamas which clung to my limbs were strange. Nothing seemed to be my own. Nowhere could I piece together those fragments of memory in my mind. Then my eyes leaped towards something on the wall exactly opposite the bed, and everything flashed back. The red light was burning!

CHAPTER VI

I THINK it could have been a matter of seconds only before I was in my sitting-room, feeling eagerly along the wainscotting for the spring which opened the hidden door. Whilst I stood there, it rolled open before me, and Beatrice Essiter appeared. She was perfectly cool, but there was urgency in her voice.

"Put out your light," she ordered.

I had turned on the switch as I had entered the room. I stepped back and did as I was bidden. We stood there then in an intense darkness.

"Joseph is on his way down," she announced. "We didn't expect him to-night, or Uncle would have sent Minchin to see you. He seems to have made up his mind suddenly. He is only bringing one carload of men, so I imagine he is more out for carrying the girl off by a quick rush than a fight."

"What time did they start?" I asked.

"An hour ago," she answered. "They may be here at any time. Put some clothes on quickly. Our other men are at their posts already. You can turn on the light in your bedroom if you are sure the curtains are drawn. I should get outside by your private door and keep in the shadow of the house. You will find Huntley, the red-haired footman who served you, on your left."

"How many are we?"

"Let me see," she reflected. "We shall have to leave out Miles. He certainly won't be any use as a fighter to-night. There can't be more than ten or a dozen of them, and there probably won't be as many as that when they get to close quarters."

I heard the click of the door and knew that she had gone. I hurried into a few clothes, caught up a leaded stick which Huntley had brought me in after dinner, and, with my automatic safely in my pocket, cautiously opened the door and stepped outside. At first I could see nothing in front, and behind me the house itself seemed dark and lifeless. There was not a sound to be heard from the road or the open spaces beyond. I crouched against the wall, listening intently. Owing no doubt to a regrettable streak of brutality in my character, fighting, even for its own sake, has always made an appeal to me, and I felt the joy of the coming battle already throbbing in my veins. As my eyes grew accustomed to the darkness, I could distinguish Huntley crouching a few yards on my left, but so far as I could apprehend there was no sign as yet of the attack. Then, when I was still leaning forward, peering into the obscurity around me, the air was suddenly rent with a sound as though a million telephone bells set in different keys were clanging one against the other. Simultaneously, from the tower came a blinding stream of light, passing slowly in a semicircle from the house. By its illumination we saw that the invaders were close at hand. Barely forty yards away, a wormlike procession of dark forms in a single file were creeping towards the house. Caught in that sudden blaze of light, they hesitated, and although the situation was tense enough, for I realised at once that we were very much outnumbered, my first impulse was to laugh. They swayed and staggered about as though they were drunk. Then the leader made a spring forward, and with a hideous cry leaped into the air and fell over motionless. The invaders were quick enough to recover themselves. They stepped over the fallen body and came running towards the house in the form of a semicircle. Huntley, a few yards off, cursed softly.

"Bad work!" he muttered. "Some one's done a split. If they hadn't come singly, the wire would have had the lot. Look out, sir!"

As it was, the attack seemed a little demoralised. A second searchlight from the other tower, flashing unexpectedly in the eyes of the invaders and blinding them with its intense brilliance, created something of a panic. One man stood with his face buried in his hands and his back to the house; another fell over; a third unashamedly ran back to where I could see a tumble-down looking motor *char-à-banc* waiting in the lane. The sound of alarm bells died away, however. The searchlight could only play upon one section at a time. A tall figure from the centre of the attackers blew a whistle, and the result was electric. The skulkers returned, and they were at us.

So far as I could tell, we were outnumbered about two to one. We were better fighters, however, and although they were possessed of a sort of ferocious cunning, their methods were of less use in the open. I saw no trace of weapons at first, so I went ahead with my fists, and the first man I hit—I admit he was taken by surprise—finished the month in Bringford Hospital. The next—a sallow-faced, loose-limbed youth, with long arms and astonishingly nimble feet—dodged me so cleverly that I very nearly overbalanced myself, and gave him a momentary advantage. Then I saw the flash of steel in his hand as he crept round me, and just in time I sent him smashing over with a short upper cut to the jaw. The sight of his craftily concealed knife, however, had angered me, and I caught up my leaded stick and swung out with it fiercely at my next assailant. Up till then no guns seemed to have been used, but suddenly there was a sharp report, and Huntley went spinning over on his side. The next few minutes were a little hazy, for my corner seemed to have become the centre of the attack. I was never very clever with any sort of a blunt weapon, and I only half diverted the strength of two blows from a life preserver, either of which might have knocked me out for the night. As it was, I was dizzy for a moment, and, being hard pressed, was feeling for my gun when I saw one of the smallest of the gang trying to sneak round behind me, with that ominous glitter protruding from his sleeve. The state of fury into which I fell seemed to give me the strength of a dozen men. I lifted him by the collar and leg and flung him to the ground on his face, where he lay until he was picked up by the ambulance some hours later. Then for a few minutes I went for every one I could see. Twice a knife grazed my shoulder, and I felt the blood from a cut upon my cheek, but otherwise the luck was with me. In the midst of it all there was the sound of a long, shrill whistle. The two men with whom I was at that moment engaged slunk away, and I gathered that for some reason either a parley or a cessation of the fight was indicated. Then, full in the searchlight which was playing once more, I saw a tall, thin figure, wearing a black mask—the young man of the motor car in the afternoon, I was convinced—step boldly forward.

"Rachel!" he cried.

There was no reply. Suddenly the front door opened, and there shot out into a little semicircle of light Martin Hews in his small carriage. He appeared to be unarmed, but one hand was underneath the rug.

"Come and fetch her," he invited, in his queer high-pitched voice. "No doubt she is pining in her room. Come and fetch her, Joseph."

"Very well, I will," was the calm reply.

The masked man took a few steps forward. The rest of the gang who had been making for the *char-à-banc* hesitated, and some of them retraced their steps. The fight seemed about to recommence when I heard a voice from one of the lower windows. I looked up. A shadowy form was standing at the casement of a darkened room. As soon as she spoke, I knew that it was Rachel.

"Look out, Jo!" she warned him. "The little man has a gun under the rug."

Joseph paused. He was now about twenty paces from where Martin Hews was sitting in his chair, with Miles, the most terrified person I have even seen in my life, standing by his side. Joseph waved his hand to the window.

"Very well," he called out softly. "We'll dine at Shirley's before the week's out, kid."

She laughed mockingly.

"I don't know as I want to. You let Jim get away."

I had recovered my breath and was ready again for action, and it seemed to me no impossible task to cut Joseph off from the gang who were lining out some distance behind him. He saw me move, however, and swung round. We had one another covered, but neither pressed the trigger of his gun. No one had called for an armistice, but the fever of fighting had abated. It was like shooting a man in cold blood. Joseph faced me, and although, when he spoke, his words were clearly pronounced, I think that he must have known we were due to meet again, for his voice was disguised.

"If you fire," he said, "my men will tear you to pieces, and it really wouldn't be worth while, for you would probably miss me. Goodnight, everybody. Goodnight, Martin Hews."

"Take this with you," the latter replied, turning suddenly with a venomous look to Miles. "Out you go, you common informer. Take your rubbish, Joseph."

Miles staggered out into the night with the terror still on his face. Martin Hews reversed his little carriage into a dark corner where he was out of sight. I doubt whether any one but myself saw his hand steal up from underneath the rug. The darkness was stabbed by a quick flash. Miles spun round and round, gave one shriek of agony, and fell. . . .

They were all running for the *char-à-banc* now—Joseph, with a cigarette in his mouth, sauntering on behind. A sudden desire came upon me to take him alive. My luck of the night, however, forsook me. I was trying to cut him off from the others by circling round a strip of marshland, and I put my foot into one of the deep holes filled with mud and water with which the whole of the marshy land was pitted. I struggled to my feet but before I was thoroughly steady I was caught up in the wire of the electric signal cord, and over I went again. A bullet whistled above my head, and probably the second fall saved my life. Before I could stagger to my feet, the *char-à-banc* was throbbing and grunting its way citywards.

CHAPTER VII

I FOUND lights streaming from every window of the Mansion and the front door wide open. The first person I saw as I stumbled in was Martin Hews, seated in his chair with Minchin by his side. In the far distance, Miss Essiter was bandaging Huntley's arm.

"Dear me, dear me, Major!" my employer chuckled, as he inspected my appearance. "Another one to add to the list of casualties, I fear."

"Major Owston!" Miss Essiter exclaimed, looking across at me with the first suggestion of a human expression in her face I had ever seen.

For the first few seconds after my arrival, I was incapable of speech, even of hearing. Every fibre of my body was responding to the emotion of the moment. A murderer! There he sat, a few feet away, his eyes challenging mine. I had seen fighting of all sorts in my life and bloodshed of every description, but I had never before seen a man shot in such stony-hearted fashion. Again I fancied that I could see the stab of flame and the man's convulsive gesture of agony as he spun round—Miles too, the perfect butler, placid, emotionless, suave! Perhaps because I was a little delirious with pain and excitement, the face of Martin Hews seemed suddenly to fade into the likeness of an old gargoyle carved over the porch of a *château* in Normandy where I had once been a guest—an evil, leering thing, with Satanic questioning in its eyes. I knew very well, even in those dazed moments, what he was asking me. Then, with an effort, I pulled myself together. Beatrice Essiter, her task accomplished, was hastening towards me. There was a shocked look in her face.

"You must come and let me look after you at once, Major Owston," she insisted.

I realised then that the blood was streaming from the gash in my head, down my cheeks and on to my clothes. There was a cut in my trouser leg where I had narrowly escaped being knifed, a bruise on my chin, and a flesh wound on my arm from which the blood was dripping. To complete my dishevelled appearance, my clothes were soaked with mud and water from my fall. She made me stoop over a table upon which was a great bowl of water and some lint.

"They have handled you roughly, I am afraid, Major," Martin Hews remarked, gliding a little nearer towards us.

"Serves him right," cried a shrill voice from the top of the banisters. "Crikey! A great fellow like that never ought to have been let loose amongst a lot of undersized 'uns. They didn't half cop it. You big bully, you ought to be ashamed of yourself."

I looked up, startled. Rachel was leaning over the oak balcony of the first landing. She threw me a kiss flagrantly.

"That was one of my boys whose neck you nearly broke," she continued reproachfully. "Taken me to the pictures many a time, he has."

"You will have to come to your room, Major Owston," Beatrice Essiter announced. "Huntley, if you feel strong enough, can you find any sort of a change of clothes?"

"In the meantime," Martin Hews observed, "I shall send for refreshments. Our staff is crippled, but still mostly on its legs. Dear me, we shall miss Miles! Grateson, I see you have your head bound up, and are looking more yourself again now. Will you bring in wine and spirits? Major Owston will be glad of some refreshment as soon as he has been attended to."

The man departed, and I was hurried away. With indifferent but skilful fingers, Beatrice Essiter washed the blood from my face and dressed the wounds. Huntley presently arrived with a change of clothes, and soon I began to feel myself again.

"You are still rather a pathetic looking object," she remarked. "I suppose you had to go and plunge into the thick of it like that."

"I rather thought that was what I was here for," I reminded her.

She made no reply. Suddenly we heard the stopping of a car outside.

"The police at last!" she exclaimed, a little anxiously. "I expect you will be wanted."

Two policemen and an Inspector in uniform were in the hall when I arrived, and a surgeon who had come with them in an ambulance was out in the grounds. My presence was evidently not required for the moment, so I went to the sideboard and helped myself to a stiff whisky and soda. When I returned, the Inspector had departed for the grounds to take a note of the casualties, and my employer was leaning back in his chair as though exhausted. He beckoned me to him, however.

"New sort of fighting for you, Major," he remarked, his eyes, more beady than ever, seeming to protrude from under his inflamed eyelids.

"It was an undisciplined sort of scrap," I acknowledged. "We had the best of it, I think, but we ought to do better next time with a little method."

"Every one of my men, as you doubtless observed," he continued, "has been a fighter. I watched you, Owston. I am satisfied with my bargain. As usual, I was right in my judgment. It is really an amazing thing how seldom I make a mistake."

"I wish I had gone for that fellow Joseph earlier in the evening," I confided.

"I am glad that you did not," was the response. "Joseph, they say, is a terrible fellow to deal with, and a wonderful fighter. We might have lost your help."

"What I cannot understand," I told him, "is why they all cleared off so suddenly. I won't say that they were getting the best of it, but they were certainly pushing us very hard when they chucked it."

Martin Hews nodded.

"I can tell you why they went," he said. "I know Joseph's methods. They had a man near Bringford Police Station, and directly the police got the message and started out, he sent a warning. They got away at precisely the right moment. But for an act of treachery, Major, there would have been many more of them who never got away at all. We should have filled the cells of Bringford Police Station."

"Treachery?" I repeated.

His eyes held mine.

"Miles," he explained simply. "He went up to London during the afternoon, and I thought it as well to have him watched. He was lost in Shoreditch within a hundred yards of Joseph's headquarters. There isn't the slightest doubt as to the nature of his business there. Joseph arrived to-night with a plan of our defences. If his men had attacked as usual, in a semicircle, there wouldn't have been half of them able to swing a fist or raise a knife. They wouldn't have got over the shock by now. As it was, they came in single file, feeling for the wire, and only one man got it. '*De mortuis*,' you know, Major! We'll let it go at that, but it is a very curious thing— traitors pay. They always pay. Miles, you see, is our only fatal casualty—the man who turned informer."

"So that was the reason," I muttered.

"That was the reason," Martin Hews assented suavely. "I ran no risk of a mistake. I put him in the chair, and when he had done shrieking, he confessed. You are a soldier, Major. You understand the treatment of spies. The death of Miles was an ethical act of justice. It must be regarded as such. I trust that you agree with me."

I swallowed hard, and for a moment I could find no answer.

"Perhaps," he went on softly, "you are inclined to doubt my word. You need not. A deliberate lie I have never told in my life. My niece knows of this business. She will confirm what I tell you. A traitor, Major, must die a traitor's death."

"I suppose so," I agreed.

He nodded, and his face seemed to relax. I well understood, that, so far as I was concerned, and I was the only man who had seen the shot, the affair was finished.

"Show me again that little upper cut, Major," he begged. "You were only just in time with it. I could see the fellow fumbling for his knife. Just there, eh? . . . Capital! It was neatly done. Pray help yourself to another whisky and soda."

I did as I was bid, and he beckoned me once more to his side. He himself was the calmest member of the household. He had the air of one who has been the witness of some agreeable spectacle. His face, with its little dab of pink colour, was unruffled. There was not a gleam of nervousness in his manner. He was evidently well pleased with himself, and apparently with me.

"You like life, Major," he continued. "I can see that. Well, you will have plenty of it here for the next month or so. Joseph isn't likely to be content with what he has got to-night. It is almost his first reverse, but he would have run off with the girl all right if one of my men in London hadn't seen Miles skulking out of the Bethnal Green Road this afternoon. We were just in time to make a few changes, although we couldn't alter the main wiring. Joseph won't be content with this, however. He'll try again for the girl whilst we are still disorganised—before many hours are passed, I dare say. You find her attractive, Major?" he asked, looking at me with a contortion of his features which I can only describe as a leer.

"In her way, I suppose so."

"Scarcely a Helen. Attractive beyond a doubt, but a little crude according to modern standards. You know, Owston, I look upon it as rather a humanizing feature in these desperadoes that they set such store by their womenkind. I shouldn't be surprised to find that there was more sexual fidelity amongst that class than in our own circle. What do you think?"

"I can't say that I have studied the subject much, sir," I admitted. "I never heard before, in this country, of a gang vendetta like this on account of a girl."

"It broke Donkin," Martin Hews sighed. "Bad luck, for he was serving me well."

The Inspector returned—apparently a much graver man. There was a studiously official look upon his face, and I felt at once that he wished us to understand that his attitude towards the household and the whole happening had undergone a change.

"This is a more serious matter than I had imagined, sir," he announced. "We have found a dead man outside, shot through the back, and three or four others, dangerously wounded."

"The dead man is my own butler," Martin Hews scowled. "I had just trained him into my ways, and his loss is a great inconvenience to me. As for the miscreants who tried to storm my house, the only regret I have is that every one of them wasn't badly wounded."

The Inspector listened without change of expression.

One gathered that his attitude towards us was not particularly sympathetic.

"I notice that your house, sir," he continued, "is fitted with nearly every burglary alarm I have ever heard of. You have, too, a most unusual number of menservants, and a powerful searchlight fitted up in the tower."

"And why not?" my employer asked irritably. "I am a nervous person, and as you may have heard, I have been a collector of treasures all my life. Naturally I take such precautions as I think are wise. As regards the constitution of my domestic staff, I am a wealthy man, and I choose to be well served by those who can help in such a situation as to-night's."

"The ordinary householder," the Inspector observed, "is as a rule content to rely upon the police for protection. If he has exceptional treasures, he does not bring them to such a lonely and out-of-the-way neighbourhood.

"I am not an ordinary householder," Martin Hews snapped. "This house suits me—its locality suits me, and with all due deference to you, sir, I claim the right to make such arrangements as I think necessary to protect my own property. If we had waited for you to answer our call to-night, you can imagine what might have happened. Any ordinary householder would have been overpowered, there would have been serious bloodshed, and I should have been half a million pounds the poorer."

The Inspector closed his book without pursuing the subject further.

"I won't detain you any longer, sir," he said. "I still have your servants to question."

"If you will pardon my interfering with what is without a doubt your business," my employer observed, "I should like to point out that this household will be here to-morrow or the next day, and that there is a good deal more to be learned on the road between here and London

than in my house. I presume your business is to arrest the
burglars who were guilty of this outrageous attack."

"I have taken such steps as are necessary in that direction, sir," the man replied. "Every police station in the
vicinity has been notified, and Scotland Yard men are now
watching the approaches to London in the districts from
which these men probably came."

"Intelligent," Martin Hews admitted—"very intelli-
gent, Inspector. That's where the telephone comes in.
Block the holes, eh? Of course they'll separate. I hope
Scotland Yard will send their men out far enough."

"They know their business, sir," was the somewhat curt
rejoinder.

"The man I want to see arrested," Martin Hews wound
up vigorously, "is the instigator of this raid or attempted
burglary, or whatever you like to call it. I am perfectly
convinced that you have the chance now of breaking up a
famous gang of criminals. In that undertaking I wish you
every success. My household is, I fear, a little disorganised, but my secretary, Major Owston here, will be
glad to offer you some refreshment."

He swung round in his chair, paused for a moment at
the foot of the stairs to allow his wheels to enter the
grooves, and flew up them with a speed and unexpectedness which left the Inspector gasping.

"God bless my soul!" he exclaimed. "Ain't he a mar-
vel!"

I made no reply. My own convictions with regard to
Mr. Martin Hews were best kept to myself.

CHAPTER VIII

It must have been, as I afterwards discovered, about a quarter to three, an hour after I had retired to bed, that, notwithstanding my fatigue, I woke with a violent start. My first impulse was to look at the globes on the wall opposite to me. Not one of them was burning. I touched the electric switch of the lamp at the side of my bed and I received a genuine shock. There was no result. Stiff in every limb, I tumbled out of bed and tried the other switch. Still no result. Then, as I stood there, I heard a soft tapping. I threw open the door. A figure, at first undistinguishable, was standing there, holding an electric torch. Directly she spoke, I realised that it was Beatrice Essiter.

"What's wrong?" I asked.

She crossed the threshold, and still holding the door handle, listened for a moment intently.

"I can't tell," she confided. "For one thing the whole of the electric installation seems to have gone wrong. There isn't a light in the house. The secret doors won't open, nor will the telephone ring."

"That's queer," I muttered. "Could any of Joseph's gang have got at the engine?"

"That's what I have been wondering," she replied uneasily. "Jenkins, the electrician, never appeared after the fight was over, and I fancied just as I was getting into bed that the lights were becoming fainter."

I struggled into some clothes.

"The police searched the whole house," I remarked. "Did they visit the engine room?"

"I believe they did. I remember how surprised the Inspector seemed to be at the size of our engine. Jenkins must have been on duty then, or they couldn't have got in without breaking the door down—and there's something else."

She paused and listened again. From where we were on the ground floor to the roof, the great house seemed almost ominously silent.

"I was just going off to sleep," she went on, "when I fancied that I heard voices in the room where that little Jew girl is. It was then I found out that the lights weren't going, and I am afraid I made some noise in groping about before I could find the torches. Anyhow, she was alone when she opened the door to me."

"Did she let you in?"

"Of course. I looked all around. There was no one there."

"Did she seem uneasy?"

"I fancied that she did."

"Do any of your secret passages connect her apartment with any other portion of the house?"

"Yes. If she knew where her door was, and had a plan, she could find her way almost anywhere. The only thing is that none of the switches which open the concealed doors are working now, as the power has broken down. You know that one of the plans is missing? Miles confessed this evening that he had stolen it and sold it to Joseph."

I reflected for a moment.

"You are sure the Inspector actually visited the engine room?" I asked.

"Quite certain. If any one of the raiders had used the plan to find their way in there by the secret passage, and done any damage to the plant or to Jenkins, he must have found it out."

"What about the girl? Did you tell her that you thought you had heard voices in her room? Had she any explanation to offer?"

"She was simply rather impudent. Declared that she must have been saying her prayers."

"You haven't communicated with your uncle, I suppose?"

"I tried to get into the library," she confided, "but I couldn't open the door. There is another way, of course, but I thought I had better come and find you. I don't know why," she concluded, with a little tremor in her tone, "I am not nervous as a rule, but at the present moment I am absolutely terrified."

"I don't think you need be," I assured her. "Why, the police searched the place thoroughly and they've only been gone an hour or two. Where does your uncle sleep?"

"In a room leading out of the library," she explained. "He very seldom goes to bed at night, though. He generally writes and works out plans for the next day until six o'clock, and goes to bed until twelve."

"Then he should be in the library now?"

"I imagine so," she answered, after a moment's hesitation. "I suppose if I hadn't been so foolish, I should have gone to the other door."

"Much better to come for me," I told her—"especially if you were feeling jumpy. I'll go up at once. You haven't another torch, have you?"

She handed me the one she was carrying.

"I have two more in my pocket. I'll show you the way up by the stairs, and—"

"Well?"

"It is foolish of me, of course, but bring your gun. This may be just silliness on my part, but it isn't often I get like this. There are one or two other things which I don't quite understand."

I loaded my automatic quickly and slipped it into my pocket. In the case of a fight, I knew that I should have to use it, for my arms and legs were still stiff, and my wound painful. Then I followed her out into the now deserted hall and mounted the stairs with her. We paused first when we arrived at the third storey outside the door which opened and closed only by the electric appliances from Martin Hews' desk. I pressed the button, but nothing happened. There was no actual sound to be heard in the room, and yet I too was conscious of an uneasy feeling. A thin stream of light was just visible under the door, but that was not unusual if Martin Hews remained there all night. Beyond that, however, if such a thing were possible, I should have said that I was conscious of waves of sound which never became absolutely definite, and yet left me with a disturbed sense of movement, of action, in the closed room.

"Where is the other door?" I whispered.

"This way," she answered.

She led me a few paces down the corridor and directed my fingers on to a small, ordinary door knob.

"Open it and go in," she enjoined, "and make some excuse to Uncle if he is alone. If there is anything wrong, I will go and fetch help."

I gripped my automatic with my right hand, turned the handle with my left, and looked in from the threshold upon a queer and thrilling sight. It was a matter of seconds only before my appearance was discovered, but those seconds were quite enough for me to take in every detail of that amazing scene. Martin Hews was seated at his desk, stiff and rigid, his hands palms downward upon the table, his eyes protuberant, his mouth a little open. He was watched over by the Inspector, still wearing his uniform, but with the upper part of his features now concealed by a black mask. He was only a yard or two away from my employer, whom he was covering with a vicious-looking automatic. In the middle of the room were two large kit bags, one of them already filled and strapped, ready for removal. The rosewood-rimmed show cases, which contained a collection of gold medals and some priceless, uncut precious stones, were already empty, and the taller of the two policemen, also in a mask, was in the act of cutting a small Corregio which hung over the door from its frame. The third policeman had lifted his mask for a moment whilst he held an exquisite pink pearl up to the lamp, by the light of which they were working, before finally approving of it, and seated on the back of a divan, facing me, with a cigarette in the corner of her mouth, was Rachel. Never in my life have I looked upon so thrilling a scene as that dimly lit apartment—the three men, with their sinister black masks, Martin Hews, his face dark with terror, his eyes almost starting from his head, and the girl lolling there, with a cigarette dangling from her red lips. . . .

My entrance had been so noiseless that I had time to take all this in before I was observed, and there is no doubt whatever that if I had been anything but a fool I should have stepped softly back and waited for the result of the alarm which Beatrice Essiter had no doubt already given. Before I had fully realised the situation, however, Rachel saw me. Her great eyes glowed across the room, and the cigarette fell from her fingers. For what reason I could not at that moment surmise, in the act of screaming out, she seemed to change her mind, and stifled the cry in her throat. Her start, however, had been sufficient. The man who was examining the pearl looked quickly up, swung round and faced me. I covered him at once.

"Hands up! Both of you!" I cried. "Quick!"

The man who had been cutting the Corregio from the frame obeyed. The nearer one hesitated. I could see the wicked flash of his eyes as he dropped the pearl from his long, skinny fingers, and ducked. His hand was on its way towards his hip pocket, and with the other man to look after, I dared not hesitate a second. I shot at his legs, and although I missed them the first time, the second bullet must have broken his kneecap, for he went spinning round and the gun slid out of his hand on to the carpet. The other man had crept a step nearer to me, but his hands were still upraised. I had him covered again whilst his companion lay writhing upon the carpet.

"Shoot him, you b——y fool!" the latter shouted. "Take a risk, can't you?"

"Gun's in my helmet upon the table," the man spat out. "Kick me yours."

The wounded man made an effort to roll over, but stopped at the sound of my voice.

"Touch the gun, and you're a dead man," I warned him. "Keep your hands up, you there!"

What followed seemed to me at that moment, as it has done many times since, the strangest part of the whole amazing episode. I was beginning to think that I had won my way through and was master of the situation. The man on the ground had fainted with his last effort to reach his gun. The other was standing obediently well away from the table, with his hands up, and, according to his own admission, unarmed. Then suddenly I heard Rachel's voice—a hoarse, passionate whisper.

"Look out, you fool! Look out, behind the curtains!"

Even as she shouted, I remembered the third man at the far end of the room. His chair was vacant. Martin Hews, unguarded, was leaning forward across the table, his face distorted with mingled rage and fear, and a miniature automatic, with a specially made butt, clenched in his hand. The man who had been guarding him had disappeared, but Rachel's cry had disclosed his plan. The

whole of the left-hand side of the room between the two
doors was hung with magnificent tapestry, towards which
she had pointed. I saw the bulge in it grow nearer every
moment as the pseudo-Inspector crept up towards me.
About three yards from where he now was came a parting
in the tapestry. I watched it with burning eyes, watched
for the glitter of a gun, expecting to see it pushed through
at any moment. With it all, too, I realised another im-
minent source of danger. Rachel could have handed the
gun to the man who had been cutting the picture from
the frame, and I would have been powerless to interfere. She sat there instead, watching—as I watched—that
bulge behind the tapestry drawing closer and closer. The
man with his hands up, who had already been making
gestures, hissed over his shoulder.

"Give me that gun, you little devil!"

Rachel made no movement. It was hard work to watch
everything, but the bulge was still more than the length
of a man's arm from the parting, and I allowed myself
one glance at Rachel's face. I caught only a glimpse of it,
but it was enough to tell me that so far as she was concerned I was safe.

"Get your own gun, you clumsy bungler!" she shouted.
"Calling me names too! Three of you against one man,
and him a toff! Gawd, I wonder what Jo would say to the
mucking lot of you? Watch the bulge, guv'nor."

I watched, though my gun was still covering the other
man. Nearer and nearer came that quiver behind the
tapestry. Just as I expected, I saw an inch or two of dull,
sinister metal slowly forced through the opening. Shooting men in cold blood in the library of an English country
house was nothing to my fancy, but in another second,
when his eye had crept up to the chink, I was his mark.
I swung around and pulled the trigger of my gun twice
in succession, trying to hit the arm which held the pistol.

The other man, who had been watching his opportunity, leaped forward the moment he was uncovered, but in a second there was the spit of a shot from behind him, and he staggered round to fall with a sickening crash upon the carpet. Martin Hews, steering his chair beautifully between the bodies of the two wounded men, drew up at my side, also covering the partition in the tapestry. We waited breathlessly. The man in hiding was evidently hit, for there was no movement, and no sound but his groans.

"Don't trust any of them, sir," I shouted. "Keep your hand upon your gun. The man on the floor's coming to."

Martin Hews smiled. Throughout the whole of my somewhat tangled memories of that scene, I remember his smile. There was ugly humour, there was the blood lust, there was ferocity, all there.

"Well spoken, my gallant Major!" he cried. "My preserver, and a made man from this moment. Little lady on the divan, we will find you a prince for a sweetheart, not a guttersnipe."

She had slipped to her feet. Her air was one of bravado, but I think that even then she began to realise what she had done, that she had turned against her people, that she would probably never again dare to show herself in her old haunts. Perhaps she knew. At any rate, she shrugged her shoulders and wiped the cigarette ash from her sleeve.

"They fight dirty," she declared. "They've got what was coming to them. Jo would say the same if he was here."

Then I heard the tramping of feet, the panting of men running, and we knew that our ordeal was over. Minchin was first into the room, followed pell-mell by Huntley and Grateson. In the background I caught a glimpse of Beatrice Essiter, and all the chill ill humour had gone from her face, and her eyes were glowing with a great relief.

CHAPTER IX

EITHER owing to purposeful avoidance of me, or by a
series of coincidences, I saw nothing whatever of Beatrice
Essiter during the unsettled but comparatively calm days
that followed. In common with several other members of
the household, I seemed to spend the greater part of the
time at Bringford, the nearest county town. I was merci-
fully spared any direct question as to the cause of Miles'
death, and heard the open verdict returned without any
particular qualm of conscience. The three members of
the gang whom we had handed over to the police were
duly committed for trial, notwithstanding the fact that
a famous lawyer from London, who had come down specially for their defence, had fought their cause gallantly.
In the end, however, the verdict of murder was returned
against the three of them, and they were removed to different quarters, to await their trial on the more serious
issue.

During the remainder of the time things proceeded
uneventfully at Breezeley Mansion. My meals were served
alone. I saw nothing of my employer except that always
after my return from Bringford he sent for me and questioned me closely as to what had taken place. I was
quickly convalescent from my various injuries, and although I never recovered from my first almost superstitious aversion to the whole neighbourhood, I fell into the
habit of taking an evening walk about four o'clock as
far as the river. It was on my third excursion of this sort
that I encountered Beatrice Essiter.

She was half a mile away when I first saw her, the only

human being in sight upon that dreary stretch of marshland. I stood in the wet grass, with my back to the river,
and watched her swinging her way along the top of the
raised path—the swamp on one side, the miserable
apology for a road on the other. As she drew near, I advanced to meet her.

"Is there anything wrong?" I asked. "Am I wanted at
the Mansion?"

She shook her head.

"What else is there to go wrong?" she rejoined. "I
had no idea that you were out, even. I wanted to walk
somewhere, so I came to have a look at the river."

We stood side by side on the edge of that garbage sink
of desolation, beneath our feet the cinders, around us the
feebly growing marsh grass. Up the grey bosom of the
sullen river a great lighter, surrounded by screaming
tugs, was making its cautious way, followed by other
craft—a few coasting steamers, a Norwegian barque
laden with timber, a coaling barge, a dredger passing on
its dreary errand to vanish in the grey mist which hung
over the distant bend. She turned away with a little
shiver.

"What a neighbourhood for any sane person to live
in!" she exclaimed bitterly, as we commenced our homeward walk. "Isn't it rather like my uncle's distorted attitude towards life to bring the beautiful things of the
world to such a place?"

"I can't imagine why you stay with him," I told her
bluntly. "It must be hideously depressing."

She shrugged her shoulders.

"It doesn't really matter very much," she remarked indifferently. "Certainly you can't have found the last few
days monotonous."

We were well on our homeward way now. Behind us the
sirens from the steamers hurrying up the river to catch

the tide shrieked out their warnings. In the distance ahead, we could see the lights from the signal posts along the railway; nearer still, the black outline of the Mansion, stark and ugly, with its unnatural blaze of illumination.

"Monotonous?" I reflected. "Two inquests—one of them resulting in a verdict of wilful murder—a police enquiry, two scraps in one night! No, it hasn't been monotonous. Has any one from Bringford been over this afternoon?"

She shook her head.

"I think now that our three desperadoes have been committed for trial, they'll leave us alone for a time," she replied. "The Chief Constable told my uncle that they'd been putting them through a sort of third degree to try to get some information about Joseph."

"Any luck?"

"Not the slightest. I believe they'd all three go to the scaffold sooner than give him away."

"I don't suppose I should be any good at that sort of a job," I said, "but if your uncle has no work for me soon, I should rather like to potter about in the East End for a week or so. I know the district these fellows come from, and a man can't be at the head of a gang of nearly a hundred of the worst criminals in London and keep for ever in the background."

"Ridiculous!" she scoffed. "Any one of them would know you in a minute down there. Besides, I don't think Joseph will ever be found in the East End."

"Where then? Park Lane?"

"I shouldn't be surprised."

"How do you account for Rachel then?"

She shrugged her shoulders again.

"Men have queer playthings," she remarked. "She is pretty enough too. I wish some one could get her to talk."

"Why?"

"Because she is just the one person who knows all about Joseph, and we shall have no peace here whilst he is at liberty."

We were drawing nearer and nearer to our gaunt palace of desolation. They were trying out a new searchlight from the tower, and we had to turn our backs for a moment to escape being blinded by the quivering beam of fierce illumination. Within its narrow orbit, we could distinguish every stick and stone and puddle all the way to the river.

"It's a queer business, all this," I muttered, half to myself.

"It's all right for you," she rejoined bitterly. "You can get away when you want to, but it's my daily life and I can't escape from it. Ever since I can remember him, my uncle seems to have had the desperadoes of the world for either his friends or his enemies. He gets rid of his enemies generally, but fresh ones come. I don't think he has ever been so bitter against any one as Joseph, though."

Miles' successor admitted us—a middle-aged man named Johnson, apparently as well trained and well mannered as his unfortunate predecessor. He delivered what seemed to be an urgent message to my companion, whose face darkened as she listened. She left me without a word and made her way to the lift. I turned into my own apartments and found, to my surprise, Rachel, unceremoniously curled up in my easy-chair.

"Hullo, young lady! Who gave you permission to come in here?" I asked.

She leaned over, struck a match, and lit a fresh cigarette.

"I've had a quarter of an hour with the old ogre," she confided, "and I've given my—what is it you soldiers call it?—parole. I've promised not to attempt to wander back

home on my lonesome. I'm going to wait until Jo comes
for me."

"Well, he came for you the other night," I reminded
her, "and you are still here."

She looked at me with a crooked little smile.

"That's like a man—that speech," she said reproachfully. "I shouldn't have been here if I'd let Ned pot you."

I hastened to apologise.

"Quite right, young lady," I admitted. "I was rather
a beast to say that. Jolly sporting effort of yours it was.
Don't think I've forgotten it. I haven't, and I'm never
likely to."

"Then be a bit more pally," she begged. "I'm for the
gang, of course, and my own boys, but I can't stand dirty
fighting. Besides, it was Ned's fault, really. They'd had
you all for mugs, with their sham uniforms and ambulance: they'd got our wounded chaps away and all the
swag they were told to collect, and yet he must stay for
that picture. I bet he'll cop it when he gets out."

"I don't think that will trouble him much," I remarked.
"He'll get seven years at least, even if they bring it in
manslaughter, and I don't think Joseph will be at the
prison gate then to meet him—not outside, at any rate."

"He'll get something extra, I dare say," she reflected,
"for personating the police. A bit green you folks were,
you know. I knew those weren't real cops the moment I
set eyes on them."

"I dare say you've a larger experience of the Force,"
I retorted. "Besides, you must remember we were all
pretty well done in and dazed, and we were expecting the
police. May I ask for how long you're going to give me
the pleasure of your company? I have some letters to
write."

She settled herself down a little more comfortably.

"I am going to stay just as long as I like," she de-

clared. "I could have been clear away from this place
and you'd have been buried by now if it hadn't been for
me. Just you remember it and be a bit decent."

I felt suddenly a qualm of self-reproach. The girl
spoke the truth.

"All right, I won't bother about the letters," I decided, filling my pipe and drawing up a chair. "You can
stay and have a cocktail with me, if you like."

"It's a pal to talk to I want," she confided, smiling at
me graciously. "The maid who waits on me is a mute, and
there's lots of things I want to know. How many of the
gang had to be sent to hospital?"

"We don't know ourselves," I explained. "When the
sham inspector and police came and made such idiots of
us, they brought an ambulance of their own and took
away all the wounded. No one on our side was seriously
hurt except poor Jenkins, the electrician, and Miles."

"Serve the butler right," she remarked complacently.
"He was the man who squealed."

"You can't be sure of that," I remonstrated.

"I jolly well am!" she contradicted. "Why, I've seen
him with his old soapy face down our way when the gang
was meeting time after time. It was from him Joseph got
a plan of your secret staircase, a set of keys to the house,
and a list of the valuables in the study. That's why they
knew just what to take and what to leave, besides being
able to get into the house and find their way about. It
was him as gave 'em a key to the electric tower, so that
they could do in your electrician and muck up your
plant. He deserved all he got, that chap did, and Joseph
won't worry either. He don't like 'em any better when
they peach for him than when they peach against."

I listened to her story of Miles' misdeeds with satisfaction, and afterwards found myself studying her thoughtfully. There were times when she was a wild-looking

creature enough, but this morning she was neatly, even primly dressed. She was still wearing her gown of vivid red, but her black hair showed signs of careful arrangement, her fringe was cut shorter, and the fierceness had gone from her eyes. Her expression was almost childlike, her tone at times wistful.

"You seemed very unconcerned the other night," I remarked. "Supposing we hadn't chipped in; were you going with those men willingly?"

Her face clouded over. Her red lips were pursed. She was apparently considering the matter.

"Well," she confided, "I don't know as I'm stuck for life or death on Jo. He's got more brains than any of you people—I will say that for him—but he gets kind of sarcastic sometimes, and he plays the toff too much to be exactly my fancy. All the same, what's a girl to do? I couldn't live cooped up here for long with you frozen faces. I've got to have a man, and dancing, and all I want to smoke and all I want to drink, and the pictures whenever I want to go to them."

"But doesn't it matter what man?" I ventured.

"Not much," she admitted frankly, "so long as I take a fancy to him. You'd do all right, if you set your mind to it."

"I'll think of it seriously," I promised her.

She laughed across at me with a touch of her usual devilry. There was invitation both subtle and obvious in her eyes.

"You'd better look sharp," she warned me. "I am here now, but Joseph wants me bad. He gets tired of the classy West End dolls. He'll be after me again before long."

"The sooner the better. We're ready for him."

She laughed scornfully.

"Likely to get him, aren't you? You may be something of a fighter—I won't say you haven't pluck—but brains—lordy, the day that Jo makes up his mind to walk in here and take me away, he'll do it, and I shouldn't be surprised, Mister," she went on, "if it wasn't soon. I bet after the other night you've got him on the raw. I was his girl first, before Jim took me away. He swore he'd get me back. You've got me now, although you don't seem to have much idea what to do with me, but somebody's got to pay for that night, and pretty badly too. That's why, if I were you, I'd be looking for another job. If you're going to sit down here and wait, your number's up, my big man, for all your muscles."

There was a knock at the door. The new butler presented himself, with a card upon a silver salver. I picked it up and read it:

DETECTIVE INSPECTOR BLOOR

"The gentleman would like a few words with you, sir," he announced.

Whatever the object of his visit, the Inspector evidently intended to give me no time to prepare for it, for almost simultaneously he entered the room. Rachel jumped from her chair and fled, throwing a kiss to me from the door. Johnson followed her with a glance of stately disapproval.

"Take a chair, please," I invited. "What can I do for you?"

The Inspector accepted my invitation, but declined the cigarette I offered. He was in plain clothes, a man of medium height, with exceptionally full eyelids which gave him at times a rather sleepy expression. His other features were undistinguished, but his mouth was firm and straight. His complexion was sandy, and his hair of the same colour, although closely cropped, was so thick that it stood up in all directions. His voice when he spoke was unexpectedly pleasant, his speech cautious and well-balanced. The impression he produced upon me was curiously favourable, although at the same time I felt instinctively the need for great circumspection.

"Major Owston," he confided, "I am here in a sense professionally, but I have another reason for visiting you. Captain Joyce is an intimate friend of mine."

"Leonard Joyce," I repeated. "One of my oldest pals. It was he who gave me the letter to Mr. Martin Hews."

"So I gathered. I saw a good deal of Captain Joyce at one time. He was in the Intelligence Department—M.1. 7A, I think you called it—and we had several little affairs to straighten out together. A very good fellow."

"One of the best," I agreed.

I fancied that I was being subjected to a very close scrutiny from underneath those heavy eyelids, but it was almost impossible to tell.

"You may have gathered from my card, Major," he continued, "that I am in the Detective Service at Scotland Yard. You will not object if I ask a few questions concerning recent happenings."

"Go ahead!" I invited. "I have been through it all with the Essex police, but you can have it all over again if you want to."

"You occupy some post in the household here, I believe. May I ask what it is?"

"Well, I am not quite sure that I know myself," I confessed. "We never put it into actual words. A sort of secretary, I should imagine."

"Secretary?" my companion repeated, in his soft, pleasant voice, which at times was almost a drawl. "Typing letters, and that sort of thing?"

"Nothing of that sort at all," I assured him. "To tell you the truth, I have only been here for ten days, and we've been rather upset most of the time, as you doubtless know. I expect my duties will be more clearly defined later on. Up till now, life seems to have been a hotchpotch of scraps and inquests and police court proceedings."

"You took rather a prominent part in the defence of the household the other night, I understand. Mr. Hews speaks very warmly of your services."

"I did my bit, naturally."

My visitor reflected for a few minutes.

"I should perhaps tell you, Major Owston," he went on, "that my visit is made at the instigation of the Chief Commissioner, who is particularly interested in recent events here. I want to suggest to you that in your own interests as well as in the interests of the law, you are quite frank with me."

"Why not?" I rejoined. "Ask me anything you want to, by all means.

"Capital! I am sure that you have nothing to conceal, and a little extra frankness on your part may perhaps help us to solve certain curious problems which have arisen. To begin with, then, hasn't it struck you that your engagement here is of a very singular nature?"

I hesitated.

"To tell you the truth," I confided, "even if that idea has sometimes cropped up in my mind, I haven't allowed myself to think of it. I've been out of a job for nearly two years. I came with Joyce's letter, having precisely ninepence in my pocket. Mr. Martin Hews offered me a position in the household and promised to explain the nature of my duties more clearly later on. A man who has been rescued from starvation, or from borrowing from his friends—which is a trifle worse—isn't very particular what he does, so long as it's on the level. When this scrap came along, I was only too thankful to be of any assistance."

The Inspector nodded sympathetically.

"Very natural—very natural indeed. Still," he went

on, "it seems unreasonable, Major, that you shouldn't have asked yourself 'what manner of a job is this I'm taking on? What am I expected to do to earn my money?' "

"Under ordinary conditions, I dare say you're right," I agreed, "but you must remember that first of all I was too grateful to get any sort of job at all to worry much about what my duties would be, and secondly this scrap has disorganised the whole household and driven everything else out of my thoughts. I imagine that presently Mr. Hews will take me a little further into his confidence. Then I shall have a clearer idea of what he expects from me."

"Quite reasonable," my questioner admitted. "Quite reasonable. You were never in the Intelligence Department yourself, were you, during the war?"

"Never," I told him. "I never had any staff appointment of any sort. My soldiering was nearly all regimental work."

"Nevertheless," the Inspector continued, "Captain Joyce always spoke of you—your name cropped up often in our conversation—as a person of common sense. I put it to you, as they say in the law courts, that you must have been struck by certain mysterious things concerning this household."

"In a sense, of course, that is true," I agreed. "On the other hand, a soldier gets into the habit of minding his own business. If I see things I don't understand, I don't worry about them."

"This—er—network of secret passages, doors that only open by electricity, and searchlights which are played around the countryside?"

I shrugged my shoulders.

"Mr. Martin Hews himself," I pointed out, "is a very exceptional person. He is a cripple, and he has here an immensely valuable collection of curios. I should take it for granted that he was justified in any means he adopted to protect himself."

"But all these contrivances," my visitor persisted gently, in his silky, pleasant voice, "are really not so much use, after all, as a means of protection. They failed him, for instance, the other night."

"That was because the whole show was given away by a member of the household who was in league with the burglars," I pointed out— "Miles, the butler, the fellow who got shot."

"Quite true. Nevertheless, I understand that the whole system is being reinstalled, and a successor to the unfortunate electrician who was murdered already appointed. Now I should like to ask you this question, Major. Remember that I am speaking on behalf of the custodians of the law of this country, and that you too are one of the king's servants. I ask you, has it never occurred to you that there is something mysterious about this whole house? I suggest that there might be something going on here which may be—I am speaking quite frankly —of a criminal nature?"

"There are possibilities of every sort, of course," I acknowledged. "I am not of an imaginative turn of mind, however, and so far as I have thought about the matter at all, I have remembered that Mr. Hews, like a great many deformed people, is probably of a freakish turn of mind. These devices appeal to him and he is rich enough to install them if he wishes. Nothing in connection with them which has come under my notice could in any way be considered an offence against the law."

"Five footmen," my visitor murmured.

"I don't see anything in that at all," I declared. "There is surely no reason why a wealthy man, who can perfectly

well afford it, shouldn't keep a few extra servants to help
him guard his treasures?"

The Inspector listened to me without change of coun-
tenance. I was telling the truth, but I had no idea whether
he believed me or not.

"There is a young lady, at present an inmate of the
household, who was mentioned as being one of the causes
of the attack. Why does Mr. Hews protect her?" he
enquired. "She was, as I dare say you know, the companion of Donkin, the leader of the rival gang of hooligans, until a few days ago."

"Mr. Hews is upstairs," I replied. "Why not ask him
such a question for yourself? He has not taken me into
his confidence."

"But it was you," my *vis-à-vis* persisted softly, "who
aided Donkin to escape. You knew, I presume, that he
was a criminal?"

"I knew nothing about it at all," I insisted. "I hadn't
been in this house more than an hour when Donkin arrived. I saw him into a motor boat. That was all."

"Aiding and abetting a criminal to escape!"

"How was I to know that he was a criminal?"

"You were merely an agent, without a doubt," the In-
spector allowed, "but Mr. Martin Hews knew all about it.
Now one is driven to ask oneself, why did a gentleman in
Mr. Martin Hews' position take such an interest in Jim
Donkin as to assist him to escape from justice and give
shelter to his lady companion?"

"From what I heard of the conversation, Inspector," I
told him—a little maliciously, I confess—"I gathered
that it was Joseph from whom Donkin was anxious to
escape. He didn't expect the police for about a week."

"*Touché!*" my visitor admitted with a smile. "But you
must remember those fellows naturally knew more about
one another's movements than we did. I am afraid I am

wearying you a little, Major. I am sorry, but we are up against a very ugly problem at Scotland Yard, and somehow or other it has to be solved. We want Joseph—we want him very badly."

"You can't want him out of the way any worse than Mr. Martin Hews does," I confided.

"That statement of yours, Major," the Inspector declared, stretching out his hand for his hat, "opens up the way for a suggestion on my part. I propose that we should work together. You are still a soldier of the king, and I am the representative of the law. We are equally concerned in the war against crime. And, believe me," he added, rising to his feet, and suddenly looking at me with wide-open eyes which I discovered to be unexpectedly blue and bright, "Joseph and his men will be discovered in time, discovered and brought to justice. Pay me a visit some time at Scotland Yard. I will show you some of the statistics. It is an amazing thing how seldom a criminal in the long run escapes. The law wins, Major Owston. Try to bear that in mind, and let us have that call from you at Scotland Yard whenever you feel inclined. It will give me pleasure to find myself working with a friend of Captain Joyce."

We shook hands. The fellow had an indescribably attractive manner, and somehow or other, although his questions embarrassed me all the time, I felt that it was impossible to dislike him. I had a grim foreboding that before long I might find myself between two stools.

CHAPTER X

THE yellow telephone tinkled shortly after Inspector Bloor's departure, and in obedience to its summons I mounted to the third floor and presented myself in the library. When I entered the room, I found Martin Hews apparently deep in contemplation of a small bronze, which he had placed upon the table before him. He motioned me over without turning his head. His beady, unblinking eyes were rivetted upon the figure. His lips were a little parted, the lower one protruding. He might have been, as indeed he was, engaged upon an act of worship, but he looked more like that gargoyle than ever.

"You are not an artist, Major Owston?" he murmured.

"I am afraid not, sir," I agreed.

"Yet what does it matter?" he went on, in his thin, metallic voice. "Does it take an artist, I wonder, to appreciate the exquisite and etherealised triumph of a great work like this? Consider the Cupid for a moment, his attitude—a poem in itself—his shy adoration, tinctured with that faint hint of desire."

"Wonderful!" I assented.

"As for the Psyche," he continued, his voice becoming shriller, as usually happened when he was greatly intertested, "not even Walter Pater could translate into words and phrases her exquisite charm. Look at that curve, Major, the curve beginning at the middle of her back downwards, the tapering legs, the modelling of her knee. Men made war in the old days for women and for gold. Is it any wonder that they make war to-day for the possession of such treasures as this?"

I remained silent. His eyes were still wandering over the two figures, and although there was no trace of the idealist in his expression, I had the feeling that for the first time I had heard him speak with perfect honesty, perfect sincerity.

"Donkin got that for me," he confided. "It was once in the famous Mason Collection. A thousand guineas it cost, and I very nearly lost it. It was in that fellow's bag the other night when you shot him. Joseph wanted it, I suppose. Blast him! Come over to the table, Owston. I have a few words to say."

I watched him with an interest which never seemed to slacken, as he threaded his way through the medley of furniture, replaced the statuette upon the bracket from which he had taken it, and with a single turn of the wrist glided round and drew in again under the knee hole of his desk. He motioned me to the chair by his side, sometimes occupied by his niece.

"You are promoted," he said. "The chair of death—as somebody once called it—is no longer for you. I am beginning to be convinced that I was right about you, as I usually am. A brave man, dogged of purpose, not over-intelligent, but with sufficient brains to adapt himself to a difficult situation. A trifle expansive with our friend Inspector Bloor, perhaps, but you were taken by surprise. On the whole, I liked your manner, I approved of your reticences. Bloor was disappointed, I think."

"You overheard then?"

"Naturally. It was very important that I should overhear. I was within a few feet of you on the other side of the wainscotting. It interests me very much to learn that Scotland Yard is becoming suspicious about my house and my manner of living."

My momentary annoyance vanished. This was, after all, part of the game.

"It is twenty years, Owston," my employer reflected, "since I first committed an offence against the statutory laws. I think I may safely say that until this time I have never even been suspected. I can see, however, that from now on those things will become more difficult. This may affect the arrangement between us."

"You are not going to send me away?" I exclaimed, with a sudden fear that he was mocking me.

"Nothing," he declared, "is further from my thoughts. My plans, however, must be altered to meet the new conditions. You will be my ally, but I cannot keep you by my side so continually as I had intended. From to-morrow you will find yourself in possession of chambers in town, where you will spend the greater part of your time. The work you will have to do there will explain itself as the hour for action arrives, but its main object will be concerned with the determination to which I have come during the last few days. These two gangs of criminals—Donkin's and Joseph's—have at times in the past been of great assistance to me. From henceforward it is finished with them. It is too dangerous a game for any one who has attracted the attention, however indirectly, of Scotland Yard. Donkin's has broken up naturally, with the flight of its chief; Joseph's I shall destroy. Afterwards, I shall conduct all my operations myself. I have no longer any need of either of my disreputable allies."

There was the usual signal to which apparently he replied favourably, for a moment later the door opened, and Beatrice Essiter came into the room. She did not even glance at me. She stood before her uncle with her fingers upon the table.

"There is a serious matter to speak of," she told him.

I took a step towards the door, but he checked me promptly.

"Proceed," he directed.

"The police have been to Grafton Street."

His lips parted a little, but he remained silent. Only his eyes burned out their question.

"They found nothing," she went on hastily. "They lingered over the Mallowfield Ruby, but they seemed satisfied with Isaacs' explanations. They asked a good many questions about some of the gems in the Hereford Chest, but Isaacs insists that he satisfied them. They knew nothing about the vaults. At any rate, they did not ask to be allowed to inspect them. Isaacs is convinced that the visitation has no particular significance."

"He had better come down here," Martin Hews decided. "The topazes were in the vault?"

"Yes."

"He can bring them to me by hand."

"I should leave him alone if I were you," she advised. "He has gone home to Hampstead by this time. He told me that he was shaken all to pieces. His voice sounded like it. Here is a telephone message which you may find even more interesting. It came from a call office in Piccadilly."

Martin Hews took the slip of paper in his hand and he read it aloud, partly, I believe, for my edification:

"A car will wait at Breezeley Station until ten o'clock to-night. If it returns empty there will be more trouble. Isaacs has sent for a nerve specialist."

Martin Hews leaned forward across the table. His tiny fists were clenched until the knuckles were white. I have never seen so horrible an expression as the one which distorted his face. For a moment he lost control of himself. He used words which made me glance in horror towards Beatrice Essiter. She seemed deaf, however. When he had finished he rubbed his lips with a thin cambric handkerchief. Then she lifted her head.

"I should let the girl go," she recommended.

For a moment I thought he would break out again. This time, however, he controlled himself.

"Would you?" he rejoined dryly. "On the contrary, I am not one of those who offer gifts to their enemies. Never before has any one dared to bribe one of my own people to turn informer against me. Miles lies dead—a merciful death. Joseph is alive—to-day."

"Alive, unidentified, and undiscovered," she reminded him.

This time he seemed to have regained complete possession of his self-control. He listened to his niece's comment without anger.

"Undiscovered and unidentified," he repeated coldly, "because he was always more useful to me as a mythical figure. Donkin I never dared deal with openly after he disclosed himself. Joseph has declared war against me, and I have accepted the challenge. Within a month's time, his gang will he broken up as Donkin's is, and Joseph, if he has a wish left in his body, will be wishing that he were where Donkin is. . . . Now, you can leave us, Beatrice. I have something to say to Major Owston."

She obeyed in ungracious silence. Her uncle waited until the door was closed.

"Owston," he asked, turning to me, "does it strike you that I have become an old man within the last forty-eight hours?"

"I see no change, sir," I told him.

"Yet," he went on, "this is the first time within my memory that my niece has questioned any command of mine, the first time she has ever shown the slightest doubt of my being able to carry out my plans."

"It is rather a large order, isn't it, sir?" I ventured.

He stared at me out of his beady eyes as though I had

spoken heresy. His attitude resolved itself, however, into that of one dealing with an ignorant child.

"When you have known me longer, Major," he said, "you will understand that the thing I have pledged myself to do is always done. I have pledged myself to deal with Joseph, and Joseph will be dealt with. My ordinary methods," he continued, with a queer little note of pomposity in his thin voice, "would lead me to success within a reasonable time. I have evidence; I have signposts. I have a wonderful scheme all carefully thought out. But within the last few hours a new idea has come to me. I have thought of an easier, a surer way, which will lead us to our goal without even a week's delay. You will be one of my helpers?"

"Gladly, sir," I assented.

I waited tentatively. I had no idea of what was coming.

"Do you know much about women?" he asked.

"Not a damned thing," I assured him, "I beg your pardon, sir, I mean that I know very little about them—haven't come my way, somehow."

"I rather gathered that," my employer agreed dryly. "You would be surprised then if I told you that with the very slightest encouragement, that little *gamine* in the west wing would be in your arms, and after that you would know all you wanted to about Joseph."

I felt the colour slowly mounting to my temples. My first impulse was towards blasphemy. I tried an old trick I used when I was in the regiment and noted for a violent temper. I counted ten before I spoke. Then I looked across at him.

"You also overheard my conversation with Rachel, or rather hers with me?" I asked.

He chuckled.

"Certainly I did. The young woman's attitude towards life amused me exceedingly.

"I am sorry, sir," I said, "but I wouldn't take on a job of that sort for the world."

Again there was that hard stare in his soulless eyes, the slight protuberance of his quivering underlip, the gathering scowl.

"Why not?" he demanded shrilly.

"I don't mind the fighting," I explained. "I don't even mind being a trifle the wrong side of the law at times, but I'm not going to try to turn a child like that into a common informer."

He thrust his hand into one of the drawers of his desk, took out a packet, and threw it towards me.

"There is a bank book there, and a cheque book, which should belong to you," he remarked. "You may find your balance interesting. If you have scruples, you needn't go too far with the girl. If she thinks she's once got you, she'll fall fast enough."

I am only human and I looked longingly at that packet, but I shook my head.

"It can't be done, sir," I decided.

My employer had the air of one endeavouring to maintain a judicial attitude under exceedingly trying circumstances.

"You have to remember," he continued, "that the girl herself is utterly devoid of morals. She has been the mistress for the moment of any man who has taken her fancy. Whatever she feels to-day is forgotten to-morrow. You have to remember, also, another thing," he concluded, a vicious little threat creeping into his tone, "to refuse one of my commissions means—the open door."

My heart sank. The ways of luxury even for this brief space of time had made a different man of me.

"I am afraid the matter doesn't admit of discussion," I

said. "It's just bad luck. Personally, I don't believe that
the girl was doing more than teasing me when she made
those slight advances you seem to know about. If I had
taken her seriously—"

"Try and see," he suggested.

There was an ugly cynicism in his smile. He was honest
enough in his belief—I could see that—honest enough,
too, in his judgment of Rachel. He may even have been
right. Yet even then the thing was still impossible.
Perhaps he thought because I remained silent I was
hesitating. He leaned forward. His mouth took one of
its worst curves. His expression was the expression of a
satyr.

"Listen," he proposed. "Your dinner table must be
sometimes lonely. Send for her to-night and let her dine
with you. Tell her you are leaving here to-morrow for
rooms in Mayfair. Ask her to come and share them with
you for a week or two. You can promise her something
worth having—*carte blanche* at any dressmaker she
chooses. If she doesn't jump at it, I shall have been wrong,
and we'll call the matter off; if she goes with you, she'll
have chucked Joseph, and she'll tell you all I want to
know. Believe me, my modest young man," he wound
up, with a final Satanic smile, "I will back my opinion this
time to the extent of a hundred pounds to one on the result."

"Sorry I have not made myself clear, sir," I apologised.
"I won't touch the business."

"It's that or the open door," he snarled.

I rose to my feet.

"Sorry, sir," I regretted.

I could see the whole of his small frame quivering, and
I knew he was passionately angry. He once more opened
the drawer and drew out two twenty-pound notes, which
he passed over to me.

"You have earned that," he said. "Take it and go to hell."

My hesitation was only momentary. I came to the conclusion that I had earned them, and I had in any case no fancy for walking back to London. I took the notes, buttoned them in my waistcoat pocket, and turned away.

"I thank you very much, sir," I said.

"Go to hell," he repeated.

I walked downstairs a little dazed, took my hat, which was all that remained of my previous apparel, from its peg, and went out of the house. I made my way along the rough lane until I reached the stile where the cinder path ran past the deserted brick kiln to the station. Then I turned for a moment and looked back. Grotesque as it appeared to me when I had first caught sight of that loathsome structure, my hatred of it now seemed to have grown in intensity. Against that empty background, rising from its flat plain of desolation, it stood out like a gewgaw building, planted there by the machinations of some evil spirit, devoid of every possible line of beauty, every curve, every dash of colour that could please. But for its size and its distance from the river, it might have been the sorting house for pilgrims awaiting their dread passage across the Styx. I shivered as I looked at it; I shivered as I looked away. Yet so curiously are we constituted that when I vaulted the stile on to the cinder path and set out for the station, I knew that there was nothing I wanted so much in the world as to hear the voice of Martin Hews calling me back, to find myself once more an inmate of that house of mystery.

The affair was no longer any concern of mine, but I must confess that it gave me a little thrill of interest when in the far corner of the station yard I saw a small, powerful-looking limousine in the charge of a dark-

liveried chauffeur. I spoke to the solitary porter.
"Is that a taxi?" I asked him.

The man shook his head.

"There ain't no such thing in these parts, sir," he told
me. "I don't rightly know what it is. The man's been waiting there for over two hours. There's been a plenty of
trains in and out, but he's never even looked at the passengers coming or going. To my way of thinking, he
seems to be expecting some one from the Mansion."

"Have you spoken to him at all?" I asked.

"I wished him good afternoon, but he didn't make no
reply. I asked him an hour ago if his feet were getting
cold, and he sat like a block of wood."

I strolled across to the car. The chauffeur merely
turned his head at my approach and went on reading his
newspaper.

"Having a long wait, aren't you?" I remarked.

He looked at me and made no response of any sort.

"It's not my business," I went on, "but as a matter of
fact, I don't think the young lady is coming."

He showed no signs of interest or intelligence but deliberately returned to his perusal of the newspaper. Just then
I heard the whistle of the approaching train and I left
him.

CHAPTER XI

I HAD trouble at the booking office with my two ten-pound notes, and I travelled to London with the understanding that I should pay for my ticket upon arrival. Whilst I waited upon the platform at Liverpool Street for the Inspector to bring me change for one of my notes, a respectable-looking, middle-aged man in dark clothes raised his bowler hat, and accosted me.

"Major Owston?" he enquired.

"My name," I acknowledged.

"I am to show you to your rooms, sir," he announced. "I have a taxicab waiting. I found that they were rather scarce, so I took the liberty of engaging one."

"Aren't you making some mistake?" I asked him incredulously.

"No mistake at all, sir," he answered confidently. "I received all my instructions half an hour ago from Breezeley Mansion."

My spirits began to rise. Perhaps, after all, Martin Hews had relented. I tipped the Inspector who brought me my money and followed the man out of the station. He held open the door of the taxi for me.

"You will excuse my riding with you, sir, please," he begged. "Passengers are not allowed outside. . . . Number 3a, Down Street," he directed the driver.

"Down Street?" I repeated, as we drove off. "Quite a pleasant neighbourhood."

"You have not yet visited the rooms, I think, sir?"

"I have not."

"You will find them small but quite comfortable," the

man assured me. "I hope I shall give you satisfaction. My wife is a very good cook, and I am used both to valeting and waiting at table. My name is Smart."

"I have no doubt that we shall get on together excellently, Smart," I told him. "That is, if I stay."

"I hope that you will be staying the month at any rate, sir. Mr. Yardsley has engaged me for your servant on trial for that period."

"Who the mischief is Mr. Yardsley?" I enquired.

My companion coughed.

"I understood that he was the solicitor acting for the gentleman who rang me up from the country," he replied hesitatingly.

After that I asked no more questions. We duly arrived at our destination, and I was ushered into a very pleasant and even luxurious suite of bachelor rooms. They were not only ready for my occupation, but whisky and soda, cigarettes and cigars were upon the sideboard, and a variety of brand-new articles for my use in the bathroom. Mrs. Smart—a pleasant-faced, somewhat diminutive woman—came almost at once to take my order for dinner.

"I may be going out to a restaurant, Mrs. Smart," I demurred.

She looked at me in pained protest.

"The message was, sir," she ventured, "that you would probably be dining in to-night. I have been cook in gentlemen's families for many years and always given satisfaction."

I gave my order without further comment, deciding that some one was probably communicating with me that night, and that I had better not stir out. As soon as she had departed, I looked into my bedroom and found the drawers full of all manner of hosiery, ties, shirts and collars, and every imaginable article of men's wear. There

were two suits of clothes and a coat from a well-known
tailor, with a note to say that his cutter would come
round any time if I would communicate with them by telephone, to see what alterations were necessary!

I helped myself to a whisky and soda, and, crossing to
the window, looked over Piccadilly towards the Green
Park. Every now and then I found it exceedingly hard to
realise the sudden change in my position, after a year's
desperate struggling. At no time, however, had the fantastic unreality of the thing appealed to me more than at
this moment. Little more than a week ago, I had been
literally a beggar. The last bed I had slept in before my
excursion to Breezeley Mansion was in Rowton House.
The sudden return to the almost forgotten luxuries of life
almost took my breath away. There was no doubt, however, about my immediate surroundings. Everything was
real, matter-of-fact, and deliberate. The clothes had evidently been ordered for me, and from the bedroom came
that delightful before-dinner sound—the soft running of
water. Smart once more presented himself.

"Your bath will be ready directly, sir," he announced.
"You will probably feel more comfortable to change early.
If you will allow me, I will prepare your clothes now. I
was a little doubtful about the dinner suit when I un-
packed it. Since I have seen you, I am quite sure it will fit
all right."

A certain vein of philosophy, which had kept my head
above water in difficult times, reasserted itself, and I proceeded to comport myself as the well-established tenant
of these very pleasant apartments. I wallowed in a warm
bath and finished up with a cold spray. I lingered over
the drawing on of silk underclothes and approved of
the quality of my evening socks. I recognised the cut of
an expert in my shirt, showed Smart my own particular
way of tying a black bow, joined with him in his en-

thusiastic approval of the set of my dinner jacket, and strolled into the sitting-room, where Mrs. Smart was laying the cloth, in about an hour's time, with an amazing sense of well-being tingling in my senses. The woman merely glanced up at my coming.

"Smart will be bringing you a cocktail in a few minutes, sir," she confided. "He is supposed to be a very good mixer."

The cocktail arrived in due course, accompanied by the evening papers, and I was forced to admit that Smart was an artist. I lit a cigarette and amused myself by reading of the futile efforts of the police to make any further arrests in connection with the Breezeley Mansion burglary. It appeared that I was a little before my time, for half an hour passed without any signs of dinner. I replenished my glass from the shaker and had ensconced myself once more comfortably in the easy-chair when my complacency was suddenly disturbed. Smart threw open the door of the room.

"The young lady, sir," he announced.

I stared at Rachel for a moment without comprehension. Then I understood the trick of which I had been the victim. A fit of fury seized me, none the less intense because of the mocking laugh which parted her lips. She had undergone a transformation so complete that her appearance alone would have kept me tongue-tied. She was wearing a small turban-shaped black hat and a fashionable black afternoon dress of some soft and clinging material. Truly, I said to myself, this man Martin Hews was the devil incarnate.

"Shall I lay another place, sir?" Smart enquired.

"No," I shouted.

The man remained silent, but his air was one of respectful expostulation. I am convinced that he understood the whole situation. Rachel only laughed.

"Aren't you going to dine, then?" she asked, drawing off her gloves.

"Whose flat is this?" I demanded angrily.

"Ours, isn't it?" she mocked me. "Can I have a cocktail?"

"Certainly, miss," Smart replied, seizing on the excuse to hurry away.

She came across the room and sat on the edge of my chair, derision in her eyes, but looking more like a human being than ever I had seen her.

"I say, now, what's all the trouble?" she remonstrated. "I sha'n't eat you."

"Where did you get those clothes from?" I asked sternly.

"A young woman met me at the station, took me to her shop in Bond Street, and rigged me out from head to foot," Rachel explained, slipping from her place and pirouetting around. "Don't you like them? Can't say I'm stuck on black, but these West Enders ought to know, and the *crêpe de chine's* O.K., I can tell you."

My momentary fit of anger melted into laughter. After all, there was a humorous side of the situation, and I was a fool to lose my temper. Just at that auspicious moment, Smart returned with a cocktail which he handed to Rachel. Without further comment he began to lay another place at the table.

"Cheerioh!" Rachel exclaimed, raising her glass. "Why, that's too bad. You haven't got one."

"I had my second half an hour ago," I told her. "Mrs. Smart kept on making some excuse for not serving dinner. She knew all about this stupid business, I suppose."

"I don't think it's a stupid business at all," Rachel declared, coming back to the arm of my chair, and swinging her leg, with the obvious idea of admiring her own stockings. "I call it a very nice party. I believe he's gone to get another cocktail for you. I shall wait before I finish mine."

"I shouldn't," I advised her. "To tell you the truth, I'm rather thinking of going out and dining at my club."

She made a little grimace.

"You wouldn't be so unkind," she pleaded. "I should get into such trouble when I got back."

"When you got back?" I repeated hopefully. "You are returning to Breezeley then?"

"Unless you invite me to stay here," she murmured brazenly.

She leaned nearer to me, her lips very close indeed to mine.

"If you come an inch nearer, I shall box your ears, you little hussy," I warned her.

She indulged in a further grimace. Then her prophecy came true. Smart entered silently, with another cocktail upon a tray.

"I have taken the liberty, sir," he acknowledged, "quite a light one. My own special fancy. I shall be serving dinner now, sir, directly."

"Cheerioh!" Rachel repeated, raising her glass once more.

"Cheerioh!" I grunted.

Dinner appeared, and we took our places at the table. Rachel's deportment on the whole gave me no cause for anxiety. It is true that she moved her place a little closer to mine, and that she once or twice felt tentatively for my hand, but this, I noticed with satisfaction, was between the courses, and her first attention was directed always towards her food, to which she did full justice. She demanded champagne and was promptly served with it. I asked for whisky and soda and drank sparingly of that. I permitted myself a glass of port when the excellently cooked meal had been served, and in a glow of after-dinner humanity, remembering that I had still nearly forty pounds in my pocket and that the young lady had not declared herself, I allowed her searching fingers to rest for a moment or two in mine. Then the inevitable crisis arrived. The cloth was cleared, the coffee and liqueurs stood upon a small table between us, and Rachel curled herself up upon the hearthrug at my feet, smoking a cigarette.

"Now, young lady," I suggested, "let's get to business."

"Business?" she murmured. "You are funny!"

I ignored the provocative gleam in her eyes and continued.

"Do you know what you're here for?" I asked.

"I can guess," she answered.

"Your mission here," I went on, "is to vamp me à la cinéma, and when you have shorn my locks—"

"When I have what?" she interrupted.

"My fault," I apologised. "Put it this way. When we are sitting google-eyed, hand in hand, or probably with my arm around your waist, swearing to be true to one another for the rest of our lives, I am to begin gently and tactfully to pump you about Joseph."

She nodded.

"I rather thought that was the game," she murmured. "Give me some of that sweet white stuff."

I filled a liqueur glass with white crême de menthe for her, which she sipped appreciatively.

"Quite a scheme, ain't it?" she ruminated.

"Does it appeal to you?"

She slid towards me until her head was perilously near my knee.

"I like the first part of it all right—Henry, your name is, isn't it?—I like the first part, Henry, but when it comes to the rest—well, you know you're fine to look at—I always did like big men—but you know, Mister, up here—" she tapped her forehead—"I don't think you or Mr. Martin Hews have anything on me. If you began to ask me questions about Joseph—my, how clumsy you'd be! I should soon fill you up with a lot of faked stuff or else let you know where you got off."

I nodded approvingly.

"That's honest," I said. "Then tell me why you came?"

She leaned back deliberately, her head against my knee.

"Please don't do that," I begged.

She laughed at me and remained where she was.

"Don't be silly," she rejoined. "This is very comfortable. If you want to hear why I came you'll have to keep quiet. You wouldn't like to brush my fringe back, I suppose, with that great hand of yours? It's getting into my eyes."

"I would not," I answered sternly. "Go on, please."

"Well, of course I saw through the game the moment the old man sent for me," she continued. "I was to come up and have dinner and drink wine with you, and try to find out whether you were on the square. That was how he put it to me. That was what he wanted me to believe. On parole, of course. Very nearly gave himself away, the old fool! 'What time am I to be back?' I asked him, as innocent as possible. 'Any time you like,' he replied, with a funny sort of grin, 'so long as when you do come you come straight from Down Street.' Artful old guy! I knew all the time what he was after. It wasn't you he wanted to test. It was me he wanted to peach about Joseph. If it wasn't that I thought it would be such fun to come, I'd have given him what for."

I was beginning to feel more at my ease.

"I am inclined to wonder," I observed, "whether Martin Hews, clever man though he is, understands men and women as well as he thinks he does. Girls are too good sports to give their sweethearts away for nothing. After all, Joseph is your man."

"Is he?" she interrupted. "Steady on there, guv'nor! I'm not so sure. I've been crazy about him at times. There were other times I liked Jim Donkin just as well. I ain't at all sure about you, Henry," she continued, with an upward little flash of the eyes. "You're a good 'un in a scrap. That's what I like. I love to see men fight."

"Then you ought to be ashamed of yourself," I told her.

"Why?" she enquired curiously. "A man has either to fight or steal. Joseph is good with a knife or a gun, and he's as foxy as they make 'em, but he always seems to keep outside things. He ain't what I should call a fighter —not like you, Henry."

"Well, are you going to tell me where I can find him?" I asked her.

Her eyes flashed lightnings at me. She pushed herself away, suddenly trembling with anger. Underneath her filmy black dress I could see her small but beautifully shaped bosom rising and falling passionately.

"You pig!" she cried. "You know I'm not. You're not a fool muddling about outside the world like Martin Hews. You know that even if you kissed the last breath out of my body and my lips were aching for more, tortured me in any way you can think of, you'd never get me squealing. I don't pretend I'm crazy about Joseph any longer. I'm faithful to a man as long as I feel what I want to feel for him, and when that's finished, I don't bother any more about him. You folks call that wicked, I suppose. I don't. I call it nature. I live as I am made, not according to the books. Listen!"

She sprang to her feet. Every fibre of her seemed

quivering with emotion. She pointed to the door and swung round to me.

"I tell you this, Henry; if Joseph were to walk into the room at this moment, I'd send him packing if I could, but there's no torture has ever been invented could make me tell you or Martin Hews or the cops how to lay your hands upon him. His day will come some time, and maybe I sha'n't wear mourning for him, but it won't be me who'll give him away. Why, Mister," she went on, dropping once more back to her old place at my feet—"I mean Henry—don't you know that's the reason why Joseph's lot have smashed Donkin's, why they'll smash any other gang that comes up against them, and why the police can only get one or two at a time, like they did at Breeze-ley? They're tight-lipped, every one of them. Two men have tried squealing, and they've been dead in twenty-four hours. That's where Joseph's clever. He'd swing himself, before he gave a pal away. So would every one of them. They're mostly Jews. They're as wicked as you like, they're up to any dirty trick. They'd stab you in the back as soon as look at you, but they'd stand tor-ture, as I would, sooner than turn informer. If that fool Miles hadn't been shot the other night, Joseph would have seen that he got what was coming to him all right, though he paid him a thousand pounds in hard cash for what he'd done. He knew very well that he'd do the double cross if he didn't."

"Well, this is all very interesting," I admitted. "Pity you didn't tell it to Martin Hews."

"Likely to, wasn't I?" she scoffed. "I should have spent the evening down there moping. Henry, aren't you ever a little bit affectionate?"

"Very seldom," I assured her.

"It seems a pity," she sighed, smoothing my hand. "Don't you like girls, Henry?"

"Very much—in my own fashion."

"Show me your own fashion," she begged, laughing up at me.

"Look here, my child,"I said, withdrawing myself from her closer proximity upon the pretext of reaching for a cigarette, "we'd better have an understanding, hadn't we? I like you, I think you're very attractive; I like you more and more every time I see you, but that's all there is to it."

"Ain't you queer," she murmured.

"You're faithful to your men, aren't you, Rachel?" I asked.

"I'm faithful until I like some one else better."

"There's Joseph," I suggested.

"But I like you better than Joseph—dear," she whispered.

Then a flash of inspiration came to me.

"Listen, Rachel," I said. "You were in love with Joseph once, I suppose?"

"Fairly dotty," she assured me.

"If any other man had tried to make love to you then—"

"I'd have knifed him," she interrupted.

"Very well. I'm in love with another girl."

The smile left her face, and the tantalizing light died out of her eyes. She crouched in her place, looking up at me, her lips parted, her eyes dim.

"You don't mean that? Say you don't mean that, Henry?"

"I mean it."

There was a moment's silence. I gripped hold of myself, terrified of a sudden weakening, for I was as human as most men, and the pathetic break in her voice made a more dangerous appeal to me than all her wiles.

"It isn't his niece, is it?" she asked wistfully. "She's

beautiful, but she ain't got any life. She'd never love like I can, even though I'm a common little thing."

"Never mind who it is, Rachel," I said. "She exists all right. I wish she didn't."

She threw her arms unexpectedly round my neck. Her burning lips brushed my cheek.

"Forget her," she begged. "We don't need to think of any one else but ourselves, just for now."

I lifted her up and carried her back to her chair. She clung to me convulsively. I could feel her whole frame shaking with sobs, but I set her down and left her. Her arms fell to her sides listlessly. She turned her head away. I tiptoed my way to my own room and locked the door. I had a telephone there to Smart's quarters and I called him up. As I held the receiver in my hand, I saw the handle of the door turn and then go back to its place.

"Smart," I asked him, "is there a car waiting outside?"

"Yes, sir."

"Very good," I said. "The young lady will be down directly."

I waited for five minutes. Then I returned to the sitting-room. Rachel was leaning back in her chair, with a full glass of liqueur in one hand and a cigarette between the fingers of the other. She had dabbed rouge on to her cheeks, the pallor of which had alarmed me, and her lips were becarmined.

"I say," she complained, "have I got to go home without a cinema or a dance or anything? That old spider said you'd give me ever such a good time."

"I'm afraid you'll have to go, Rachel," I insisted. "I don't know anything about cinemas, and if you danced with me once, you'd never want to again."

She sprang to her feet.

"Let's try."

She half sang, half hummed, very musically, one of

the most fascinating of the modern fox trots. We danced round the table and backwards and forth until we were breathless. Then she drew away with a laugh which was almost natural.

"You're all right," she declared. "Give me my cloak."

I picked up the sort of black silk wrap which she had been wearing, threw it around her shoulders, and rang the bell. She took my arm for a moment.

"The first time in my life I've been turned down," she confided. "I don't like it, Henry. I thought I was just angry at first. I ain't sure, though," she added, "that it don't hurt."

I bent down and kissed her.

"Friends, please," I begged.

She shook her head.

"I ain't sure," she answered, as the door opened.

CHAPTER XII

As soon as I had heard the car turn the corner of the street, I settled down with a pipe, a whisky and soda, and the evening paper. Barely a quarter of an hour had passed, however, before the telephone bell at my elbow rang. I hesitated for a moment before I took up the receiver. I had an alluring but terrifying vision of Rachel, with her turbulent femininity, back again with new graces and devilments. I might have spared myself the fear, though. Rachel was already heading for the marshes of Essex, and the voice that spoke to me was cold and precise.

"Is that Major Owston?"

"It is," I answered. "Who are you?"

"Beatrice Essiter. I am speaking from Breezeley. I am sorry to disturb you, but I have a message from Mr. Hews."

"You are not disturbing me at all," I assured her. "I was only reading the paper."

It might have been my fancy, but it seemed to me that there was a great change in her tone when she spoke again.

"All alone?"

"All alone. The enemy has effected a graceful retreat. I am enjoying a pipe and a sense of barren triumph."

"I gather that the young lady is on her way back here?"

"Unless she breaks her parole," I replied.

"Do you care to know that I am glad to hear it?"

"I can't think of anything else in the world just now," I replied, "that I would rather hear."

She laughed down the telephone—the first time I had ever heard her indulge in so light-hearted an effort, and I am quite sure that the old wire had never throbbed to anything more musical.

"Poor Uncle!" she murmured. "His devilish scheme gone wrong! He will lose faith in you, Major Owston."

"So long as you don't," I began—

I think that perhaps the personal note was too marked. She interrupted.

"Major Owston, I rang you up to say that one of my uncle's agents, his lawyer, who arranges many matters for him in town, will call upon you to-morrow morning. He will bring you some memoranda about Joseph."

"Good," I told her. "I shall like to be getting to work."

"My uncle wishes to impress upon you," she continued, "that there are two Josephs. One is an out-and-out East-Ender, akin with his gang, a desperate, bloodthirsty person who sticks at nothing. The other is a wealthy young Jew, moving in quite exalted social circles, probably a member of a good club, possibly even one of a famous family, exploiting his position simply in search of places to rob."

"I follow you," I assured her eagerly. "Very interesting indeed, it sounds."

"Now, listen to me attentively, please," she went on. "We don't want you to go after Joseph the East-Ender. We could tell you his haunts, but you would never reach them alive. We have another class of person taking care of that end. What my uncle wants you to do is to try and get in touch with him through the social side of his life."

"I see," I murmured a little dubiously. "It may take some time, I am afraid. My only club is a Service one, which wouldn't be of much use, and I have avoided all my friends during the last two years."

"Naturally. That does not matter in the least. Your friends will be found for you. All that you have to do is to accept the invitations you receive and watch the people."

"Shall I ever be allowed to come back to the Mansion for a week-end?" I ventured.

She laughed again, and it was hard for me to believe that it was indeed she who was indulging in such an act of graciousness.

"How can you want to come back to such a horrible place?"

"But I do," I declared emphatically.

Then, after a moment's pause, I added what I should never have dared to say face to face.

"I want to see you again."

She made no immediate reply and I began to regret my temerity. Then she spoke once more.

"You may see me sooner than you expect. My uncle wishes me to attend some of the festivities for which you will receive cards. I may have to ask for your escort."

"I shall be delighted. I am not sure that I number a tail coat amongst my possessions yet, though."

"I think that will probably arrive. Uncle is very thorough, and he is wonderfully served. . . . Now for the next part of my message. Are you listening?"

"Rather!"

"You are to be at Christie's at three o'clock to-morrow afternoon. Just take a chair, buy a catalogue, and watch the bidding. If no one speaks to you, then come away in the ordinary course. My uncle simply wishes you to be there."

"That's all right," I promised. "By the by, I see they are selling some wonderful miniatures."

"Yes. It is the Martellion Collection in which my uncle is interested. . . . Good night, Major Owston."

"Good night, Miss Essiter."

"And, Major Owston?"

"Yes."

"I am glad our young Helen is on her way back."

After that, any few regrets or sense of loneliness from which I might have been suffering departed. Smart brought in the whisky and soda and asked for my orders for breakfast, after which I dismissed him for the night. In due course, not too early, I prepared for bed. I admired myself for a few moments in the looking glass in a suit of very choice lemon-coloured pyjamas, opened the window a few inches, and tumbled off to sleep as soon as I had turned the lights out. I closed my eyes with the confident expectation of sleeping until Smart brought me my tea. I awoke, however, within a few hours, with a violent start, to find the electric light turned on, and a figure who seemed somehow or other very near to me, leaning over the end of the bed.

"What the devil!" I gasped—

There was no immediate reply. I never even finished my sentence. I became suddenly very wide awake indeed. My visitor was wearing a black silk mask, completely concealing his face, and a hand of incredible steadiness was gripping an automatic, pointed directly at me.

"Don't move," he said softly. "Above everything, don't call out. Are you awake now?"

"Yes," I answered. "What do you want? How the mischief did you get in here?"

"Don't be silly," my visitor begged contemptuously. "You know who I am, right enough. I am Joseph. You can't seem to be able to lay your hand on me, so I've come to see you. I don't like the way you're drawing your knees up. If you move as much as a foot, I'll let 'daylight into you."

I decided to wait for a better opportunity to assert

myself. In the meantime I watched my visitor keenly. Already two things had struck me. First that his cockney accent seemed scarcely natural; secondly that the dirty and neglected state of his hands was a little overdone. Underneath some smudges of black, I could see on one finger the traces of a remarkably well-manicured nail.

"You want to know what I'm after, I suppose. I'll tell you. I came after my girl. If I'd found her here, you'd have been stiff by now. Where is she?"

"Search the place if you think she's here," I invited. He chuckled.

"A nice chance that would give you, wouldn't it?" he murmured. "No, Major, I've been in both the other rooms. You've saved your skin for a few minutes. I've got another bone to pick with you though. You're Martin Hews' new man, aren't you? You're after me, they say."

"And so far as that is concerned," I replied, "I shouldn't be surprised, Joseph, if I didn't get you."

"An excellent nerve," he remarked approvingly. "I suppose you realise that your life is wobbling in the balance. I may pull this trigger at any second."

"Somehow or other," I said, "I don't remember to have heard of Joseph shooting an unarmed man lying down."

"Pooh!" he scoffed. "That's nothing. I'd shoot my grandmother in the back if I had to."

"Well, then, there is another reason why you will probably behave like a sane person," I told him. "You enjoy your life too much to want to end it with a rope around your neck. I have a manservant sleeping in the next room, with his wife."

"Stupefied, both of them," he confided. "Softest job you can imagine. Their supper was laid out when I happened to stroll through the kitchen—jug of beer and a bottle of whisky. I bet they're lying across the table now."

"Let's go and see," I suggested.

There were creases in his mask, and I think he smiled.
"Pity you didn't join up with me and play the big
game, instead of becoming Martin Hews' mercenary," he
said. "I like a man who can grin when the trick's against
him."

"I'm not a mercenary," I objected.

"What else are you?" he demanded. "You call me and
my men criminals, but we fight for what we want. Martin
Hews is a far dirtier type of scoundrel, with his cheque
book, his hired assassins, and his receiving offices—and
as for you, he pays you for fighting, I suppose. What else
are you but a b——y mercenary and one of the worst?"

"You're calling me very unpleasant names," I reminded
him. "If you'll put that thing away for a moment we
might settle this."

"I should look well, shouldn't I?" Joseph smiled. "Over
six feet, aren't you? I heard of your fighting the other
night."

"You saw me," I told him. "And if I'd known who
you were before, and if I hadn't put my foot in that
damned pothole, you would never have got away."

He sighed maliciously.

"So you recognised me! Rather a pity you mentioned
that. Before, there was just about one chance in twenty
that I might have left you with a few words of caution.
Now—well, it can't be done. A man who has seen me out
with my lads and has recognised me can't be allowed to
live. Say your prayers, if you want to, Major. Your number's up."

"Is it?" I rejoined. "What about your own?"

I had drawn my legs up inch by inch and stiffened every
muscle in my body, preparing for the spring forward.
It was a useless effort though. I failed to reach the automatic by at least a yard, and Joseph's hand had never
quivered. I heard a wicked little spit, saw a stab of

flame, and suddenly felt a queer, terrible sensation just over my heart. I saw a pair of black eyes bending down just as the room began to go round, fragments of words seemed to reach me, fierce, yet freighted with the spice of diabolical mirth:

"That will teach you . . . to leave Joseph alone . . . and his women . . . in this world, and . . . "

Then the room faded away and blackness came.

CHAPTER XIII

My awakening recollections were confused and fantastic. Smart, in most unpicturesque *déshabille*, was standing with his handkerchief to his mouth, gaping at me. A young man, with a black moustache and horn-rimmed spectacles, a few feet farther away, was smoking a cigarette, and I myself had come back to the world with a strong inclination to be sick. Both windows were wide open, although a drizzling rain was beating in. Furthermore, there was the most abominable smell in the room.

"Capital!" the young man exclaimed. "Hope you don't mind my cigarette. This chemical concoction of your friend's makes the most ghastly stink I ever came across."

There seemed to me no reason why I should not be in another world, but I had a firm conviction that I was still in my bed, and also that there was very little the matter with me.

"But he shot me," I declared, sitting up. "The fellow with the black mask. I saw the flash, felt the stab just over my heart."

The young man nodded.

"He shot you with a freak invention of his own," he explained, producing what seemed to me to be a piece of burnt wadding. "He apparently used an ordinary pistol, but a specially made cartridge. The wadding burst against your chest, and a small phial full of the most villainous dope broke against your skin. Naturally you went off pop—quaintest thing I ever heard of. I've got the whole of the stuff together to be analysed."

"Who are you?" I enquired.

"I'm a doctor from across the way," he explained. "Your servant fetched me. Seems he went to sleep in the kitchen after supper. He declares he was drugged, himself. When he woke up, he came in to see if you were all right and found you unconscious. Perhaps this will help you to understand the matter," he went on, handing me a square of paper. "I found it pinned to your pillow."

I held it up and read in printed characters:

"I came here with two automatics—one to use if you were alone, the other if you had company. If I had used the other, you would have been safely out of my way for ever. Take my advice, and keep out.

JOSEPH."

I folded up the piece of paper and thrust it under my pillow. Smart brought me in a cup of coffee.

"If you can drink it," the doctor said, "it will do you good. We've opened all the windows in the flat, and the smell will soon be gone."

I took the coffee and felt better with the first sip.

"How did the fellow get in?" I asked Smart. "You locked the outside door, I suppose?"

"Indeed, I did, sir," the man replied earnestly. "He must have got a pass-key from somewhere."

The doctor felt my pulse and murmured a word of commendation.

"Nothing more I can do for you," he announced. "You can have these bits of stuff back after I've sent them for analysis. So far as I can see, there will be no harmful effects whatever."

"Right-o!" I answered drowsily. "I'll send you a fee across in the morning if I may."

Then I dismissed Smart also and slept until I could smell coffee and bacon and eggs, a few hours later.

At half-past ten, Mr. Yardsley was announced. In clothes and general appearance he was the most legal-looking person I had ever seen, from his black satin stock to his broad-toed boots. He introduced himself, and we shook hands.

"I have instructions, Major Owston," he announced, "to put you in possession of certain information. You appear to have entered Martin Hews' service rather hurriedly."

"That is quite true," I admitted.

"Into my client's history and past life there is no necessity to enter. It is sufficient for you to know that Mr. Martin Hews is a very famous, a very wealthy gentleman. He is one of the greatest collectors of curios in the world, and like a great many other collectors he is, I regret to say, sometimes utterly unscrupulous as to the means by which he gains possession of his treasures."

"I can imagine that," I murmured.

The lawyer coughed. I caught a gleam of something in his cold eyes, and I knew very well that if ever there was a rogue in the world Stephen Yardsley was one.

"Professionally," he went on, "it has suited my purpose of later years to devote my whole energies to Mr. Martin Hews' affairs. They have brought me some very interesting work in various branches of the law."

"I should imagine," I suggested, "that they have even brought you very near the criminal courts on more than one occasion."

"At times, I must confess to you, Major Owston," my visitor acknowledged, "that I have had difficulty with my client. He is a very shrewd man, but he has the spirit of a buccaneer—a buccaneer, Major—for whom there is very little place in this police-guarded and law-abiding world of ours."

"He seems to edge his way into trouble sometimes," I

observed. "We've had two very pretty scraps down at Breezeley Mansion already as you may have heard, Mr. Yardsley. Not altogether unexpected either, I should gather."

"We will not speak too much of matters which are still *sub judice*," Mr. Yardsley begged. "What you have to remember is that the contents of Breezeley Mansion would be under-insured at two million pounds, and owing to the peculiar way in which some of those treasures came into my client's possession, he is not in a position to insure them. Any man, under such conditions, would be justified in adopting strong measures for the protection of his property. It is one of my duties to keep my client within the law, so far as possible."

"Very interesting," I remarked. "Now what about this fellow Joseph?"

The lawyer leaned back in his chair, his fingertips placed together.

"You may or you may not know, Major Owston," he went on, "that during the last five years there has been a curious change in the workings of the criminal world. Years ago, it was every man for himself. To-day it is a sort of fraternity. A humorist in my profession remarked lately that they would soon be setting up a trades union."

The idea tickled me, and I was able to raise the necessary smile.

"During the last few years," Mr. Yardsley continued, "the public has been curiously deceived by the press in certain matters. You read continually of fighting between rival bands at race meetings, of knives being thrown, and occasionally of a man being killed. The men of whom these bands are composed are not ordinary hooligans at all. Race meetings have only a secondary interest for them, and the worst of the quarrels certainly do not start upon any race course. They are the originators of most

of the criminal exploits of the day, and by banding together they make the position of the police far more difficult. Within the last few months, two of these gangs,
Joseph's and Donkin's, have practically wiped out the
others, and barely a fortnight ago Donkin killed a man
in a fight and has had to fly the country. Now I am going
to admit to you, Major Owston, that Mr. Martin Hews
has been at the back of Donkin's gang in a good many
of their exploits. He has financed them when it was necessary, and he has even gone so far as to suggest to them
various privately owned treasures which he wished to
acquire, and for which he was willing to pay a considerable sum. These affairs are naturally conducted through
an agent who keeps a second-hand art shop in Grafton
Street."

"But surely," I ventured, "this is a criminal proceeding?"

"Morally, Major Owston, without a doubt it is," the
lawyer assented. "It is my business to overlook the transactions in such a way that Mr. Hews remains technically
outside the law. That has always been done. After this
preamble, we now come to the difficult situation which has
arisen since Donkin's flight. His gang is dwindling away.
Most of them have joined the enemy. To-day Joseph's
gang is omnipotent."

"And Joseph, I gather, is not exactly on friendly terms
with Martin Hews."

"For some reason or other," Mr. Yardsley confided,
"there exists the most bitter and intractable enmity between them. Only a month ago, we know for a certainty
that the Borghese Medallions came into Joseph's hands.
An amazing daylight robbery, that! There was no limit
to what my client was prepared to pay for these. Isaacs,
his Grafton Street agent, did everything that was possible. Every proposal he made was met with stony silence,

and Joseph sold these medallions to a New York millionaire. Mr. Martin Hews had no sleep for a month. The same thing was repeated with a fifteenth-century Italian landscape—a reputed Leonardo da Vinci—for which my client was prepared to give five times its claimed value. Joseph calmly sold it to an Argentine railway man, again completely ignoring Isaacs. Now recent events have made things worse. Mr. Martin Hews was entirely responsible for Donkin's escape, and he has given shelter at Breezeley Mansion to the young woman whom Donkin sometime previously had taken away from Joseph. So far, Joseph's efforts to regain possession of her have been, I understand, unsuccessful, and he has lost several of his best men. Things now, I fear, have reached a very dangerous crisis. I have done my best to restrain my client, but there are times when one might as well talk to a creature of granite. Knowing all the circumstances, Major Owston, I must pronounce it as my considered opinion that before many weeks are past either Joseph will have Martin Hews' life, or one of Martin Hews' people—it may even be you, Major—will get at Joseph and kill him."

"Is your office in Lincoln's Inn, Mr. Yardsley?" I asked, perhaps a trifle irrelevantly.

The lawyer was mildly perplexed.

"It is in the immediate vicinity," he admitted. "Why?"

"I really don't know," I confessed. "It seems to me that you ought to be talking about conveyancing deeds and drawing up wills and mortgages, and that sort of thing, and to hear you calmly discussing which of these two men, both in London, will succeed in murdering the other seems a little quaint."

My visitor smiled thinly.

"I was brought up," he confided, "in one of the strictest of legal schools, and I served my articles with a purely conveyancing lawyer, but I may as well tell you, Major

Owston, since you know so much, that the criminal world has always had a fierce attraction for me. I gave up a splendid practice in order to enter Martin Hews' service. He chose me, because I was, in a sense, above suspicion. I still keep a portion of that conveyancing business. I am still looked up to as a lawyer of the old school, by a great many people. A few may guess at my other activities, but they never have evidence. I appear to you to be out of my vocation. I never feel so thoroughly in it as when I am organising some scheme for our friend Martin Hews, so that he may get what he wants and remain free of the law. His great desire, I may say his passionate desire, at present is, as I think you know, to get rid of Joseph. I think there is no price he would not pay for that man's life."

The lawyer's cold grey eyes, which had flickered for a moment, rested upon mine. I knew quite well that this highly respectable legal practitioner was inciting me to murder,

"But what about the police?" I asked. "They have three of the gang in their hands already."

"Very true," Mr. Yardsley assented, "but that will be of no assistance, so far as the capture of Joseph himself is concerned. Joseph's men are never informers. That's about all the religion they've got, but they've got that. And there's just one thing more, Major," the lawyer went on reflectively. "Supposing they got Joseph, and he was sentenced to a long term of imprisonment, I am not quite sure how that would suit Mr. Hews' book. Joseph, under such conditions, might prove himself to be a very dangerous enemy."

"In short," I put in, "what you would really like would be for Joseph to be killed in a fight or quarrel. Pity I didn't sleep with an automatic under my pillow last night, and I might have arranged it for you."

So far as my visitor's parchment-like face was capable of showing emotion, he displayed it then. He leaned forward in his chair, his thin lips parted, the lines about his mouth deeper, his pale grey eyes staring into mine.

"Do you mean that Joseph has been here?" he demanded.

I told him the story and handed him the scrap of paper. He read it and handed it back without a word. He made no comment at all upon my story. He sat looking into the fire steadily, and I could almost feel his brain at work, thinking the matter out in every detail. Presently he glanced up.

"I suppose you know what happened to your predecessor?" he asked.

"I didn't even know for certain that I had one."

"A young fellow named Fotherway," Mr. Yardsley confided. "Things hadn't developed quite so far as at present, and he thought he could do a little good as a spy down in the East End. He went off one Saturday night, following a clue Donkin had given him, to a house somewhere Limehouse way. They found his body in the Thames the next morning. That was the work of Joseph's gang, without a doubt, but they were never able to bring a scrap of evidence against him. I am telling you this, Major," he went on, "not because I want you to think that your position is more dangerous than it is, but because I want to warn you that now you are known to be in Martin Hews' service, you must be prepared for trouble at any time. Frankly, I cannot understand why Joseph did not make an end of you last night. I imagine he spared you because it wasn't quite a safe environment for him. I can think of no other reason. I have not, I may say, one iota of belief in that gesture of chivalry. I am not a man of violence, Major Owston, but I have watched this business for some time, and I should like to warn you that you must never be without your revolver or automatic pistol, whichever of the two it is that you carry. You must never be misled by anonymous letters or messages inviting you to strange rendezvous. Your business, such as it is, will centre round the West End. Keep to the West End."

"All right," I conceded. "Now, is there anything definite I can start on? I am getting a large salary, and I want to work."

"Quite natural," he agreed. "It is my business to give you all the assistance I can. In the first place, during the course of the day, you will begin to receive invitations for various functions, chiefly from what I should call the upper, middle wealthy class. Accept them all, but especially those from Jewish families, and watch."

"Watch for what, particularly?" I enquired.

"We know for a certainty," the lawyer explained, "that Joseph goes as a guest to many of the best known houses in London, and that it is from the information he has gleaned as a guest that some of his most daring burglaries have been planned. He gets to know the geography of the house, and, from a personal inspection, the jewels which are really worth taking a big risk for. From what I can gather, it is very seldom indeed that he goes near the East End nowadays. There are a score of police at work around that particular little district, not far from the heart of the City, where they think his headquarters are, and they are also watching his place in Shoreditch, where it is reported that he has been seen, but my own belief is that he hasn't been near any of these haunts for months, that he has spent the whole of his time in the West End, and that when he moves eastward again, it will be for a very brief visit, and to an unknown rendezvous."

"You have spies of your own about, then?"

"Certainly," he admitted. "I have six men, each of

whom has served his apprenticeship at Scotland Yard, and I can assure you that it is very seldom that my client needs any information that we are not in a position to give him. We were able to warn you of the raid the other night. We are able to telephone down valuable information nearly every day. I will tell you frankly that one of these men is now watching you."

"Any more hints for me?" I asked.

Mr. Yardsley produced a paper from his pocket.

"Besides these invitations which I am already arranging," he said, "there are several restaurants and night clubs where Joseph is reported to have been seen—the Milan Restaurant, for instance, and the Blue Skies Night Club. There are others, but these are the most likely. Lunch or dine at the Milan whenever you have the opportunity, and make a point of visiting the Blue Skies Night Club as soon as you have an evening to spare."

"Rather like looking for a needle in the proverbial haystack?" I ventured.

"It may seem so," Mr. Yardsley agreed. "Nevertheless, Major Owston, any detective will tell you that the most amazing captures in the history of crime have been made by chance. The luck may be against you, and your visits to all these places may be profitless. Mr. Hews takes that risk. He begs you to persevere."

With that, Mr. Yardsley picked up his hat—a flat-topped bowler of the sort affected a generation ago by racing men—drew on one glove, shook out his umbrella, and bade me good morning. He had left a card upon the office."

"You will find my address and telephone number there," he said, "but whatever you do, don't communicate with me personally; in other words, do not come near my office."

More than a little pompous, extraordinarily legal, neat

and precise in his movements as in his dress, my visitor took his leave. I watched him descend the stairs. It seemed to me that of all the strange figures in this strange world into which I had been projected, his was perhaps the most unexpected and incomprehensible.

CHAPTER XIV

I DULY presented myself at Christie's at the appointed time, and from the moment of my arrival I was attracted by the appearance of a singular-looking man who was seated in a sprawling attitude in a large oak-backed chair just underneath the auctioneer's rostrum. He was an elderly Jew of the fine Old Testament type—a Jew who disdained the semi-disguise of a Savile Row tailor, and whose clothes and general appearance seemed chosen with the idea of deepening beyond a possibility of mistake the line of demarcation between himself and the smug, hook-nosed, keen-eyed crowd by which he was surrounded. His long grey beard reached to his chest. His hair, of the same colour, silvery and well cared for though it appeared, had evidently known little of the barber's skill. He wore an old-fashioned black frock coat, dark grey trousers, a quaint, enormous watch chain spread across his waistcoat, and two or three cornelian rings upon his fingers. His spectacles were steel-rimmed, his cravat a little wisp of black, tied in a bow. He would have commanded attention in any crowd, and the auctioneer, when he mounted to his post, greeted him respectfully. I was not in the least surprised when some one leaning over addressed him as Mr. Isaacs.

The sale, to commence with, was a dull one. Isaacs scarcely glanced at the catalogue and made no bids. A collection of Bartolozzi engravings failed to evoke any enthusiasm, two or three pictures by little known Italian masters produced only languid offers. About half an hour after proceedings were opened, however, there was a brief pause. I heard the flutter of catalogues and realised that there was a distinct stir in the room. The auctioneer coughed and leaned forward.

"We come now," he announced, "to what is perhaps the most famous collection of miniatures in the world, the property of our late esteemed friend, Mr. Mark Rosenfeldt. Mr. Rosenfeldt was a great patron of these rooms and a friend of most of us. More than any one, I may say, I regret the necessity for this sale. Since it has arrived, however, I ask you to treat the collection with respect, for I am not sure that I would be saying too much if, small though it is, I proclaimed it to be absolutely the finest in the world. I shall commence with the comparatively modern miniatures of the seventeenth and eighteenth centuries and conclude with the Martellion collection."

The miniatures were passed around—very exquisite pieces of work, as even I easily appreciated. Bidding for the first started at a hundred guineas and finished at seven hundred. The ten offered realised something like five thousand pounds. The bidding for each was brisk and carried with it an air of finality. Isaacs, however, did not once lift his head or show the slightest sign of interest in the proceedings. It was not until the earlier lots had been disposed of that he abandoned a whispered conversation with his neighbour and readjusted his attitude, turning more directly towards the rostrum. There was a preliminary murmur of voices, and then a silence. One felt the thrill of suspense which was in the atmosphere. Several men, obviously dealers, who had been in the background, pushed their way to the front. The auctioneer leaned forward.

"The Martellion miniatures, ladies and gentlemen," he said, "will not be passed round, as I am quite sure that any of you who appreciate their significance and intend to bid already know them well enough. There are seven of them, all absolutely authentic. They are the sole existing work of a painter who, if he had lived, would easily have challenged the supremacy of Watteau in this particular branch of art. Apart from that, the frames are of paste, unquestionably and entirely unique—of paste, gentlemen, the secret of making which has long since departed, and of which I state confidently that no other examples exist. The history of these miniatures is as well known to you as to myself. They were brought over here at the time of the great Revolution from the *château* of the Duc de Gramont, and bought by the Marquis of Southampton, in the possession of whose family they have remained ever since, until they were removed for purposes of sale to these rooms a fortnight ago. My instructions are to offer them first *en bloc*, and if I fail to get a satisfactory price for them to ask you to bid for them singly. I would suggest an initial bid of seven thousand guineas for the seven miniatures."

I glanced round the room, trying to guess who the bidders might be at such a price. Before I looked back again at the auctioneer, the bidding had reached eleven thousand, and I had not detected as much as the flicker of an eyelid from any one of the company. I watched Isaacs closely, and for the first time I saw a faint nod. It was scarcely a gesture—more an increased wrinkling of the forehead and a slight closing of the eyes, but he went on until the price stood at twenty thousand guineas. The auctioneer paused for a moment.

"Gentlemen," he said, "I congratulate you. We have now reached a price for the miniatures which would not be considered by my clients an undignified sacrifice. The bid rests with Mr. Isaacs at twenty thousand guineas. May I say twenty-one, my lord?"

A tall, youngish man from the back of the room shook his head.

"I have finished, Mr. Adams," he declared pleasantly. "Too hot going for me."

It appeared, as I learned afterwards, that almost from the start the bidding had lain between Isaacs and this very well-known peer, a noted collector of *objets d'art*. The general expectation, therefore, was that with his withdrawal, the miniatures would be knocked down to Isaacs. The auctioneer raised his hammer.

"Sorry, my lord," he said. "The bid is twenty thousand guineas with you, Mr. Isaacs. Going then at twenty thousand guineas. Going—"

"Tventy-von," came a strange foreign voice from somewhere in my vicinity.

There was a noticeable flutter of astonishment. Every one turned round, I amongst them. The man who had suddenly entered the arena endured the general scrutiny without changing a muscle. He seemed also the least likely person in the world to have bid twenty-one thousand guineas for a collection of miniatures in an assembly where even the dealers, except Isaacs, had withdrawn. He was a long, lanky man in a light brown suit of foreign cut, tan, buttoned boots, a flowing tie, and linen which one could scarcely call irreproachable. His thin, yellow fingers, cigarette stained and with broken nails, were clenched together as though in excitement. He stared at the auctioneer through large, concave spectacles, with horn rims and sides. There was a distinct hook to his nose, his complexion was sallow, his black hair unruly and streaked with grey. From his appearance, I should have imagined him to have been the proprietor of one of the smallest of the second-hand clothing establishments in the purlieus of Soho.

"You bid twenty-one, sir?" the auctioneer repeated, trying hard to conceal his own surprise.

"Tventy-von," the new bidder reaffirmed.

Isaacs flashed one glance over his shoulder, and it seemed obvious that he too failed to recognise the newcomer. His responsive gesture was swift.

"Twenty-two."

"Tventy-dree."

"Twenty-four."

"Tventy-vive."

"Twenty-six."

"Tventy-zeven."

"Twenty-eight."

"Tventy-noin."

"Thirty."

"Dirty-von."

The last bid remained with the stranger. The auctioneer paused, and turning to one of his staff, who was loitering in the background, whispered to him. The latter at once approached the unknown bidder. I had changed my place during the last few minutes and was exactly behind him, so that I could hear every word.

"Might I enquire your name, sir?" the clerk ventured.

The mysterious bidder looked up at his questioner. It was obvious that he was very much a foreigner.

"Vat vor you vant that?" he muttered. "I vant those leetle pictures. I can pay if I buy."

The young man was somewhat taken aback, but he persisted.

"It is customary in transactions of this size to be acquainted with our clients," he whispered.

The stranger felt in his waistcoat pocket, produced a shabby leather case, and handed a card to the young man.

"I am vrom Van Doorns in Amsterdam," he announced.

The name was evidently known to the young man, whose manner became more respectful.

"You understand the terms of the sale, sir?" he enquired.

"Quite vell."

"You will be prepared to pay for the miniatures if they are knocked down to you before you leave the room?"

"I shall pay for dem, and I take dem away."

The young man still hesitated.

"The name of your firm is well known to us, sir," he said, "but in a transaction of this size I am afraid a cheque would not be considered."

The stranger, with a suspicious glance on each side of him, produced from a hip pocket a capacious wallet. He bent back a great wad of notes, brushing them with his thumb, drew one out and held it towards the young man.

"Dese are von dousand pounds," he pointed out. "Dey com from your Bank of England, dis morning. If I buy, I pay. If I have not enough, I bid no more."

The young man retreated and made his report. The auctioneer once more took up his hammer.

"The bid remains with the representative of a well-known Amsterdam firm," he announced, bowing slightly across the room. "Shall we recommence the bidding? Thirty-one thousand guineas I am bid, Mr. Isaacs."

I settled down to watch the duel, feeling a new species of excitement in my blood. By this time the room was crowded, and a very distinguished company it was. There were many whom I knew by sight, obviously habitués of the place, attracted by curiosity—a well-known statesman, a couple of Members of Parliament on their way down to Westminster, a sprinkling of women—all interested in this sudden flash of drama which had found its way into the struggle between the Jew and the Dutchman. Amongst the company I saw a leaven of hard-faced, shrewd-eyed dealers, watching with not a little malicious satisfaction Isaacs, one of the great figures of the room, pressed hard by a stranger. Probably a rumour of what was happening had spread, for every now and then newcomers came hurrying in. More than once the auctioneer had to appeal for silence. In the meanwhile, the price crept up. The flicker of an eyelash from Isaacs, still statuesque and crouching in his chair, meant a thousand guineas. His opponent's bids were made in a guttural and almost unrecognisable accent, but lest there should be any mistake, he was standing up now, and he waved his arm each time he spoke. At forty thousand guineas there came another pause. I leaned forward from my chair and saw my neighbour apparently counting his wad of notes. Then quite unexpectedly he rose from his place, returned the notes to his pocket, and shook his head angrily at the auctioneer. He glanced across at Isaacs and brandished his fist.

"He have gif more than the vorth," he shouted. "He can haf the lettle pictures."

Muttering to himself, he strode out of the room, and I followed him. Twice he looked round as though for the purpose of making a final gesticulation, and each time he saw me. A sudden idea flashed into my brain. I quickened my pace and arrived on the pavement just in time to see Mr. Van Doorn of Amsterdam step into a powerful limousine. I looked around for a taxi, but as ill luck would have it, there was not one in sight. Then to my surprise, the unsuccessful bidder leaned out of the window and beckoned me to him.

"Yong man," he said, "I haf been disappointed about the lettle pictures. Now you—you will be disappointed. I gif you lettle tip, because you com see me off."

He thrust something into my hand, and the car shot away. I unfolded the slip of paper and stared at it in amazement. It was a bank note for a thousand pounds.

CHAPTER XV

To search London for an eighty-horse-power car, which had disappeared five minutes before I was able to find a very ordinary taxicab seemed to me simply waste of time. I contented myself with making a guess at the quickly vanishing number, which I jotted down on the back of an envelope, and drove instead to my rooms with the idea of telephoning to Breezeley. Smart met me in the hall.

"A gentleman to see you, sir," he announced. "I hope I did right. I asked him to wait. He is in the sitting-room now."

"Any name?"

"A Mr. Bloor, sir. Connected with the police force, I believe," Smart confided.

I mounted to the sitting-room and shook hands with my visitor.

"Comfortable quarters here, Major," he remarked.

"Very comfortable indeed," I admitted.

"I have always thought," he went on, settling himself into the chair which I had indicated, "that if I were a young man with nothing particular to do in life, this is precisely the locality in which I should choose to live."

"Supposing we agreed not to waste time with banalities," I suggested. "Join me in a whisky and soda—say when—and tell me what you want?"

Inspector Bloor looked at me across the room, or rather he did not look at me, for those heavy eyelids seemed to have descended like curtains before his eyes.

"I like mine rather short," he said. "Just a splash

more soda water. Thank you, Major. To get on with it
then. I hear Joseph has paid you a visit. Are you in a
position to identify him? If so, we might make a deal together."

Inspector Bloor had certainly played up to my suggestion. I pushed the cigarettes towards him, helped myself to whisky and soda, lit a pipe, and sank into my easy-
chair. As a matter of fact, although I wasn't telling him
so, I was particularly glad to see him just at that moment.

"How did you know?" I asked, "that I saw Joseph last
night?"

"Not your business," he answered promptly. "You see,
I'm on your track. Let's cut out the immaterial. He was
here last night expecting to find the girl. He didn't find
her, and he let you off light. Are you any nearer being able
to identify him?"

"I certainly am not," I acknowledged. "Joseph is full
of fantastic gestures but I imagine he's no fool. He wore
a mask, he talked broken cockney, one nail was manicured,
and the others were filthy."

"The East and the West, eh?"

I nodded.

"So you see, I am still not in a position to help you,
Inspector. On the other hand," I added, "it is just possible that you may be able to help me."

"Straight to the middle of it, Major. Here I am, and
the law is with me."

"What should you think if a man gave you a tip of a
thousand pounds for shadowing him out of an auction
room and bowing him into his limousine car?"

"I should damn well bring out my magnifying glass and
look at the note," was the blunt reply.

I felt in my waistcoat pocket and smoothed out the
bank note before him.

"Handed to me casually," I confided, "by Mr. Van Doorn of Amsterdam, who had bid up to forty thousand guineas for some miniatures at Christie's this afternoon on the strength of a wad of these."

"Not another word," the Inspector begged. "Wait!"

He took a magnifying glass from his pocket and studied the note carefully. When he had finished—and it was an affair of nearly five minutes—he leaned back in his chair.

"This is very interesting, Major," he admitted, looking into the fire. "Pray don't think that I was all that time deciding whether the note was genuine or not. That it was a forgery I knew in ten seconds. What I wanted to make up my mind about was whose work it was. Rather important to us that, you know. I think I can put my hand upon the man. You wouldn't mind, perhaps—it might be worth while—just a word or two as to how it really came into your possession?"

I told him everything in a few sentences. He seemed curiously unmoved. In fact, he finished his cigarette and lit another before he said a word.

"I cannot imagine," he observed at last, "why the Germans should be the worst detectives in the world."

I just looked at him enquiringly. It saved a few words.

"You see," he went on, "psychology is the favourite study of the thoughtful German, but it is the most neglected one with us. Now that little story of the salesrooms at Christie's explains itself, simply because in a crude way we are beginning to understand something about Joseph. Don't you see that when a man with such a Puck-like sense of humour is up against even the greatest issues, he cannot resist yielding to it? You understand, of course, what Joseph has done. He has sent a puppet, or even come himself—who knows?—to that sale, with a bundle of forged notes as his guarantee, and has made

Martin Hews pay twenty thousand pounds more than he need have done for the miniatures. He completes the triumph of the afternoon by giving you this little offering, so that Isaacs shall know how he has been bluffed."

"Wait a moment," I interrupted. "Supposing Isaacs had left off bidding at any time?"

The Inspector shrugged his shoulders.

"He would probably have denied the last bid and got out of it that way. I am sure he never meant to use the notes except as a matter of bluff. The one thing I don't think he quite realised," the detective went on thoughtfully, "was that the note he gave you might come into my hands. May I use your telephone?"

"Certainly."

I indicated it with a nod. In a moment or two he was talking to a subordinate.

"That you, Holmes?" he enquired. . . . "Look here, I want Cogswell—Ed Cogswell. Run through the tickets of leave. You'll find him somewhere Maida Vale way, I expect. Bring him up right away. . . . No, don't arrest him. Nothing of that sort. Say I want a little friendly chat. And—wait a moment!"

He covered up the receiver and turned towards me.

"Would you mind if I had him here and asked him a question or two?" he begged. "These fellows get scared to death of being taken to the Yard, and I want him in a good temper."

"Bring him here by all means," I agreed.

Bloor turned back to the telephone.

"Holmes," he went on, "bring him up to me, at Number 3a, Down Street. Ask for Major Owston's rooms."

He rang off and leaned back in his chair.

"If you are interested in the criminals of the world, Major," he continued, "you should certainly meet our friend Cogswell. He is a man, I should say, of not more than fifty-four or fifty-five years of age, and he's spent at least twenty of these in prison, and yet if he had been born under different circumstances he would have been a great artist. . . . Now then, Major," he broke off, his tone once more matter of fact, "no more gossiping. I'm all for your way of playing the game—straight at it and no chat. Where's the number of that car?"

I produced the envelope upon the back of which I had jotted it down.

"Y P 7872, so far as I could see," I replied.

The detective folded up the envelope, and placed it in his pocket.

"You couldn't do anything with this yourself," he pointed out. "Tracing cars is our job. I shall know to-morrow whether it's a faked number or not. Personally, I think there's no doubt of it. The *char-à-banc* which brought those people up from Breezeley the other night changed numbers at least three times. It's done with a switch—the easiest thing possible. Now, Major, I'm going to speak to you as man to man—as one friend of Leonard Joyce's to another."

"Fire away."

"You know what your job is, I suppose? If not, I'll tell you. You're after Joseph, and Joseph is not the slightest use to you alive. What could you do with him? You'd have to hand him over to us, and that wouldn't suit your employer's book in the least. The last thing he wants is Joseph in the dock. He wants Joseph dead— killed—and he's come to the conclusion you're the man to do the job. He doesn't care a damn what happens to you. You're his tool, nothing more nor less."

"That's all very well, Bloor," I reasoned, "but if ever I kill Joseph, it will be in a fair fight."

"Don't you kid yourself too much about that," he warned me. "Killing a man's a serious business in this

country, and where's your excuse for the fight? Why, I
can hear the prosecutor even now explaining your connection with Martin Hews to the jury. You'd be lucky
if you got off with five years. That's if you kill him, remember. There's always an exceedingly good chance that
he may kill you."

"Are you trying to get me scared, Inspector?" I asked
him quietly.

He smiled and passed his hand through his shaggy
hair.

"Too hard a job for me, Major, I'm afraid," he remarked, traces of the smile still lingering in his face. "All
that I care about is that we don't play around in this
matter like children. You want Joseph; I want Joseph. It
may not suit your patron's hand altogether, but you will
have done your job just as well if we find him as if you find
him. The man may be a wild animal, but you can't treat
him as such without asking for serious trouble. Amateurs
can't hunt men, you know, Major, in a country where
there is an established police force. We won't let the fellow off, I promise you. We've got enough against him
to put him out of the way during Martin Hews' lifetime."

"But have you?" I ventured. "I agree with you as to
what Martin Hews really wants from me, but I believe
that's because he is afraid that Joseph will wriggle out
of any charge you can bring against him. He'll have the
best lawyers in the world, you know, and they say that he
has perfect alibis, and a whole array of witnesses to dis-
prove any charge which can ever be brought against
him."

The Inspector nodded reassuringly.

"Very well put, Major," he admitted, "but we have
prepared for all that. There have been occasions," he went
on—"I am talking now confidentially—where we have
been holding a man whom we have known to have been

guilty of a serious crime, but who has been extremely clever in the way of stultifying the proper evidence, when we have been compelled in the interests of justice to stretch a point ourselves. For instance, supposing there is a minor charge against him where the evidence is more conclusive, we get him on that first with a maximum sentence, and before his time's up we've generally managed to knock the bottom out of the other defence."

"They call it 'framing a case' in the States, don't they?" I asked.

"They may call it what they like. It's common justice. What I want to impress upon you, sir, is this fact. If Joseph gets into our hands, we are not going to let him slip. I can promise you that, and, between ourselves, I'll go further. We've nothing against Martin Hews at the moment. If we get Joseph, I think I can assure you that we sha'n't be too inquisitive as regards the past. You could drop him a hint of that some time. Now, what do you say, Major? Do we work together? Mind, you've got to take the responsibility on yourself. I can't make any bargain, official or unofficial, with Martin Hews. What about it, Major?"

I held out my hand, which he promptly grasped. There were footsteps upon the stairs, and we didn't bother about words.

CHAPTER XVI

Mr. Cogswell, it appeared, had been easily found; for, some time before we had expected him, he was ushered into the room, escorted by a burly-looking plain clothes policeman. Bloor dismissed the latter with a wave of the hand.

"You'll wait and see Mr. Cogswell home, Constable," he enjoined. "Well, Ed," he went on kindly, "so you're out again?"

The door closed behind the retreating officer. His charge advanced farther into the room and I looked at him in amazement. He was a bent, shrivelled-up little figure of a man with snow-white hair, a tremulous, sensitive mouth, and one of the gentlest expressions I had ever seen.

"Yes, I'm out again, Mr. Bloor," he said, and his voice was just as soft and inoffensive as the man himself, "and this time I hope for the rest of my life."

"That remains with you, you know, Ed," the detective reminded him. "Put your hat down and take a chair. This is Major Owston, who is interested in a little matter I want to ask you about."

The newcomer returned my greeting, deposited his hat upon one chair, and seated himself upon another.

"I can't imagine what you want with me, Mr. Bloor," he remarked anxiously. "Surely you don't believe that I'm doing any work again. My ticket of leave doesn't expire for a long time yet. Besides, I've finished. I couldn't stand another stretch."

"Got enough put by for the rest of your life, I hope," the detective observed.

Mr. Cogswell looked at his questioner reproachfully. He removed a pair of light gold-rimmed glasses he was wearing and wiped his eyes.

"Not quite a professional question, that, Inspector," he complained—"not quite like you, sir."

"Bless your heart," Bloor assured him, "I only asked out of curiosity. Some one must have made a lot out of your skill, and I only hope you had a share of it. I have nothing to do with you, so long as you keep straight. As a matter of fact, I have asked you to come up this evening just as a personal favour to me."

"Anything I can do for you, Mr. Bloor," the little man replied, with somewhat dubious fervour. "You have always treated me like a gentleman. The accidents of my profession," he sighed, "have sometimes made our relations difficult. Otherwise, I have had nothing to complain of—nothing at all."

He turned towards me, as though to be sure that I had been the auditor of his confession. He was a trifle wistful—more than a trifle anxious. Bloor produced the bank note.

"This is your work, isn't it, Cogswell?" he asked quietly.

The little man shrank away from the oblong slip of white rustling paper in something very much like horror.

"Mr. Bloor," he protested, "I have been in jail for five years. I have only been out three weeks. Ask my landlady, ask any one at my lodgings. I have done nothing except read for an hour or two at the British Museum each day and sit in the Park. I haven't a tool, a—"

"That's all right, Cogswell," the detective broke in soothingly. "Don't you worry, there's a good chap. I'm not trying to fasten anything on you. This is an old matter entirely. We have nothing against you—nothing whatever. Any one can tell from the look of that note that it isn't new stuff. Besides, you know as well as I do, Cogs-well, that your people were always clever in that way. They had enough capital to keep the stuff for a year or two before they used it—gives it a better appearance. I hate a new bank note myself. This is just curiosity, Cogswell, and it gives you a chance to do yourself a good turn. Have a look at it."

The man accepted the note, reluctantly, as it seemed at first, yet when once it was in his possession, with a curious feverishness. His fingers strayed over it almost affectionately. He took a small magnifying glass from his pocket and examined the lettering. The longer he looked, the more pronounced was that faint smile. He nodded silently.

"Your work, eh, Cogswell?" Bloor enquired.

"You know as well as I do, Inspector," the other assented, with a note of self-conscious pride in his tone, "that no other living man could have turned that out. I've done my bit for it, sir. That's dead stuff enough, so far as I am concerned. If any one's been trying to flash those about now, that's their trouble. I don't belong in that. None of the people I've worked for were as green as that. As soon as a batch is spotted, the remainder's either burnt or sold for anything they'll fetch abroad. There's no trouble coming to me from these."

"Of course there isn't, Cogswell," the detective reassured him. "As a matter of fact, no one has even been trying to pass them. They have just been used for a very annoying practical joke."

"Ah!"

The little man permitted himself a deep-drawn sigh of relief and pushed the note away from him.

"There is no charge of any sort," Bloor went on quietly, his blue eyes very wide open and fixed benevolently upon the man on the other side of the table. "No charge of any sort to be brought against any one in connection with these notes. No one has tried to pass them. But, as a matter of curiosity, Cogswell, I wonder if you could remember and tell me who had the handling of that particular batch?"

There was a brief silence. Bloor was trying hard to appear as though the question were unimportant, almost a casual one. The note forger seemed to have aged within the last few seconds. He moved his chair a little farther back from the table.

"So that's it, is it, Mr. Bloor?" he muttered.

"Well, there's nothing very serious about it, is there?" the detective rejoined good-humouredly. "I tell you that we have nothing against anybody for trying to pass those notes. There's nothing in the world for you to look scared about. What about a drop of whisky and soda? I am sure the Major wouldn't mind."

"Of course not," I assented. "You will find everything on the sideboard, Bloor."

The little man held out his hand.

"Thank you, gentlemen," he declined. "I never take spirits. In fact, I never drink at all, except a glass of wine with my dinner, and that chiefly when I'm abroad. . . . Of course I know, Mr. Bloor, who had the handling of that batch of notes, and you know that I know, and you also know, Mr. Bloor," he went on, his voice gaining in strength and a sort of desperate courage, "that I value my few remaining years of life too highly to dream of answering your question. If this is what you've sent for me for, sir, you have wasted your time. I think you ought to have known me better. There are gentlemen even amongst forgers, and I have always been considered one."

"You haven't got this exactly right, Cogswell," the detective remonstrated. "I am not asking you to squeal. I have told you as plainly as I could that there's no charge to be made in connection with the notes, because no one has tried to pass them. Surely that lets you out? On the other hand, I should like to know to which of the four or five of the gangs at home and abroad you used to supply, those notes went."

"You have," Mr. Cogswell murmured, "a highly trained and very efficient staff of detectives under you at the Yard. They could probably find out anything you wanted to know. As for me, I was ill in prison. I have lost my memory."

Bloor threw away the end of the cigarette which he had been smoking and tapped another throughtfully upon the table.

"Cogswell," he said, "we will leave off fencing with one another. There is a reward which would mean a competence for life upon the head of the man to whom I believe those notes belong. What about a little villa in your beloved Italy—Fiesole, or one of those places, you know? Plenty of leisure to paint your pictures—yes, I know that you were an artist once upon a time—and ample means to live out the rest of your days in the sunshine. All this is yours for a word, and, mark you, I'm not asking you to inform about anybody or anything. I give you my word of honour no charge shall be made against any one with regard to these notes."

The little man rose to his feet and picked up his hat. There was a shamed look in his face. He had the air of a person whose intelligence or whose probity had been doubted.

"Mr. Bloor," he protested, "you know as well as I do to whom that packet of notes belongs. You know as well as I do that you are up against brains which you can't match from your Chief Commissioner to your latest recruit. It wasn't very nice of you, Mr. Bloor, to try to bring me back into this. You know very well that even if

I knew where he is these days and what he is doing, and gave you the clue you want and are not clever enough to stumble upon yourself, no money I could draw from you, a thousand pounds or a million, would be of any use to me in this world."

"Italy is a long way off," the Inspector reminded him. "There are quieter places even than Fiesole."

Cogswell shook his head.

"You must know that I should never reach Italy at all, Mr. Bloor," he said reproachfully. "I should be lying upon my back within a very few days in some quiet spot, with my eyes turned up towards the sky, and I shouldn't know whether the sun was shining up there or whether the stars were looking down at me. I must wish you good night, gentlemen."

The Inspector shrugged his shoulders, and our visitor passed out. From the window I saw him, with his escort, stepping into a waiting taxicab—a shrunken, pathetic little figure with his coat collar turned up and his hands deep in his overcoat pockets. I realised at that moment how merciless and awe-inspiring must be the rule of this man of whom his myrmidons stood in such abject fear. . . .

Smart brought us in cocktails, and it was Bloor who first broke the rather curious silence.

"I'll hand this one thing to Joseph," he pronounced, his glass in his hand. "There isn't a person who's ever worked for him—not one of his East End gang or his West End accomplices—from whom we've ever been able to draw a single word, a single hint, as to the man himself. He's got them bound to him either by the direst terror or some other means. That poor devil Cogswell would give his soul to end his days in Italy. Yet he believes what he says. He sees himself a dead man if even one little hint were to pass his lips."

"Well, it's a rotten way anyhow of getting your man
—through an informer," I declared.

"Quite right, Major, it is," the detective agreed, toss-
ing off the remainder of his cocktail, "but you must remember that what's sport to you is our daily bread. You
may not realise it, but half—more than half of the famous criminals who have been brought to justice have
been brought in if not actually by an informer, by just
a hint from some one in the know. When a man succeeds
as Joseph has done, in establishing a crowd of helpers
of whom not a single one dares to even whisper his name,
I tell you, Major, that man's hard to get at."

There was a discreet knock at the door, and Smart
brought me in a note—a large, square envelope upon
which my name was hastily printed. I tore open the flap
eagerly. I knew perfectly well from whom it came:

"My dear Major,
I quite forgot to warn you, don't try to pass that note.
I meant it just as a keepsake. The dawn of the sleuth
hound in your ingenuous self, when you followed Mr.
Van Doorn out of the salesroom, was irresistible. Martin
Hews can have the miniatures. I went in to examine them
the other afternoon, and I found number four a trifle
faulty, and the paste brilliants of number three did not
please me. Twenty thousand guineas I can chalk up to the
credit of my account. I hope the dear little monstrosity is
not too angry. Come out and look for me one evening
soon. I shall be somewhere about the West End.
                                        Ever yours,
                                        JOSEPH."

Inspector Bloor read the note at least three times.
He searched in vain for a watermark upon the paper.
Then he folded it up and placed it carefully in his pocket.
He was slouching in his chair, with the palm of his hand

upon the table. His head was downcast, and his eyes hidden.

"There are three things," he expounded, "one of which in the long run usually ends the career even of the greatest criminal. The first is the informer, the second is a woman, and the third is vanity."

I poured out another cocktail. Bloor drank it and rose to his feet.

"Here at least, in this impudent note, we have a clue to one of Joseph's weaknesses," he continued. "He amuses himself at the expense of the man he hates. He could no more keep his cheap triumph to himself than could a boy who has made his first century at cricket. He has to preen himself about it. Well, if the informer doesn't come along, and the woman fails us, there is always this third. Some day or other he will write just one note too many. Good evening, Major."

"What about my note?" I asked. "I shall have to show it to Martin Hews."

"You shall have it back in two hours," my departing visitor promised. "Our expert must see it and photograph it first. Don't forget, Major, that even though we are not advertising the fact, we are in this show together—for our mutual benefit, I hope. I shall be turning up at all manner of times—now and then, very likely, when you'll be uncommonly glad to see me."

"Six to seven is my hour," I told him.

"Suits me admirably," my visitor observed, as he picked up his hat. "I take mine usually a shade dryer."

CHAPTER XVII

Turning into Grafton Street on the following morning, in response to an urgent telephone call from Isaacs, I
was in time to witness a singular and impressive sight.
One of the largest limousines I had ever seen, with a
specially wide door, drew up outside the premises which
I was on my way to visit. A burly-looking man in plain
clothes, whom I thought I recognised, descended from
the front seat and opened the door. Huntley and Grateson, in mufti, alighted, a slab of wood was adjusted from
the inside of the car to the pavement, another on to the
step of Isaacs' shop, and in a few seconds Mr. Martin
Hews in his wonderful carriage flashed out of the car,
to the utter amazement of the passers-by, swung through
the door of the shop, described a graceful curve and
pulled up in front of an old French mirror. I crossed the
threshold a moment later in time to see his questioning
glance around, a glance that asked almost childishly for
the admiration of any possible witness of his exploit. Two
loiterers in the shop gazed at him open-mouthed. I also
responded to the call honestly enough, for his skill in
handling his amazing carriage always seemed to me almost supernatural. He smiled in what was for him a good-
natured fashion.

"Good morning, Major," he greeted me. "Your arrival was opportune. You see, it is not only in my library
that I can perform miracles. And here are our friends,
Isaacs and Yardsley, both looking a little gloomy. Never
mind. To your safe, Isaacs, this instant! The miniatures
—I must see the miniatures."

"They have cost you a prodigious sum," Isaacs groaned.

"I know, I know," Martin Hews interrupted. "I will hear your story afterwards. We will see what can be done—but the miniatures!"

We passed into the more retired portion of the establishment where only a few were permitted to wander, and from there into Isaacs' sanctum, a very marvellous room, a copy, I was told afterwards, of the famous Rose Chamber at Versailles as it was in the old days. A great safe had been built into the wall and concealed by a screen. Isaacs produced his keys and opened it. Glancing around, I saw that behind us, just outside the room, in a casual semicircle, although they were enacting their rôle of dilettante connoisseurs, were the three men on guard. Nothing disturbing seemed to be in the air, however. The safe swung open, and from one of the shelves Isaacs produced the casket which I had seen in the auction rooms. He set it on the table in front of Martin Hews, touched a spring, and the miniatures were disclosed, hanging from bent hooks in a row, with a background of ancient purple velvet. There was a low gurgle from Martin Hews' throat, which sounded more like the gluttonous ecstasy of some wild animal falling upon its prey than any human form of expression. I am quite sure that in those moments he forgot us, he forgot the whole world, he forgot the great price he had been forced to pay for his treasure. Nothing, it seemed, could bring a single touch of spirituality into his features, but there was a light of intense absorption in those protuberant eyes, a distinct and humanizing quiver of his lips. One by one he handled the miniatures lovingly, and I will swear that mentally he kissed them. Then he hung them back on their hooks, but still he gazed from one to the other, motionless. All the time there was silence. The sounds in the shop were muffled by the thick carpet. From the street came only the honk of passing motors, the falling of footsteps upon the pavement. Not one of us dared to breathe a word or to move. It was almost as though we were assisting at some rite at which the high priest of our religion was officiating. . . .

The spell was broken at last. Gently and reverently, Martin Hews himself dropped the lid of the box.

"Another triumph," he murmured, in a tone of self-congratulation. "More happy hours. Isaacs, I will drink a glass of your Amontillado, or of your Golden Madeira. Major, you shall drink wine which will make you loathe the garbage you call cocktails. My friend Yardsley, with the sombre face, you too shall feel your palate tickled, feel the blood burn in your cheeks."

He beamed on all of us. It was one of his moments. He was in supreme good humour. I was beginning to learn that his moods and tempers followed one another like the checks upon a crazy quilt. Each was as intense as it was brief. From a lacquer cabinet, Isaacs produced a dust-covered bottle which he opened with jealous care, and poured its contents into priceless long-stemmed glasses. The wine was like honey without its cloying sweetness. With the first sip one felt that great though its age might be its body had endured.

"To my success!" Martin Hews proposed, with the smile of a conceited child. "To my continued success! I am the greatest treasure hunter in the world. To-day I own the Martellion Miniatures, which kings have desired. Next month—wait!"

He looked around. The door was closed.

"Next month," he repeated, dropping his voice, "I may possess the greatest treasure left upon this ransacked earth—"

Isaacs had risen suddenly to his feet. With his outstretched arms and distraught mien, he was like a prophet of old.

"Mr. Hews!" he cried. "Sir! I beg! I implore! Not a word!"

There was a moment's uneasy silence. My employer's fit of exultation had passed. He raised his glass sulkily to his lips.

"My tongue ran away with me," he admitted. "Until one knows, one must not speak of this thing. Let us change the subject. Yardsley, what have you to say concerning the *contretemps* of yesterday?"

The lawyer advanced a little from his place somewhat in the background.

"I have had an interview with the firm this morning," he announced. "The point raised is without doubt a curious one, but to my mind admits of little argument. Mr. Adams is here at the present moment and is anxious to speak to you on the subject."

"He shall have the opportunity," Martin Hews conceded. "Let him be brought in."

A very worried-looking auctioneer presently made his appearance. Martin Hews swung round to meet him, with a scowl upon his face.

"So, Mr. Adams," he said, "you are a wonderful judge of curios, but you cannot tell a good bank note from a bad one!"

"Not unless I see it, sir."

"The whole situation has been explained to me. I suggest that you put the matter before your client. The last serious bidder for the miniatures was Lord St. Walmer, at nineteen thousand guineas. They were mine at twenty thousand. Owing to your accepting the bids of an imposter, I was induced to pay forty thousand guineas. What about that twenty thousand guineas?"

"The equity of the position," Mr. Adams acknowledged, "would seem to demand that the sale should be entered to you at twenty thousand guineas. At the present moment, however, I am not sure how my client will regard the matter. Mr. Yardsley has explained to me the legal aspect, but his arguments do not seem to me to be entirely sound. There is, for instance, no absolute proof that the other bidder was not prepared to pay if his bid had been accepted. On the other hand—"

Martin Hews' hand flashed out. It was a little habit he had when he wished to end a discussion.

"You are getting wearisome, my friend," he complained. "Put the matter to your client. He can return me the twenty thousand guineas if he thinks well. If not, it really doesn't matter. The miniatures are mine."

In a sense it was a magnificent gesture—a little spoilt by the fact that he looked into the face of every one of us for our approbation. Isaacs only groaned.

"Mr. Hews," he protested, "twenty thousand guineas, it is good money. Mr. Yardsley is sure that the law is with us."

"I have the miniatures," Martin Hews repeated.

From a slim gold case he produced a cigarette and lit it.

"Half-past eleven," he announced, glancing at his wrist watch. "I shall return at once. Major, your presence will be an additional protection. You shall ride with me and tell me the story of your last night's adventure. Was the wine not strong enough—or was the lady unwilling? You shall lunch at Breezeley, Major. I will send you back. Call in my men. Give me the casket."

We left the place, a curious little procession. The wooden platforms were readjusted, and again Martin Hews performed his amazing feat, ending in a recess of the car built to hold the carriage so that he really seemed to be ensconced amongst the cushions of the back seat.

I took my place by his side, two of his protectors faced us, and one climbed on to the seat by the chauffeur. Martin Hews was looking anxiously out of the window.

"Did any one see that?" he asked me. "I thought I heard a lady scream."

"There were two ladies who screamed," I told him, "one man who swore, a child who yelled, and a policeman who was, I think, stricken dumb for life."

"There is no one else who could perform such a miracle," he boasted, with a grin, "and all the time on my knees were the Martellion Miniatures. . . . Now, Major, tell me about last night."

I gave him a faithful account of all that had happened, and he listened attentively.

"Apparently then," he remarked, "if my little scheme had succeeded, and I really had no doubt but that it would, the result would have been—er—disastrous to you?"

"I think he meant it, sir."

My companion sat for a few moments absorbed in reflection.

"This craze of men for a particular woman is one of the most baffling problems in life," he murmured. "It exists. The pages of history are scored with tragedies to prove it. Are you built the same way, Major?"

"I expect I am, sir," I admitted.

"Dear, dear, dear! And on his part he would have killed you and risked everything—risked his own capture!"

There was a momentary gleam of disappointment in Martin Hews' eyes. I knew quite well he was regretting the fact that I was not a dead man and Joseph beset with the fresh peril of my murder. With the complete ingenuousness of a child he even betrayed his thought.

"Ah, well," he sighed, "after all, I should have been deprived of a very useful helper. Is that the whole story? You have nothing further, Major, to tell me?"

I produced the note with some hesitation.

"This is a copy, sir," I told him. "It was simply found in my letter box last evening."

He read it through and gasped as he came to the last sentence. He crushed it in his fist. His unusual amiability had departed. His eyes became so protuberant I was really afraid they would drop out of his head. His lips were drawn back, his features convulsed with passion. He swore and blasphemed until words failed him. All the time, the two men opposite sat silent, with folded arms. Presently he leaned back as though exhausted. He did not speak again until we were nearing our destination. Then he opened his eyes and looked out of the window, pointing with his forefinger to the grim and hideous edifice which we were approaching at something over sixty miles an hour.

"Wonderful!" he exclaimed. "A wonderful house, that, Major!"

"Wonderful, indeed," I agreed.

"The ladies of the household," he chuckled, "will be glad to see us. We will give them a treat, Major. I will celebrate alike my acquisition of the miniatures and this last nail which Joseph himself has driven into his coffin. They shall lunch with us. It is not often that I exercise hospitality. You will do me the honour, Major? . . . Good!"

We drew up at the door which was immediately thrown wide open. My employer waved me to descend.

"Hurry inside, all of you," he enjoined. "Hurry, you three men. You have luncheon to serve. Now, Major. Stand clear of the steps. I will show you something."

Another platform had been put down, and from the spot indicated in the hall I witnessed a repetition of his

Grafton Street exploit. He looked up at me with his head a little on one side, as he swung his chair round.

"A trifle unusual, I think, Major, such skill? I can turn in the thousandth part of an inch."

"It is more than wonderful; it is uncanny, sir," I told him.

He shot upstairs. I made my way to my sitting-room and felt almost a sense of home-coming as I entered it. A cheerful fire was burning in the grate, and several bowls of flowers were arranged upon the sideboard and table. There was also a surprise. Curled up in my easy-chair, a magazine in her hand, a cigarette between her lips, and a glass by her side, which I shrewdly suspected of containing port, was Rachel.

"Hullo!" I exclaimed.

For a moment she remained quite rigid. When she answered, she did so without turning around.

"What are you doing here?"

"I like that!" I rejoined. "You're very welcome, but I should think I could ask you the same question."

Then she faced me and indulged in a somewhat elaborate yawn.

"Had to change rooms," she confessed. "I'm so deadly bored. I'm going to take back my what-do-you-call-it and slip my halter. There's nothing for me to do down here —not even a gramophone in the house. I'm fed up."

"You had better go and do your hair," I advised her. "There's a luncheon party to-day."

"Get on with you! What sort of a luncheon party down here?"

"Well," I admitted, "it's rather a family affair. The Chief, you, Miss Essiter and myself."

"You're kidding?" she scoffed.

"I swear I'm not," I assured her.

She stood up and yawned once more, stretching herself

with her arms over her head so that her slim body seemed to resolve itself into one lithe line. There was a knock at the door, and Johnson appeared.

"Mr. Hews presents his compliments and hopes that you will take luncheon with him, miss," he said, addressing Rachel. "In half an hour, if you please."

Rachel nodded, and waited until he had departed.

"All very toney, isn't it?" she remarked. "I suppose you're used to it. I ain't."

By this time I realised that she had not been told of Joseph's nocturnal visit to me. I decided to keep it to myself for the present, however. She lifted her arms and danced a few steps towards the door, humming to herself.

"I say, I'll be scared to go in there alone," she confided. "Can I come here for you?"

"Certainly, if you like," I agreed. "We will face it together."

CHAPTER XVIII

In my earlier days I had visited wealthy friends, both at home and on the Continent, but I had never before sat down to a luncheon served more luxuriously. The dining-room which was on the ground floor, and which I had never previously entered, was panelled to the height of about five feet in old Dutch oak, and the red-lacquered walls above were hung with a dozen or more marvellous old masters. The table and chairs might have come from the palace of a Venetian Doge, the glasses were Italian, with faint gold rims and strange pictures in strange colours, fading with a hundred years of use. The silver was Georgian, the linen Florentine. The wine and one or two of the principal dishes were served by the butler, whose two subordinates, to my surprise, proved themselves to be excellent footmen. At the head of the table sat Martin Hews with his casket in front of him, the miniatures displayed in full view. Opposite him was his niece, and facing me, Rachel, and a more uncomfortable *partie carrée*, so far as conversation was concerned, could never, I should think, have been brought together. Beatrice Essiter was once more the indifferent, almost morose young woman of my earlier recollection. She neglected even her duties as hostess, scarcely once addressing either Rachel or me. For the rest, Martin Hews seemed quite content to monopolise the conversation. He gave us a dissertation upon miniature painting. He quoted all the masters from the sixteenth century and explained why this particular art had languished rather than progressed during the Renaissance.

"I wonder, sir," I remarked, during one of his brief pauses, "why you don't write about your treasures? Articles, at any rate, if not a volume."

"In my later days, Major," he said, "when I have ceased to collect, I probably shall. I pick up magazines at times, containing articles which profess to deal with subjects in which I am interested, and drop them in disgust. I read volumes reviewed at great length in florid phraseology, volumes upon pottery and china, volumes upon pictures and art, statuary and bronze, and again, my dear Major, the ignorance displayed by the authors is sometimes appalling. There is not one of these subjects upon which I am not a master. I have thought of writing, but what do I owe the world that I should enlighten it? I am content, at present at any rate, to sit amongst the most wonderful collection of beautiful things any great artist has ever brought together, and find food and drink and all the thrill of life as the joy of them passes through my senses. . . . You are drinking Tokay, Major, from the cellars of the late Emperor of Austria. I sent an agent from Paris to be certain of securing some."

"A wonderful wine, sir."

"It is to your taste, I hope, Miss Rachel?" he asked her. "I trust you have appreciated the perfume."

Rachel took a sniff.

"It smells all right," she admitted. "I must say I like that port they bring me after dinner every day. I beg a glass in the mornings sometimes. We don't get port like that down—"

"Down where?" Martin Hews asked insinuatingly.

"No, you don't !" she scoffed. "You don't catch me like that."

Our host smiled.

"There is no doubt," he acknowledged, "that a life of

action such as you, I imagine, have led, Miss Rachel, sharpens the wits as well as the tongue. What do you think, Beatrice?"

She raised her eyebrows as though a little bored at being addressed.

"Really, I haven't thought about it," she replied. "Rachel seems to be possessed of a very useful spirit of independence. I dare say there are times when she needs it."

"I have needed it," Rachel declared doggedly, "since I left the board school for young Jews and Jewesses at eleven years old without a job and had to find the money somehow or other for my mother's funeral. Being alone in the world teaches you independence, all right. You don't get soppy, anyway."

I plunged clumsily into the conversation.

"I was once told," I ventured, "that your schools are better than Christian ones."

"Maybe," Rachel agreed indifferently. "Didn't teach me much, but that was because I didn't want to learn. I've generally been able to find out what I wanted to know."

"But listen, my dear young lady," Martin Hews begged, turning the row of miniatures more directly towards her. "Can't you realise the beauty of an education which could teach you to understand the subtle and hidden perfection of work such as this?"

"They're pretty pictures enough—a little faded to my mind," Rachel replied. "I should call it a funny education which could make me see any more in them. I know a second-hand shop down our way where they've got some chromos of Venice and other places abroad with real colouring, not faded stuff like that."

Martin Hews indulged in the artist's shiver and, turning to me, abandoned the conversation hurriedly.

"What do you think of my friend Yardsley?" he enquired.

"Well, he looked to me like a typical, old-fashioned,
family solicitor," I replied. "When he began to talk to
me about affairs in which we were interested, he amazed
me. I should think you must find him very useful."

Martin Hews chuckled.

"He is supposed to keep me out of the dread clutches
of the law," he said. "Sometimes I try him high, I am
afraid. It has always been the curse of my life," he went
on, "that when I have wanted a thing, I have wanted it so
intensely that I can find no brake to my desires. Sometimes such a temperament leads one into indiscretions.
Hence Mr. Yardsley. . . . You are admiring my pictures, I hope, Major. You recognise the Meissonier, of
course. The Claude Monet you may not have seen. The
Velasquez very nearly got me into trouble, but there it
hangs for the world to see. The two Gainsboroughs please
a great many people. I myself find them rather florid examples. Life, after all, is a queer business," he muttered,
with a sudden access of depression. "What use are sixty
or even seventy years to a man? Even I, with artistic
perceptions which have been granted to few, know of un-
trodden fields where I shall never find time to wander. Art
is eternal, and life is an insignificant little chart of days,
dealt out to us as though by a malevolent deity."

Johnson discreetly filled my glass, and I abandoned
myself for a few seconds to the joy of the golden wine.
Rachel winked frantically at me across the table. Martin
Hews, intercepting her message, glowered down upon us.

"It matters nothing to the brainless rabble," he
snapped. "Seventy or eighty years are too long for
them to spend munching the grass of ignorance. It is men
who understand who should live through eternity. For example," he went on, "look at this miniature. I understand

it. I detect a beauty in it none of you others could ever recognise. That gift of perception, that instinctive reverence for beauty, should carry me on through the ages long after you others are dust and ashes—and it won't. That is the accursed, the damnable part of it."

The wine had given me courage. I ventured upon a word.

"Well, we don't know much about things yet, do we, sir? You may be collecting treasures in another world a hundred years hence, and I may be shooting criminals."

He looked at me with malice in his eyes.

"I can conceive no useful reason for your continued existence, Major," he said. "Muscle and brawn will be found created anew in every cycle. As to your future profession—shoot me the criminal I want to see dead before you make your plans."

"Perhaps he ain't such a criminal, after all, compared with some of you," Rachel insisted bravely.

"Perhaps not," Martin Hews agreed, with unexpected suavity. "After all, what is crime? Who made the laws? I have no doubt that in private life our Joseph, for instance, is a very reputable person, but all the same, nothing would make me happier than to wake up to-morrow and to hear that his throat had been slit."

Beatrice Essiter, who had been leaning back in her chair with a supreme lack of interest in her face, both with regard to our conversation and life in general, intervened voluntarily for the first time.

"Isn't the discussion becoming a little bloodthirsty?" she remarked. "Why not give them an exhibition of your latest accomplishment, Uncle, and then have our coffee in the library? You can at least show them something no one else in the world has ever done."

He welcomed the suggestion with obvious pleasure. Once more the childishness in him leaped to the surface. There was about him something of the bashful delight of a precocious child invited to play his piece on the drawing-room piano.

"I am glad you reminded me of that, Beatrice," he said. "Certainly you shall see, you two, what no one else in the world has seen, except my niece and Minchin, my servant. You shall see what no other person could do."

Our hostess rose, and the servants fell into their places. Martin Hews circled around the hall, made a momentary adjustment and flashed up the stairs. We joined him a few minutes later in the library. He took the centre of a little clear space and waited, his hand upon the controlling wheel of his carriage, his eyes following his niece's movements. Beatrice produced a small but wonderful gramophone in a black ebony case, put on a record and closed the lid. The music of a waltz stole out into the room. Martin Hews leaned forward ecstatically, one hand beating time to the music. Then, with a gentle glide of his chair, he danced. Rachel and I watched, open-mouthed, Beatrice, with that steady but tolerant contempt which seemed to be her attitude towards most things in life. Never out of time, reversing at the corners, up the middle, across and down the sides, the chair flashed in and out, and always the quaint little figure in the seat moved his body to the music. He kept it up until the end. Then he looked at us with that almost imbecile smile of the vain and nervous child awaiting approbation.

"Crikey!" Rachel exclaimed. "Why, you'd make your fortune, Mr. Hews, on the halls!"

"I couldn't have believed such a thing possible, sir," I declared.

"It is impossible for any one else," he agreed. "Take some coffee. Afterwards I must rest. Owston, you must go back to London. A car shall be ordered for you. There is work for you during the next few days. Drink a little of my Napoleon brandy, but mind the glass. The National Debt couldn't replace it. Cigarettes? There they are upon the table."

"What about me?" Rachel demanded. "I'm fed up with this, I am."

"You are under parole to me," he reminded her. "You have, I believe, pledged your word to Jim Donkin not to move from here willingly until you hear from him, except with my permission. You can go up to London with Major Owston, if he'll promise to take care of you," he added, with a grin.

She bit her lip, and at that moment I half expected to see her priceless coffee cup go hurtling through the air. She restrained herself, however.

"I'm sick of what you call my parole!" she exclaimed. "And if old Jim's made such a muck of things as to have to go into hiding, I'm not going to hang on here waiting for him."

"Haven't you some relatives, Rachel, who would make themselves responsible for you?" Beatrice asked, from the depths of her easy-chair. "My uncle fancies himself under obligations to Jim Donkin. He would no doubt be willing to find you money."

"Keep your damned money!" Rachel retorted fiercely. "There's no call for you to interfere."

Beatrice brushed away a little ash from her cigarette which had fallen upon her tweed skirt. She looked across at Rachel with a faint smile.

"My uncle has his reasons, I suppose, for keeping you here," she said, "but it seems a pity to burden ourselves with an unwilling guest."

"Then why don't he let me go?" Rachel demanded. "I'm unwilling enough. I'm fed up with you all. This silly house, with doors that won't open in a Christian way, and electric alarms if you put your foot across the threshold, and

lights springing out, too, from all manner of places—
I'm fed up with it. I tell you this, Mister," she went on,
"that parole of mine can hold good for another week,
and at the end of that time out I go by hook or by crook.
If Jo comes and fetches me I'll go with him. If he don't,
I'll get off by myself. There, that's fair and square, ain't
it? One week from to-day, and to hell with my parole! I
want a bit of life, I do."

She rose to her feet and without a backward glance
at any of us left the room. Martin Hews watched her
thoughtfully. There was something in his eyes which I
hated.

"A crazy witch!" he muttered. "The makings of a very
elegant woman, though. A pity you're not able to make
an impression upon her, Major."

"If I had," I reminded him, "they'd probably have been
reading the funeral service over me to-day."

"Quite true," he acknowledged. "Still, she knows.
A pity we are not in the Middle Ages. There were so
many delightful expedients in those days for soliciting
the confidence of people in her position. We are too
humane nowadays. I ask you whether it is not an absurdity to think that that young woman, moving about
this house as she pleases, could tell us where to find Joseph."

"I doubt whether she could," I answered. "Joseph is
almost as much a mystery to her as to us. She may know
some of his haunts, but I believe he changes them every
week."

"All the same, set her loose near any of them, and
we'd have him," Martin Hews predicted. "We've traps
enough going, but they want baiting. Anything to say to
me before you go back, Major?"

"Well, there is, sir," I told him. "Bloor wants to work
with me—the man who was down here from Scotland

Yard. He knows more than I do already. He has the whole force at the Yard behind him, and he's a clever fellow."

"But I hate Scotland Yard," my employer declared passionately. "They're too inquisitive. They pry into my affairs."

"I don't think Inspector Bloor wishes to do that, sir," I assured him. "He gave me a hint that there is a good deal which he is perfectly willing to forget. All that he wants is Joseph."

"And if they got him," Martin Hews muttered, "what would it mean? Three years—five years. I want Joseph dead. Nothing else."

"That may come. If ever I meet him when we are equally armed, I promise you that it will be a fair fight, and I won't spare him. On the other hand, there may be circumstances when a fight is impossible, and if I can take him alive I must hand him over to Scotland Yard. They want him badly, sir. They won't let him off, as you seem to think. As soon as they've got him safely in prison, on one charge, his band will be broken up. Some of them will lose their terror of him then. There'll be one informer at least amongst the gang. The police will get the evidence they want. They're just as anxious to put Joseph away for life as you can be."

Martin Hews sat for a moment deep in thought, his underlip protruding, his ugly eyebrows close together.

"Very well, Owston," he conceded at last, "have it your own way. Work with Bloor, if you must, but if you meet Joseph, and if a fight should come of it, and you should kill him, I shall pay into your banking account the sum of twenty thousand pounds."

"I don't fancy blood money," I told him. "Joseph is a dangerous criminal, and if I find him and he won't give himself up, which we know he won't, well, we'll fight, and if we fight I fancy it will be until one of us is dead, but I won't touch money for it."

He waved me away with a contemptuous gesture.

"No wonder you've made such a failure of your life, Major," he scoffed. "Sentiment is a fine thing in its place, but maudlin sentiment is detestable. I cannot force my money upon you. Leave it as you say. . . . Leave it as you say," he repeated, "but for God's sake," he added, lifting his hands and clawing the air, "get me Joseph."

Johnson was already holding the front door open for my departure when I heard footsteps in the hall, and, turning around, saw Beatrice approaching. She motioned me to join her on the large divan which stood before the open fireplace.

"I expected to find you in your room," she said.

"I didn't go there," I replied. "I thought perhaps I had better get away. I seem to be rather in trouble with every one."

"Your little friend Rachel was waiting for you. She spends half her time curled up in your easy-chair."

"She has never been there at my invitation."

She remained silent for a moment but showed no disposition to move. Her manner was still ungracious enough, but I fancied that she was struggling to say something. Suddenly she looked me straight in the eyes.

"Were you honest with my uncle, Major Owston," she asked, "when you told him that you would not take twenty thousand pounds blood money?"

"Absolutely," I assured her.

"You need money."

"Of course I do. I haven't a shilling in the world. That isn't any reason why I should turn assassin."

She looked away from me into the great wood fire which was burning in the hearth. Her face relaxed, her lips quivered. Then, almost for the first time, she smiled at me. It was an amazing transformation. She was no longer the sullen, scornful young woman, whose sole idea seemed to be to make herself as ungracious as possible. She was suddenly attractive in a very wonderful manner, and I knew that, stupid though I might be in many ways, I had fashioned her faithfully in my thoughts.

"I should like to tell you, Major Owston," she said, "that I very much appreciate your attitude. I have heard so many of these bargains, and it has sickened me of my life here, of life altogether. My uncle thinks he can buy the stars out of heaven. By-the-by, he sent me to see you."

"I hoped you'd come on your own account," I confessed.

"Since you have said that," she replied, "I will admit that I should have come, but I expected you were in your room, and I knew that the little Jewess was waiting for you. I am glad you were not. My uncle wished me to tell you that on Friday evening, and probably Sunday or Monday, you will be faced with the hardest task he has yet exacted from you."

"Tell me the worst," I begged.

"You have to be my escort to some of these parties. Do you mind?"

I was not very eloquent, but I think that I succeeded in being convincing. Anyhow, she stood upon the steps and waved her hand to me, and, looking back at Breezeley Mansion, for the first time I quite forgot its horrors.

CHAPTER XIX

A few evenings later, I dined with Bloor. In his dinner clothes, which in their way were correct enough, he presented a more rough-and-tumbled appearance than ever. His masses of sandy hair were still indifferently controlled, in spite of obvious evidence of a barber's efforts, and, although everything else about him was in order, he wore the heavy boots of an ordinary policeman with rubber sides. His smile, however, was just as kindly, and he had always a quiet air of self-possession and gentleness which seemed curiously out of keeping alike with his profession and with his exterior.

"Any news?" he enquired, as we seated ourselves at a chosen table in a popular grillroom.

I handed him over another of the square envelopes.

"Smart found this in the letter box during the afternoon," I confided. "He had opened the door only a few seconds before, and he declares that there was not a soul in sight."

Bloor read out the few words printed as usual in rough characters:

"Get out of this, Major. It's not your job, and you'll be hurt."

The detective stared at the message thoughtfully and placed the half sheet of paper in the breast pocket of his coat.

"I will return it to-morrow," he promised. "Fellow seems to take a queer interest in you, doesn't he?"

"Seems so," I admitted.

"I am beginning to wonder about it," Bloor confided. "He might have done you in the other night, if he had been keen. Another killing wouldn't have made much difference to him. What's he mean by it, Major?"

"I can't imagine."

Throughout our first few courses Bloor was thoughtful. Then he asked me an abrupt question.

"Do you know anything about Martin Hews?"

"Not a thing," I acknowledged.

"Ever felt any curiosity about him?"

"Who wouldn't?" I rejoined.

"Shall I tell you his history?"

I hesitated.

"I am not quite sure," I reflected, "whether it's altogether decent, so long as I'm working for him. He's probably told me as much as he wants me to know, and that's nothing."

"You'll have to learn to be a little less finicky, Major, if you're going to carry your job through. However, I'll let you off lightly. The Hews, of West Yorkshire, have been one of the principal county families there for three or four hundred years. Colonel James Hews, who was the head of the family, was killed during the war, and our friend Martin, who was his younger brother, succeeded. There was plenty of money, but on his accession Martin Hews sold the whole of the family estates, disappeared with two trained nurses from England for nearly three years, came back and began to lead very much the sort of life you see him leading now."

"Has he been crippled like this from birth?" I asked.

"Since the day of his birth. A horrible affair it must have been, but he was apparently born without legs. One gathers that he spent those three years mostly in Paris, Madrid, and Florence. He paid one visit to Egypt and left hurriedly. He was reported to have said that half

the antiquities there, even in the tombs, were faked.
One year he spent in the East, but we have no records of
him there. Upon his return, he rented a great mansion
in Berkeley Square. Pictures, bronzes and curios began
to pour in from every part of the world. Then—eleven
years ago, I think it was—one of the most daring burglaries ever planned stripped him of half of his treasures.
He was uninsured, and from that moment he seems to have
been inspired with a feverish hatred of the police who, I
am sorry to say, utterly failed to make a single arrest.
That burglary, to my mind, was the work of Joseph—and
the beginning of his career. Afterwards, Martin Hews retired to that extraordinary building on Breezeley
Marshes which he added to until, as you know, it is now
colossal. From that time—I speak confidentially, Major
—he has been, at various intervals, under police super-
vision."

"Better not tell me any more," I suggested, "except this
—Miss Essiter?"

"His only sister's child," Bloor confided. "I know noth-
thing about her, except that her mother was married in
New York and that she went to live with Martin Hews
some years ago. A strange household, Major—a very
strange household indeed!"

"A very uncomfortable one for the young lady," I declared.

Our conversation was broken in upon for the next few
minutes by the service of dinner. As soon as we were alone
again, Bloor leaned across the table.

"Tell me," he invited, "how you have been employing
your time the last few days?"

"Unprofitably," I admitted. "Just a rotten grind,
that's all."

"Meaning?"

"I've squeezed my way in to three receptions," I con-

fessed, "listened to some awful music, danced with some
very unattractive young women, and drunk some very
bad champagne. I haven't seen a soul who even suggested
to me what Joseph might be like. I have followed women
about who were wearing wonderful jewels until I became
an object of suspicion myself. I have eschewed my rooms
and dined and lunched alone at restaurants until I am
sick of them. Not a thing has happened to me except
the note you know about."

"I thought Miss Essiter was to go to these night shows
with you," my companion observed.

"She was, but she rang up during the afternoon of the
day I was down there for lunch and told me that her
uncle could not spare her. She is coming to-morrow night
for the big show that Lady Bonofar is giving in Grosvenor Square. If Joseph really goes to social functions
at all, I don't see how he could miss a party like this."

"I suppose not," Bloor assented thoughtfully.

"I wonder if you'd think it presumptuous," I went on,
"if I ventured upon a word of criticism. It does seem
extraordinary to the layman—take myself as an example
—that with the whole of your organisation at Scotland
Yard, all your resources, your records, your small army
of detectives of various classes, you still have no idea
where to lay your hands upon an established, a really famous criminal who is known to be the head of a gang. It
seems just a little helpless, doesn't it?"

My companion smiled across the table at me—a
thoroughly good-humoured, pleasant smile. He nodded
sympathetically, and, stretching out his hand for the
menu, turned it over, face downwards.

"A very reasonable criticism, Major," he admitted,
"but let me assure you that very few people have any
idea as to how slowly it is necessary for us to work when
we are after big game. If you miss a single step, you may

come to grief. All the same, we move, we move all the time. We don't spring, perhaps, but we advance. Two months ago we had no certain information as to any of Joseph's haunts, or as to his personality. Now look here."

He drew a little plan, starting from the Bethnal Green Road, and working eastwards towards the river. This he enclosed in a circle, and passed it over to me.

"Joseph's headquarters," he pointed out, "are somewhere within that circle. A month ago the orbit was much larger. Now every day my men close in a little upon it. I have twenty-three men living apparently harmless, civilian lives within that circle, Major, and at our present rate of progress there will be less than half a mile to guard at the end of next week."

"Well, that's something," I acknowledged.

"We have at the present moment marked down in that locality seven men guilty of various crimes, whom we could arrest and bring to justice to-morrow. We keep our eye on them, but we're waiting. We want the lot. We want Joseph. Now wait a moment."

He drew back the menu and made another rapid little pencil sketch. To my amazement, my own street was there, Clarges Street and Half Moon Street, and Shepherd's Market. Again he drew a circle, and this time there was very little space indeed enclosed.

"Somewhere there," he confided—"a close neighbour of yours, you see—our friend has a shelter of a different sort. It consists of two rooms only, and so far we have found it impossible to locate him. It is, I believe, very seldom used, but he was there, without a doubt, on the night when he paid that visit to you. The place we should really like to discover, though, is the place to which Mr. Van Doorn of Amsterdam drove when he left Christie's, and I will tell you this much about that. He passed Lord's Cricket Ground and took the road to Finchley. There, alas! he disappeared, but if you were to go for a little motor trip one fine day along the North Road, you would probably find a few more motor bicyclists about than usual. Those are our men, and each one of them has a very good idea of what he is looking out for."

"I apologise, Inspector," I said.

"Then you come to the question of Joseph himself," Bloor continued, and his eyelids dropped a little as he glanced downward at the plan which he was tearing into small pieces, "and here we have to contend with a great difficulty. Joseph could never have remained free for a month, instead of all these years, but for his amazing gift of disguise. Against our will, Major, even the professional outlook is obscured and prejudiced by such a presentation as that of Mr. Van Doorn of Amsterdam. Subconsciously it haunts us, even though we know that it was a disguise. What you have to do is to forget that you ever saw Van Doorn. When you meet Joseph, if ever you do, face to face, I can promise you this—he will be a person of an utterly different type."

"One might find out something by careful enquiries at the stage doors," I reflected. "Joseph must have assistance in his making up, and it's probably theatrical. If we could hear now of some dresser with a special reputation who had fallen upon more prosperous days."

Mr. Bloor beamed upon me kindly.

"An excellent idea, Major," he acknowledged. "We shall make you one of us, after all. We will put some men on the job to-morrow. You have no special news from Breezeley Mansion then?"

"Everything seems quiet there," I replied. "Rachel is sulking and sending out notes and letters which are regularly intercepted and destroyed. Martin Hews still spends an hour or two daily gazing at his miniatures, but he has also some other business on hand which involves a lot of correspondence. Miss Essiter has twice proposed to come up to these infernal receptions, and each time the little monkey has stopped her at the last moment."

The detective sighed.

"I had hoped," he admitted, "quite hoped, that Joseph would have made some move to release the young lady. That, of course, is also Martin Hews' idea. That is why he keeps her there. I have six men working on the roads between the station and the Mansion, and a dozen along the river banks, the way I rather fancy Joseph would choose. Not a sign of him, not a movement, not even a scout. And all the time, Major, I can't help thinking that Joseph is watching from somewhere with his tongue in his cheek, watching the trap without bait, watching my poor fellows wet through half the day, and laughing softly to himself."

A waiter paused at our table. He handed a slip of paper, folded up, to my companion, and hurried away. Bloor opened it slowly, read it without moving a muscle, and passed it across to me:

"Sorry to see you drinking a '19 wine. The '11s are still on the list.

JOSEPH."

Of course all our enquiries came to nothing. The waiter who had handed us the slip of paper had received it from another one, who thought it was from a gentleman in the restaurant. Anyhow, he remembered nothing and knew nothing. Bloor accepted the little episode with calm and happy content.

"Major," he prophesied, "my words will come true. "No criminal can afford to have a sense of humour."

CHAPTER XX

THERE was a moment almost of hesitation on my part before I stepped forward in the centre of the lounge at Claridge's on the following evening to greet Beatrice Essiter. I had met her and been with her in such strange places, in such an atmosphere of doubt, tragedy and suspicion, that to find her calmly moving towards me, dressed, as even my masculine eyes convinced me, more wonderfully than any other woman in the room, her beautiful hair fashionably arranged, a row of lustrous pearls around her neck, the frown gone from her face, the sullen discontent from her lips,—to see her like this gave me for a moment a sense of curious unreality. Perhaps she felt something of the same sort of thing, for her own greeting was a little constrained.

"We remind one another of that new Russian Ballet," she laughed, almost immediately regaining her poise—"hobgoblins and fairies turned into ladies and gentlemen of fashion. Nothing about my uncle's staff work inspires me with greater admiration than his genius for providing clothes. I am surprised that you did not find your correct regimental tie with your lounge suit and linen."

"Your uncle is a most amazing man," I remarked.

She smiled without smiling, a trick she had sometimes —a little flutter of the eyelids, a deepening of that attractive line at the corners of her mouth.

"Yes, I suppose he might be called that," she agreed. "Just now he is depressed. He has come to the conclusion that there is at least one other man as clever as he is in the world, and he doesn't like it."

We moved into the restaurant and towards the table which I had engaged.

"No sign of Joseph, then?"

"Not the slightest. Helen remains upon her balcony and sighs in vain. Hector's love is less than his cunning. So the Mansion is still under arms, and the flashlights search the countryside every night. . . . You know the sort of evening that is in front of us?"

"I have already spent three this week at minor affairs," I groaned. "This, however, should at least be a spectacle worth seeing. They tell me that there are two thousand invitations issued, and that nearly every one has accepted, because Lady Bonofar is going to wear her diamonds. Think of it! Two thousand people, and Detective Bloor told me last night that Joseph was the greatest artist in disguise the criminal world has ever known. Makes our chances seem a trifle slim, doesn't it? Personally, I would rather fancy myself in the East End."

"You are very foolish to talk like that," she said severely. "Do you read the newspapers?"

"Lately I have."

"Did you happen to notice an account of a man found dead upon the steps of the old wharf at Rotherhithe?"

"Yes," I admitted, "I saw that."

"Did you read yesterday about two more having been found near Blackfriars' Bridge, one throttled, and the other with a broken skull?"

"Yes, I saw that too. 'Terrible result of a fight near the Docks,' was the heading."

"Then there was a man found dead on the line near Brentwood."

"I missed that."

"Did it not strike you," she asked, "that there were a good many deaths by violence in the course of three days?"

"One or two of them might have been suicides," I reminded her.

"Well, these weren't," she assured me. "I am certain my uncle knows, and he told me that every one of these four were men from Donkin's gang—the few who haven't gone over to Joseph. He isn't going to run any risk of their turning informer, you see. Joseph's secret service in the East End is perfect. You couldn't stay there for twenty-four hours without joining this little list."

"Well, I don't see what use I'm going to be up here," I sighed. "Joseph seems to be able to come and leave notes in my letter box whenever he likes. I feel somehow all out of place. I am more at home in a scrap, but when it comes to brains, well—"

"You have brains enough," she interrupted pleasantly, "to get one of the best tables in the room and to order a very excellent dinner. I call that a good deal, you know."

"You are laughing at me," I complained.

"Then I'll be serious," she promised. "Listen. Of course, my uncle realises that you've had no experience in this sort of thing, but he chooses to employ you deliberately, and I'll tell you why. It may surprise you to hear it, but he is exceedingly superstitious. Nearly every day I see him looking, for half an hour sometimes, into one of the most wonderful crystal globes I have ever seen."

"Do you believe in that sort of thing?" I asked incredulously.

"If you lived at Breezeley Mansion you would," she laughed. "Anyhow, he has come to the conclusion that you have luck. You certainly have come off rather well in one or two little affairs. You were lucky not to have been knocked about worse in the scrap at the Mansion. You were lucky to escape being shot in the library afterwards. You were lucky not to have kept Rachel with you that night in Down Street."

"That wasn't altogether luck," I said, leaning a little towards her.

She looked me in the eyes very steadily and with some return of that sphinx-like expression of hers.

"What was it then?" she asked. "Indifference?"

I wasn't going to lie about it, anyhow.

"No, it wasn't exactly indifference," I replied. "I'm just the same as other men. Rachel is fascinating in her way, and I expect I felt just the same sort of attraction for her as any other man might have done. I got out of it by telling her that I cared for some one else."

"And do you?"

There was not the faintest curiosity in her tone, but her eyes were still holding mine.

"I am beginning to," I acknowledged, summoning up my courage.

Anyway, I scored, for although still indifferently, she looked away, and continued her dinner.

"We have wandered from the point, haven't we? I was telling you that it is my uncle's belief in your luck which makes him reluctant to part with you. .He knows that Scotland Yard are at work, and he has schemes of his own for tracking down Joseph. With it all, he firmly 'believes that you are the one man who will succeed."

"If I could only once see the fellow," I sighed.

"You probably have. It may lead you into slight difficulties, but if I were you, I would concentrate upon the idea that he is somewhere close at hand always, and be on your guard against even the most innocent-looking person who seems to take an interest in you. That is what we must do to-night at Lady Bonofar's. It is our only chance. Let us try to persuade ourselves that he may be even dining in this restaurant at the present moment."

It was a quaint idea and rather appealed to me. I looked round the room curiously. It was a little early for the fashionable world, for it was part of our programme to see the people arrive at the reception for which we were bound, but there were quite a sprinkling of smart people dining. There was only one, however, who, according to my ideas, could possibly have been the man of whom we were in search. He was seated by himself at a corner table—a tired, sallow-faced man who was eating his dinner languidly, and only occasionally glancing up at a passer-by. I directed my companion's attention to him.

"What about the man in the corner?"

She glanced at him curiously.

"So that's your idea of Joseph," she observed. "Well, he has just that air of being able to look like some one else if he wanted to. Shall we ask your friend the *maître d'hôtel* who he is?"

One of the head waiters who was an old acquaintance of my more prosperous days, and who had been very attentive to us, was passing, and I summoned him. He smiled at my question.

"Yes, indeed, sir," he acknowledged, "we all know that gentleman. He only arrived from America last night. That is Mr. Stanley Caton. They say that he is the richest man in the world."

"From America last night," I repeated. "Has he been away long?"

"For a little over three months, sir, and I am sorry to say that he is leaving again to-morrow—for Russia, I think. His wife and two daughters are with him. To-night they have gone to the theatre."

The waiter passed on, and I permitted myself a little grimace.

"Number one's a blank anyhow."

"You mustn't be discouraged," she insisted. "We will

probably have to put up with a good many blanks before we get anywhere near our man. However, I sha'n't mind the quest being a long one, if I am allowed to come up and join in it and you order dinner as carefully as this."

"Your chef at Breezeley is so wonderful that I was really a little nervous," I told her.

She shrugged her shoulders slightly.

"Do you know," she confided, "that I scarcely realise what I am eating there. Everything tastes the same to me when my uncle is at the other end of the table. Did any one ever succeed in running away from Uncle Martin, I wonder? . . . Not until he had finished with them, I am sure. Not until he had used all their brains and their youth till only the husks were left," she added bitterly.

I had to sit tight and remember—remember all the time —that I was Martin Hews' man, living on his bounty without a shilling of my own in the world. The moment passed. When she spoke again, it was in a different note.

"You have given me your impressions of a possible Joseph," she remarked. "I will give you mine. There! The man behind Lord Farendon, just coming in."

A small party of newcomers were filing into the room. Two I recognised as well-known Members of Parliament, and I also knew by sight Lord Farendon, who was a Cabinet Minister. The man whom my companion had indicated was a stranger, but his appearance was certainly somewhat striking. He was slightly over medium height, with a pronounced stoop, black hair, pale complexion, somewhat sunken cheeks, and dark eyes inadequately concealed behind horn-rimmed spectacles. The lines of his mouth were curled upwards, giving his expression a touch of cynicism. He was dressed a trifle foppishly, considering that he was amongst a company where the least eccentricity of attire is considered out of place. His black bow tie—the men were all in dinner coats—was a little larger than ordinary and almost resembled a stock. His links and his studs—the latter, so far as I could see, of finely chosen pearls—were also jet black. He seemed quite at ease amongst his companions, but at the same time he had the air of being almost a stranger to them. There was a brief delay about taking their places, which function was directed by Lord Farendon, who was evidently host. The man in whom I had been interested was to be on his host's right, and as he seated himself he glanced across the room in our direction so that, although quite casually, our eyes met. There was something about that glance, unpremeditated though it was, something about the man, the poise of his body as he leaned over his chair, which brought me not exactly any sense of actual recognition, but which thrilled me in a most mysterious way. There was not a line of him, or a feature, which directly reminded me of any one I had ever met before in my life, yet I felt curiously and strangely affected by his presence. It was as though I were meeting some one whom I had known in another personality, under perhaps forgotten conditions. He himself apparently reciprocated none of my interest. His eyes had passed from mine almost at once and rested upon my companion. There they remained. So far as a man with every appearance of breeding and good manners can stare at a beautiful woman with whom he is unacquainted, he committed that unpardonable sin. He looked at her without changing a muscle of his face, yet I could read well enough his interest, and I felt that strange mixture of sensations, which still kept me speechless, change into anger. I glanced at my companion. There was, perhaps, the slightest possible tinge of colour in her cheeks, but although her eyes met his steadily, there was not the faintest glint of that hauteur in their expression which had so depressed me on our first few meetings. She seemed to have accepted the challenge of his interest and in a sense to have reciprocated it. I beckoned to a *sommelier* to fill our glasses, and when I looked back again the man at the opposite table was talking to his host, and my companion was resisting the importunities of a waiter who was trying to press some more asparagus upon her.

"Well, what do you think of my choice?" she asked.

"Honestly," I admitted, "that man is about as near my idea of Joseph as any one could be."

The tinge of colour had gone, and left her, it seemed to me, paler than ever. There was something in her expression which reminded me of the moment when we had met upon the threshold of my room at Breezeley Mansion, when the red light was burning upon my wall. Some fear seemed to have been born in her.

"Those things don't happen, do they—not in real life?" she murmured. "We are in search of one man out of seven million, and we are scarcely likely to find him the first time we dine together in a public restaurant. Besides," she went on, "although I have a great idea of Joseph, I can't really imagine him dining with Dukes— there is a Duke there, isn't there, besides a Cabinet Minister? I think we shall have to go a little farther afield for our victim. Lady Bonofar's reception rooms still seem to me a more likely place."

"What a pity!" I sighed. "I like the atmosphere here much better, and I hate a crowd."

Our meal drew on towards its end, but something seemed to have disturbed the growing intimacy between us which had filled me with so much pleasure. I noticed too, very much to my annoyance, that the man who had so manifestly shown his interest in my companion had in no way abandoned it. He was contributing his full share to the general conversation of the table, but whenever he had an opportunity, he looked across at us, and his eyes sought hers in almost challenging fashion. I summoned my *maître d'hôtel* and whispered in his ear. He bowed and departed towards the office.

"I have asked him to get me a list of Farendon's guests," I explained. "That fellow looks at you all the time. Have you ever seen him before, that you know of?"

Her fingers toyed uneasily with her cigarette case.

"I can't exactly remember that I have," she replied, "yet there is something about him—how foolish we are! We have worked ourselves into this state, you know. Anyhow, if your waiter succeeds in his mission, we shall know who he is."

The *maître d'hôtel* returned presently and laid a little strip of paper by my side. My companion and I read it together:

> "Lord Farendon
> The Hon. Peter Gateson
> Mr. R. C. Croome, M. P.
> Mr. Prayson Taylor, M. P.
> Sir Godfrey Mandon
> The Duke of Medchester
> Mr. X."

I looked up at the *maître d'hôtel*
"Which is Mr. X.?"

"The gentleman seated at his lordship's right hand, sir. He is a guest who does not wish his name in the paper."

My companion and I exchanged glances.

"A man of mystery, anyhow," she murmured.

As though he knew we were talking about him, he suddenly leaned forward in his place and shot a swift, searching look across the room towards us—a look which seemed individual enough, and yet which included both of us. In cold words it is impossible to describe the effect it had either upon my companion or upon myself. There was something cynical, something defiant, in the stony imperturbability of his features compared with the almost threatening blaze of his eyes. I realised at once that he knew we had been making enquiries about him and resented it.

"You must have met a great many people at different times at your uncle's?" I suggested to my companion. "Are you sure that you never met him there? He talks to both his neighbours, yet whenever he has a minute to spare he looks at us."

"My dear man, do you think that I don't know it?" she laughed nervously. "After all," she went on, a moment later, "why shouldn't he if he wants to? He just escapes being rude. Don't you think that we are getting a little jumpy about our quest already? Joseph may be a very extraordinary person, but he is scarcely likely to be a friend of Lord Farendon, or to be sitting on his right hand at a dinner party at Claridge's."

"Yet," I reminded her, "every one has warned us that we must look in the unexpected places for him. Any ordinary criminal Scotland Yard could have laid their hand on long ago."

She shrugged her shoulders ever so slightly. She had the air of wishing to abandon the struggle.

"Dinner has been quite delightful," she said, as she looked into the mirror of a marvellous onyx and diamond vanity case, "and as an escort, Major Owston, I find you so far a complete success. You don't mind my telling you that, do you?" she added, shutting the case up and smiling at me.

"Rather not. As a matter of fact, I find it very reassuring."

She nodded.

"I know what you mean. I can be disgustingly ill-mannered," she confessed, "and my life down at Breezeley makes me bad-tempered and irritable. Shall we go? We mustn't forget the business of the evening has yet to come."

I paid my bill, and we left the restaurant. Mr. X. was apparently engrossing the attention of his whole party by the recital of some adventure as we passed. He did not glance in our direction, nor did Beatrice, whom I was dutifully following, turn her head. I watched his faint gesticulations, however, as his fingers flashed through the air, listened to his voice, dry but not unmusical, and I told myself that somewhere in this world, either in a crowd or in some foreign place which I had half forgotten, on a steamer perhaps, or during that twelve months I had spent in the desert, or even on the battlefield, Mr. X. and I had met before.

CHAPTER XXI

LADY BONOFAR's party had been deservedly heralded
by the entire press as one of the events of the London sea-
son. Her house in Park Lane, architecturally superb,
and garlanded with the choicest of flowers in amazing
profusion, had more the appearance of a royal palace.
The finest music in London was played by alternate or-
chestras in the magnificent ballroom. Three of the greatest chefs from Paris had ransacked Europe for delicacies
to grace the supper table, but one could scarcely fail to
notice that the people who mounted the stairs and passed
presently from room to room, who talked scandal with
one another, flirted, chaffed and exchanged gossip about
their mutual friends, were of the world one meets day by
day in every restaurant, theatre, and at every resort of
Europe. Men or women of any noticeable distinction or
divergence from type were rare. Later on, the surging
crowd presented an increasingly Bohemian aspect. Several
well-known actors and actresses mingled with the social
throng. So far as our personal quest was concerned, we
met with no success. There were hundreds of men who
might possibly have been the person of whom we were in
search, but not a single one who seemed in the least different to the others. We saw the famous Bonofar diamonds encircling the neck of our hostess, and we had no
difficulty in picking out the detectives who were shadowing her wherever she moved. As the evening grew later, we
partly abandoned our enterprise and permitted ourselves
some amount of relaxation. We danced to the wonderful

music, and I fancy that there were moments when my companion as well as I myself forgot altogether the grim purpose which was mingled with our evening's amusement. Wherever we went, I noticed that Beatrice attracted a considerable amount of attention. Even I, an absentee for so long from the world where such things are understood, knew that her toilet was as nearly as possible perfection. Her jewellery, her vanity case, cigarette box and other trifles were all not only costly but exquisite. The dancing, and perhaps the evening's respite from the sinister influence of her dreary home, had brought colour to her cheeks and had banished altogether the discontented, lowering expression which was associated with my first memory of her. She was not only extremely attractive to look at, but she was unusual. Evidently our hostess had to answer many questions, for eventually she came over to us.

"You are Mr. Martin Hews' niece, are you not?" she asked Beatrice. "I am afraid I have forgotten your name. Do tell me, please."

"My name is Beatrice Essiter," she replied, with a smile. "I have heard my uncle speak of you. This is Major Owston, my escort for the evening."

I murmured a word or two of thanks for her hospitality, to which Lady Bonofar listened graciously.

"I wonder if you could spare a few dances?" she asked Beatrice. "So many men have asked to meet you, and I can find plenty of partners for Major Owston."

To my intense relief, my companion shook her head.

"Would you mind, Lady Bonofar, if I asked to be excused from dancing any more this evening?" she begged. "We've been here already a terrible time, you know, and we were just going when you spoke to us."

"You must meet my brother, anyhow," Lady Bonofar begged. "I insist upon that, or rather he does. . . .

Samuel, the young lady is going to be good-natured and give you one dance, although she won't have anything to say to my young men. My brother, Mr. Leopold—Miss Beatrice Essiter—Major Owston."

Mr. Leopold, who had been hovering in the background, was a middle-aged man of rotund figure, with a wrinkled face, sallow complexion, small black eyes and uncompromising features. He departed with Beatrice, and I resigned myself to dance with Lady Bonofar. At close quarters her diamonds were really the most wonderful I had ever seen, and I was amused to observe, all the time upon the outskirts of the dancing floor, Bloor's myrmidons watching us suspiciously.

"Tell me," my partner asked presently, "do you know that amazing uncle of Miss Essiter's very well?"

"I haven't known him very long," I replied, "but I am really a sort of secretary of his. That is why I was allowed to bring his niece to-night."

"I had no idea," she confided, "that Beatrice Essiter was a young woman of such distinction. I remember her as a sulky, ill-mannered child when she first came back to England. If she went out more here, she would become quite the vogue. Three of the diamonds in my new necklace, by-the-by, came from Mr. Martin Hews. He has an astonishing knack of getting hold of fine jewels. I suppose he is fabulously wealthy, and dealers go to him when they must have money."

My employer's jewel-collecting propensities was a subject I thought it best not to discuss, but my partner seemed scarcely to notice my reticence.

"Of course, it's a terrible misfortune for him to be deformed like that," she went on, "but at any rate it has given him an opportunity of concentrating upon his hobby. My brother is a strange character, too. I never know in what part of the world he is. Sometimes I don't see him for years together. He has a house in Java, a bungalow in Rangoon, a flat in New York, an *appartement* in Paris."

"A genuine cosmopolitan then," I ventured. "He has an amusing time, I expect."

"I don't know what he does," my partner confessed, looking up at me with a pleasant smile but slightly wrinkled eyebrows. "I sometimes wish he would confide in me a little more. He makes and loses fortunes with equal facility. Lately I am glad to say he is rather more by way of making them. I expect your charge of the evening is wishing that he had taken dancing lessons at some time during his life. How he has the nerve to go hobbling round the room like that I can't imagine, especially with a girl who has been dancing with you," she added, with a final smile. "I will take pity on Miss Essiter."

We waited for them and sat out for a few minutes in a corner of the winter garden, where footmen in gorgeous liveries passed to and fro the whole of the time, and the atmosphere was heavy with the exotic perfume of stephanotis, lilies and gardenias. We drank old vintage champagne, and presently our host—a dapper little man whom I had not met—looking a good deal less than his sixty years, came and bustled his wife off to greet some late arrivals. Leopold also took his leave, and Beatrice and I made our way downstairs.

"You didn't get much of a show in the way of dancing, I am afraid," I remarked.

She turned to me with a little grimace.

"The oddest man," she confided. "He was once a great friend of my uncle, he assured me, but they seem to have had some disagreement, and he begged me not to mention his name. He divides his time, it appears, between collecting precious stones in Rangoon, gambling on the New York Stock Exchange, shooting pigeons in Monte Carlo, playing baccarat at Cannes, and visiting his sister in London."

"Can't say I took a great fancy to him," I admitted. "I wonder how he passes his time over here?"

She shrugged her shoulders.

"I really don't know what a man of that type could do in London," she acknowledged.

The hall was thronged, and we had to edge our way towards the great flight of steps, where we found at least a score of people waiting for taxies. A very handsome car, of a well-known make, was drawn up in front of the door, and Mr. Leopold appeared behind us, pushing his way a little unceremoniously through the crowd. He recognised us, however, and hesitated.

"Can I drop you anywhere?" he asked, without any particular cordiality. "There aren't any taxies."

Beatrice looked out at the driving rain and accepted at once. I followed the two down the steps.

"Where to?" Mr. Leopold asked, without removing the cigar, which he had been smoking, from his mouth.

"Claridge's, if you please," my companion begged.

He gave the address to the chauffeur, seated himself by her side, and pulled down an arm-chair for me.

"Dull party!" he declared, stretching himself out with an air of relief. "Can't think why Sarah gives them. Never went in for entertaining myself—perhaps because I never married. You young people off home?"

"Well, it's nearly two o'clock," Beatrice remarked, glancing at her wrist watch.

"Pooh! What's that?" our host scoffed. "Too much sleep, not enough exercise, and too little to drink are the three worst things in the world. Let's go to a night club. I know a beauty. Just half an hour, eh?"

Now I can declare quite honestly that it was my intention to refuse that invitation. I had commenced an earnest effort during the last few days to school myself into an attitude of caution towards every stranger in the world, and Leopold, notwithstanding his relationship to our late hostess, was certainly a stranger of a peculiar type. My companion, however, settled the matter before I could open my lips.

"I should love to," she agreed.

"Want to go to the Embassy?" Mr. Leopold suggested. "Pretty well empty by this time, though. I'll take you to a place that only has eighty members or so, but they're all there every night after two. Wonderful music, good wine, and the best deviled marrow bones in London. Hi, John!" he shouted down the speaking tube. "Go to the Blue Skies."

We slackened speed, passed Claridge's, and turned towards Oxford Street. Soon, so far as I was concerned, we were lost. The window panes were dripping with rain, and we had left the main thoroughfares. Suddenly we pulled up in a small street which seemed chiefly occupied by warehouses. Mr. Leopold reinstated the temporarily deposed cigar in his mouth, stepped out, and was saluted at once by a giant commissionaire, who appeared through the handsome swing doors of an unpretentious-looking building. We followed our host into a pleasantly lit circular hall, with a vista on our left of a delightful dancing floor lined with supper tables. The waiters and *maîtres d'hôtel* seemed to be of a superior class, and several of the men and women standing about in the hall and dancing I recognised as having been present at Lady Bonofar's reception. Our host motioned towards the ladies' cloakroom opposite.

"Will you leave your things in there, Miss Essiter?" he begged. "You won't mind signing in the secretary's room?" he added, turning to me. "This is a quaint little place, but it's the most exclusive of its sort in the world.

You have to sign personally and have your proposer and the secretary countersign."

Naturally I had no objection, and I followed him into a room farther down the passage. A man was seated at a plain mahogany desk, writing by the light of a heavily shaded green lamp. He looked up as we entered and smiled at the expression of astonishment in my face. The door behind me closed with a little click. We were suddenly plunged into complete and utter darkness.

CHAPTER XXII

IT took the whole of my first few moments of recovering consciousness to realise where I was. There was
a blank in my mind against which I struggled in vain. The
secretary's office at the Blue Skies, with its soft carpet,
shaded green light, the face of the man seated at the desk,
so utterly unexpected, his head raised at my entrance,
that thin, sardonic smile upon his lips—and afterwards!
A faint, imperfect thread of recollection was swept away
in a spasm of horror. I suddenly knew that I was in a
police cell. . . . There were voices outside, some one was
coming in. I sat up on the hard pallet and, struggling
against a deadly sickness, rose with difficulty to my feet.
A policeman entered, accompanied by an unmistakable
doctor, carrying a small black bag.

"Getting over it?" the latter asked curtly.

"Getting over what?" I demanded. "Why am I here?
Who brought me in?"

The doctor smiled indifferently. I suppose he was used
to such questions.

"You were brought here at three o'clock this morning,
drunk," he said dryly. "Very drunk indeed," he added, as
an afterthought.

I sat for a moment with my head between my hands.
The thoughts were forming themselves already in my
brain. I began to apprehend the full nature of the devilish
cunning with which my clumsiness was confronted. Then,
like a stab, I remembered Beatrice.

"Can you tell me where the young lady is I was with?"
I asked.

The doctor shook his head. He had taken my wrist and was feeling my pulse. He looked into my eyes and stepped back.

"I know nothing about any young lady," he assured me. "Where was he when he was found, Constable?"

"Sitting upon the pavement, with his back against the wall in Chatham Street," the man replied, with a grin. "Drunk as ever I did see a gentleman in my life," he added.

"Well, you seem to have pulled yourself together," the doctor remarked. "I thought I had better have a look at you before you went into Court, but you're perfectly all right now."

"You are prepared to certify that I was drunk?" I enquired.

"I certainly am," he replied. "I should imagine you're not going to deny it, are you?"

"I was drugged," I told him emphatically.

He was a not unpleasant-looking little man, and a gleam of humour shone in his eyes as he smiled.

"I've heard that story pretty often," he confided. "We are used to it here. You may have been drugged, but you smelt of whisky enough to knock a man down."

"I never tasted a drop of whisky all last night," I declared.

The smile faded from the doctor's face, and he turned his back upon me. A police sergeant put his head in at the door.

"Better bring your case along, Jim," he enjoined. "Mr. Horton is sitting."

In my disordered evening clothes, unwashed, and with my hair unbrushed, I was led out of the cell. My head was clearing quickly, and I tried hard to think. The harder I tried, the more improbable, I realised, would any story sound which I might tell. To my relief, as we entered the courtroom, I saw that there were barely a score of people present. The magistrate looked up from his papers.

"Charge?" he enquired laconically.

"Ordinary drunk and incapable," I heard the clerk whisper.

The policeman who had brought me in stepped into the box, gripped the Testament, and stood at attention.

"Police Constable Dethbridge," he announced. "At three o'clock this morning, I was on duty in Chatham Street. I saw the prisoner seated with his back to a wall, apparently asleep. I tried to rouse him, but failed. He smelt very strongly of whisky and was evidently drunk. He is a heavy man, and I had to call a taxicab to bring him to the station."

The magistrate nodded.

"Any questions?" he asked.

I shook my head. The doctor took the place of the policeman.

"I examined the accused at about a quarter to four this morning," he said. "I came to the conclusion that he was hopelessly drunk. He smelt strongly of whisky, and I should think, from his condition, he had been drinking it neat. He was utterly incapable."

"Any statement to make?" the magistrate enquired.

"Yes, I have a statement to make," I said. "I have never been drunk in my life, and I was never less so than last night. I had dined at Claridge's with a young lady, where we had one bottle of champagne and one liqueur. I went afterwards to a reception where I had one glass, or perhaps a glass and a half, of champagne at supper, and another glass later in the evening with my hostess. A gentleman to whom we were introduced there gave us a lift in his car, and invited us to accompany him to a night club. I entered the club perfectly sober and was conducted to the secretary's room to sign my name in the visitor's book. I remember nothing more until I awoke in the cell this morning."

The magistrate looked at me, and if ever disbelief lurked behind a pair of cold grey eyes there was disbelief in his.

"You remember nothing of what happened to you in the secretary's room of the club?"

"Not a thing."

"Can you tell me the name of the club?"

"I never heard it."

"Can you tell us the name of the young lady with whom you dined?"

"I should prefer not to."

The magistrate leaned back in his chair and tapped impatiently upon the table with his pencil.

"What about your friend who introduced you to the club?"

To my intense surprise, Leopold suddenly arose from the back of the Court.

"I am here, sir," he announced, "in case my evidence is required."

Obeying a gesture of the magistrate's, he stepped into the witness box.

"I met Major Owston for the first time last night," he testified. "He seemed to me, when we were first introduced, as though he had been drinking a good deal, but he was still sober. I offered to take the young lady and him to a very respectable night club. I think that the night air was probably bad for him. He seemed a little unsteady on entering, and I made a point of taking him to the secretary's room to sign his name before I introduced him into the club proper. Unfortunately, as it happens, the secretary offered us a whisky and soda, and Major Owston had no sooner drunk his than he collapsed."

I looked across speculatively at Leopold. His eyes met mine a little reproachfully.

"It was a very awkward position for me," he continued. "Fortunately he happened to have told me where his rooms were, so we put him into a taxicab and sent him home. I suppose on the way he insisted upon trying to come back."

"Forty shillings and costs," the magistrate pronounced curtly.

There was a brief whispered conversation between the police sergeant and the magistrate's clerk. I gathered that no money had been found upon my person. Mr. Leopold stood up again and handed some notes to the latter.

"As I was responsible for taking the young man to the club," he said, "I should like to pay the fine."

"Can I appeal?" I asked the magistrate.

"You can, but I should advise you not to," was the uncompromising reply.

I stepped down, and somehow or other made my way outside. A good-natured policeman called a taxicab to the side entrance, and a quarter of an hour later I let myself into my rooms. Smart greeted me with an air of grave distress.

"A bath quickly," I ordered. "Any telephone calls or messages?"

"Nothing of any sort, sir."

"No note?"

"Nothing."

I took up the telephone receiver and asked for Claridge's Hotel.

"Is Miss Essiter staying in the hotel?" I enquired.

There was a brief delay. Then the reply.

"Miss Essiter is staying here, but she is not in."

I made my way to the bath-room, and began to throw off my clothes.

"Smart," I confided, as he brought in the towels, "I spent the night in a police cell, and probably you will see in the papers this evening that I have been fined forty shillings for being drunk. The charge was entirely unjust. That is all I have to say about it. Do the best you can with these clothes. Put me out a clean lounge suit, get me some strong tea, and eggs and bacon."

"Very good. sir."

"I bathed, dressed, and changed as quickly and carefully as possible. Then I ate my breakfast and walked to Claridge's. I think that never before in my life had I felt more nervous than when I presented myself at the bureau and enquired for Miss Essiter. The reception clerk listened to me with a certain hesitation.

"Miss Essiter was staying here yesterday, sir," he admitted. "I am not quite sure whether she has left. Will you take a seat for a minute or two."

He passed on my card to a *chasseur*, and I waited in a high-backed chair, watching the people coming and going through the swing doors. Mine was entirely an idle scrutiny, but suddenly I sat upright. I felt my muscles stiffen. I had a feeling, too, such as I imagine an animal must experience when the hair stands up all down his backbone. Mr. Leopold, clad with almost offensive perfection in town clothes, a black frock overcoat, fitting tightly into his pudgy figure, a silk hat, and with a big cigar in his mouth, entered the hall, and strolled across towards the lounge. Arrived almost at the threshold, he stopped as though to relight his cigar, and in that moment a man, dressed in dark clothes and having the appearance of a servant, stepped forward from the obscurity of the further entrance, and without preamble or any form of salutation, handed him a letter. Leopold asked no questions, made no remark. His hand slid with it into his overcoat pocket. He finished the lighting of his cigar, and without a glance towards the retreating figure of the messenger, he continued his progress. I was half inclined to follow him. Then I reflected that he was safe there, at any rate for some time. Presently I heard the clatter of the gate. The *chasseur* stepped out of the lift. I felt a sensation of positive horror when I saw that he was still carrying my card in his hand. Instead of bringing it direct to me, however, he went to the bureau and talked for several moments to the reception clerk in charge. After some delay, the latter approached me.

"Miss Essiter is staying here, sir," he announced, "but she is not in at present."

"Do you mean that Miss Essiter has gone out already this morning?" I asked.

The young man hesitated. He looked at me surreptitiously and probably took note of my agitation.

"Are you a relative of Miss Essiter's, may I ask?" he enquired.

"I am her uncle's secretary," I told him. "She was in my charge last night, and through an unfortunate accident we were separated. I came round to be sure that she reached the hotel safely and to see her if possible."

The young man looked me over and apparently decided in my favour.

"Miss Essiter has not yet returned, sir," he acknowledged.

I received the news with greater calmness than I had believed possible. I felt a queer little choking in my throat, but I fancy that there was nothing unusual in my manner.

"Has there been any message?" I asked. "Are her clothes still in her room?"

"There has been no message," the young man replied, "and her clothes are still there."

"Has her bed been slept in?" I persisted.

"Apparently not," the clerk answered. "The chamber-maid went to call her as usual this morning with tea, and found that the room had not been occupied."

His manner was almost too perfect. The ugly thought flashed into my mind that he was not altogether unused to young ladies staying alone who failed to return at night.

"Something must have happened to Miss Essiter," I said. "I shall telephone to her uncle and communicate with the police."

"Just as you think well, sir," was the suave reply. "Of course, as you know, I dare say, sir, some of these parties keep it up pretty late nowadays. The young lady may have stayed and had breakfast with her friends after-wards."

"Quite so," I agreed. "Thank you very much."

All the time I had stood facing the hall, so that no one could pass out of the lounge unseen. I took my leave of the reception clerk now and made my way towards it. For about thirty seconds I stood just outside the thres-hold, my fists clenched, and my nails digging into my flesh. As soon as I felt sure of myself, I entered. Mr. Leopold was seated in an easy-chair, reading the paper, with a large cocktail by his side. He looked up at my approach, and though I watched him closely, I could find no signs of apprehension in his manner.

"So you've pulled yourself together, young man, have you?" he asked coolly.

"More or less," I answered. "I have brought you back your forty shillings, Mr. Leopold."

He accepted the money with a gesture of indifference. His little bright eyes were all the time scrutinising my appearance.

"Would you be so good as to tell me," I continued,

"what became of Miss Essiter after you packed me off last night?"

"Certainly," he assented. "You have observed, I hope, that I was very careful not to mention the young lady's name in court. I waited until she came out of the dressing-room, and then I explained the situation to her as tactfully as I could, and told her you had felt it best to take a taxi straight back to your rooms. I asked her whether she would care to accept my escort and have a dance or two, but she preferred to return here. I put her into a taxicab, and wished her good night. A very charming young lady! I am proposing to send my card up to her presently and invite her to lunch."

"Very kind of you," I acknowledged. "By-the-by—you must forgive my questions, but my mind is really curiously blank about a great part of my evening—did Miss Essiter seem surprised at what you told her? I was all right coming along in your car, wasn't I?"

"I wouldn't go so far as to admit that," Mr. Leopold said, his keen little eyes watching me furtively. "I know what it is, though, with you young fellows in the army, especially if you've been in the East. You can, and do, take a terrible lot to drink, and then, all of a sudden—phut!" he exclaimed, waving his hands. "In the car coming along, I must confess that I fancied I saw some signs of that. That is why I took you into the secretary's office myself. I wanted to have a word with you—just a word of warning, you know. Unfortunately, old Daggers made us have that whisky and soda, and I suddenly realised that it was all up with you."

I groaned.

"You are quite right, Mr. Leopold," I admitted. "I perhaps exaggerated a little in court when I said that I had never been drunk. If ever I am, it comes on like that. You don't know the trouble I'm in, though. You say that you put Miss Essiter in a taxicab, at the club?"

"I certainly did," he assented. "I would have sent her in my car, but unfortunately I had just told the man to go and get some supper."

"And you directed the man to Claridge's?"

"Naturally I did. What about it?"

"Miss Essiter has not returned here," I told him. "She did not return at all last night. Her room is still empty."

Mr. Leopold stared at me with an incredulity, which, if it was assumed, was exceedingly well done. His mouth was open, although his eyes seemed to have partially concealed themselves beneath the creases of fat at the top of his cheeks.

"God bless my soul! Not returned?"

"You can enquire for yourself if you like."

"God bless my soul!" he repeated, with the air of one deep in reflection. "You are sure," he added, after a moment's pause, "that this is not her way of indicating that she does not wish to see you? She is probably annoyed. She might very reasonably be annoyed, Major, at your defection last night. She might not unreasonably tell the clerk to say that she was not in if you called. What do you think of that?"

I shook my head.

"I am afraid there is no doubt whatever," I told him, "that Miss Essiter did not return last night. You can go to the office and enquire for yourself. In fact, I should very much like you to do so. We shall see then whether there is anything in your idea."

"I will do so with pleasure," he agreed, swinging his short legs to the ground and rising to his feet. "There is certainly something in your suggestion. I will make enquiries in my own name and send up my invitation to lunch at the same time."

He hurried off. I felt my cheeks burn and a little tingle

go all down my spine as I watched him. I was about to commit an action of which I had never been guilty in my life. As soon as he had turned the corner, I thrust my hand into the pockets of his coat which he had left hanging over the side of his chair. The first one was empty; the second contained a single letter, still enclosed in an envelope, although it had been opened. I transferred it unseen to my own pocket without daring to glance at it. I replaced the coat, and when he returned he found me seated in the same attitude of utter dejection in which he had left me. With his assumed expression of gravity, he rather suggested a travesty of a fat mute at a funeral.

"You have unfortunately been correctly informed, Major," he announced. "This is very unpleasant. I have seen the manager himself. He assures me of the fact that Miss Essiter has not returned. What can we do?"

"Well, what do you advise?" I asked him. "Of course, it was chiefly my fault for leaving her alone, but it was you who put her into the taxi and sent her back here."

"We must consider the situation," Mr. Leopold declared, beckoning to a waiter and giving an order. "We are men of the world. We are equally involved in this matter—no, I will not say equally. I offered my escort to the young lady, and she refused it. My share of the blame is small, but still it was I who invited you to the club. In your condition, I should not have done that. We must put our heads together. You are looking ill, Major. No wonder, of course. Drink that," he added, as the waiter returned with two cocktails upon a tray.

He watched me craftily, and although the impulse was strong to dash the glass and its contents in his face, I resisted it successfully.

"I am older than you. I have had a wider experience of life," he went on. "Miss Essiter is, I am sure, a charming young lady, but heredity tells, and her uncle is one of the cranks of the world. He has friends in every walk of life. No doubt Miss Essiter has her own little circle. She would naturally be furious with you. She would be precisely in the mood to look up some of these other friends. What do you think, Major?"

"Quite possible," I admitted.

"Under those circumstances, I suggest that we give the young lady a chance before we create a scandal. Give her, at any rate, until this evening. If, at the end of that time, nothing has been heard of her, we had better take the obvious course. If you like to leave it to me, I will see that Scotland Yard is informed, and you can go down and interview her uncle."

"You don't think we ought to let the police know at once?" I asked dubiously.

"I should give her another hour or two," Mr. Leopold urged. "Remember that if she went in for a spree—and young people go pretty far nowadays—it was partly your fault. Give her a chance. Give her until evening before you go down to see her uncle, and at the same time I'll let the police have all the particulars. Better for me to tackle Scotland Yard, because it was I who saw the last of her. I can tell them exactly what time she left the Blue Skies, and it is very possible that the commissionaire may remember which taxicab he fetched. There is no possible harm that could come to her, you must remember, Major. We must give her a chance of turning up on her own account. The press in these days is far too free in such matters. We mustn't compromise the young lady, if we can help it."

I rose reluctantly to my feet. I hated to leave Mr. Leopold, but I felt that I had reached almost the limit of my endurance.

"Very good, sir," I told him, "I'll leave the matter in your hands, and I'll wait for a time before I go down to

Breezeley. Can I see you anywhere this evening in case you have any news?"

"Certainly, my lad," was the cordial reply. "I'm damned sorry about last night, but it can't be helped. Don't worry about it too much. I've seen men in Johannesburg go off like you did after a week's drinking, and not come to for days. It's all in a lifetime, you know. I have no doubt the young lady will forgive you. I'll see you to-night with pleasure. Where am I dining now? Can't remember. Anyway, will you come to my rooms —Number 27a, Berkeley Street—and have a cocktail with me whilst I change for dinner. Half-past eight, eh? How does that do?"

"Very well indeed, thank you," I assured him. "I'll be there."

I walked dejectedly towards the exit. Halfway there, however, Mr. Leopold recalled me. He was fumbling in the pocket of his overcoat.

"I say, you didn't notice a letter lying on the floor or on my chair when I went to the office, did you?" he asked.

"I am afraid I'm not in the humour to notice anything this morning," I regretted.

He frowned. His little black eyes looked slantwise into mine.

"Nothing important, I hope?"

He shook his head, apparently satisfied.

"It was just a message. I never carry important papers about with me. Sorry to have called you back. I'll see you later in my rooms. Half-past eight to-night, eh?"

"If I get back from Breezeley alive," I replied dolefully.

I sent an urgent note to Bloor, abandoning with some reluctance my first intention of going down to Scotland Yard myself. Afterwards. I summoned up all my courage and started off for Breezeley.

CHAPTER XXIII

ONCE again I swung over the stile at the end of the
long cinder walk, facing that gaunt, incredible building
which arose from the sodden, unwholesome-looking marsh,
a leering gesture of Brobdingnagian architecture. It was
wrapped in darkness when I left the station, but in those
last few minutes of my tramp it suddenly flashed out into
light from cellar to attic, a sign, as I had gathered before,
that some one had left the station and was approaching.
A wind was blowing from westwards, rolling the river
mists before it, bringing the obnoxious odours of chemical
and soap factories from the other side, and wafting little
showers of smuts which seemed day by day to have fallen
upon the land and to have choked the life and heart out
of all growing things. I shivered as I drew nearer and
came under the shadow of the huge edifice, shivered as the
front door opened without any summons from me, and
Minchin, more like a Chinaman than ever in his sinister
immobility, bade me enter. The house was incredibly still.
He led me to the lift.

"The master is waiting for you, sir," he announced, and
this time I was sure that there was a note of malicious
pleasure in his tone.

We glided up the three storeys and passed along the
corridor until we arrived at the fateful door. The usual
signals passed, and I was ushered in. Life in these days
was teaching me self-control, and I advanced as bravely
as I could into the little circle of light thrown from Martin Hews' red lamp—the only illumination in the room.

"Sit down," he ordered me briefly, without looking up.

I obeyed. My employer was bending over the table, studying what seemed to me to be a chart. He had pins in it which every now and then he moved, after consulting some notes by his side. His mouth was slightly open and drawn sideways, giving a most unpleasant twist to his face and disclosing his fanglike teeth which I could never see without an inward shiver. His beady eyes seemed more prominent than ever, his flaxen hair was brushed so smoothly that it positively shone in the lamplight. I watched him with fascinated eyes. There were times when it seemed almost impossible to believe in his humanity. His white fingers, with their shining nails, no bigger than a baby's, played hesitatingly around the pins before he moved one. He was dressed as usual with the utmost care. His rich satin tie was fastened by a pin, mounted on which was an exquisite pearl. The minutes went on, and, so far as he was concerned, I seemed to have no existence. It was at least a quarter of an hour before he spoke to me, and then he did so without lifting his eyes from his task.

"So you are good for nothing except drayman's work, after all, Owston?" he said.

"It seems so, sir," I admitted.

He removed a pin and still stared at his chart. He had the air of being entirely engrossed by it. Anything he said to me might have been the indifferent commonplaces which are the gesture of a great general engaged in mighty work.

"You were sent to the West End of London to establish yourself there for a certain purpose. On practically the first night, you stepped guilelessly into a booby trap. You cannot now enter a single night club in London. Your name is being posted as an undesirable person upon the warning lists. You will need courage to show yourself wherever people of the world into which I wish you to penetrate are gathered together. The cards of invitation for the functions which I wanted you to attend with my niece have been, or will be, of course, withdrawn. You have destroyed your whole utility to me in a single evening."

"That is all quite true, sir," I acknowledged, "but it is not the full extent of my folly. You have probably received my telephone message, and you know that a much more serious thing has happened through my blundering. Your niece, of whom I was in charge, has disappeared."

He leaned back in his chair now and looked straight across at me. It was obvious that he was enjoying my misery.

"Disappeared?" he repeated. "Explain yourself, if you please. Your message was too vague."

"Miss Essiter went with me to the Blue Skies Night Club at the invitation of a Mr. Leopold, brother of Lady Bonofar. When we arrived there, I was asked to visit the secretary's room, where I was damned fool enough to allow myself to be drugged, and woke up this morning in a police cell. This morning I went to Claridge's, and I learned that Miss Essiter had not returned. I have seen Leopold, and he declares that he put her into a taxicab at the club a few minutes after I had left. Nevertheless, no one seems to have seen her since. This afternoon I received one of those polite communications from Joseph. Here it is."

I handed to him the note which had been found in my letter box a few minutes before I had left. He read it through slowly:

"A fair exchange, my dear Major. I have altered my mind. I have decided that I will not raze Breezeley to the ground to snatch away your prisoner. Rachel is, after all, a little creature of the slums and alleys, but Beatrice —Ah, well, it would not be for you, dear clumsy enemy,

*to appreciate how wonderful a woman she is. I think that
I shall rest content."*

Martin Hews read with the dawn of a devilish smile the
words which had brought sobs to my throat.

"A delightful fellow, Joseph," he chuckled. "Good taste
too. His little trollop has charm, but Beatrice—well,
when she forgets to scowl, and the pleasant things of life
come her way, I am inclined to consider my niece almost
a beautiful woman. What do you think, Owston?"

I made no reply. I think that he scarcely expected one.
He sat there with his finger tips pressed together, his
repulsive eyes dwelling upon my face, gloating over my
misery.

"And temporarily," he continued, "she has taken
Rachel's place. She is now the Helen of the moment in the
hands of the enemy—not with the same result, I trust—
I fondly trust. Still, we must be prepared for the worst.
Joseph is a man and a lover of women. Who knows?"

I felt the veins of my forehead almost bursting, but I
kept silent. My employer tapped lightly upon the blot-
ting paper in front of him with the tip of his ivory pen.

"You are a wonderful escort, are you not?" he went
on, with a sneer. "You ruin my plans, and you expose
my niece to the most terrible dangers with which a young
woman can be threatened. Yet you look well and contented—carefully dressed too, I see. Evidences of a visit
to the barber. You lunched as usual, I trust."

I knew that he was trying to goad me into losing my
temper. There was challenge in his eyes with their glint
of contempt. I ground my heel into the carpet, and I
answered him with composure.

"Naturally," I replied, "I have lived my normal life."

He was obviously disappointed—a little surprised too,
I think.

"My niece would be flattered," he murmured. "Poor girl, if ever we succeed in rescuing her, we must tell her the story of your heroic composure. Perhaps you had better explain to me once more, in as few words as possible, exactly what happened."

I recounted everything, up to my first glimpse of Leopold in the lounge at Claridge's. He nodded resignedly and held out his hand, as soon as I mentioned the man's name.

"You needn't tell me what happened," he groaned. "You remembered, of course, that you were a British officer, and that instead of brain you had been endowed with the muscles of an ox. Leopold is, I presume, in hospital. Another police court case to-morrow, eh?"

"Not at all," I assured him coolly. "I tried my best to make friends with Mr. Leopold."

He looked at me with expressionless face. I could see that he was suspending judgment.

"If you will read the account of my appearance before the magistrate," I went on, "you will see that I contradicted nothing that Mr. Leopold said. I allowed him to pay my fine. I did not appeal. I only went so far as to deny that I was drunk, and that, I take it, any man in my position would have said as a matter of course, whether he was or wasn't."

"But when you went to Leopold in the lounge of Claridge's—surely you played the muscular hero then?"

"I apologised for the trouble I had given him, I thanked him for having seen Miss Essiter to the taxicab, I confided to him the story of her disappearance. I accepted his suggestion that we should do nothing about it for some hours, and I agreed to leave it to him to make the subsequent enquiries. I am to see him again at half-past eight this evening in his rooms."

Very slowly indeed a wrinkle stole into Martin Hews' protruding forehead.

"Is it possible," he murmured incredulously, "that you are not quite a fool? Why did you adopt that attitude?"

"Frankly," I replied, "because I felt perfectly certain that the obvious one would be a mistake. I preferred Mr. Leopold to believe that I accepted his story and did not connect him in any way with Miss Essiter's disappearance. I thought that by keeping in touch with him I might learn something."

"And you are seeing him again to-night?"

"That is so, sir. We shook hands at parting, and whilst he went, at my suggestion, to the hotel office to make enquiries for himself, I stole a letter from his overcoat pocket."

"You are beginning to interest me curiously," my employer confided, with a little curl of the lips. "I cannot make up my mind whether it is a development on your part, or whether you are indeed a singular mixture of imbecility and common sense. Show me the letter."

I produced it and laid it upon the writing table. It consisted of two lines only, written upon perfectly plain note paper. Martin Hews read out:

'2—39—21—20—18—37—18—8—1—1—19—9.'

"A communication in cipher!" he murmured. "Well, have you been able to make anything of it, Major?"

"I am afraid not, sir," I admitted. "I thought you might be able to do that."

"You flatter me," was the cynical rejoinder. "Can't you see that this is not a code which lends itself to any of the ordinary methods of deciphering? It is a made-up one, the key to which remains in the other person's hands. Of course it may be an important communication. Did Leopold seem disturbed at having lost it?"

"He certainly did."

"Well, there's only one thing for you to do," he pointed out, handing it back to me. "Leopold must have the key. You are seeing him this evening. Possess yourself of it."

"Thank you very much for the idea, sir," I replied. "I will see what I can do."

He chuckled almost like a human being.

"Upon my word, Major, you are improving," he declared; "you certainly are improving. If I had the time to spare, I dare say, after all, I should be able to make something of you. As it is, well, I'm afraid you must go back to Rowton House."

"Very good, sir," I replied, rising to my feet. "I am sure I deserve it."

"Sit down, you fool!" he enjoined. "Of course you deserve it, but I shall probably be weak enough to give you another chance. You are responsible for my niece's disappearance. You must get her back."

"I should have set to work at that, sir, whether you had sent me away or not," I assured him.

"As a matter of interest," he proposed, "tell me just how you were going to set about it. The methods of others are always appealing."

"Inspector Bloor will be coming to see me sometime this evening," I announced. "I should have gone down to Scotland Yard myself, but I have an idea that I am being watched."

"What, that horrible man!" Martin Hews exclaimed irritably. "Don't you know that I object to the police interfering in my concerns, except in a case of absolute necessity? I won't have them about here, asking questions all the time. Do you hear, Owston? If calling in the police is all you can do to find my niece, you had better get back to Rowton House. I don't want them. I won't have them. I've more brains in the tip of my little finger than you'll find in the whole of Scotland Yard."

"I can quite believe it, sir," I replied, "but Inspector Bloor is rather by way of being a personal friend of mine. He has already promised to avoid unnecessary enquiries into your affairs. In a disappearance case like this, the help of the police is really worth having. In any case, the responsibility of having lost Miss Essiter is partly mine, and I must do what I can to find her."

"Pooh!" Martin Hews scoffed. "You will go down to the Blue Skies, I suppose, you'll cross-examine the concierge, you'll discover the taxicab driver, and in the end you will have learned nothing. Quite all right, as a matter of form, of course, but you won't arrive anywhere. As to getting any information from the taxicab driver, it's an absurdity to think of it. They are all in the pay of the night-club proprietors. Still, you'll find him all right, I expect. He'll tell you his story and receive the sovereign, or whatever your generosity may suggest. You'll be put off by a possible clue. You'll have wasted a few evenings, and then you'll have to start all over again. You won't find my niece that way."

"Perhaps you could suggest something, sir?" I ventured.

He made no reply. His right hand slid into that wicked little drawer, where, amongst other things, I knew that he kept his miniature automatic, produced a key, and thrust it across the table towards me.

"You needn't bother about Scotland Yard," he said. "That will bring my niece home."

"What is it?" I asked.

"The key of the wing where Rachel's apartments are situated. We have had a little trouble with her the last few days, and I have been obliged to be severe."

My air of bewilderment seemed to please him. He started his engine, glided back in reverse from his desk, swept around the table, across the room to a far stretch of the bookcases. Arrived there, he scanned the volumes in front of him.

"Number seven," he said, pointing to it. "Get it down, will you? I think the frontispiece is what I want."

I obeyed him. It was a mighty volume and of staggering weight. The title, I noticed, was "Savage Animals of the West African Interior."

"Lay it upon that table," he directed. "Open out the frontispiece."

We looked at it together—a great illustration four times doubled. In the far left-hand corner of it, stealing along through tropical grasses, dense shrubs, and in the shadow of enormous trees, was a strange, fierce-looking animal like some sort of a huge cat. Its head was close to the ground, its eyes were set in an almost terrifying stare. In the background, following it closely, I saw a man in bush clothes, with poised rifle, creeping along.

"He wants the male," Martin Hews confided. "See here."

He leaned over, and with his forefinger traced the way through more shrubs, round the huge trunks of trees, past bunches of nauseous-looking fungi, and a whole shrubbery of exquisite flowers, through dense masses of undergrowth to a slight clearing. Here were two more of the animals lying at ease, a male and a female, the remains of a half-consumed animal between them. The head of the male was raised, as though he were listening. Martin Hews looked up at me with a smile which was almost fatuous in its conceit.

"A little lesson, my dear Owston, for you amateur detectives, and a great one for Scotland Yard, who are far too mechanical—so mechanical that they ignore psychology and sentiment and cling to the methods of Inspector Bucket. So foolish! The driving power of the world is human nature. Here, in this primitive forest, we see it. The hunter wants a male specimen of that exceedingly disagreeable animal. What does he do? He follows the angry female."

There was a ring of triumph in his tone. He looked at me with the air of one expecting applause. I began dimly to see what was at the back of his mind, but I kept silent.

"Think, Major," he went on patronisingly. "Keep on thinking, and perhaps you will understand why I threw that key upon the table. Give her Joseph's letter and let her go. My bargain with Donkin, which I faithfully kept, is at an end. He died yesterday on the boat. I received a wireless this morning. Rachel will find my niece, all right. Replace the print carefully, please, Owston. The book has great value."

I did as he bade me, returned to the table, and picked up the key.

"Stop!" my employer exclaimed. "This task, simple though it may be, requires perhaps a little more finesse than you are capable of. Besides, she must understand—"

He broke off and spoke down one of his telephones. In literally a few seconds, a hard-faced woman who might have been a matron in a lunatic asylum, except that she was dressed in shiny black silk, made her appearance. Martin Hews handed her the key.

"Bring the young lady here," he ordered.

The woman accepted the key in silence. He leaned back in his chair.

"We must make up our minds, Major," he went on, the tips of his fingers pressed together, "whether it is possible for me to make any further use of you. The purpose for which I engaged you was to watch the West End of London, gaining entry, so far as you could, into such quasi-fashionable haunts as might be accessible to Joseph, whilst my other gangsters tightened the cordon around him in the East End. I know to a few hundred

yards," he continued, glancing downward at that chart,
"where Joseph's East End headquarters are. I am not
sure that I could not narrow them down to a single street,
but the fox has to be there before I dare stop the holes,
and the fox very seldom ventures near nowadays. It's the
West End that's calling to him, Major. I have an idea
that in that part of town with which he is not so familiar,
he sometimes loses that marvellous cunning which en-
ables him to steal about the sewers of East London untouched. Some day, I believe that the man's own character, his vanity, his love of pleasure, his sense of humour,
his constant poses, may bring him into the last passage of
life."

He was silent for a few minutes, scowling at the
opposite wall. I knew that this was no time for me to
interrupt. It was for me to sit in wondering silence whilst
a great man planned his campaign.

"One false move on our part down East," he reflected,
"and we should have to begin all over again. I have a
good man there whom you have never met and never will
meet. Yardsley tells me that he is aching to cast his net.
I hold him back. I want a certainty. I want to see Joseph
where escape is not possible—not in the hands of the
police; he'd wriggle away from them somehow—I want
to see him with a bullet through his heart and the glaze
of death in his eyes. I had hopes of you, Owston, in the
West End. Joseph has been too clever for us. He has cut
the ground away from under your feet."

"I shall venture to disagree, sir," I objected firmly.
"The Blue Skies isn't the only night club in London, and
I have friends of my own whom I could look up, now that
I have the means, who could get me into a dozen. As to
those evening parties, I am willing to take my risk of a
snub. There were half a dozen more cards of invitation
this morning. If I go anywhere where I am not received,

I will make the best of it. Remember, too, I have not quarrelled with Mr. Leopold."

"That," Martin Hews admitted, "may probably be your salvation. Let us refresh our memory concerning him."

From a drawer on the left-hand side of his desk he drew out a black morocco-bound volume, fastened with a Bramah lock. He selected a key from his bunch, opened it, glanced down the alphabetical index, and studied two closely written pages. At the bottom of the latter was a small photograph. He held the book out to me.

"Your friend, I think."

"That is the man," I assented.

Martin Hews read carefully from beginning to end what was evidently some sort of a *dossier*. Then he pushed the book away.

"Leopold's career," he confided, "has points of interest. In his younger days, he was a suspected I. D. B. and had to leave Africa at a moment's notice. He was also tried for murder, and there seems to have been no doubt that he and two of his associates really did shoot the man to whom the Reitzvontein Mine belonged, and by a fraudulently signed agreement became the sole owners of the property, instead of holding only a tenth share. His later enterprises are connected with the floating of various doubtful companies, and his reputation in the City is not what it was. At the same time, he appears to be rich, and spends a great deal of money, although the mine is no longer a paying concern. He would come into touch with Joseph quite naturally on this I. D. B. business, and there is not the slightest reason that I can see why he should not be connected with him at present. That is for us to discover."

"I might have a stroke of luck there, sir," I ventured.

He looked across at me speculatively.

"That is possible," he admitted. "No one is so likely to succeed with a clever man as a man whom that clever man believes to be a fool. You're a blunderer, Owston, but you have qualities. I should have given you credit for more common sense than to have accepted the invitation of a stranger to go to a night club whilst out with my niece. On the other hand, I should never have expected you to have used that discretion which you did use when you met the man who was responsible for taking you there. I may still be able to make use of you, Owston. I am not sure for the moment how, but I have an idea. This little wildcat leans to you as much as to her own men. Something may come of that."

"If I could find your niece and bring her back, sir," I assured him, "I should be quite content to have you chuck me out afterwards."

"If you could do that," he acknowledged, "there is no telling what might happen, for you would relieve me of a great anxiety. I like to live with a clear mind and a clear conscience. You may think that I run great risks. I do not. I have one of the best lawyers in the world to protect me and to see that I evade the penalties of my necessarily sometimes illegal actions. I have at least a dozen fighting assassins to protect my person, to watch me and deal with those who would do me harm. I have a secret-service agency in London in which I employ a certain number of trained and highly capable men. My house here is, since that accident the other night at any rate, impregnable. No one can reach this apartment in which I am, against my will. I live here in joy, because I live with more of the world's treasures to worship than any human being knows of. In a secret chamber which you have never seen, Major, I have pictures—stolen pictures, many of them—from most of the great galleries of Europe—some of them stolen at my behest, all of them joy for my days, warmth for my life, food for my soul. But I have a secret—a secret which only two people know. One is seldom very far from the end of my revolver; the other is my niece. That is why I want her back."

I stared at him fixedly. It was hard to conceive of egoism so absolute. In a moment or two he went on again.

"In this matter of the return of my niece, you will be able to help, if not directly, indirectly. You probably are one of those human beings who make a special appeal to women. I see that there are lines underneath your eyes to-day, a grim set about your mouth. You are disturbed about my niece, perhaps."

"I am more than disturbed about Miss Essiter," I assured him. "I have not seen a great deal of her, naturally, but I have the greatest admiration and respect—if I dared to say so, I would add, notwithstanding our brief acquaintance, affection for your niece."

Martin Hews indulged for a moment in the grimace which always filled me with horror. He laughed. It reminded me of nothing so much as of a rough sketch of a devilfish leering at its mate, which I had once seen, made by a futurist artist in a moment of intoxication at an all-night party.

"Excellent!" he murmured, as he sat looking at me with parted lips. "Several millions my niece will probably inherit, some day, unless I found a museum, Major Owston. A young lady to inspire affection, without a doubt!"

There was the usual summons of a visitor demanding admittance. Martin Hews pressed the knob. The door opened, and Rachel came storming in.

CHAPTER XXIV

Rachel's outburst of anger was short-lived, and the words seemed to die away upon her lips. There was something about the atmosphere of this so curiously impressive apartment which seemed to almost sterilize passion, to have something of the same effect upon the ordinary tempers and emotions of life as entrance into a great, cold cathedral from the heat of a summer's day. Her voice had been raised and she had evidently come in with the idea of making herself thoroughly disagreeable. Before she had finished a couple of sentences, however, she broke down. Martin Hews pointed to a chair. His manner had become very grave and subdued. A stranger might have believed that he was really sympathetic.

"Young lady," he confided, "I have bad news for you. I beg that you will prepare yourself for it. The news will distress you, I am sure, but there is a redeeming feature about it. It will give you your liberty."

"Well, that's something, at any rate!" the girl exclaimed. "I'm sick of this old barracks—fed up with it. I suppose it's Jim? Have the cops got him?"

"Jim Donkin is dead," he announced. "His wound gave him great trouble on board ship and an operation became necessary under which he succumbed. I received a wireless message from the captain this morning."

"So that's that!" the girl muttered, looking with hard eyes straight in front of her.

"I was under a promise to Donkin to give you shelter here and protection from Joseph. I have kept my word. At his death my responsibility ceases. You are free to go when you choose."

"Well, that will be now," the girl declared, without hesitation. "Poor old Jim!" she added, with a sudden break in her voice.

For a moment her head was buried in her hands. Martin Hews looked across at her with an air of gentle curiosity. There seemed to be nothing that I could say.

"Poor old Jim!" she repeated at last, looking up. "I'm sorry. He had to go, though. I knew very well that Joseph was the better man. Joseph was his master, although Jim did steal a march on him once. Joseph would have had me in the end, anyway."

Martin Hews sighed.

"Joseph is a very troublesome fellow," he observed.

"Has he been spoiling any more deals?" the girl asked, with a shadow of a smile upon her tear-stained face.

"He has done something a great deal more offensive to me," was the grave reply. "Show the young lady the note you received this afternoon, Owston."

I handed it across to her.

"What's this mean?" she demanded suspiciously, taking it into her hand but not at once reading it.

"A great deal of trouble for us," Martin Hews acknowledged. "Keeping my bargain with Donkin has cost me dearly. I am plunged into the depths of distress. My niece, Miss Essiter, whom you have seen here, has disappeared."

"Get on with it," Rachel enjoined eagerly. "Do you mean that Joseph has copped her?"

"My niece was dining in the West End with Major Owston here last evening, and afterwards they visited a night club. Major Owston was inveigled into the secretary's room and declares that he was drugged. At any rate he woke up in a police cell, and my niece has disappeared."

The girl was mercurial in her emotions. Her momen-

tary spasm of grief seemed to be forgotten. She threw
herself back in her chair, and her fine white teeth flashed
as she shook with laughter.

"Bravo Jo !" she exclaimed. "That's what you get for
cooping me up here."

Then, for the first time, she seemed to remember the
letter in her hand. She took it up and read it through
word by word. Its sense appeared to steal into her comprehension gradually. She dropped it in the end as though
stung.

"So that's it, is it?" she muttered viciously. "'A creature of the slums and alleys,' am I? Taken your niece
for his girl, has he? We'll see !"

"Joseph is scarcely likely to proceed to such ex-
tremes," my employer said soothingly, but with an evil
note of banter in his tone. "He is probably holding her
as a hostage until I give you up. That time has now arrived. You can go to him at once, tell him that Donkin is
dead and that you are free. You can let him know also,
if you like, that I think it is almost time we stopped cutting one another's throats. I never part with a friend
whilst he is alive. Donkin was my man, and I stuck to
him. With Donkin dead, things have changed. He knows
whom to approach if he wishes to get into touch with
me. You can tell him to start with I'll give him thirty
thousand pounds for the Borghese Medallions. He
won't be able to show them even in America for years to
come."

It is my belief that the girl had scarcely heard a word
he said. She was all the time seated with her eyes rivetted
upon that sheet of paper. It was only the silence when
he had finished which at last seemed to distract her
from it.

"So I can go?" she said.

My employer nodded.

"Our friend, Major Owston here, is returning to London by the next train. There will be a car waiting at the door for you in a quarter of an hour. He will escort you to London. If you need money or anything of that sort until you rejoin your friends, Mr. Yardsley, of Elm Street Chambers, will provide it."

She stood with one arm akimbo, her other hand flat upon her smooth, shapely hip.

"I want none of your money," she declared scornfully. "What if I go straight to the police station? I've been kept a prisoner here, haven't I? It's a free country. You see what you've done. You've kept me away from my man, and he's took another. What have you got to say about that?"

"I can only say that I hope most sincerely that you are mistaken," was the equable reply. "If I thought that Joseph had dared to molest my niece—"

"Shut up!" she interrupted. "Joseph's a man like the rest of them. He's got his way with women, and they generally fall for him. I expect that pasty-faced young missis has gone the way of the others."

I felt the blood run cold in my veins with horror, but Martin Hews' expression of half-cynical tolerance remained unchanged.

"Well, we shall see," he said. "In ten minutes, Major Owston will be downstairs in the hall waiting for you."

She flung round at me.

"I haven't much use for him, either," she scoffed. "Swallowed a ramrod when he was young, I should say. Full of blood and fire, ain't he? That's what I want in my men. That's why I like Jews. Besides, he's balmy about your niece. Feeling you'd like to get at Joseph, eh?" she asked me mockingly.

"I expect I'm feeling towards him just about as you are," I replied.

"Feeling towards him just like I am!" she exclaimed, and her eyes seemed filled with lightnings. "Feel? You don't know what it means."

She left the room. My employer watched her with expressionless face. As soon as the door was closed, his cheeks were puffed out, his lips parted. He grinned across at me.

"Did you see how I handled her?" he demanded, conceit reeking in his tone and every movement. "Got her on the raw every time. She's not going to look about her very much. She wants a word or two with Joseph. If they give her the chance, Major, I shouldn't be at all surprised if she didn't pay me a visit, or you, before many hours are passed. Do you know, I am feeling quite reconciled towards your stupidity. I am not sure that this temporary separation from my dear niece may not bring about our greatly desired end. A furious woman has been the ruin of greater men than Joseph."

All the time he knew he was torturing me with his damnable cynicism, his blatant indifference as to what might have happened to his niece. His little eyes were watching me, as if to discover some signs of my suffering. Outwardly, I fancy that I kept cool enough. Inwardly, I was fighting furiously against the aching impulse to set my heel upon him, as one does upon some poisonous insect. I think that he realised exactly the condition I was in, and that my struggle afforded him intense amusement.

"Any other matters to report, Major, before you leave?" he asked.

"There is one thing more, sir," I told him. "I believe that I have seen Joseph."

He flashed a quick and breathless glance across at me. "Where?"

"At a dinner party given by Lord Farendon at Claridge's, and again at the moment I met with my misfortune in the Blue Skies Night Club."

"You really are developing gifts of reticence," my employer sneered. "It amazes me to think that you have sat there for the best part of an hour, talking about comparative trifles, and have not vouchsafed me that interesting piece of information."

"It is because it can't exactly be called information that I haven't mentioned it before," I explained. "It is just an idea—an inspiration, if I may use the term. He sat facing me, at a table in the restaurant, and he looked at both your niece and myself—how shall I say?—with the air of one who recognises and expects to be recognised. His eyes deliberately mocked me. I could imagine him distinctly as the man who led his gang in the attack upon this house, and I could imagine him also as the man leaning over the end of my bed. I couldn't identify him, of course, but from the bottom of my heart I believe that man is Joseph. One thing I am certain about, and that naturally strengthens my conviction. It was this same man who looked up from behind the desk in the secretary's office at the Blue Skies and grinned at me five seconds before I passed out."

"Your suggestions," my employer admitted, "are full of interest. Try your hand at describing him."

I did my best, although it was not an easy task. I looked through a dozen snapshots he pushed across to me and could do no more than find a vague likeness in any one of them.

"If he really is a man who has the *entrée* to society of that sort," Martin Hews continued thoughtfully, "it might account for several little things which have happened to me during the last year. After all, why shouldn't he? Any one can dine with a lord nowadays, provided his bank account is large enough. What name was he passing under?"

"I got a *maître d'hôtel* to bring me a list of the guests," I said. "There was something queer about that too. He was put down as simply Mr. X."

"Not so good," my employer regretted. "A man as clever as Joseph would have a name and an identity, and plenty of corroboration ready at hand, just in the same way as he would never commit a murder without having established an alibi. You have a list of the guests with you, Owston?"

"Here, sir," I replied, handing it to him.

"It may amuse me," he remarked, glancing at the names, "to set this affair in train after your departure. Report to me anything the young woman says or does of significance during the journey, and do not—you would scarcely, I am sure, be guilty of such imbecility—attempt to follow her at Liverpool Street Station. I may yet find a place for you in life," he went on, "but it will not be as a sleuth-hound. If only, with your open and ingenuous expression, your apparent lack of intellectual qualities, you could really combine permanently a little of the discretion which you have exercised during the last twenty-four hours, you might in time be very useful to me."

"There is only one way in which I wish to be useful just now, sir," I reiterated, as I rose to my feet. "I want to find your niece."

"Quite correct," was the unenthusiastic reply. "Quite in accord with the proprieties. Personally I have but one anxiety in connection with her disappearance."

The man's colossal selfishness appalled me. I knew quite well that he was thinking only of his miserable secret, and I left the room for my journey back to town with a shudder.

CHAPTER XXV

I COULD make little of Rachel on the way to London. She sat curled up in a corner seat of the first-class carriage, her eyes looking steadily out of the window, a disfiguring scowl upon her face. She waved away impatiently the cigarette I offered her and scarcely took the trouble to reply to my few efforts at conversation. She had all the appearance of a woman either in pain or nursing evil thoughts. There was a sombre fire in her eyes. Every now and then, her thin fingers twitched. Her clothes were untidy, her hat she had thrown into a corner the moment she had entered the carriage, and her fine blue-black hair seemed to have lost all its lustre just as her eyes had lost their glow. Only once her lips moved; and she was evidently talking to herself. I fancied then that she repeated that unhappy sentence—"a creature of the slums and alleys." Her eyes were all the time tearless. She showed no interest in the familiar places we passed; neither did her liberty seem to be affording her any particular pleasure. She watched our progress into that far-flung mass of life around Bethnal Green Junction without movement or any sign of excitement. As we drew near Liverpool Street, I was obliged to speak to her.

"What about money?" I asked.

"Keep it," she answered. "I have plenty."

She rose to her feet, shook out her skirts, smoothed her hair, and accepted the hat which I had picked up. She studied her reflection in the looking-glass and made an almost obscene grimace.

"Ugly, ain't I?" she demanded, facing me defiantly.

"I have seen you look beautiful," I told her. "The night you came to me in Down Street, for instance."

For one moment there was a natural expression in her eyes.

"Beautiful, eh?" she murmured. "I didn't get much out of it, did I? You were too much in love with Joseph's last fancy, I suppose. Well, she's gone down the sink anyhow along with the rest of them."

I took her by the shoulders and shook her none too gently.

"Don't dare to say such a thing, you little ragamuffin!"

"All right, all right!" she jeered. "You wait. You may get a surprise before long. Lot of stick-in-the-muds, ain't you? There's Mr. Martin Hews, as cunning as they make 'em, your old lawyer fellow Yardsley who was to pay me money if I wanted to go to him; there's Bloor, the Scotland Yard detective, and the Lord knows how many of them,—all after Joseph. And you can't find him. You don't know what he's like. You don't know whether he's a gentleman or a coster, and I could tell you—I could tell you all about him. I'd be found on the pavement the next morning, and I'd be buried before the week was out, but I could tell you, all right. He's clever, Joseph is. Talk about brains, there's none of you can match him, but he's a devil all the same. He's a bigger devil than that Puck-faced mummy of yours over at the Mansion."

"Why did you leave him for Donkin?" I asked.

"Because he brought another girl down," she confided. "That's the reason, if you want to know it, Mister. Jim was all right, but he wasn't in Joseph's class. I did it in a temper, you see. I do things sometimes like that. I'm always afraid that some day—"

She broke off, realising the interest with which I was listening.

"Talking a bit, ain't I? Never mind. No harm done.

And you're thinking—shall I tell you what you're thinking about?"

"You'd be clever if you could," I replied.

"You're wondering what I'll do if I find Joseph with
her. That's what's dancing up and down in your mind.
You'd like to tell me what to do, wouldn't you? That little
ogre back at the Mansion would, anyway."

I leaned forward in my place. We were drawn up on a
great tangle of tracks just outside the station, lights
flashing on each side, and trains everywhere coming and
passing."

"Rachel," I said, "listen to me for a moment. I want to
get Joseph, if I can. That's part of my job in life, but
more than that, by a long way, I want to make sure
that Beatrice Essiter comes to no harm. I want her back
again safely. Do you get me?"

She nodded.

"I'm not going to follow you," I continued. "I don't
care where the devil you go to. If you're off to the slums
looking for Joseph, I know jolly well you won't find what
I want there, for if your man isn't a fool—if he's serious
about her—he isn't going to begin by dragging her down
to that part of the world. It isn't there I'm coming to look
for her, at any rate, and there's nothing else I want to
do but just that one thing. I want to find Beatrice Essiter,
and after that I don't care what happens. Joseph can
go to hell his own way, or any way you like to take him."

She was roused at last. She sat up, and her eyes
sparkled.

"You're the first man I've met, anyway," she declared,
"who put the girl before the job."

"You haven't lived long," I told her curtly, "and you
haven't lived very widely. Anyway, you know the truth
now," I added, as we glided into Liverpool Street Station. "You say you don't want any money, and there's

nothing else I can do for you. Well, then, off you go, young woman, and the best of luck to you!"

She gave me her slim, nervous hand, hot and feverish in mine.

"You're a good fellow of your sort," she said, a little awkwardly, "and Joseph's a devil. I sometimes think he's Satan himself, but if I lived to be a hundred years old, he'd be my man."

I last saw her sprinting across the broad platform towards the first of a rank of waiting taxies. I saw her pause on the step of the first one whilst she looked around. A flickering light flashed upon her face, and its lines seemed suddenly strained, almost ominous. She stood on tiptoe, as though to whisper the address to the driver. Then she sprang inside and disappeared.

I found a hastily written note from Bloor at my rooms, explaining that he was very busy, but would come round the moment he could leave the Yard, probably between nine and ten, and at eight o'clock that evening, looking perhaps even more dejected than I felt I was ushered into Mr. Leopold's very luxurious suite of rooms in Berkeley Street. My host, partly dressed and wearing a magnificent plum-coloured dressing gown of thick satin, greeted me warmly.

"The cocktails at once, Maurice," he ordered, addressing the man who had admitted me. "Sit down, Major. Well, how goes it?"

"Badly," I admitted.

"No word of the young lady?"

"Nothing. We have an idea, though, as to what has become of her, and her uncle is furious. He has turned me out of the house and given me the sack, and I don't blame him."

"Dear, dear me, that's bad!" Mr. Leopold sympathised.

"You say that you have a clue though, as to what has become of the young lady. What do you mean by that?"

"Not exactly a clue," I explained. "We have had an anonymous letter from a man who has a grudge against Mr. Martin Hews, from which we gathered that by some means or other she has fallen into his hands. What it all means I scarcely understand. I have only known Mr. Hews a week or so, and the whole thing is a mystery to me."

"Sounds as though it might be a mystery to any one," Mr. Leopold observed. "Perhaps it's one of those things better not looked into too closely, eh? In the old days it used to be 'Boys will be boys'; since the war, it's 'Girls will be girls.' Well, here's better luck, Major. I think you'll find that as good a cocktail as there is in London."

The cocktail was certainly good, and potent enough, as I discovered from my first sip.

"I'm terribly sorry about last night," my host continued, eyeing me, as I fancied a little stealthily. "How many drinks did we have in the office? Was it one or two?"

"I have no idea," I confessed. "Of course, it sounds ridiculous, but the story I told before the magistrate was practically the truth so far as my memory goes. I just remember stepping in there, feeling a little giddy, and then everything seemed to go dark."

"Just as though all the lights had gone out, eh? It was exactly the same with me the last time I was bowled over. Well, now, tell me, Major, is there anything I can do to help? You've been to Claridge's again, I suppose?"

"I was there half an hour ago. They have heard nothing of Miss Essiter."

"Would you like me to telephone to Scotland Yard or step down there?"

I shook my head gloomily.

"Very good of you, sir," I replied, "but I don't think I should do anything of that sort for a day or two. Of course, there's always a chance that Miss Essiter may have joined up with some friends. Breezeley Mansion's a dull enough place for any girl."

"My own idea precisely," Mr. Leopold agreed, almost eagerly. "No good making a fuss before it's necessary. Have you any clue at all you can give me as to who this person may be who sent the anonymous letter?"

"Not the slightest in the world," I admitted. "As a matter of fact, he's the man we've been trying so hard to find."

"A gentleman?"

"Oh, no," I answered hastily. "He's the head of a gang of roughs down in the East End somewhere. I shouldn't think he's ever set foot in Bond Street in his life."

"Head of a gang of roughs," Mr. Leopold mused, his narrow little eyes still scrutinising me keenly. "Well, the police ought to know something about him then, oughtn't they?"

I appeared to hesitate for a moment.

"Mr. Hews doesn't care much about the police," I confided.

Mr. Leopold grinned, a humorous, flesh-creasing performance. Every moment, he seemed to be becoming more at his ease with me.

"I don't wonder at it at all, Major Owston. If you'd been with that scarecrow many more months, you'd probably have understood the reason well enough."

I permitted my glass to be replenished. My host glanced at the clock.

"If you'll just excuse me for a moment," he begged, "I'll finish dressing, and then I can drop you anywhere you want to go. I'm dining at the Hyde Park Hotel at a quarter to nine. Help yourself to anything you want. The cigarettes are on the table."

He disappeared into an inner room, and from that to an apartment beyond. I strolled over to the table and let my fingers linger in a cigarette box. The details of the room were easy to assimilate. The writing table was of ormolu and ebony and had only three drawers. They were wide open. The two cabinets were filled with china, top and bottom. The rest of the room was mostly taken up by bookcases. The obvious depository for papers or any form of valuables was unmistakably—almost flagrantly—evident. Let into a panel of the plainly decorated walls was a safe so cleverly concealed that only the yale key-hole and the slight difference of colour at the hinges betrayed its presence. . . .

In the distant room, I could hear Mr. Leopold talking to his valet. Anything hidden in that safe was, so far as I was concerned, as secure as though it were in the vaults of the Bank of England. It was something, however, to know where the code book of which I was in search was likely to be kept. I strolled back towards my chair, looking at the titles of the books in the cases, wondering what Mr. Leopold's tastes in literature might really be. There were some very beautiful volumes, a surprising edition of Daudet, richly bound in white calf, Guy de Maupassant's short stories flaming in orange, green and purple, an *édition de luxe* of Mademoiselle de Maupin, and then the only volume which had evidently been taken out recently—an old book, bound in limp leather, hastily replaced, and still projecting beyond its fellows. I bent down to look at the title and resumed my seat, smiling to myself. The idea of Mr. Leopold indulging in half an hour's solitude each day with the Bible amused me.

"Well, young fellow," he exclaimed, as he rejoined me, the last word in perfumed and correctly tailored masculinity, "if you're ready, I must get along. How are you spending the evening, may I ask?"

"I'm not quite sure," I confided, as we passed out of the door and stepped into the lift. "I did think of going to the club, but I decided it was rather early to face it."

"What club?" he demanded.

I told him, and he was visibly impressed.

"My dear Major," he protested, "don't dream of going there until this thing has blown over. Take my advice and keep away."

"Well, then," I said, "I shall probably dine in my rooms. I have a few little matters to clear up, and there may be a message about Miss Essiter."

"Don't you worry too much, young fellow," Mr. Leopold advised me earnestly. "You're doing the right thing, I am sure, in not making too much fuss about it. I expect you'll find the young lady has just slipped off for a bit of liberty. The girls of to-day will do it, you know, and I'm not sure that we don't like them all the better for it, eh? A good-looking girl like Miss Essiter is bound to have some pals."

I refrained from kicking him with difficulty, and we glided smoothly off.

"My fifth Rolls," he confided. "No cars like them. It's a lot of money to pay to start with, but they never give you any trouble afterwards. Money's easily earned nowadays, too."

"Is it?" I rejoined. "I wish you'd tell me how?"

"Would you like a job in the Colonies?"

"I'd like a job anywhere where the work wasn't crooked."

My companion looked at me as though I were some sort of natural curiosity.

"That sounds odd after you've been working for Martin Hews," he observed. "Wouldn't tell a lie, eh, or play a part, or deceive anybody? Well, you know there are places for your type—not very highly paid places, I am afraid, though. In the money world, it's the man who knows how to bend things to his own advantage the nearest and quickest way who comes to the front, and that can't always be without a little hanky-panky. I suppose you would stretch a point sometimes, if there was a bit in it for yourself as well as for your employer?"

"I've got to live," I answered dejectedly.

The car came to a standstill at the corner of Down Street and Piccadilly. I prepared to descend.

"I'll think things over and let you know," Mr. Leopold promised. "And don't worry too much about the young lady. A bit fantastic, that theory of yours that she may have been carried off by some one or other. Those things don't happen nowadays. Shouldn't be surprised if you didn't hear that she was safely at home by now."

I thanked him cordially for his hospitality and sympathy, escaped a handshake by a glance at his immaculate white kid gloves and an apology as to the condition of my own hands, and stepped out on to the pavement. I watched the car start off and mingle with the traffic going Kensington way. Then I walked a few paces towards my own front door, a little wearily. I might have succeeded in gulling Mr. Leopold to a certain extent, but the main object of my visit to him remained unaccomplished. What sort of a book, I wondered—!

The idea came to me as I turned the key in the lock and crossed the threshold. I sprinted up the stairs, two at a time, and directly I had reached my sitting-room, I rang the bell.

"Smart," I asked a little breathlessly, as soon as he appeared, "have you a Bible?"

"Have I—a—I beg your pardon, sir, what was it you said?"

"A Bible," I repeated. "You or your wife—any one. I want a Bible."

"What cocktail would you like, sir?"

"I don't want a cocktail, Smart. I want a Bible," I reiterated.

He hurried from the room and was away almost ten minutes. When he returned, he was still blowing the dust off a large and mouldy volume.

"It belonged to the missus's mother," he announced, placing it upon the table. "I'm afraid it hasn't been opened for a good many years, sir."

I seized it eagerly, and carried it to my writing-table. I had only just brought out the cipher letter which I had stolen from Mr. Leopold when Smart returned.

"Mr. Bloor to see you, sir," he announced.

CHAPTER XXVI

FORTUNATELY, my evening meal was equal to the demands made upon it by an unexpected though diffident guest. I followed the latter's lead and refrained from embarking upon serious topics until we were alone with our coffee and liqueurs.

"I got your note, Major," he said. "Couldn't come before. Things have been a bit parky with us to-day. So you found a spot of trouble last night?"

I nodded gloomily.

"They were too clever for me," I admitted.

"Let's have the whole story, please," he begged.

I told him everything. He listened with his eyes fixed upon his coffee cup.

"Damned clever," he conceded. "And suggestive too. All goes to prove your theory that Joseph's turned West Ender. They don't want you poking about in these parts evidently, and they took the cleverest means of stopping it. You're banned from the Blue Skies now as an ordinary visitor, and from all the affiliated night clubs where we fancy that Joseph sometimes meets his friends. I suppose the cards of invitation will stop too. I see the point. What I don't quite get is why he's taken this big risk for Miss Essiter. Had he ever seen her?"

"Not to my knowledge," I answered. "I rather imagine it's a counterstroke to Martin Hews. You see, Donkin and Joseph were all the time fighting for little Rachel, the Jewess. Donkin was Martin Hews' man, and when he got into trouble, Martin Hews helped him to escape and shut up the girl at Breezeley."

Bloor was looking a little grave.

"I don't like the sound of that," he admitted. "Tell me about the young lady, Major. You knew her fairly well, I suppose?"

"I have only known her since I have known Martin Hews," I reminded him. "I should say that she'd had a very unhappy life lately, and that she was a little embittered. She's inclined to be supercilious, she is undoubtedly fastidious, she is not in the least nervous, has plenty of courage, and I should think she'd make a brave fight anywhere, anyhow."

Bloor looked at me for a moment kindly.

"Rotten sort of show for you last night, Major."

"I would sooner have lost my right arm," I told him, "than have had it happen. As it is, there isn't a single thing in the world I can think of except getting her back. I don't care a damn about the rest of the business. If I want to get at Joseph still, it is simply to tear the life out of him if he's hurt her, and, by God, I'll do that!" I declared, letting myself go for the first time.

"We'll get her back," Bloor promised cheerfully. "Sometimes I fancy, Major, that there's a sort of rude chivalry about Joseph. I don't think he'd dare to do anything brutal, even though she is Martin Hews' niece. I don't suppose you've had any news of her during the day?"

"Nothing except this," I replied, handing him Joseph's latest communication.

He read it carefully.

"My God, what a nerve!" he muttered. "You showed this to her uncle? What was his reply?"

"He passed it on to Rachel, the little Jewish girl, and let her loose."

Bloor was a big man, and a man with a big nerve. Nevertheless I saw him shiver, and I knew that he was experiencing that same cold wave of horror which had swept over me when Martin Hews, with his cynical leer, had first expounded his scheme.

"It's damnable!" he muttered. "The girl knows where to go to, all right, but—"

There was a pause. Neither of us cared to utter our thoughts.

"Did he have her followed?" Bloor enquired.

"I don't think so. He was too clever for that. The girl would have been up to every trick of that sort."

My visitor pulled out his pipe and filled it with savage fingers.

"If one could only know where she went," he muttered—"east or west. If one knew where to pull down the curtain."

I had never seen Bloor so depressed. I made some remark about it as I refilled his cup with coffee. He nodded.

"You're in trouble all right, Major," he acknowledged, "but so are we. There's hell to pay at the Yard. We had the Home Secretary down this afternoon. I suppose you don't bother much about the papers these days?"

"Not much," I admitted.

"Golders in Cheapside was burgled early this morning, the watchman shot, and fifteen thousand pounds' worth of jewels taken clean away. I'm confident the men came out of a bolt hole in Joseph's section. One of my men saw them go, but we're trying to keep things quiet down there, so he didn't interfere. He only obeyed orders. The idea was that they'd come back again if they were out on a job. Well, they didn't come back, and I should think they're not likely to now. It was a marvellously planned coup. All that we know is that the men went off in a closed motor car travelling westward."

"A bad business," I observed, with as much sympathy as I could muster for any one else's trouble.

"It's a very bad business indeed for us," Bloor agreed, "because it's the seventh affair of this sort within the last few weeks. There are three men dead and two in hospital, and sixty thousand pounds' worth of jewels gone. The Chief and I, and the rest of us, are just as certain as any one can be that it is Joseph's gang at work, and I'm damned if we can lay a finger upon them. The only important capture we've made at all was thanks to you, Major, down at Breezeley, and of course, quite properly, the Essex police got the credit for that. I tell you we're getting hell down at the Yard. We'll have to do something, or there'll be half-a-dozen resignations asked for."

"You know where the gang are," I pointed out. "Why don't you rope them in and have done with it? You may not get Joseph, but he can't do much mischief without his men."

The Inspector filled his pipe quietly.

"It will have to come to that, I'm afraid," he admitted. "It's a perfect nest of criminals, and we should be certain to get at least half-a-dozen convictions, but what the hell's the use of that? We shouldn't get the men who did this last job, and we shouldn't get Joseph. Only a week ago, we got two of his outside men, besides the three over at your place, but do you think they'll squeal? Not one of them. They're just going to take what's coming to them, and they'll never open their lips. There's one old chap we took not long ago, for burglary. Must have been fifty-four, if he's a day. He got ten years. There isn't a chance in twenty that he'll ever come out again. We went nap on him because we knew he was in Joseph's area. If he'd have told us what we wanted to know, he could have walked out of prison a free man in three months, with a thousand of the best in his pocket. He just grinned at us—never even hesitated."

"How the devil does any man get such a hold over this class of person?" I wondered.

Bloor folded his arms and looked into the fire. His eyelids were very heavy to-night, a sign that he was tired.

"I figure it out," he explained, "that he gets it in two ways. The first is fear. Now in our records you will find that there are six cases within the last five months of men having been found dead with no certainty as to whether they had committed suicide or been murdered. We let it go at that, but we know all about it. Five out of the six, at any rate, were Joseph's men—not in the inner circle—who had given away just the trifle they knew about the gang and the mysterious chief they never saw. They got theirs, anyhow, though their information wasn't worth listening to. The first hold Joseph has over them, Major, is fear."

"And the second?"

"Self-interest. Now there was a young fellow, Hobson, got three years some time ago. He really could have told us something, for he was an expert typist and shorthand writer, and we are convinced that for some time he acted as Joseph's secretary. He hadn't a penny when he went to prison, nor a relative in the world. He came out six weeks ago. He was married almost at once. He's got a small motor car, and he's back at his original job of tailoring down in Wandsworth. Joseph looks after his men. Hobson went to prison cheerfully, because he knew that when he came out he was going to be cared for."

"That's the right principle," I admitted, "especially with that class of person. We've done most of our colonising like that when we've had savage tribes to deal with. Knocked the fear of God into them first and rewarded them afterwards beyond the dreams of avarice if they ran straight."

Smart made a brief reappearance with the whisky and soda. I filled our glasses and produced my own pipe. Then Bloor asked me a question concerning the matter which I knew had been puzzling him.

"Supposing you tell me now what you were doing with the family Bible when I came in?"

"I will with pleasure," I assented, "but first of all, do you know anything about Mr. Leopold, a brother of Lady Bonofar?"

Once again the eyelids were half lifted. He shot a quick glance at me.

"The man who took you to the Blue Skies?"

I nodded.

"He took us there, and I am convinced that he knew what was going to happen to me when he made an excuse for getting me into the secretary's office. It was he, too, according to his own story, who put Miss Essiter into a taxicab to go home. I have come to the conclusion, Inspector, that Leopold is one of Joseph's West End associates."

Bloor was listening intently. He made no observation.

"For that reason," I went on, "when I saw him yesterday morning, I resisted my first impulse to take him by the throat and choke the life out of him. I decided that to give him the hiding he deserved wouldn't do any good. I pretended instead to accept his story. I had a cocktail with him at Claridge's, and I stole a letter out of his overcoat pocket."

"Good for you!" my companion murmured. "What was in the letter?"

I passed it across to him. He glanced through it with declining interest, and finally shook his head.

"I'm afraid it is scarcely worth while taking it to our code department," he pronounced.

"Why not?"

"Because it is obviously one of those codes," he pointed out, "which are made up by arrangement between two people, and probably changed with every communication. It wouldn't lend itself to any form of regular transcription. The only thing you could do would be to get hold of the homemade key—the particular one, I mean, upon which this is based. Now this was sent, you say, to Leopold. Very well, somewhere in Leopold's possession you might find a corresponding cipher, but even that is not necessary. It could be based upon a copy of the daily newspaper, a magazine, anything, but unless you knew what it was, you might try in vain for the rest of your lifetime to decipher the thing."

"What about a book?" I suggested.

"A book certainly, but then what book? You see that would probably be decided upon *viva voce*."

"What about the Bible?"

"Quite a possibility. Where did you get the idea from, though?"

"Well, I'll tell you. I went to Leopold's rooms to-night, as I have told you, to have a cocktail and give him the opportunity of persuading me once more not to move hastily in the matter of Miss Essiter, but to leave it in his hands. He had a magnificent collection of books in the room, but the only one which looked as though it had been disturbed for weeks was the Bible, and that was half out of the shelf."

Mr. Bloor rose almost hastily to his feet. He came over and patted me on the back.

"Well, I'm damned, Major!" he exclaimed. "Whether this works out or not, it shows you've got more of our instinct in you than I gave you credit for. Come along. Let's get at it!"

We pondered over the code for some minutes and then made our first essay. Number 2 we took as being the second book of the Old Testament; 39 we accepted as the chapter; 21 as the verse. I counted the words until I arrived at 20. A queer little whistle broke from Bloor's lips. My own exclamation was profane but exultant, for the verse was this:

And they did bind the breastplate by his rings unto the rings of the ephod with a lace of blue, that it might be above the curious girdle of the ephod, and that the breastplate might not be loosed from the ephod; as the Lord commanded Moses.

And the 20th word was BLUE!

After that we went at it breathlessly. Eighteen was the Book of Job, and the eigtheenth verse of the thirty-seventh chapter was:

Hast thou with him spread out the sky, which is strong, and as a molten looking glass?

And the eighth word was SKY.

The First Book was Genesis, and the nineteenth verse of the first chapter ran as follows:

'And the evening and the morning were the fourth day.'

"Blue Sky Thursday!" Bloor exclaimed. "Major, I hope you haven't any engagement?"

I laughed at him, and we made our plans.

CHAPTER XXVII

An hour or so later, we left our taxicab at the corner
of the narrow street in which the Blue Skies Club was
situated and walked down as far as the entrance. Bloor
drew me back into the shadows and looked around. Across
the street from us a man was selling matches; another was
standing on the kerbstone, with a bundle of evening papers
under his arm. A taxicab driver was seated upon the front
seat of his vehicle, smoking and reading the latest sporting edition. A chauffeur, in a small two-seated car, was
facing him on the other side of the entrance. There was
plenty of space between them for any one to take up or
set down a passenger at the Club, but their places were so
arranged that any one passing in or out would be within
their reach. Bloor beckoned to the newspaper man, who
touched his hat and hurried across. We both of us selected
newspapers, we both of us needed change, and all the time
Bloor talked.

"You understand, Richards," he said, "it isn't the people who are coming into the club you need be interested
in; it is the people who come out."

No reply, only a little nod. The young man was labo-
riously counting out change.

"Any one who looks to be a messenger from the club,
whoever he is, is to be detained," Bloor went on. "You
have plenty of men to fall back on. There are six policemen at the next corner, and six at the Oxford Street end.
'Apple' is the word. You understand? We want a man who
is expected here to-night, and we want to stop any mes-

sage being sent out to warn him against coming. We will see to the telephone ourselves."

The young man, pocketing his change, touched his cap and ambled off. I watched him in some admiration. He stopped to beg a fag end from the taxi driver and a light from the chauffeur, and during those few moments he passed on to both the message he had received. According to our arrangement, I presented myself alone at the swing doors of the club, and what we had expected promptly happened. A commissionaire, holding out his hand, blocked my further progress.

"I beg your pardon, sir," he said gruffly, "but are you a member of the club?"

"I am not," I acknowledged, "but I wish to have a word with the secretary."

His hand fell heavily upon my shoulder. He was a Goliath of a fellow, but I affected to hesitate.

"I have a friend outside," I confided.

"Well, out you go to him," was the brusque reply. "You're not wanted in here. Manager's orders."

The swing doors revolved once more, and Bloor stood by my side.

"What's the trouble?" he enquired.

"This fellow won't let me in."

"Not you nor your friend neither," the man declared truculently. "Out you go, both of you. I don't want your card," he went on, as Bloor produced one. "If you're not out of here in ten seconds—"

Bloor slipped back his coat. The man gazed at his badge transfixed.

"If you don't wish for my card," the former said, "let me tell you who I am. I am Detective Inspector Bloor of Scotland Yard. This gentleman is with me. Go and tell your secretary that we wish to see him and don't stop anywhere on the way."

The man still hesitated, his eyes fixed upon me. Evidently his orders, so far as I was concerned, had been decisive.

"You know that this gentleman was turned out of here for drunkenness last night?" he asked the Inspector.

"I know all about it," was the terse reply. "Do as you're told."

The man turned reluctantly away. A few yards from us, he paused, and seemed about to enter the dancing room. Bloor moved across to him swiftly.

"Straight to the secretary's room," he ordered. "If you want to keep out of trouble, my man, you won't trifle with the law."

After that, there was no further delay. The door of the office through which I had passed was opened, and a middle-aged man wearing gold spectacles and looking a little heated came hurriedly out.

"What's the trouble, Inspector?" he asked.

"None, I hope," Bloor answered. "I wish to make a few investigations here. We should like to go straight to your office."

The secretary turned towards me.

"Delighted to assist you in any way, Inspector," he said, "but this gentleman has been struck off the rolls of the club."

"He was never a member," was my companion's curt reply. "At present he is accompanying me. If you are wise, you will make no further difficulties."

The secretary stood his ground.

"You know that he was fined forty shillings and costs this morning, sir? It's in all the papers. Major Owston of Down Street."

"Quite enough of that. Show us the way to your office."

The secretary led us there, mumbling to himself. I crossed the threshold exactly as I had done on the pre-

vious night and stood inside, looking around. The room
was precisely as I remembered it, except for the absence
of Mr. X. from his place by the desk.

"I don't really see, Inspector, the object of this visit,"
the secretary said nervously. "We did all that was possible as regards Major Owston, both for our own sake
and his. The moment that we realised he was incapable,
we sent him off in a taxicab to his rooms."

Bloor did not even take the trouble to listen. He walked
slowly around the office, tapping the walls here and there,
even lifting the carpet in places. Finally, he seated himself
at the secretary's table.

"Really, sir!" the latter remonstrated. "I must protest."

Suddenly the room was plunged into complete darkness. All that I could see was the red light from the
end of the cigar which Bloor had been smoking. Then
I heard his hand hit the desk and the sound of a scuffle,
and from the altered position of his cigar I knew that he
had risen to his feet. The lights blazed on again. The secretary was lying on his back upon the carpet. He rose to
his feet, trembling with agitation.

"This is the most extraordinary behaviour, Inspector,"
he exclaimed. "I shall telephone to your headquarters at
once."

"You will probably save me the trouble of doing so in
a few minutes," Bloor rejoined calmly. "Now, if you're
a sensible man, you'll get up, answer my questions, and do
the best you can to help me in the execution of my duties.
What is your name?"

"Cranford."

"That's a lie to begin with," Bloor rapped out. "Your
name is Ernest Rees. You were liable for prosecution two
years ago in the Messor case, but we let the matter hang
over."

"Not another word, sir," the man begged, in a completely altered tone. "What do you want me to do?"

"Answer my questions, first of all. How long have you been here?"

"Seven months."

"Was it through Mr. Leopold you got the post?"

"Yes."

"Now listen. Answer this question, and mind you answer it truthfully. Why is there a control here under my chair, turning out every light in the room, and another to switch them on again?"

"It was there when I came, sir. They use it at times, I think, to get rid of any one they don't want in the club."

"How is that managed?"

"Dope, sir, I believe. I can't explain any more than that. I am always sent out of the room when that sort of thing is on."

"It was used last night when Major Owston came in?"

"I believe so, sir."

"Do you know why?"

"I do not, sir."

"Do you know by whose orders?"

"By Mr. Leopold's, sir. He is a member of the committee."

Suddenly those heavy eyelids of Bloor's seemed to disappear. He swung round in his chair. His blue eyes were full of brilliant, questioning light.

"There was another man here last night who sat at this desk and who dealt with Major Owston. Who was he?"

The man was shaking in every limb. He held up both hands.

"Before God," he cried, "I don't know!"

"You don't know his name?"

"No, sir. When he comes, I am sent away to a little office behind."

"How often does he come?"

"About once every ten days, sir."

"Was it he who took the young lady who was with Major Owston away from here last night?"

"Before God, sir, I don't know," was the passionate reply. "They don't trust me here. I'm not one of them. They keep everything secret from me. Whatever goes on here, sir, I'm not in it—I swear to God I'm not."

"I don't want to be hard on you, Rees," Bloor said, after a moment's silence. "Honestly, I'm inclined to believe you, when you say that you know very little about what goes on here, but this man who comes every ten days—you could describe him, perhaps."

"I would if I could, sir," the secretary answered fervently. "I can assure you, Mr. Bloor, there's nothing I wouldn't do to serve you."

"Very well then," Bloor said in a calmer tone, "don't fluster yourself. So long as your sympathies are in the right quarter we don't want to hustle you. This little visit of ours may turn out to be very much to your advantage. We never forget those who help us, Rees, and this is rather a serious matter we have come up against. Now tell me quietly, as man to man, why do you find it difficult to describe this person?"

The change in Bloor's victim was amazing. A few minutes ago he had seemed on the point of hysteria. Now he was back again, his old self, calm and earnest. The detective's diplomacy had done its work.

"Mr. Bloor," he said, "I'll tell you the truth, and I only hope you'll believe me. That gentleman comes here, as I have told you, about once in ten days, but unless you were within a few yards of him, unless you heard him speak, as I have done, unless you saw him in here in the office with Mr. Leopold or in the little retiring room behind —next door on the left, sir—I swear that you wouldn't recognize him from one time to another. He comes here in disguise, sir. That's what he does."

"Wait one moment," Bloor enjoined. "You spoke of a little retiring room. What does he use that for?"

"Supper parties with ladies, sir, generally," was the prompt reply. "It has a private exit on to the street."

I gave a little start. Bloor motioned me to keep silent.

"Did he take supper there last night?" he asked.

"He may have done, sir. I was sent off on an errand immediately Major Owston arrived."

"Very well. Now we'll go on where we left off. You think he comes here in disguise, yet you always recognise him."

"I've recognised him once or twice, sir," the secretary admitted, "but it's my belief that he's been here dozens of times when I haven't. He's not so careful about me, because he knows that I'm on the brink of trouble all the time. He knows you people still have one up against me."

"You may count that written off, Rees," Bloor promised him. "You are behaving like a white man to-night, and you shall reap the benefit of it. Now, can you tell us anything about the disappearance of Miss Essiter last night?"

"Not a thing. They don't trust me here. They sent me all the way to the Milan, and I didn't get back till it was over."

"You saw the man we are enquiring about last night?"

"I saw him come in."

"Describe him as he seemed to you then."

Rees reflected for a moment.

"Well, he was a little above medium height,—slim, just the sort of figure the young gentlemen try to give themselves nowadays, a little pale, and with what I should call a sardonic expression."

"Should you know him again if you saw him?"

"If I saw him again in the same make-up I would, sir."

"What name does he go by here?"

"Rather a ridiculous one, sir—Polly Harten. If word comes in that Polly Harten is going to be in the club any particular night, everything is a little altered. We have extra men on duty. We send away some of the waiters, supper is laid in the retiring room in case he wants to use it."

"I see," Mr. Bloor murmured. "Does he ever come two nights following?"

"I have known him do it. Not often, though."

"You haven't had any word of his coming to-night?"

"None at all."

Bloor was silent for several moments.

"Rees," he said, "this mysterious patron of the place is wanted. We want him very badly. We want him so badly that we will pay a reward of five hundred pounds—I think it might even be made more. Can you help?"

Once more the man was back in a state of abject terror.

"Inspector," he begged, "don't ask me any more about him. There was the head waiter here before Guido. He got talking to a private detective employed by some gentleman down in the country. He came swaggering in to me, saying how he was going to make five hundred pounds with just the wave of his arm one night. The next day they found him dead not fifty yards away from here. The questions you ask me I have to answer, but I can't do more, sir. Indeed, I can't."

There was the sound of hasty footsteps outside. The door was thrown open. Mr. Leopold, looking very agitated indeed, stood upon the threshold.

CHAPTER XXVIII

I THINK that never before have I seen an expression of such blank amazement as that with which Mr. Leopold confronted us for the first few seconds after his entrance. My presence, in particular, seemed to render him, at first, speechless.

"Hullo, Owston!" he stammered at last. "How on earth did you get in here?"

"I brought him in," Bloor acknowledged, rising to his feet. "Do you happen to be a member of the committee, sir?"

"I certainly am," the newcomer assented.

"Mr. Leopold?"

"That is my name."

"You will forgive my coming round in a sense quite unofficially, sir," Bloor continued, in a conciliatory tone. "The fact of it is, I wanted to ask you a question about the young lady you were kind enough to see into a taxicab last night. Her friends have communicated with Scotland Yard. You know, I dare say, that she has not returned yet to Claridge's Hotel where she was staying, and the last place she was seen was here."

"But who are you?"

"Detective Inspector Bloor of Scotland Yard, at your service."

Mr. Leopold turned angrily towards me.

"I thought it was distinctly understood between us," he said, "that such enquiries as were made should be made through me as representing the club."

"Major Owston is blameless in the matter," Bloor put

in quickly. "I called for him in accordance with instructions received to-night, and I asked him to accompany me here."

"Then I should like to know, if it isn't Major Owston, who is behind all this disturbance," Mr. Leopold protested, with an air of bluster. "There are a dozen people who will tell you that Miss Essiter left here alone in a taxicab within a few minutes of Major Owston's removal. That ends our connection with the matter. I may say that I resent this visit of the police just as our guests are coming in."

"I am in plain clothes, sir," Bloor pointed out deprecatingly. "Surely you cannot object to the young lady's people placing the matter of her disappearance in our hands."

"The young lady's people?" Mr. Leopold repeated, with a frown. "Who may they be? Do I take it that you are acting for Mr. Martin Hews?"

"Don't know the gentleman, sir. As it happens, we are instructed by Claridge's Hotel."

Mr. Leopold divested himself of his coat and hat. He appeared to be slightly reassured.

"I have a guest outside," he confided. "I will take her in to the restaurant and join you again."

"Certainly," the detective acquiesced. "Pray don't hurry, sir. Very sorry to inconvenience you."

Leopold disappeared, and as soon as the door was closed, Bloor turned once more to Rees.

"Give me your keys," he ordered.

The man handed them to him without hesitation.

"Now hurry off. Get into my taxicab, drive to Scotland Yard, and wait there for me. Ask them for my room. I'll send you home afterwards all right. You have probably done yourself a bit of good to-night. If any one stops you outside, say 'Apple.'"

Rees obeyed promptly. Bloor turned to me.

"Don't interfere in this more than you can help. Try to keep on the right side of Leopold, if you can. Do as I wish now and question me afterwards. Go out to the telephone booth and ask for a number—any number—and let me know the result."

I made my way to the hall, and the commissionaire sullenly directed me to the telephone booth. Just as I reached the door, Mr. Leopold emerged from it, nearly bumping into me.

"What's the matter with the telephone?" he called out to the commissionaire.

"Didn't know that there was anything wrong, sir," the man replied. "Now I come to think of it, no one's rung up for at least an hour."

He hurried into the booth. Leopold held me by the lapel of my coat.

"Owston," he exclaimed nervously, "what the devil's the meaning of this? I've treated you right, haven't I? Is it you who've brought the police here?"

"I can assure you that it isn't, Mr. Leopold," I was able to tell him with perfect truth. "The Inspector inside called on me and insisted upon my coming here."

"What the devil business of the hotel's is it?" Leopold demanded furiously. "It was ten to one against Martin Hews daring to go to Scotland Yard, and you were —forgive me, Major. I am a little upset. Now look here. Do you want to do me a good turn?"

"I'd be very glad to," I assured him.

"I have been able to show you that I wanted to be your friend," he went on. "I turned up at the police court this morning, on purpose to get you off light. Persuade that fellow to clear out as quickly as possible. There's nothing to be learned here. I'll give you my word as to that. It does a club harm to have him seen hanging about."

"I'll do my best," I promised.

"I shall have to write a note," he continued, a little more quietly. "It won't take me five minutes. Afterwards, I'll come back to the office. What's wrong with the telephone, Graves?" he asked, as the commissionaire reappeared.

"Completely out of order, sir," the man reported. "I can't get a reply from anywhere."

Mr. Leopold was getting hot again. There was a distinct moisture upon his forehead and a return of the scared look in his eyes.

"Damned odd," he muttered. "To-night of all nights, too! Send a message to the nearest call office to report the line gone wrong, Graves. And, Major?"

"Yes."

"I want to send a note away. Keep the Inspector where he is for a minute or two."

"I will if I can," I assented.

He bustled away, and I returned to the office.

"The telephone has been cut off, all right," I announced. "I met Mr. Leopold coming out of the box. He's gone to write a note."

"Step outside quickly," Bloor enjoined. "Call over the newspaper man. Tell him to pass word to the others that on no account is any one to leave the place who looks as though he was taking a note anywhere. He should be stopped by force if necessary, and the note is to be taken from him."

I hurried out and executed my errand. The commissionaire stopped me on my return journey.

"Say, guv'nor, what's going on?" he asked curiously. "Trouble about last night, eh?"

"It's about the young lady who was with me when I came," I confided. "She hasn't returned home, and her people are making a fuss."

"I saw her go away," the man reflected.

"Well, there's a reward of five hundred pounds," I told him, "for any one who can give any definite information as to where she went."

A sudden cupidity shone in the man's eyes. He moistened his lips and looked at me thoughtfully.

"Five hundred quid!" he repeated. "My God!"

"Easily earned money," I went on. "The amount will be paid over to any one who is able to give information concerning the young lady's whereabouts, if they just step down to Scotland Yard and ask to see Inspector Bloor, or they can come to see me—Number 3a, Down Street."

The man looked about him nervously.

"I'd be more at home with you, sir," he confided, in a half whisper. "If I'm that way to-morrow morning, perhaps—"

I nodded and hurried off. I had only just time to make my report when Leopold reappeared. He had obviously fortified himself with a drink and was smoking a cigar. He seemed to have abandoned for the moment his suspicions of me, but he was very far from being at his ease with my companion.

"Inspector," he announced, "I have been making a few enquiries on your behalf. The commissionaire who called the taxicab for the young lady is ready to answer questions, and I think we could find the taxicab driver. I have sent a boy out to see. The cloakroom attendant, too, can tell you that she saw the young lady leave the room, cross the hall, and step into the taxicab. This, of course, merely supports my own testimony, but the chauffeur may have something to tell you."

"Quite so," Bloor assented. "I'll take the matter up with pleasure in a few minutes, Mr. Leopold. In the meantime, I am sorry to have to tell you that, although my errand here to-night chiefly concerns the matter of this young lady's disappearance, I had another reason for coming, and a more strictly official one. May I ask whether you know your secretary's name?"

"Perceval Cranford, he calls himself. Surely he hasn't been getting into trouble."

"His correct name is Ernest Rees," Bloor confided, "and he has been wanted by the police for some two years. I have been obliged to send him away under arrest."

"God bless my soul!" Leopold exclaimed. "Well, well, this is a surprise, Inspector, if you like!"

Now I was watching Leopold pretty closely, and it was perfectly obvious to me that this disclosure as to his secretary's real name was no surprise to him at all. Furthermore, I was convinced that for some reason or other he was immensely relieved. He unlocked a cabinet and produced a box of cigars.

"I wish you'd told me the real object of your visit at once, Inspector," he said. "We'll do all we can to find out what's become of the young lady, of course, but I never looked upon it as a police matter. Try one of these. Pretty good stuff you'll find them, I think. Help yourself, Major."

"Thank you," Bloor replied. "I never smoke when on duty."

"Take a few for later on," Leopold insisted. "Fill your case, Major. Cranford a wrong 'un! God bless my soul!"

There is just one thing more," Bloor observed, feeling in his pockets. "I shall be bound, as a matter of formality, to search Cranford's desk. He has left me the keys."

I could never have believed that so much change in a man's expression was possible in so short a time. Leopold, during the last few moments, had completely recovered his composed demeanour and was becoming positively genial. His terror now was a revelation to us both. His complexion, unwholesome at the best of times, had become ghastly. He dabbed at his forehead nervously with his over-perfumed handkerchief. Fear shone out of his eyes.

"But that is impossible," he protested. "Cranford has no desk of his own. That one belongs to me. The papers are mine. Those are my keys which he has given you."

Bloor shook his head regretfully.

"This man Rees has been receiving letters which it is necessary the police should see," he announced. "I am afraid that I have no alternative but to search for them."

"Any letters he received were put in the rack," Mr. Leopold insisted. "He answered them in the writing room or at home. I don't know where. He never made use of my desk. He had not access to it."

In his terror, he had gone one too far, and Bloor was upon him like a flash.

"But he was seated before it when we arrived. It was open and he was busy sorting some papers."

Mr. Leopold gripped at the side of the desk.

"Then he had no right there, I tell you," he declared angrily. "The desk is mine. Its contents are mine. I must ask you to hand me back the keys."

Bloor gently but firmly shook his head. For once, notwithstanding his ruffled hair, his freckled complexion and heavily lidded eyes, he thoroughly looked the part of a Scotland Yard detective engaged on serious business.

"Mr. Leopold," he said, "any private papers of yours of a personal nature will be respected. My duty, however, necessitates my searching that desk."

There was nothing more to be said. Bloor commenced his task, blandly deaf to Leopold's continued protestations.

CHAPTER XXIX

THE next quarter of an hour was one which I shall not easily forget. Outside, everything was normal. We heard the music of the gay little orchestra, sometimes the swish of feet moving across the dancing floor. We heard the taxies and automobiles drive up, the exchange of jovial greetings in the hall, and in the distance a clatter of plates and the popping of corks. The habitués of the Blue Skies Dancing Club found everything as usual on their arrival there, but, in that little office behind, Leopold, as I could very well see, was sweating blood. His eyes watched feverishly every one of the papers and letters which Bloor selected for further inspection—already a formidable little heap. Then, in the midst of it all, the private telephone which stood upon the top of the desk, rang. Leopold sprang towards it. He had no chance, however, Bloor brushed him on one side with a swift stab of the elbow and took off the receiver himself.

"The Blue Skies," he said. "Who is speaking?"

I gasped in surprise. Bloor's imitation of the secretary's voice was wonderful. Nevertheless, there was a pause. I took off the additional earpiece and listened.

"Is that Cranford?"

"Cranford speaking."

The next question came in a marvellously distinct voice. For some reason or other, it gave me a thrill when I heard it. It seemed to match so well the cynical, lowering personality of the man who, the last time I had seen him, had been sitting in Bloor's place.

"Is it all right for Polly Harten to come in to-night?"

"Perfectly all right," Bloor answered smoothly. "When?"

"Presently," was the curt reply.

Afterwards there was silence. Bloor hung up the receiver and looked speculatively at Mr. Leopold.

"I wonder," he murmured, "whether there is such a person as Polly Harten?"

Leopold moistened his lips with his tongue.

"You will find her name on the books of the club," he answered.

"Then, if she is a member, why does some one ask in a man's voice if it will be all right for her to come here to-night? I should rather like to see Polly Harten."

An ugly smile broke crookedly upon Mr. Leopold's lips. For once he said something which sounded perfectly natural.

"I don't think you would," he declared.

There was a moment's silence. Bloor turned back to the desk.

"I see you are thoroughly satisfying your curiosity with regard to my private affairs," Leopold observed.

"I feel very much ashamed of myself," Bloor confessed, without a quiver of sarcasm in his tone. "At the same time, I must do my duty. So far, Mr. Leopold, I may tell you that I have come across very little—very little indeed which should cause you any anxiety."

"You will find nothing there to justify your highhanded proceedings to-night," Mr. Leopold assured him, with the air of one recovering his courage. "You will find nothing there to justify yourself when you are called up before the Chief Commissioner to-morrow morning."

"I am sorry you take it that way, sir," Bloor said, continuing his task. "We have to make our failures sometimes, you know, but we try to do our duty. That fellow Rees is a thoroughly bad lot. We are compelled to regard with a certain amount of suspicion any place where he has been employed. You must admit that there are some things even about this room which seem to require explanation. This, for instance."

The room was suddenly plunged into darkness and a few seconds later flooded with light again. Mr. Leopold was making his stealthy way to the door, but paused at Bloor's somewhat peremptory injunction.

"Don't hurry away, please," the latter begged. "I was going to ask you about these switches."

"There's nothing to tell about them. They turn out all the lights at once."

"But why should they be placed under your foot as you sit here, I wonder?" the detective mused. "You see, I should have quite a long way to go to the door, if I made use of them, in the pitch darkness, and plenty of odd pieces of furniture to bark my shins against. Why weren't the switches by the door, Mr. Leopold?"

"No idea," the latter growled. "A notion of Cranford's, I suppose."

"Ah!" Bloor murmured. "A quaint fellow, that Cranford. He seems to have some quaint correspondence too. Hullo, some one else ringing up! Don't go, Mr. Leopold."

Again the same voice.

"The Blue Skies?"

"Yes."

"Is that Detective Inspector Bloor speaking?"

Even Bloor gave a little start. I nearly dropped the receiver. It was the same voice, slow, distinct, with its gibing undernote of mockery.

"Our dear shock-headed friend," it went on, "sitting in Cranford's chair and poring over a pile of secret documents! Not much there, Bloor—not very much, I am afraid. Still, it is a move. I grant you that. It is distinctly a move. You're getting on. You're a little better than Martin Hews' people, for instance. They seem to spend their time, I am told, haunting the pubs down Bermondsey and Shoreditch way. Shoreditch, Inspector, do you know, is a place I very seldom go to. And that fine fellow Owston, who met with such an unfortunate accident last night. I dare say he is with you. I shouldn't be at all surprised if he is shadowing the place where he lost his lady love. . . . No denial, I notice. Tell me about your health, Bloor. I saw you the other night dining with the gallant Major, and I thought you looked a little peaked and worried, and why the devil don't you go to the barber sometimes? That head of hair of yours is perfectly disgraceful. . . . You shouldn't worry so much, Bloor. I dare say the Chief gets difficult sometimes. I shall drop in and see him one day, and I'll certainly give you a leg up if I can, Inspector. . . . Not in the humour for conversation, eh?"

"I like to listen," Bloor confided. "Your voice is a little unusual, you know. I am trying to listen so well that I shall never forget it."

"I have a nice voice," our sardonic enemy went on; "clear—it has even been called musical—but just a trifle inclined towards ribaldry. All my friends, you know, consider me too frivolous for the highest type of criminal. You know I'm Joseph, of course? It is Joseph speaking."

"How are you, Joseph?" Bloor rejoined. "I'd like to see you down here. Are you bringing Polly along this evening?"

"Not to-night," was the regretful reply. "I meant to, you know, although how the mischief you knew it I can't imagine. Never mind. I shall be at the Blue Skies one evening before very long, Inspector, and I shall dance there and drink a bottle of that Cliquot '15, and I shall walk out just as happily as I entered—only, Inspector, I shall choose my night. See? By-the-by, if Major Owston is there, would he like to have a message from a young lady?"

"I'll give it to him," Bloor promised. "What is it?"

There was an instant's silence. Then once more the mocking voice, only this time I fancied that it contained a suggestion of something more sinister.

"The young lady will bring it to him herself, Inspector. Good-bye."

The connection was broken. Bloor rang up the Supervisor of the telephone first, and afterwards Scotland Yard. Then we sat and looked at each other. In Leopold's presence, however, we refrained from speech.

"Are you two going to occupy my room all night?" the latter demanded harshly.

"We shall be leaving in a few minutes," Bloor assured him. "Don't let us keep you any longer though. I remember you mentioned that you had a guest here. Pray return to her whenever you like. There are a few of your papers I am taking the liberty of removing to look over at my leisure, and there was a little plan here—very interesting—but never mind that now. I am afraid we shall have to have another talk with you about the club, Mr. Leopold. By-the-by," he asked, a little abruptly, "what is this half bottle of whisky doing here, so tightly fastened down?"

"Sample bottle," Mr. Leopold replied, with a malicious gleam in his eye. "Pre-war stuff, Inspector. Have a sniff."

Bloor lifted it up and held it to the light. There was a sort of coating of frost on the outside of the bottle. His lips pursed themselves into a whistle.

"You won't mind my depriving you of this?" he asked. "We're a little short of pre-war stuff at the Yard."

This time I thought that Leopold would have a fit. He sprang for the bottle, but Bloor easily held him away.

"Look here, sir," he said quietly. "I am being very patient with you, but you know as well as I do that the man whom I have been compelled to arrest this evening was a dangerous criminal. He has been associated with this place for some time; so have you. I am obliged to take serious notice of that fact."

"Blast you, you're lying!" the little man shouted. "It's all camouflage about Cranford. You and your Simple Simon there, both of you—a couple of b——y liars, trying to be clever! I wish to God you'd opened the bottle and drank it!"

We left the room, the door of which my companion carefully locked on the outside.

"Aren't I going to be allowed in my own office?" Mr. Leopold asked angrily.

"After to-morrow," the Inspector promised. "Really, I am treating you very well. There are several documents there and some letters which demand a good deal of explanation. Until to-morrow morning." . . .

Evidently some whisper of impending trouble had spread, for the club was almost deserted as we passed out into the street.

"After all," I reminded Bloor, as we turned westward, "he is certain to have a spare key."

My companion smiled.

"Precisely," he said. "I am hoping that he has. There are several documents there which were quite inexplicable to me. I have left them all. To-morrow I shall see which he takes the trouble to destroy."

We walked homeward in a slight drizzle of rain. It must have been three o'clock. It was still pitch dark, and the streets were almost empty. I opened my front door with a latchkey.

"You'll come in and have a drink, Bloor," I invited.

"I certainly will, if you don't mind," he assented. "When one comes to think of it, for a member of the committee of a club where a good deal of wine is consumed, Mr. Leopold was inclined to be inhospitable. I'll admit that I am thirsty. I'm curious, too, to know if Joseph's last message meant anything."

I was staring at a note, in Smart's handwriting, which had been scrawled on a piece of paper and stuck up against the wall to attract my attention.

"A young lady waiting in my sitting-room!" I exclaimed. "Come along, Inspector."

We tore up the stairs, and I threw open the door of the sitting-room. My first sensation, looking across towards my easy-chair, was one of disappointment. There was certainly some one there, but it was not Beatrice. I turned on the switch and almost instantly that faint sensation of disappointment passed into one of overwhelming horror. I swayed upon my feet for a few seconds without any power of movement. Bloor, on the other hand, never lost his presence of mind for a moment. He literally sprang past me at the chair with a knife all ready in his hand. What we had to face in that brief but timeless interval is utterly indescribable. It has passed into the chamber of horrors in the dark corners of my memory. A sob was tearing at my throat before I was able to be of any assistance to Bloor. Rachel was lying back in the chair, bound with the cruellest of ropes. Her eyes were open, but glazed and set with terror, and every particle of colour had left her cheeks and lips. But the rest of her! The beautiful silky eyebrows of which she had been so proud—gone! Just flesh where they had been. Her silky blue black hair, every shred, every particle—gone. And the bald scalp! She had the appearance of some terrible mummy dragged from its grave by an over-curious civilisation. As we cut the rope, there were tears in my eyes and blasphemy on Bloor's lips. When the last one was severed, and she fell limp into my arms, I took her up like a baby and kissed her. Bloor was already at the telephone, talking rapidly. As soon as he had put back the receiver, he hurried to the sideboard, came back with a glass of brandy, and forced some between her blue lips. A card fell from her chest and lay unnoticed upon the floor. For a time I held her tightly, smoothing her arms, patting her cheeks, saying every wild thing I could think of. Slowly a little colour came back. She began to breathe naturally. Bloor, who had been watching, forced still more brandy between her lips.

"Let me die, please," she moaned. "They brought me a looking-glass. I want to die."

I forced a laugh. I don't know what sort of a sound it was.

"You foolish child!" I cried. "Why, you'll be dancing in a month."

"Number 10, Eldon Street," she faltered. "She's there with him. They'll have moved by now, unless you're quick. Number 10, Eldon Street. It's the other side of the river. Kill him—one of you, kill him, please."

"Eldon Street," Bloor repeated. "My men are within a hundred yards of there now."

He was at the telephone again, and she tried to creep away from me. I leaned over and turned out the light. She breathed a sigh of relief and curled up in my arms.

"Oh, my God!" she sobbed. "The agony! And I saw —I saw!—They must have followed me here. Your man let me in and said I must wait for you. I sat here, and I must have dozed, and when I woke up there were two of them, and there was a gag in my mouth."

I reached out my hand for the brandy. She swallowed some greedily.

"They've cut my legs too," she cried hysterically. "One

man said he was a surgeon. He said they wouldn't look pretty again for a long time. You'll kill Joseph? Promise me you'll kill him."

"I'll try," I vowed. "I killed a man before for less, and went to prison for it. They can hang me this time if they like."

She was crying quite naturally now, and I let her alone. Presently Bloor, who had hurried out of the room at the sound of an automobile horn below, came back.

"Carry her down, Major," he begged. "God, she's got both legs bandaged! I'll wrap her up in something."

He fetched a silk dressing gown from my room, and we carried her down the stairs, her long, thin arms wound fiercely round my neck. Outside was a police ambulance, and a nurse waiting on the pavement. She helped me to lay Rachel upon the stretcher and together they drove off, Rachel waving her hand feebly. . . .

Bloor and I once more mounted the stairs, and the first thing I did was to pick up from the floor the card which had been pinned upon her chest:

JOSEPH
AT HOME
10 Eldon Street,
E. C. 4.
INVITATION BY HAND
COME WHEN YOU PLEASE.

We mixed ourselves whiskies and sodas of which we were very much in need, and I threw open a window. Bloor filled his pipe, and walked up and down the room, smoking.

"A foul business, Major," he groaned. "The fellow's a devil incarnate. Number 10, Eldon Street—that's the district. My men are in there by now."

"A lot of good that will do us," I said bitterly. "You

don't suppose he's waiting there to hand out refreshments."

Bloor came over to my side and rested his hand upon my shoulder.

"Pull yourself together, Major," he enjoined kindly. "Of course, it was a shock. I don't mind admitting I felt a bit squeamish myself, but remember, in a month she'll be singing again as happily as ever. It was a brutal, foul thing to do, but—he killed the men who squealed. It's all in the game, Major. She'll be well in a month."

"That child—that poor child!" I muttered. "You are right, Bloor, of course, but what she must have suffered!"

"We are all put through it now and then. God, what's that! Thunder?"

There was a faint drizzling rain falling, but not a breath of wind. I had been looking over the Green Park towards the river, and it seemed to me that a sudden flash of light had shot across the sky. Even whilst we stared at it there was a low, rumbling sound like a peal of thunder. For a moment or two we remained silent and without comprehension.

"Thunder!" I exclaimed. "And lightning too! But it couldn't have been lightning."

Bloor was a moderate man, and he had only drunk half of his whisky and soda, but he went over to the sideboard and finished the remainder at a gulp. Then he turned round with one hand upon the back of a chair and watched the telephone. I stood at the window and listened. Nothing else happened, except that a dozen fire engines from Kensington came rushing past the Park. Then at last the telephone tinkled and I took off the spare receiver.

"Superintendent Cassells speaking."

"Inspector Bloor. Go ahead."

"I took a small force down to the assistance of our men and surrounded Eldon Street as directed. We broke into the house simultaneously from the back and front. A few minutes after we entered there was an explosion. There's very little left of the house, and the next two are on fire."

"Any of our men hurt?"

"P. C. Harrison killed. Sergeant Rush left arm blown off—on his way to hospital. A few burns amongst the rest. Nothing else."

"What was it? Dynamite?"

"A timed machine. Some of us heard the hissing. Harrison himself gave the alarm, and we just got clear. The house was deserted, sir, but it had been occupied within the last hour. Very luxuriously furnished. Heaps of books and three sets of private wireless—all destroyed."

"Keep the uninjured men down there," Bloor ordered. "Prepare a report and be in my room at ten o'clock to-morrow morning."

"Very good, sir."

Bloor hung up the receiver.

"If I can't get Joseph first," he said fiercely, "we'll smash the gang. We'll try Chicago methods. I'm going to treat them rough, and the old ladies of Whitehall can go to hell!"

I heard him with exultation. I knew perfectly well that night or day there would be no rest for me now until the day of reckoning between Joseph and myself had arrived.

CHAPTER XXX

I MADE my plans for the following morning, but they were all shattered before I had finished my breakfast. By eleven o'clock I was in the train, bound for Breezeley. Martin Hews' message allowed me no room for protestation or argument. I sent a note to Bloor, received an entirely favourable report from the hospital concerning Rachel, and started off on my dreary mission.

I seemed fated to see Breezeley Mansion under awesome conditions, and this morning was no exception. I hurried from the station and broke into a brisk run as soon as I had reached the old cinder path, for there was no doubt whatever as to what was coming. There was one narrow cleft of clear sky between two great masses of purple-black, sulphurous clouds. That shaft of light seemed, as I entered the gates to be descending upon the great house. It stood out unnaturally clear in its fantastic setting, the black clouds overhead and on either side—ridiculous but impressive: a house built without foundations, without background or foreground, such a building as might come to you in your dreams, only to pass away for ever before your opened eyes. . . . The first peal of thunder sounded as the door swung inwards before me; the second as I passed into the upstairs room. The lightning in zigzag flashes almost blinded me for a moment. Then the rumblings of fresh thunder began, and there was a moment's peace. The door was closed behind me and I advanced towards the table, but at my accustomed chair I stopped short in amazement. It seemed impossible that this cowering figure was the Martin Hews of my fears.

"Don't look at me as though I had gone out of my mind," he snapped, "and can't you realise that this house is a mass of electric wiring. We shall get no news, although I am expecting the most important telephone message of my life. We shall probably have all our alarms and communicating bells destroyed. Heaven knows what is going to happen to us."

There was a flash of lightning, another crash of thunder, and his head disappeared between his convulsively twitching hands. When he sat up, he was a pitiful sight.

"Owston," he moaned, "you are seeing me in one of my weakest moments. I hate thunder. I have hated it all my life. It brings evil. Already there is trouble. Look!"

His tiny forefinger shot out towards the wall. Immediately opposite him was a small blank space. I remembered well the pastel that had hung there—a girl's face, a copy of a great master. "The Madonna of Deptford" Martin Hews had once called her.

"What's happened to your pastel?" I demanded.

"Gone in the night," he replied, with a little shiver. "Not a bell rang, not a key was turned. The room is impregnable, held in the bonds of the greatest power on earth —electricity. Yet, look! It is gone in the night."

I glanced around the room.

"One never knows who is listening here," I hesitated.

He leaned over the table and touched a switch.

"The place is soundproof now," he confided. "What was it you wanted to say?"

"Only something you'll probably turn me out of the house for," I answered. "I don't trust Minchin."

A week ago I knew very well how such a statement from me would have been received. Now he sat huddled up, his chin upon his chest, his arms resting upon the table, the fingers of both hands twitching as though with an ague. The cruel glitter had gone from his eyes. Fear lurked in their depths.

"You too," he muttered. "Beatrice said the same thing, and Minchin is the only other one who knows—Beatrice a prisoner in the hands of my enemy, and Minchin—"

His eyes wandered back to the wall. He looked at that blank space as though he saw there the writing of fate. As he gazed, the lightning once more filled the room, and the thunder shook the house. His eyes seemed to grow large, like those of a frightened child. His fingers twitched more and more convulsively. His cheeks seemed to be contracted. It was as though he were losing flesh visibly. For the first time in my life I began to feel towards him as towards a human being.

"Have you had any trouble with Minchin, sir?" I asked.

"Yes," he acknowledged reluctantly. "He wants to buy a cottage over beyond Southend and go there for week-ends. He wants to leave me for two days a week."

"Well, why not?" I questioned. "He could train another valet, couldn't he, sir, to take his place?"

Martin Hews shivered. He looked at me as though I had spoken sacrilege and merely waved my suggestion away as something unthinkable, unworthy of consideration. The thunder muttered again, this time more distant. A great relief began to creep into his face.

"That's farther away," he exclaimed. "It's going. It's lasted long enough for a thunderstorm. Look out of the northern window, Owston. Tell me which way the clouds are moving?"

I looked across the soggy waste of land upon which the blinding rain was spitting, across the Thames to the nebulous country beyond.

"The storm is over," I reported. "The clouds are all passing southwards, and the rain has come."

He was a different man when I turned back into the room. He pointed to the cupboard let into the panel between two bookcases.

"Open it," he directed. "There is just a button to press."

I obeyed him. Inside was that wonderful collection of bottles, all sizes and all shapes, liqueurs I had never heard of, and a row of Venetian glass.

"Give me some brandy," he demanded. "Choose something for yourself."

I gave him the brandy he asked for and helped myself from a bottle of light-coloured Italian liqueur which I had never before seen out of the country, and which tasted as the herbs on the Campagna smell.

"I've had a bad time, Owston," my employer confessed slowly. "It is past. Is there news?"

"None of Miss Essiter, I am sorry to say," I told him, "and bad news of Rachel."

He indulged in a little grimace.

"Do you mean that my scheme failed?"

"Utterly. I suppose the idea was sound, brutal though it was. I found her in my rooms last night, with her hair all cut off, damaged and mutilated, half conscious. She just had strength to murmur 'Number 10, Eldon Street' before she was taken to the hospital. Number 10 Eldon Street was raided in a quarter of an hour, and the house was blown up by an infernal machine directly the police got inside."

"That was Joseph?" he gasped.

"Joseph beyond a doubt," I answered. "He had been there. So, I believe, had your niece. Now, God knows where they are!"

Martin Hews finished his brandy and swung out into the room.

"Throw up the north window," he ordered.

I did as he bade me and, side by side, we looked out towards the City, he in his chair, and I standing close by. His outstretched forefinger followed the course of the great turgid streak of river as it crept forward and was lost in the masses of ugly buildings which clung to its banks. Even the torrents of rain had not cleansed the air of the lowering smoke. Unabashed, those myriads of chimney stacks continued their discolouring orgy of smuts and tiny cinders. It was one of the dreariest outlooks upon which a man could gaze, fading away at last into a black jungle of obscurity.

"She is there somewhere," he declared. "Joseph's more at home in the East End, for all his struggles to get out of it. It's there I want him run to earth, hemmed in, showing his teeth for the last bite. What's the next move, Major?"

"Scotland Yard has got the gang pretty well surrounded, sir," I told him. "They are going for them at once—perhaps to-night. That's why Joseph didn't mind so much his East End hiding places being given away. Inspector Bloor's been working cautiously, but street by street, house by house almost, he's got them where he wants them. They are cornered down there, and Joseph knows it."

Martin Hews looked out at the great gaunt wilderness of factories, the streets of smoke-stained human habitations. Much of the strength was back in his face. His eyes glistened with hate.

"If I were a man like others," he muttered, "I'd make myself like one of these accursed wolves. I'd creep from street to street, from hiding place to hiding place; I'd beg and steal and lie; I'd go to prison and come out again.

I'd fight, I'd crawl on my belly until I found him. I'd crawl on until I got nearer and nearer, until I could spit death into his heart."

"And I'd do the same if I could," I declared passionately. "Look at me—six feet three, and with, as Bloor tells me, a clumsy, British face. I can't make up even for amateur theatricals, I can't act well enough to play the footman. What chance would I have in the slums? I had to give my word to Bloor to keep away from there before he would even talk to me."

"Pull down the blind," my employer bade me. "I have seen enough."

He made his way back to his place, guiding his chair still with that unerring and marvellous skill. On his way he pressed a button in the wall. The whole place was lit at one touch with soft, lambent lights. One of the telephones on his desk tinkled gently. I obeyed his gesture, took up the receiver and listened.

"Isaacs is speaking from Grafton Street—urgent, he says," I announced.

There was a sparkle in Martin Hews' hard round eyes as he took the receiver from me, a sparkle which immediately afterwards became a blaze. His expression as he bent over the instrument was almost ecstatic.

"Listen, Isaacs," he said, when he had heard all the other had to recount, "with this, I have finished. You can go back to your beloved Hungary, and you shall take your fortune with you. You succeed this time, and you need make no further effort. I mean it. The time has come. Succeed, Isaacs, and you are rid of your burden."

There was excitement at the other end of the wire. I could tell that, though my employer's answers grew cooler all the time.

"In two hours," he announced, "Owston will be with

you. He is just the man you want for this job. You will then act. Don't hesitate. To-night."

He leaned back in his chair, and I stared at him wonderingly. Never, I thought, though I lived with him for a lifetime, should I understand this man and the things which passed through his mind. As he looked across at me, his eyes, so expressionless as a rule, were filled at one instant with the wistful light of vision; the next he was a child—a frankly excited, tremulous child.

"Owston," he declared, "for a few minutes the sterner things of life are to be forgotten. You are not fashioned of the stuff from which men of the inner understanding are made, and words alone will not suffice. Come with me."

He wheeled his chair to a distant corner of the room and stopped against the wall. For a second he was lost in what might have been a prayer, but it was evidently a mechanical effort of memory. Then he struck the panelling a number of blows with the tip of his third finger, after the manner of one transmitting a signal by Morse. Presently there was a little click. He smiled. The panel rolled upward, disclosing a miniature safe let into the wall. With a key attached to a gold bracelet underneath his left cuff, he opened it and drew out another bunch of keys—three in number.

"Follow me," he directed.

The first key, with the help of an electric button, unlocked the door close to us, which I had never seen used. We passed into a corridor, dimly lit because it was windowless. Then my guide opened another door, and we were in a gallery which must have run the whole length of the northward 'L' of the house. He touched a knob in one of the panels, and lights flamed out from the ceiling and walls. I followed him farther into the room, and a sense of wonder such as I had never felt before in all my life kept me tongue-tied and motionless.

CHAPTER XXXI

I HAD once visited what they told me was the most wonderful bazaar in Cairo, where, in an underground room, I had suddenly been confronted with the accumulated *objets d'art* of a great mercantile house, added to month by month from every quarter of the world, and displayed in that limited space with a reckless prodigality which had in it something almost insolent. This treasure house of Martin Hews was in a way reminiscent of that visit, but there was everywhere apparent a greater and finer sense of restraint; one could tell that an almost passionate love had gone to the arrangement of its sacred contents. The walls were of dark green damask, and they were covered with pictures and engravings, interrupted here and there with cabinets, mostly Chinese and Japanese lacquer work, so that not one inch of space remained but seemed to claim its treasure, yet every treasure appeared to be in the one spot and amidst the surroundings for which it had been destined. Almost meeting mine, on the wall opposite, were the placid brown eyes of a Madonna whose call to life even I knew, must have been by consecrated fingers, and there, a few feet away from me, his mouth open, teeth agleam, burning for slaughter, was a great bronze statue which had once guarded a holy temple. I walked a little farther into the room, Martin Hews in his chair moving noiselessly by my side. I had no words, but it seemed to me that he approved my silence.

"Here you learn, if you have the wit to discern it, my young friend," he said, "the secret—the major secret—

the passion of my life. Man is born either a hunter, a lover, or a treasure seeker. Perhaps fortunately for me," he added, a little bitterly, "I was born amongst the latter. Forty years of care and toil, danger and perseverance, besides the expenditure of a great fortune, have brought me these. Every one has come to me with a thrill, every one has brought me its meed of joy. What matter, I think, sometimes, if I die to-morrow? I shall have known happiness such as few others are capable of feeling, and if I fear death, Owston—and there are times when I shrink from it—it is not because there is anything in life itself which calls or holds! it is the leaving these. The Madonna who smiles at you there, from whom day by day you could learn a new lesson of beauty, was painted in 1519 only a square away from where Andrea del Sarto was sweating out his life and powers to pay the debts of his wife's lovers. It is by Raphael. Ah, you know enough to start! You recognise it perhaps. Yes, it was stolen, I admit. It was stolen first from Versailles in the time of the Revolution, and afterwards from the Pizzio Collection. Perhaps you recognise my two Greuzes, that Claude Monet the cleverest detectives in London and Paris searched for in vain. See the Golden Horn and Temple of Thaïs. Look at that Buddha. Eleven men were killed in the attempt to regain that. The scroll in that basket of gold with the jade sides is part of the manuscript of Confucius, traced by his own hands. Look at the parchment. We lived in caves long after that was fashioned. . . . What do you love best? Pictures, bronzes, jade, tapestry? Tell me, and I'll show you something that the world cannot match. . . . Pictures," he went on, interpreting my half-muttered reply. "Good. Here is variety for you. You see that panel of yellow satinwood? Look at the images. The dairy maid in gala costume, the fine lady in her court dress, the gallant who dances with her, the children, the steps covered with roses. Look at it well, my young friend. You have never seen the like before. You may never see it again. That is Watteau's *chef d'œuvre*. He started it for his lonely love, waiting for him in Normandy whilst he disported himself at Court. It was finished for a queen, paid for, they say, with her love, but who knows? . . . Pictures! You are right, perhaps. There is something stupendous about the slow creeping into life of one of those great paintings which the gods of the Renaissance gave to the world. Something immortal too, mind you, my young friend. The canvas may perish, the men whose eyes have been gladdened by it crumble into dust, but it has been, and its influence is there throughout all future generations. My only religion, Owston. Nothing in which there has been a single gleam of inspiration can die. Pictures! . . . That landscape of Turner's. Look at the solemnity of the trees, look at that shaft of light that comes from what seems to be an Italian background, to shed that unearthly illumination upon the open country. That was stolen, Owston— stolen from the castle of an English nobleman fourteen years ago. What a fuss there was! It has all died out now. Look at the picture by its side, the river, the brooding mists, and those spectral lights glimpsing down from the row of buildings there. A Turner too. One of his latest. They say if he'd kept on like that and lived a dozen years longer, he'd have founded a new school. Whistler would have been an interpreter instead of a prophet. . . . More pictures? Well, next to it, look—a Gainsborough. Forty-five thousand guineas they asked me for that at Christie's when a famous duke found that to buy diamonds enough for his new mistress he must give pictures. I didn't buy it, Owston. It was Donkin's first exploit. Cut from the frame it was, as neatly as though by electricity. It hung here six weeks after they had refused my cheque

at Christie's for forty thousand guineas. . . . China?
No, you know nothing about china, I can see. Yet your
eye may be pleased with colouring and shape. It is useless for you to handle it. Texture would mean nothing to
you. Look at the collection in that cabinet. Look at the
rose pink around that bowl. China! There are pieces here
which men might commit murder for. There are many
pieces here, as a matter of fact," he went on, "which have
cost men their lives to steal or to protect. . . . Now you
know more of me than most men. This is my Temple.
This is the pool into which I have emptied my life and
soul. Men have robbed or stolen, or killed for love or
jealousy or power. I for what you see. Leave me here,
Owston. Walk around the room and stare. Give thanks to
the Unknown for what you see that speaks to you.
Abase yourself for the ignorance which leaves you merely
gaping and marvelling. Leave me alone until I call you."
    It is not too much to say that I was stricken with some-
thing like awe. I left him carefully manœuvring his chair
so that the light fell upon the picture of a girl standing
on the parapet of a castle looking down across a plain
to a distant city. It was an unknown Leonardo da Vinci,
I learned afterwards. The figure of the girl was scarcely
even defined, yet one felt somehow the significance and
wonder of it underneath those loose garments, the message of the pinched face, the pleading air; the steadfast
eyes haunted me so that more than once I turned back in
my restless wanderings. I walked along the carpeted passage much as though I were wandering in some sanctuary.
Actual life seemed to have fallen away. I was the victim
of a species of enchantment. Ignorant though I was, thrill
after thrill assailed me, whether it was from the full red
lips of an ancestress, perhaps, of Carmen, or from the
thinner, more passionately sensitive mouth of a great
Italian lady in her Renaissance robes and head-dress. A

statuette almost took my breath away—a shrieking
figure of despair, her robes torn to shreds, borne into
captivity by a giant on horseback, a giant with flaming
eyes, a horse whose muscles swelled under the strain, the
panting breath from whose open nostrils you could almost
hear mingled with that agonised cry of the woman. . . .
There was a model of a ship which made me look for the
sea underneath, a cavalier whose eyes mocked mine to
combat, a Burmese woman, slim and alluring, modelled,
it seemed to me, from solid gold, holding out her long,
delicate arms and calling to me through the obscurity
of her oval eyes. . . . An unimaginative man, I was
amazed at myself that day, for a sudden queer idea seized
me, bringing with it a wave almost of terror. To me they
were all alive, these seducing, mocking, smiling women,
these defiant, angry, lustful men. From canvas, from
metal, from fancy scroll, they seemed to take their place
in that stormy afternoon, endowed with a vivid yet
ghostly life from a world in which they had never breathed.
I stepped almost hastily away from a Chinese idol, just
as Martin Hews glided silently to my side.

"Come," he enjoined. "Less than a dozen men before
you in twelve years have crossed this threshold."

We passed out together. He locked the doors and replaced the keys. Silently he made his way back to his
place before the desk and waved me to my chair. He looked
at me keenly, and what he saw seemed to please him. Away
from his enchanted chamber, his strange characteristics,
his childishness, his conceit, began to reassert themselves.
There was patronage in his tone when he spoke to me.

"I will explain to you, Owston, why even an unemo-
tional person like yourself feels as you do," he said.
"You may walk through any art gallery, any museum,
any private collection in the world, and, mingled with
the true and beautiful, you will find a leaven of only su-

perficially pleasing and the counterfeit. Therefore your fancy is perhaps a little excited, but you remain normal. To-day you have been in one of the great treasure houses of the world, Owston, brought together by perhaps the greatest connoisseur, the greatest artist in selection the world has ever known. Not one of the treasures you have seen, not one picture, not one statue, not one piece of carving, one fragment of china, is other than the really true expression of its maker's heart. Lovingly and carefully, I have slaved, selected, and bought, and because a mistake is impossible to me, my treasure house is a different treasure house to any other. It is a treasure house of truth."

It seemed strange to come down to earth again and talk in the language of the police courts, but I forced myself to do it.

"You called it a treasure house of truth," I remarked, "yet half its contents are stolen."

"Three quarters of them," he admitted calmly. "They were stolen because money could not buy them. That does not affect their sublimity one iota. The treasures of the world have always been amassed by rapine, fire and massacre."

"But aren't you afraid of discovery?"

"I have no great fear," he assured me. "I will tell you why. Nearly all the thefts committed in these sordid days are thefts of an article for purposes of gain. That article must be resold before the robber reaps his reward, and it is in the selling that the great danger of the proceeding arises. My treasures have been stolen for my solitary joy, stolen and locked away. The police of the world have searched for years for some of these, my most precious belongings, but they have searched in the bargain houses, they have searched in the dealers' shops of Amsterdam, London, Paris and New York. They have

searched by watching a likely purchaser and a likely
vendor—and they have searched in vain. When anything
is stolen for me, it is off the market for my lifetime."

"The contents of that room must be enormously valuable," I ventured.

He smiled in almost ludicrously patronising fashion.

"Valuable!" he repeated. "Well, I suppose that is what
occurs to the ordinary human being like yourself, Owston.
Valuable! Pounds, shillings and pence! Have you ever
asked yourself, young man, what is the value of an hour's
pure joy, what is the value of a year's, a month's happiness, what is the value of a flood of sweet thoughts let
into your brain by a divine vision? Valuable! Yes, I suppose your world looks at it like that. Well, it would tax
any museum to buy my treasures. When I am dead," he
added, with an unpleasant smile, "what a hullabaloo! All
the world coming to claim its own. A hundred laws in
conflict! Ah, well! I may plan a great surprise yet."

He sat for a moment, scowling, his underlip thrust out.
The mention of death at any time always threw him into
a sort of terror. It was the first time I had ever heard
him breathe the word himself.

"Pull down the blind of your memory, Owston," he continued, a little abruptly. "What I have shown you, I
have shown you on impulse. I don't know why. I never
shall know. Before you, Isaacs, a Cardinal of Rome, a
prince who is now a sovereign, and an artist dying partly
of consumption, partly of starvation, are the only Euro-
peans who have seen that room as you have seen it.
Minchin is with me sometimes if there is work to be done,
but when he is there, I light it only in sections."

"I am very honoured, sir," I told him, "but frankly I
am inclined to regret—"

"So you should," he interrupted approvingly. "You
have just sufficient perceptions to enable you to realise

that you have been in touch with something greater than any ordinary event of your everyday life. You will be uneasy and restless for weeks, until the commonplace world regains its hold upon you. I quite understand it. I didn't take you there out of kindness. I can imagine you lying awake at nights haunted by the call of my terrified princess, tortured by the thought that you could not tear her from the ogre on horseback and take her into your own arms. Never mind, my young friend. It is good for you to have your level march through life disturbed sometimes. I shall give you something new to distract your mind. Have you ever killed a Chinaman, Owston?"

"Never to my knowledge, sir," I replied. "I once hit one very hard in a gambling den at San Francisco."

"If by killing the Chinaman you are going to see to-night you could get possession of what I want," Martin Hews sighed, "the affair would be easy enough. Mr. Tul-Kak is too clever for that, though. In a sense, I am glad that he is. If there were killing to be done, Joseph might be there ahead of me. There is this difference between Joseph and myself. He pays when he must—that is very seldom indeed; if I want anything badly enough, I don't care whether it comes to me through payment, theft or murder. In this case, it will have, I think, to be payment. Tul-Kak is a wise man. He wants a great price, but he prefers to deal with me. I have told Isaacs that he can offer five hundred thousand pounds—a quarter of my remaining fortune, Owston—for the One-eyed Buddha."

"For the what?" I gasped.

Martin Hews smiled patiently.

"You are really very, very ignorant, Owston," he deplored. "However, I suppose I must continue to be your instructor. From time immemorial there has been not exactly a doubt, but a superstition, handed down through

all the priests of Asia, with regard to the personality
of their great god. How it came about, no one can tell,
because even in the remote ages no one dared to do more
than whisper such a thing. Nevertheless, the superstition
has lived for over a thousand years that the great
Buddha, the God of the East, had only one eye. For the
last few centuries, coincidentally with this superstition,
one has heard vague rumours of a small white jade
Buddha, watched in secret by the head priests only of a
temple in Thibet—a Buddha with only one eye. Ex-
plorers and curio dealers have lost their lives many a
time seeking for this temple, seeking for this Buddha. How
it came into India, I don't know, but it is certain that a
monk of Thibet, who was reputed to be the holiest man
in the city, left his country and travelled across the
mountains to China with the Buddha in his possession.
He paid for it with his life. Four of its successive owners
have died. Tul-Kak himself has had more than one marvellous escape. I sent Isaacs to India the year before last,
but he had only to open his mouth and his life was in
danger. I had men haunting the secret places of Rangoon,
where it was at one time reported that the statue had
been hidden, but Isaacs could make no progress, probably because he is a Jew, and in time he was forced to
leave the country in disguise. Tul-Kak has been a year
waiting for an opportunity to travel to London, and
eventually managed to pass in the suite of the returning
Viceroy. He reached London this morning. To-night, at
eleven o'clock, you and Isaacs are to see him in the Milan
Court. From what I hear of the man, he is badly frightened and only too anxious to sell quickly. Whether he
will get away with the money is another matter. You had
better go to Isaacs' shop in Grafton Street at about a
quarter to eleven. You will go armed, of course, for I
warn you that I don't for a moment believe that the

Buddha will be allowed to change hands again without a fight."

"What are we to do with it when we have it?" I asked.

"Isaacs has instructions. He has a solid iron coffer in which you will place it, and for the night it will remain in the hotel safe. I am a believer in the obvious places at times, and I think the vaults of the Milan Hotel are as safe as anywhere in the world. Don't be persuaded to try and hide it anywhere else. The vaults at the Milan Hotel. I will communicate with the manager, Mr. Bretzgel, and he will be expecting you."

"I understand."

"With regard to payment," he continued, "Tul-Kak has kept his mouth closed. Isaacs would bargain. He does not realise the greatness of this occasion. I have only one price, but it is a price which Tul-Kak will accept."

From his left-hand drawer he drew out a cheque book, filled in a form, placed it in an envelope, and handed it to me.

"Look at it," he enjoined, with a smile of vanity. "You have seen nothing like that before, Major. You'll see nothing like it again."

I drew the cheque from the envelope. It was there, plainly written in Martin Hews' beautiful copperplate hand:

Pay to the order of Tul-Kak, or Bearer,
The sum of five hundred thousand pounds sterling.

"Five hundred thousand pounds," I marvelled, "for one small statue!"

He waved his tiny hand with a gesture of supreme disdain.

"The money is nothing," he declared, "but the statue—"

He broke off. His eyes were half closed, his tone lapsed into one of ecstasy.

"With it I shall close my collection. I shall have finished. There is nothing more that I covet. I shall double my guard here and dig myself in for the remainder of my life. You know the feel of jade?"

"Not very well, sir," I admitted.

"Snow-white jade, without a flaw, two thousand years old," he murmured rapturously. "What a joy to touch, to feel, to handle!"

He sat for a few minutes in what seemed to be a state of trance. Then he rang the bell, and presently Minchin appeared.

"See that Major Owston has some lunch, Minchin," he directed, "and order a car to take him to the station."

He dismissed me brusquely, almost discourteously. An hour later, I was driven to the station through the muddy, deserted lane, with its swollen dykes and puddles of rain water standing about after the storm. The train was late, and I walked up and down the solitary platform, still a little dazed, with the experience I had gone through. It was not until after I had started for London alone in a smoky and uncomfortable first-class carriage that I realised that I was in for a new adventure, and that I was carrying Martin Hews' cheque for half a million pounds in my pocket.

CHAPTER XXXII

I FOUND a car waiting outside my rooms, and Bloor, as nearly excited as I had ever seen him, in my easy-chair.

"Good evening, Major," he greeted me. "I had a few minutes to spare, and I thought I'd look in and tell you the news. We're for it to-night."

"The raid?"

He nodded.

"Information has been coming in fast and furious," he confided. "Let me tell you this first though. We are out of one of our troubles. We got the Cheapside burglars at luncheon time. A fair catch it was, too."

"Good work!" I exclaimed heartily. "Whereabouts?"

"We got them in a restaurant down by Liverpool Street. No signs of a squeal from them, but one of our men caught Rogers—that's the ringleader of the three —trying to swallow a piece of paper. It was a note the waiter had just brought in. Evidently one of their places of call. Can't tell you what was in the note, but it means that things are moving. Then the men I planted down Shoreditch way have been sending messages up, one by one. They are all agreed the gang's full strength is concentrated in a cramped radius of a few hundred yards."

"But what about Joseph?" I asked anxiously.

"It's no good waiting forever," Bloor pointed out. "When Joseph left Eldon Street, he left the neighbourhood altogether, and we haven't a line on him yet. All the same, if we can break the gang, he'll never again be the man he was. Just cast your eye on this plan."

He spread one out upon the table, and I looked over his shoulder.

"It's a nasty district," he explained, "and the danger is that directly we're known to be there, they'll slip away from the further houses and either get us on the flanks, if they want to fight, or creep away one by one to the lodging houses by the river, which are the very devil to search. We'll have to take our chances. Here's the river, you see, and along there are the wharves. We've got the firm who own the big yards to close their iron gates, so there's no getting past those, and we've a couple of police boats patrolling the river. This row of houses here is called Tanner's Cottages, and in number 3 we know that Clooney is hiding, the man who's wanted for that bank business. That will give us something to start on. We shall open up there looking for him, and down behind, in this corner, Patt Risewell was seen yesterday sneaking out after dark to the pub there. We want him pretty badly too. The road on the other side is Fellmongers' Lane—nearly the worst spot in London. We're going to comb that out house by house with picked men who are used to handling a gun. We could have stirred things up there before, but we decided to wait until we could make the big noise, and I'm glad we did. Getting the Cheapside burglars has set our hands free. The Chief doesn't mind so much now what we do."

"Supposing they won't come out?" I suggested. "Supposing they start the Sidney Street business again?"

"So much the better," Bloor declared. "We are quite ready for that. I have an armoured car we've borrowed down at London Bridge Station now, covered up. That can be on the spot in ten minutes. We sha'n't rush it. They can take their time. These blocks of cottages have only two possible ways of exit, and we're ready for them either end. We may lose a few men, but we must be prepared for that. I've got the Chief to let me take most of them in plain clothes. That will give them a better chance. It would be like trailing our lobster backs over the Boer Mountains to leave a uniformed policeman at the corner of the street. There will be none of that this time. We shall give them a fair do. Every one who will come out unarmed and can prove himself the next morning to be an ordinary citizen, we sha'n't interfere with. Every one who doesn't come out is one of Joseph's gang, and Joseph's gang are going to pay for it this time, by God!"

"What time is the line-up?" I enquired.

"Not too early. I am sending my men down two or three at a time, all scattered around, and they are closing in as the clock strikes twelve. I don't want the slightest sign of anything unusual until then."

I drew a sigh of relief. By midnight, if all went well, I should probably be a free man.

"I'm in it, of course?" I asked.

Bloor appeared doubtful.

"You're a bit of a marked man, you know," he reminded me. "You made yourself very conspicuous and obnoxious to the gang down at Breezeley. Then, if by any chance Joseph gets to know of the fighting and comes down to help, he'll take jolly good care that you're put out of the way."

"If there was any chance of Joseph being there," I told him savagely, "it would take all Scotland Yard to keep me away. I'll be frank with you, Bloor. I've got another job on first, but the moment that's over, I'm for the East End. I know where to find you, and I hope I'll hear the guns popping when I come."

"You'll stick to me then," he stipulated. "I don't want any of my fellows to throw their lives away to-night, and I certainly don't want anything to happen to you. Besides the men I've told you about, I'm taking a hundred constables off the streets as special reserves. Frankly, I'd rather they closed in and made a siege of it. We can wait, whereas they can't. Of course, if they come out into the open, then it must be a fight. We're not afraid of that, but I hate to sacrifice good men for such scum."

We drank the cocktails which Smart presently produced and discussed from every point of view the coming enterprise. Presentiments as a rule are not amongst my obsessions, but I was surprised to find a curious wave of apprehension damping the ardour with which, in an ordinary way, I should have looked forward to such an evening.

"You're thoughtful, Major," Bloor observed, peering at me from underneath his eyelids.

I shrugged my shoulders.

"Any news from the hospital?" I asked.

"Doing excellently," Bloor reported. "Doesn't want to see anyone for a week or two. The doctor promises she'll be all right by then."

I helped myself to another cocktail.

"Bloor," I reminded him, "this is a big show that you've taken on to-night."

"It was always going to be a big show that finished Joseph," he remarked grimly.

"I wonder! You'll think I'm a dunderhead, I know, Bloor, and I dare say I am in many ways, but I've got a queer feeling about this evening."

"Out with it," he begged. "I've rather a sympathy for presentiments."

"Don't you think," I suggested, "that Joseph has made it a little too easy for you? Remember, he's never brought his whole gang together before. You've come across fragments of it in Kensington, fragments in Bermondsey, fragments in Camberwell or at Tufnell Hill, some in the

Bethnal Green Road, and others in Kentish Town. Why do you think he's brought them all together like this? Not for you just to pounce upon and destroy. I don't understand it, and that's a fact."

Bloor smoked on stolidly for a moment or two.

"I see your point of view," he admitted, "but look here, Major. The lads are there, and we want them. I don't see how he can trap us. He hasn't a very high opinion of our intelligence, remember, as he has proved more than once. Perhaps he thinks I am fool enough to try and bring Jo Clooney and Risewell in with a dozen men behind me. We're not falling into any booby trap of that sort. The men we want are there, and I'm going after them with two to one in numbers on our side. What Joseph's idea is in bringing them all together like this I'll admit I can't imagine, but at the same time, knowing they are there, we can't be such fools as to leave them alone. There's no mining, or anything of that sort, I can promise you. There's nothing going on there we haven't heard about."

He rose to his feet. I glanced at the clock and held out my hand.

"Well, here's good luck to both of us," I said, as he prepared to take his leave. "And, Bloor, I don't mind having a small bet with you?"

"What's that?" he enquired, looking back from the door.

"I bet you a bottle of the best," I told him, "that I see Joseph before you do."

"Easy drinking," he laughed. "I'm on!"

CHAPTER XXXIII

I FOUND Mr. Isaacs waiting for me outside his establishment in Grafton Street, a strange, gaunt figure in his unusually long overcoat and black slouch hat. He was carrying a brown paper parcel under his arm, which I rightly guessed to be the iron coffer.

"Well, young man," he said, eyeing me approvingly, "you are sent for my protection. You look strong, though your habits may be bad. Will you begin by carrying this coffer? You will find it heavy."

I took it from him, and a moment later his motor car arrived.

"As to those bad habits of mine," I begged, as we took our seats, "don't believe all you read in the papers. Are we up against Joseph, do you think, in this little enterprise of ours? Shall we get the One-eyed Buddha, or do you imagine he has been before us?"

Isaacs chuckled.

"I do not worry. The statuette, even though it is the world's wonder, has not the value which Joseph wants. I think we buy that statuette, all right. How much money have you?"

"More than I usually carry about with me," I admitted. "I have a draft for five hundred thousand pounds."

"I buy for less than that," he declared contemptuously. "I told our friend already over the telephone that I knew of another One-eyed Buddha."

"What did he say?" I enquired.

"The telephone girl she cut him off," Isaacs confided. "He spoke bad words. Never mind, it will do him
good."

We arrived at the Milan punctually at eleven o'clock,
but we were not allowed to ascend at once to Mr. Tul-
Kak's apartment. The concierge invited us to take seats
in the little lounge whilst he sent a special messenger
upstairs. Some impulse—I am not naturally a curious
person—prompted me to leave my comfortable easy-
chair and look through the glass partition into the Grillroom. Within a few yards of me, at a table alone, apparently at the commencement of his meal, sat Mr.
X. . . .

He might almost have been expecting me, so unruffled was his composure, so easy that faint, sardonic smile.
I set myself passionately to the task of scrutinising the
man with all the intentness of which I was capable. I
called into being all my powers of perception. His
smoothly brushed black-grey hair looked natural enough.
I traced the wrinkles on his high forehead. I took note of
the small ears, thinly cut nose, lips straight and hard,
yet wonderfully mobile. I traced that upward line of his
mouth which I honestly believe was the only natural one
upon his face, and I appreciated to the full the square,
firm chin. From a sculptor's point of view, tabulating his
features one by one, the man should have been good-
looking. Studying him as I studied him then, in what I
believe was almost a moment of revelation, it seemed to
me that there was a curious lack of vital qualities, even
in his best features. It was like the sculptor's plaster
cast of a face, rather than the face itself, but more than
ever, as I stood there looking, the obstinate conviction
gathered strength in my mind that I was indeed looking
into the face of my enemy.

I turned away and strolled over to where Isaacs was

sitting. My fingers, as I tried to light a cigarette, were shaking. My voice was scarcely steady.

"Tell me, Mr. Isaacs," I asked, "have you ever seen Joseph?"

He looked at me earnestly from under his great bushy eyebrows.

"Why that question at this moment, Major Owston?"

"Because the man whom I believe to be Joseph is seated in the Grillroom just inside there, two tables from the glass partition."

Isaacs rose from his chair and walked towards the place which I had vacated. He stood there, a tall, patriarchal figure, looking into the room with no effort at casual observation, steadily, almost severely. When he came back, his eyes seemed to have sunk a little farther into his head. He had lost something of his fine poise. I had no time then, however, to ask him a single question. A tall and solemn Chinaman, having the air of an ambassador, was approaching us. He bowed to each in turn.

"Mr. Tul-Kak very glad to see you," he announced. "Please to come this way."

We mounted in the lift to the fourth floor, traversed the long corridor, and paused before the door of the end suite of rooms. Outside, another Chinaman was standing, less ceremoniously dressed, and a most ferocious-looking fellow. The door was opened in response to our ring, by an Englishman who looked very like a police sergeant in mufti.

"This way, gentlemen," he invited, throwing open the door of the sitting-room.

Mr. Tul-Kak, who had been standing with his back to the window, bowed formally and advanced. He was a small, sallow-faced man, carefully dressed in European clothes. He waved us to chairs.

"I am Tul-Kak," he said, as soon as we had disposed of ourselves, and our guide had taken up a position facing the door. "I have with me the treasure. With which of you do I talk?"

"I am the dealer," Isaacs replied. "Let me see your treasure."

Tul-Kak moved to the sideboard, upon which was standing what I had thought at first sight to be an ebony tea caddy, but which I now saw was a very wonderful oriental casket. There were three locks to it, each one of which Tul-Kak opened with a separate key. Inside was a lining of deep violet plush, and in the middle of it, reclining there with its one eye fixed upon the ceiling, was the statuette. Tul-Kak went down on his knees for a moment and bowed his head. Then he rose up, took the statuette reverently from its place, laid it in the palms of his hands, and brought it over to Isaacs.

"Two thousand years," he confided, in a voice which trembled slightly, "have passed, and no man's hands, save the Priests of the Inner Order, have touched it. Millions of worshippers have bent the knee at a distance and passed on. Now the days of faith are finished. If curses could kill, I am a dead man already, and as it is the knives of thousands are sharpened for my life. But I, Tul-Kak, am a plain merchant, although my forefathers were priests. Take the One-eyed Buddha into your hands, Isaacs, the dealer, and buy or return."

Isaacs' long fingers travelled over the statuette, not with the loving joy of his master's, perhaps, but with the keen, close caress of the connoisseur. He looked down at it through his horn-rimmed eyeglass, turning it this way and that. I fancied that he was seeking some opportunity for criticism and failing to find it. He passed it to me, and, strangely enough, I felt a spark of almost the same reverence as had inspired Tul-Kak. It lay in my hands, its surface soft as velvet, spotlessly and perfectly white, and all the years that had passed since first its divine outline had crept into being seemed only to have lent beauty to the form, and joy to the touch. Yet as I looked at it, I felt a queer sense of trouble. The sightless eye met mine for a minute. It seemed to me there was almost a threat in its cold stare and in the curve of the mouth. I handed it back.

"It is wonderful," I murmured.

"You buy?" Tul-Kak asked Isaacs.

"I buy for my master if between us we can afford."

"I do not know that word," was the frigid rejoinder. "It is strange to me. You buy—you pay me five hundred thousand pounds."

Isaacs' shudder was a very real one. I think that the bare idea of any one parting with such a sum terrified him.

"God of my fathers!" he exclaimed. "There is nothing upon this earth worth five hundred thousand pounds. It is the price of a throne."

"It is the price of my statuette," Tul-Kak reiterated.

Isaacs made a motion to take up his hat. Tul-Kak turned to the man who had received us downstairs.

"You will telephone," he directed, "to number—"

Then I, in my great stupidity, made one of the worst of breaks. I was afraid that I saw the statuette slipping away, and I interrupted, without waiting to hear the number.

"Mr. Isaacs forgets," I said eagerly, "that our friend does not bargain. Neither, in this instance, does Mr. Martin Hews. Here is a draft upon the Bank of England for five hundred thousand pounds."

I laid it upon the table. Isaacs rocked back and forth, seemingly on the point of bursting into tears. It was business upon a scale altogether beyond him.

"The statue is sold," Tul-Kak announced calmly, as he picked up the draft and thrust it into his pocket. "There must be no writing pass. You have brought a coffer?"

I tore the brown paper from the iron box. The statuette was placed first in its own cabinet, then inside the coffer and secured.

"Where do you go with that?" its vendor asked. "No longer is mine the care, but the buyer of the Buddha buys danger with it. How far do you travel to-night?"

"Nowhere," I confided. "Martin Hews' instructions are that we deposit it in the safe of the hotel until to-morrow. After then it is no longer any concern of ours."

"He is wise," Tul-Kak declared. "Myself, I think that the Buddha is safer in anybody else's hands than mine. When I left, the whispering throughout Asia was like a wind in the palm trees. Attempts were made upon me—seven in all. I escaped. Here in London, one is safer than anywhere. Yet, do not forget, you Englishman, you Isaacs the Jew, that there are those whose priests promise them eternal life for what you have in your possession. Men die easily, believing that promise."

Isaacs shivered with fear, but I saw at that moment no great cause for alarm.

"You will permit your attendants," I asked, "to go with us to the office?"

"They are at your disposal."

Tul-Kak gave brief instructions to both the man who had been outside the door, and to the Englishman. Then he bade us farewell.

"You yourself had better remember," I warned him, "that you have half a million pounds in your possession."

Tul-Kak smiled at me. He spoke soothingly, as one to a child.

"For many years," he confided, "I have slept always

with treasures around me which two—no, not three million of your pounds could buy. I am used to that. The thieves of the night have not great courage when it is only money they seek. Sometimes, however, there is fanaticism to deal with."

He bowed us away from the door. We started down the corridor, Isaacs and I side by side, I carrying the coffer, the Chinaman who had been custodian of the door in front, the Englishman behind. So we reached the first bend. Five seconds later, I was engaged upon one of the shortest but one of the fiercest struggles of my life.

CHAPTER XXXIV

THEY must have been crouching against the wall, for they came at us as we turned the corner—three of them only, but vicious-looking fellows, and, what I hated more than anything else in fighting, they carried knives. We were walking stealthily, but they still had the advantage of the surprise, and there was no time to draw a gun. Isaacs, as was natural enough, for he was an old man and a man of peace, turned and fled with great lumbering strides, making for the room from which we had come, and both the Chinaman and I were successful in evading the first rush. Our English guide, however, was not so lucky. I found afterwards that he had been supplied through some agency, and though he would probably have been ready enough to fight in an ordinary way, his attitude towards the statuette and our precautions was that it was all bunkum. He was, in fact, actually looking behind him when we turned the corner. He paid for his temerity with many months in hospital, for the first man to spring out left his knife quivering in his shoulder, and the Chinaman and I were faced with the three of them. I narrowly escaped putting my own assailant out of action with my first blow. He half-ducked, however, and my fist, which should have got him on the jaw, slithered along the side of his face. He went reeling back, but I had no time to follow up my advantage, for I had to drop the coffer to defend myself against the second man, whose right arm I was in time to grip. The Chinaman had leaped out of the way for a moment, only to spring forward with a knife of his own, which he had drawn from some hidden place in his cumbrous attire, and he was such a ferocious-looking fellow as he hurled himself upon his assailant that the latter lost his nerve and gave way. For a second, then, I thought that it was all over, for the third man had not yet succeeded in wresting his knife back from the Englishman's quivering body, and my own immediate opponent was still dazed by the blow I had got in. I tugged at my automatic, and to my joy got it free. I could have ended the whole thing, then and there, by shooting my man—a thing I should have been perfectly justified in doing, as he had attacked me with his knife—but I shouted instead to give him a chance. His hands went hesitatingly over his head.

"Throw down your knife," I ordered.

He obeyed. The Chinaman had come to close grips with his assailant, and they went over and over down the short flight of stairs leading to the floor below, the Chinaman on top. At that moment, it was practically over. I took a step forward to possess myself of the knife which lay on the carpet between me and my special opponent, and then, with a thrill of horror I remembered the third man who had disappeared. Almost as I swung round to look for him, I felt arms encircling my neck, a blow upon my wrist which sent my revolver clattering on to the ground, and the fingers of a long, cruel hand searching for my windpipe. I struggled like a madman, but in the midst of my agonised efforts I saw the man who had been at my mercy run forward with a yell of triumph, pick up his knife and move towards me. I was holding my own against the fierce grip of that unfortunately forgotten third man, but I could do no more than that for the moment. I was helpless against the uplifted knife of the man hovering over me. That single second's forgetfulness seemed to have brought me death. My last effort, made with all the strength I possessed, practically freed me from the strangling grip of the man behind, but left me powerless against that knife glittering within a few feet of my chest. Death seemed very close indeed at that moment, and death it must have been save for what certainly was a most amazing happening. I felt a scorching on the cheek, a flick of the air, the warm blood rolling down my neck, but a miracle had occurred. The man in front, in the act of striking, his knife poised, the lust of murder in his eyes, went backwards like a log, and where he fell he lay, with a small hole in his forehead, until they carried him to the mortuary. I staggered around. Mr. Tul-Kak was standing behind me, one barrel of his ponderous, old-fashioned revolver smoking. He was calmly pointing it at the man who had been holding me from behind, as though uncertain whether or no to deal with him in the same manner. The adventure was over, however. The Chinaman came smiling up the stairs, wiping his knife upon the inside of his robe and leaving behind him a crumpled-up form upon the landing. The only one of our assailants now who was comparatively unhurt was the man who had nearly throttled me, and him I believe that Tul-Kak would certainly have shot had I not stayed his arm, with the help of which brief respite the man took a flying leap down the stairs and disappeared.

"You saved my life, sir," I told Tul-Kak. "You don't want to shoot that man like a rabbit. He'll be hung some day—a much better end for him. There'll be trouble enough, as it is."

"I am happy to have been of service," Tul-Kak said politely. "A bullet would have been well placed in the body of that ruffian, but I obey your wishes. Take my advice now. Isaacs the dealer waits for you impatiently by the lift. He has gone the other way round. Place the coffer in the safe of the hotel. Your august friend has paid me for my Buddha the price of a prince in the manner of a prince, and I desire him to have it."

I saw the common sense of Mr. Tul-Kak's arguments, and without further hesitation I picked up the coffer and prepared to depart. I permitted myself one last glance round at the scene of our struggle, clear enough in detail, notwithstanding the dim lights burning from the orange and red walls, a quaintly dramatic little tableau set in this oasis of luxurious gloom.

I had no occasion to ring for the lift, for when I reached its starting place I found it already there, the gates open, Mr. Isaacs upon the seat, muttering excitedly to himself, and the pale-faced attendant peering through the grille and listening to the sounds below.

"You have held the treasure, young man?" Mr. Isaacs gasped.

I patted the coffer.

"I have held it all right. Why the devil don't we start?"

"There has been bloodshed!" Isaacs groaned.

"Lots of it," I answered, "and there will be more if we don't get away from here. What the mischief's wrong down below?" I asked the attendant.

"I don't know, sir," he admitted, his teeth chattering with fear. "There's some sort of a riot, but what it's all about I don't know. I was waiting down there on the ground floor for the bell to ring when half a dozen young fellows—they were all wearing dinner coats, but they looked like regular East-Enders—pushed their way in through the door and made for the Grillroom. Peters—that's our concierge—he stepped out from behind the counter and tried to stop them getting at the telephones—just asked what their business might be as civil as possible—and one of them whips round and shoots the poor old chap. He's lying there right by the counter.

Listen! There's another shot! I tell you what I think it is, sir," he went on, in a terrified tone. "It's a Communist raid."

"We've got to go down, anyway," I insisted. "Come on! Start her off!"

"You stop up here, sir," he begged. "What's the good of running into bloodshed?"

"There's been a trifle up on this floor, if you want to see any," I told him grimly. "Start the lift and take me down at once."

He obeyed reluctantly, and at the second floor I stopped him. There was a tremendous clamour of voices in the courtyard below, and, although I had not the faintest idea of what was happening, I realised that to attempt to pass through the Grillroom, or to cross the paved entrance into the hotel carrying the coffer, would be at best a risky proceeding.

"Wait here until I've finished," I ordered the attendant, who was almost in a state of collapse. "I'll tell you when to start again."

I opened the coffer and took out the casket. This also, with some difficulty, I unlocked, and the Buddha almost slipped into my hands. I could have sworn, as I held him there, that his one eye twinkled at me malevolently. I thrust him into my trousers pocket and buttoned my dinner jacket. Then I relocked the coffer and hid the keys under the seat.

"You get as far as you can up towards the Strand with the box," I directed Isaacs. "If there's any one watching, they will be put off the scent, anyway. It will take them some time to get it open, and by then the Buddha will be in safety. If no one stops you, just get into a taxi and go home."

"They will kill me if they see me with the coffer," he groaned.

"Not they," I assured him. "You need not put up any sort of a fight. Let them have it right away. You will have gone before they have time to open it."

He consented to bear his part in the scheme with resignation, but without enthusiasm. The attendant started the lift again, and we glided down to within a couple of feet of the ground floor. He looked out carefully through the bars, descended another few inches and opened the doors.

"Hurry up, sir," he begged.

We stepped out, and the lift shot up again, probably to the attic! In the little hall there were scant traces of the struggle which had taken place, except for Peters lying upon his back, very white and still, an overturned chair, and the telephone receivers from the two boxes wrenched from their places and thrown upon the ground. Outside, however, pandemonium reigned. Police whistles and motor horns were all going at the same time. There was still a stream of taxicabs driving as near as they could to the restaurant and disgorging little parties of six men from each vehicle, who, notwithstanding their dinner jackets, were certainly not ordinary visitors. I looked around in amazement. The top of the glass door leading to the hairdresser's shop was smashed, and although the small lounge outside seemed to be quiet, there was a commotion of some sort in the Grillroom, to judge by the raised voices and the crashing of crockery. I pushed Isaacs out on to the pavement and found one of the porters, scared half to death and cowering against the wall. The commissionaire, a fine-looking fellow, who had attempted to deal with the first taxicab of raiders, was lying upon the pavement, stone dead.

"Don't go down towards the restaurant, sir," the porter begged me. "They're driving the people in there like sheep. There's murder going on. Look at poor Charles! It's these b——y Communists. Get up on the top floor somewhere, sir, and out on the roof if you can. I'll show you the way, if only Jim would bring the lift down."

"Are there no police here?" I asked.

"I've seen barely half a dozen, sir, and there ain't one of them alive, I should think. They seem all off the streets. A gentleman who just came in said he hadn't set eyes on a single one all the way from Charing Cross. Besides, what's the good of them in twos and threes? There's hundreds of these fellows here, and they've all got guns."

"Can't we find a telephone anywhere in the place?" I suggested.

"They went for them directly they came, sir," the man replied, "and smashed the lot. That's where Peters got his."

"Why don't you try to get a taxicab to Scotland Yard?"

"They wouldn't let me pass the corner of the street, sir," he declared. "There's a dozen of them watching every one who comes out. There's Jim coming down with the lift. Hi, you! Stop it! Stop it!"

He bolted inside. I took Isaacs by the arm and turned him towards the Strand.

"They won't hurt you," I said reassuringly. "It's only the people coming into the restaurant they're after. Goodbye and good luck to you!"

He started off with more courage than I had expected. I turned round and stepped into the vortex.

CHAPTER XXXV

THE utter confusion of the scene was beyond description. The courtyard was completely blocked with taxicabs and cars filled with men and women in evening dress who had dined, or were meaning to sup, shrieking to the drivers of their vehicles to back out, to get away at any cost. Along the pavements, the raiders were still streaming, some of them making direct for the hotel, others flinging open the doors of cars and taxicabs indiscriminately, dragging out the occupants and forcing them to enter or re-enter the restaurant. There was a great deal of shouting, and half a dozen small fights going on, but in a general way it was recognised that resistance was useless, and men and women together were being herded into the entrance hall like sheep. I joined on to one of the parties who had decided that discretion was the better part of valour, but directly I had passed through the swing doors I realised how difficult my task was to be. The system of the raid was clear. The guests as they arrived, and those who had already arrived, were being bullied and driven down into the main restaurant, where, so far as I could tell, there seemed to be at least a hundred and fifty raiders. Along the dancing floor were rows of brown leather bags, and into these fell a constant stream of glittering gems, torn from the wrists and necks of shrieking women, and an occasional morocco pocketbook. As soon as one bag was full, it was picked up and carried off to the Embankment entrance, and an empty one brought in its stead. I permitted myself only a few seconds in which to watch this amazing spectacle

—then I turned my attention to my own difficulties. I had to reach the private offices, but between me and them were the open reception desks, where there were evidences of a very fierce fight. Upon the floor space all around were at least a score of prostrate bodies—one of them of a clerk whom I had known, but mostly, apparently, of marauders. Here, as it seemed to me then, and as I afterwards found to be a fact, the most gallant and unexpected resistance had been encountered from the small company of suave-looking, well-dressed young men, mostly foreigners, who were responsible for the coming and going of the visitors. Behind the solid mahogany desks, seven or eight of them—including the bookstall man and the theatre agent—were crouching, the tops of their heads and the gleam of their guns, or whatever weapon they had been able to get hold of, all that was visible. Even as I stood there, wondering how to join them, a score of newly arrived marauders came dashing through the smashed windows by the side of the swing doors and, apparently by arrangement, flung themselves into the fray. Their leader stopped abruptly, seemed almost to lean upon the little stab of red flame, and spun round, shot dead from the cashier's desk. The second man followed him, but the third and fourth, advancing from my end, almost reached their destination. I managed to dispose of both of them, however, chiefly owing to the unexpectedness of my attack, and, taking my chance from the defenders, vaulted the desk which had been in danger and came down amongst them.

"It's all right," I called out. "I'm Owston. Message for Mr. Bretzgel."

A bullet flicked my already wounded ear and I dropped on to my knees just in time to escape another. For a moment, I hesitated. I was aching to make my rush for the office, through the glass doors of which I could see

Bretzgel, the manager, standing with an automatic in his hand, but it seemed to me that the situation here was too dangerous to leave. One of the clerks, who had risen indiscreetly, had just been shot through the shoulder, and three or four of the marauders were perilously near. I took the place of the wounded man, but action of any sort was difficult, as only a few yards behind the raiders was a screaming phalanx of guests struggling to escape. All the time the marauders were creeping closer, and one of them, half feinting at the next desk, made a sudden leap forward at mine. I hesitated to shoot at such close quarters, and, in that second of indecision, he struck the gun from my hand with his life preserver and had his knee upon the counter. He slipped a little, however, upon the smooth surface, and I sent him smashing to the floor. The man who had been preparing to take his place apparently thought better of it and took shelter behind a pillar, from which he fired a wicked but ineffective shot at me. Afterwards there was a moment's lull. I crept nearer the office and found myself next a young man whom I remembered as one of the suavest and most polite of the young reception clerks in the daily execution of his duties—his face bloodstained, his eyes on fire, his gun, which he held like one utterly unused to firearms, clenched in his hand.

"Where do they come from?" he asked me breathlessly. "Is it a revolution?"

"A gang from the East End," I told him. "There's a very strong force of police out, looking for them. They can't be long. Listen—it's quiet here now—you can do without me for a time. I must get to the safe."

I crept on my hands and knees along those last few yards to the office door. Mr. Bretzgel, who was there on guard, with half a dozen of the staff around him, drew the bolts and let me in. I stood up and drew a little breath of relief. Half of my task was now accomplished. In a

general way, this office was one of the most orderly I
have ever entered, but at this moment it presented an
amazing spectacle. The manager, with his two deputies,
was entrenched behind an overturned rosewood desk.
Three firemen were there with a hose in their hands, and
the light of battle in their eyes. There were also a moderate company of valets, porters, commissionaires, and
maîtres d'hôtel, each with some sort of a weapon, prepared to defend the safes.

"You had word from Mr. Hews that I was coming," I
said to Bretzgel. "I've just got through from the court.
You know what I want."

Bretzgel nodded and turned to one of his assistants,
who rose slowly from his knees.

"Where the devil did all this riffraff come from?" Mr.
Bretzgel gasped. "And where the hell are the police?
We've sent messages in every direction."

"Joseph's gang from the East End," I told him briefly.
"Most dangerous lot of criminals London has ever har-
boured. The police are out after them, three hundred
strong. They'll be here any minute now. What about the
safe?"

I was let into the secrets of the room. The ordinary
safe stood there, portentous, to all appearances un-
assailable. The assistant manager, however, had lifted
a magnificent rug behind where he had been kneeling,
pressed a button which released a slat of wood, turned
a key, and pulled back what I saw now was a long strip
of revolving metal, which opened and disclosed a small
vault.

"No time for receipts," he said. "Drop your treasure
in. We know all about it."

I leaned down, and I laid the Buddha upon his back
amongst great rolls of notes, and cases of jewellery. Once
again I could have sworn that that single wide-open eye

flickered, that there was something like a malicious grin upon the steadfast lips. Then the roll of flexible metal went back into its place, the slat of wood covered it, a key was turned. The Buddha was safe!

I stood up and suddenly I felt the great urge of battle upon me. I was freed of my responsibility, and even from the comparative seclusion of the office, I could hear the calling of women.

"Got any cartridges, sir, for a number four automatic?" I asked.

Bretzgel gave me a pocketful of clips. He was a man of peace, as I very well knew, with a wife and family, but he had laid all that aside and was waiting, bloodshed in his eyes, for the struggle if it should come. I charged my gun, mixed myself a drink from a bottle of whisky and a syphon of soda water which I found upon the table, and made my way to the door.

"Better stay here," Bretzgel advised. "We shall probably need you badly enough."

"You won't," I assured him. "I know something about this gang. They're planning to make off by the Embankment, and it's my belief that they're edging that way already. Your fellows at the desks are holding their own, and you'll have the place full of police soon. I'm for the restaurant."

They let me stealthily out of the office, and after lurking for a few moments behind the end counter, I crept into the hall and made a run for the front stairs. Nobody took any notice of me, and I descended. I went down the first flight without meeting a single raider. In the little space outside the cloakrooms, where one drinks cocktails before descending to take one's table, it was obvious that there had been a desperate struggle. A dozen wounded men were lying about—one, an old brother officer of mine, with a bullet in his leg.

"Anything I can do for you, Hargrave?" I asked. "Are you badly hit?"

"Not I," was the reply, "but they've got me in my sound leg, the devils. I can't move. Don't bother about me. Get into it if you can, Owston. The women need help."

I passed on and looked down for a second or two upon the most astonishing spectacle I have ever witnessed. For some reason or other, the struggle here seemed to have taken place in the shape of a hundred small fights around the different tables, some of which were still in progress. In the far distance, the raiders were passing the brown bags from one to another, and the end man was disappearing towards the Embankment entrance. Here and there at the tables were fainting women; here and there a wounded man. There was an occasional shot, but a good deal more hand-to-hand fighting of a one-sided character, for even the raiders who made no use of their revolvers carried life preservers. At one of the tables near the entrance a girl was screaming in the clutch of a man who was stripping her fingers. Her escort was already prostrate upon the ground. I made a start there, took the marauder unawares, as I frankly admit, and sent him crashing amongst the broken furniture at the next table. His companion, who had been receiving the spoils and throwing them into the bag, came for me like a wildcat, and for a minute or two we fought, whilst he struggled all the time to reach his hip pocket. I made no effort to use my own gun, for he was only a weakly guttersnipe, and in a very few seconds he was lying across his fellow. The girl by this time was in absolute hysterics. I had never seen her before, but she threw her arms round my neck, sobbing, praying me to take her out. A strange wave of brutality seemed to have dried up all my ordinary instincts. I scarcely answered her and pushed her on one side when she caught at my arm. I stood there, hesitating for a moment, at the top of the room, wondering in which direction my help was most needed, and it was in those few seconds that I received the greatest shock of my life. For some reason or other, a large company of guests were being driven from the Embankment entrance and new extension on to the dancing floor, and a certain section of them were making some show of resistance. One man in particular I saw fighting furiously to cover the retreat of a small group of women. Two of the raiders who had snatched at a necklace hanging from the neck of one of them, he shot deliberately. A third sprang forward, only to receive apparently a bullet in his heart, for he spun round and fell, a crumpled-up heap upon the edge of the floor. I took a quick step forward, meaning to go to his assistance. One of the raiders had closed in upon him. There was a brief struggle, and this man too joined the others upon the floor. I shouted encouragement and started across the room. The man who had been fighting so gallantly swung round towards me. His face and shirt front were blood-stained, his collar and tie were hanging loose. The automatic in his hand was smoking. He was standing a little free from the others, pausing apparently for breath— the protecting genius of a little line of hysterical women. For the hero of a drawing-room battle, he was a wild enough looking object, yet for all that, I recognised him —recognised him with the greatest thrill of surprise I had ever felt. The man who was fighting the raiders so gallantly was Mr. X.!

CHAPTER XXXVI

THE fighting had surged to another part of the room before I had recovered sufficiently from my surprise to embark upon any definite course of action. A little affair closer at hand, during the course of which I received a nasty scratch on the cheek, occupied my attention for several minutes. When I was free to look around again, I saw that Mr. X. was still in the thick of the fighting, and on the outskirts, also presenting a bold front, was Mr. Leopold. I watched them both closely for several moments, then suddenly a wave of inspiration flashed into my brain. I understood the whole business. Mr. X. was going from table to table, wherever the women were wearing the most wonderful jewellery, missing out the little girls with their bead necklaces and cheap engagement rings, and followed always by a thin stream of marauders. The plan was amazingly simple. He had looked through the list of tables. He knew exactly the character of the jewellery the women would be wearing, and his 'men followed his lead. When he used his gun, as often as not the man at whom he had fired went rolling to the ground, but in less than a minute he was up again. I watched Leopold. He was playing the same game—always seeming to be encouraging the defenders, always seeming to be facing with a bold front the marauders. Still bloodstained, and apparently limping badly, I saw Mr. X. stumble to a table where a woman was struggling to conceal a diamond necklace. He was followed, as usual, by one or two threatening figures, from the foremost of whom he received a blow which wouldn't have hurt a fly, but which was sufficient to send him to the floor until the necklace was secured. It was the same performance all the time: sheer bluff, made possible by his bogus automatic, and a featherweight life preserver. Every now and then, there was what appeared to be a real struggle, in which Mr. X. was always the victor, but it never once resulted in the salvation of the jewellery. I began to move now slowly towards the portion of the room where he was engaged. A minor fracas detained me a few moments, and one which gave me infinite pleasure, where I helped a pal who was hard pressed by two of the thieves, took one of them off his hands, dealt with him satisfactorily, and slipped her rings back to the woman who had been robbed. Then I braced myself for what seemed to me might be the adventure of the evening. I slipped fresh cartridges into my gun and I crossed the floor until I faced Mr. X. He had grown more audacious, I think, in the darkened light, for half the lamps seemed to have been overturned and pandemonium reigned everywhere. I saw him point to a table where a woman and two elderly men were seated. I even heard him whisper in the ear of one of the raiders, who lurked around him.

"Down the front of her dress—glinters. Make sure of them.

Then, as usual, he flung himself into the fray with apparent fury. The woman, shrieking, fell back in her chair. The man who had attacked her—a long, lithe young street Arab of scarcely nineteen or twenty—held her for a moment by the throat, whilst he ripped her dress down to her waist and drew out a handful of magnificent diamonds. Her two escorts were powerless; the only one who had attempted resistance had been thrown heavily on to his back by another raider who had been waiting to convey the jewels to his bag. Mr. X. plunged heroically in, but a push of the shoulder, which could scarcely have hurt a chicken, sent him staggering. He fired his gun at short range, and the man with the diamonds in his hand reeled over and lay for a moment quite still, whilst his companion snatched at the gems and darted off with them, the woman's shrieks ringing out. I went up to the shot man and kicked him. He opened his eyes in surprise, and I swung around to find myself face to face with Mr. X.

"Well met, my young friend," he mocked. "And now?"

"And now this," I answered, and let fly for his face, only to find myself almost overbalanced, as he slipped nimbly on one side with all the agility of a light-weight prize fighter.

He laughed derisively.

"Clumsy as usual, my dear Major!" he exclaimed. "Why beat the air trying for me?"

I had recovered my balance without falling and I kept my temper. We were facing the other way now, and I saw distinctly the man whom Mr. X. had shot crawling blantantly away.

"You are doing marvellous work, aren't you, Joseph," I mocked him, "with your sham cartridges and your sham heroism?"

He was ever so slightly disturbed—the faintest of frowns only!

"A fool with one eye open!" he murmured. "And talking about one eye, Major, what about the Buddha?"

"Safe," I told him. "Why didn't you come up to seize it? We might have settled this matter between us once and for all."

The thought of Rachel's pathetic face, of Beatrice still in his power, maddened me, and this time I made no mistake. I struck his wrist with the side of my hand such a blow that the gun he had been holding fell to the floor. I snatched it up, and whilst he was hesitating, I slipped the cartridges into my pocket.

"We'll see to-morrow," I threatened, "what the hero of to-night was playing at. I have a gun too, Joseph, and my cartridges bite."

"And I have another," he countered, his hand going round to his back like lightning. "Shall we call it quits?"

He was panting a little now, his weapon half-drawn, barely a foot or two between us. All around the screaming of women, the smashing of glass, the whole ugly work of the marauders still continued. It seemed to me to matter nothing that I looked into the dark muzzle of Joseph's gun. I had him covered, and my finger itching for its work.

"Tell me where Beatrice Essiter is," I demanded, "or I'll blow the brains out of your head even if I have to go to hell with you."

He made no reply, but there crept into his face that hideous, damnable smile. Then the passion of my life swept me into insanity. I threw my own gun to the ground and sprang at him, an action so unexpected that it succeeded. He fired a harmless shot. I snatched his automatic away and sent it clattering across the floor, and it seemed to me that the joy of my life was at hand. I had my fingers on his throat. Although his strength amazed me, and even his convulsive efforts to free himself were the movements of a practised wrestler, I had him, and he knew it. Then, in that breathless moment, I heard another sound—the sound for which I had been listening eagerly a few minutes before, but which now infuriated me. There was commotion in the Embankment Room, a dark figure came dashing into the restaurant. He swayed upon his feet even as he stood there, his hand to his mouth.

"Cops! Ten vans full of them," he shouted, and over he went, shot by a pursuer.

I looked up for a moment, and I paid. I felt a hot breath upon my neck, half turned around, and Leopold hit me with the butt of his revolver, missing my head but de-

scending heavily upon my shoulder. Joseph had his chance
then. He staggered to his feet, a ghastly sight, his collar
ripped to pieces, the marks of my fingers upon his throat,
a queer dark shadow under his eyes. He snatched up his
gun. With my left hand I sent Leopold head over heels,
stooped for a moment, and once more faced Joseph. Again
it was a life for a life between us two, but again I was
denied. We were surrounded by plain-clothes police
streaming into the place, Bloor, pale with fury, sprinting
across the dancing floor for the offices. Above the tumult
we could hear the sharp detonation of bombs, and little
puffs of green smoke came floating down, hugging the
ceiling above our heads. Then my enemy, always unexpected, always with the opportunist's sense of drama,
amazed me once more. He flung himself into a chair with
a great shout of relief. From somewhere or other, he
produced a handkerchief and began to mop his face.

"The police at last!" he cried. "It's all right, Leopold,
all right, Major. These rascals won't have a dog's chance
now."

The fellow's wits were too quick for mine. I stared at
him, taken aback. The room was already almost empty
of the marauders, except for those who were being hand-
cuffed and led away. The main body of the police had
rushed on to the entrance hall. Two or three hospital
nurses had arrived, followed by men carrying stretchers,
and a great many guests who were more frightened than
hurt were sitting up once more at their tables, and more
still were trooping from the place. Mr. X., with a word
of apology, poured himself out a glass of wine from
the bottle upon the table by his side.

"I hope you have lost nothing, Lady Robinson?" he
enquired.

"My necklace," she sobbed. "They have my necklace.
I thought you had shot the man. He went over when you

fired, but he got up again. You hit him, I am sure, because he was limping and calling out with pain, but he took the necklace."

"I am sorry," Mr. X. regretted. "These fellows take an awful lot of killing. Major," he added, "won't you have a glass of wine? . . . Another of your gallant preservers," he remarked, turning to the woman.

I took no wine, but I moved a little closer to Mr. X. He edged away at once from my scrutiny, but he was too late. One side of his face at any rate, was most amazingly made up, but there was the slightest of cracks in the wax. It might almost have been a human wrinkle, but slight though it was, I could see the change in the contour of his face. My hand rested as though by accident upon his arm.

"Couldn't we finish our little dispute out on the terrace?" I suggested. "Man to man and no weapons. What about that?"

My enemy hesitated, and Leopold whispered in his ear. I think they were cursing themselves for having waited so long. In the distance, the tumult was dying away. Law and order were prevailing.

"Wouldn't explanations of that sort be rather an anticlimax?" Mr. X. asked sweetly. "The end between us is not to-night."

"Why not?" I demanded. "I am going to hand you over to Inspector Bloor."

He laughed as though genuinely amused

"You poor fool," he scoffed, "who'll believe you? There are fifty people in the place who would bear witness to my feats of heroism. Besides which, I am well established here, well-known—not a penniless adventurer, who was in the police court yesterday morning. To every charge you could bring against me I have a perfect alibi. Come, be reasonable. What is it you want of me?"

"Beatrice Essiter, for one thing."

He shrugged his shoulders.

"You ask me to disclose the secret of my happiness!" he gibed.

Then I knew that he was purposely trying to provoke me, and I saw the reason why. Bretzgel, whom I had last seen crouched behind his desk, with a gun in his hand, was coming towards us, his arm in a sling, Bloor by his side.

"Well, gentlemen," he announced, with a smile, "the great raid is at an end. The Inspector has just been explaining to me how it was that he had three hundred police ready armed. They arrived just in time."

"The safes?" I enquired anxiously.

"They blew the office to pieces," he admitted. "They smoked us out, too, but not one of them crossed the threshold of my room. Your little deposit, Major," he confided, "is quite secure. I felt that I must come and thank you two gentlemen," he went on, turning first to Mr. X. and then to me. "In the intervals of our own siege, I saw a good deal of what was passing down here. How you, sir," he concluded, addressing Mr. X., "escaped without being shot, I can't imagine. You seemed to be in the thick of it all the time. There was a shorter gentleman with you too—"

"My friend Leopold." Mr. X. interrupted. "He made for home by the Embankment entrance directly he saw that the trouble was over. A finicky little man, who hates to be seen about with bloodstains on his shirt front. Good thing you and I are not so particular, Major."

The man was scarcely human. He looked across at me and laughed.

"Who were the fellows, anyway?" he added.

"The Wolves, they call themselves," Bloor answered curtly. "You've heard of them, perhaps. They're a gang of East End thieves with a wonderful leader who seems, I regret to say, to have escaped to-night."

"I am not sure yet," I muttered, "whether he has escaped."

"You mean that he is still hiding in the place?" Bloor demanded. "The police are searching on every floor."

"Every apartment has been entered and examined," Mr. Bretzgel confided—"even yours, sir, I am afraid," he added, addressing Mr. X.

"Quite right too," the latter remarked indifferently.

"In my report," Bloor said, "I should like to mention the names of your guests, Mr. Bretzgel, who put up such a fine fight. Major Owston, I know. May I ask this gentleman's name?"

The hotel manager appeared surprised.

"Certainly," he replied, "I thought that every one knew him. This is Mr. Ruben Sams."

"The Argentine millionaire," Bloor murmured, under his breath.

"Mr. Ruben Sams?" I repeated.

"Mr. Ruben Sams has a suite here," Bretzgel added, "of which I regret to say, however, he very seldom makes use."

I suppose my bewilderment was obvious to all of them.

"Major Owston is a little confused, no doubt," Mr. X. remarked, with a smile. "For some reason or other he was very curious as to my identity one night lately. By bribing a *maître d'hôtel* at Claridge's, he discovered that my name card at a very interesting dinner party there simply bore the inscription of 'Mr. X.' Since then, whenever we have met, he has regarded me with a great deal of suspicion. The ways of high finance are doubtless unknown to you, Major. For some time, until I collected my board for a new company I am founding, it was very inadvisable that my presence in this country should be known. I often pay visits to foreign capitals under another identity."

"I can quite believe that," I muttered.

A small army of cleaners hastily summoned before their time, had now commenced their usual labours. We all moved up together towards the main part of the hotel. The machinery of the place was once more in order, and all signs of the night's tragedy were being removed as quickly as possible.

"The Milan is never likely to witness a scene like this again, gentlemen," Mr. Bretzgel said, as he led the way, "never in our time, I trust. The Grillroom is the only one comparatively untouched. Will you gentlemen who have done such magnificent work take some wine or whisky and soda, or whatever you fancy with me there?"

"An excellent suggestion!" Mr. Ruben Sams declared. "For myself, I rarely touch spirits. I drank some of Lady Robinson's Pomery '15 and found it excellent."

As we were about to seat ourselves at a round table, I drew Bloor on one side. Ruben Sams, with his hands in his trousers pockets, leaned back and laughed at me insolently.

"Bloor," I said earnestly, "that man is no more Ruben Sams than I am."

For once those heavy eyelids were completely lifted, and I saw into the fullest depths of the Inspector's blue eyes. He was obviously astonished. He looked at me as though I had taken leave of my senses.

"I am afraid that's rather a mare's nest, Major," he expostulated. "Ruben Sams is known all the world over. Who did you think he was?"

"Joseph," I declared confidently. "I am not mad, Bloor, and I tell you that man is Joseph."

He looked at me kindly, but with a profound disbelief.

"Come and have a drink, Major," he suggested. "You have had a rough night of it."

"That," I persisted, "is the man who stood on the lawn and led his men when they attacked Breezeley. He is the man—he admits that—who was entertained as Mr. X. at Claridge's, who took such a malicious interest in Miss Essiter and myself. He is the man who came to my rooms in Down Street and who would have killed me if he had found whom he expected there. He is the man who was seated in the secretary's office at the Blue Skies, who talked to you over the telephone, and, whether you believe it or not, he led the Wolves to-night. He led them from table to table just where the women were wearing the most wonderful jewels. He had them all marked down. His fighting was a sham. When he fired his gun he used dummy cartridges and the men got up again in less than a minute. I picked some of the cartridges up. I have two or three in my pocket now."

"Show me one."

I thrust my hand into my pocket. They were gone. Bloor edged away towards the table. It was obvious that he had not a vestige of belief in my story.

"I think you're wrong, Major," he told me frankly. "Come and have that drink."

"But he talked to me to-night," I insisted. "We've spoken of Miss Essiter."

The heavy lids had descended. I knew that I was speaking against a rock of incredulity. Nevertheless, he let me down lightly.

"I tell you what I'll do, Major," he promised. "I'll have him watched. He's staying here. I'll send two of our best men up within half an hour."

We sat down at the table, and I drank a whisky and soda, of which I was badly in need. Bretzgel, after his strenuous night and a great deal of wine, soon became drowsy. Mr. Ruben Sams also drank a great deal of champagne, but his face remained as sphinx-like as ever —his eyes only grew brighter. By degrees grey streaks of dawn came creeping into the courtyard. All the time there was the tramping of feet there, the rattle of taxicabs. Reporters were arriving from most of the papers; more important journalists anxious to get fuller information; sight-seers of every description. Finally Bretzgel rose to his feet.

"You will excuse me, gentlemen," he begged. "The night has worn me out. I must barricade myself in my room and get some sleep."

Mr. Ruben Sams also prepared to take his leave.

"In such company," he declared, "I should be content to sit until the hour arrives for bacon and eggs and coffee. However, if it must be—good night. Good night, Major Owston, my gallant coadjutor to-night. Good night, Inspector, and congratulations upon your timely arrival."

He passed down the little avenue between the tables and vanished into the court—a very elegant figure of a man, notwithstanding his disordered habiliments. Bloor and I rose to our feet, and he took my arm.

"The hero of your hallucinations," he observed, as we passed out together, "has just floated an Argentine Company for two million pounds. It's in all the papers to-night. Lord Farendon is Chairman of the Directors."

"God help the shareholders," I said fervently. "No wonder Joseph prefers the West End."

CHAPTER XXXVII

I THINK that, apart from purely personal experiences, the most poignant seconds of my life were those immediately after I had passed my treasure across into the trembling hands of Martin Hews. Never in my life could I have believed in the possibility of such rapture as shone in his face: Those terrible eyes of his, as he gazed upon the statuette, became soft and positively beautiful. His lips were parted, not in a snarl, but in an absolutely beatific smile. He set it down in front of him upon the desk and drew aside the purple covering with caressing fingers. He was like a man whose emotions, so clearly reflected in his face, had generated an almost unendurable physical strain. He kept on moistening his dry lips with his tongue. Tiny beads of perspiration stood out upon his forehead. Without the slightest manner of doubt real tears stood in his eyes. So he sat spellbound, gazing, drinking in an amazing happiness, completely oblivious to his surroundings, crooning gently to himself as might have done a strangely brought-up child. His fingers wandered lovingly over that exquisite surface. The seconds passed into minutes. As often as he tried to look away, he looked back again. Finally, with the tips of his fingers still resting upon his treasure, he turned towards me.

"Well done, Owston," he acclaimed. "Well done! When the news came through of the raid, I trembled. You have brought me the last great desire of my life. Now tell me the story."

"It's a pretty serious one, I fear, sir," I warned him.

"The beginning of it was all right. Isaacs wanted to bargain, but I handed across the cheque. Tul-Kak parted all right, poor fellow. He saved my life, but they got him this morning. He was found dead in bed, as I dare say you read."

My employer nodded.

"Joseph kept his word as usual. He swore that if he dealt with me instead of him, he should die before he could cash the cheque."

"He had three men to guard him and locked doors. No good! Joseph's men got at him somehow during the raid. They could never believe that I had fought through to the office, and they imagined that I had hidden it in one of the rooms on Tul-Kak's floor. Every one of them was ransacked last night and torn to pieces."

"They pressed you hard for it?" he muttered, with a sparkle in his eyes.

"We had a bit of a scrap in the corridor of the Milan," I told him. "Afterwards we rather fooled them. Isaacs went off with the coffer, which they took from him at the corner of the street, and I reached the office vault safe with the statuette in my trousers pocket. Isaacs is all right, by-the-by. I rang him up this morning. They just took the coffer from him and let him go."

"You are a man, Major," my employer acknowledged tremblingly. "I did well when I engaged you. Now what about the raid? I have the newspapers. They speak of you as making an heroic resistance, and a Mr. Ruben Sams. Who is Ruben Sams?"

"Joseph."

Mr. Martin Hews stared at me from behind the desk. "You're laughing, Major."

I was weary of unbelief, but again I did my best to combat it. I explained the reasons for my conviction in as few words as possible.

"They all believe that he was fighting for the guests," I concluded. "Nothing of the sort. He was leading on his gang. He'd marked down every table where the jewels were worth having, and under pretext of rushing there to defend the women, he led his men to each. When he pretended to shoot, he used dummy cartridges and a life preserver that couldn't have hurt a child."

"That's a strange story, Major," Martin Hews commented quietly.

"Strange, but it's hellishly true," I answered, with some of the weariness which I felt in my tone.

"You say that he spoke of my niece?"

"I asked him where she was. He refused to disclose what he called 'the secret of his happiness.' "

My employer grinned, and if there was any time when I hated him it was when he indulged in that horrible grimace.

"I think, Major," he said, "you have run foul of a man with a sense of humour, and he amuses himself at your expense."

"Perhaps," I sighed. "It always seemed to me that it would be the easiest thing in the world, if I could once find the man whom I knew to be Joseph, to drag the truth out of him, but I can't do it. He's so damnably clever. He is always surrounded by other people who are either his confederates or who believe in him, and he always seems to be in a position to make me ridiculous if I accuse him seriously. I thought Inspector Bloor was my friend —I think he is—but he doesn't trust me. I begged him to arrest Joseph last night, and he wouldn't do it."

Martin Hews moved uneasily in his place.

"That fellow Bloor again!" he muttered. "I wish you'd keep away from him. The police are too suspicious of me. This house is watched from the front door to the river. Isaacs could have got me some of the real lacquer

which was taken from the Weindorf Palace in Vienna.
I dared not take it. Those tapestries I had last month
were brought down by motor boat to my landing stage
at Brick Bend. They are there in the boathouse still.
I daren't bring them away. There's no harm in your
being friendly with Bloor, but be very careful, Major.
Be very careful all the time. Never let him talk to you of
my affairs."

He pressed a button, and Minchin presently appeared.

"A bottle of my wine," he ordered. "Two glasses. I
get tired these days," he went on, speaking as though to
himself.

"Why don't you chuck it all now, sir?" I asked him.
"It has been a great game, I have no doubt, but is it
worth it after a certain point?"

"It is always worth it," he replied fervently, "when the
treasure is there."

"But look at what you have already," I argued. "To
my dying day I shall never forget your gallery, sir. You
have beautiful things enough to feast your eyes upon for
the rest of your life. Why run any risks? Why not ship
everything to some southern country—Italy, or somewhere amongst the quieter spots of the French Riviera,
away from this ghastly swamp. Divide your time between
the sunshine and your treasures."

He leaned across the table. Again it was the frightened child who spoke.

"I shouldn't be safe whilst Joseph was alive. You know
his oath? If I got Donkin away and kept the girl here,
he swore to steal my treasures, one by one, and then my
life. Beatrice is the beginning, I suppose. My Madonna
of Deptford followed. I know that I am in danger, but
where else in the world could I protect myself as I can
here?"

"That's all very well, sir," I expostulated, "but the

man isn't superhuman. He's beginning to get it in the neck and to get it badly. There are fifty-three men of his gang under arrest, some in hospital, the remainder in prison. Eleven are dead. His organisation must be completely shattered. The police have combed every house for miles around their old headquarters. Don't you think one of these fifty-three is likely to squeal?"

"I don't believe one of them knows," my employer confided. "They catch a glimpse of the Joseph who comes stealing down into their midst once or twice a year, from some hidden place in another quarter of the world, perhaps, but I don't believe there's one of them—even amongst his most trusted lieutenants—who could put his hand upon him at a given moment. Joseph knows all about them and what they are doing. They know nothing about him."

"How about last night?" I demanded. "They recognised him then and obeyed him.

Martin Hews smiled cryptically.

"If your theory as to Ruben Sams and Joseph being the same man is correct," he said, "I can quite understand his being willing to disclose himself. Presently I will explain why."

There was a tinkle of the bell, and Minchin brought in a long-necked, dusty bottle, with a faded yellow label and two exquisite Venetian glasses faintly tinted. He opened the bottle with meticulous care, and after he had served his master, he filled a glass and handed it to me.

"This is Berncastler Doctor, forty years old," my employer told me, holding his glass reverently to the light. "Wines of this character have their beauty, almost like the visible *objets d'art*."

He sipped from his glass daintily, with the deliberation of the true connoisseur. I followed his example as well as

I was able. The wine was the colour of pale amber, but
richer and softer, more delicately perfumed than any
wine I had ever drunk before. As he poured out his second
glass, the colour returned to Martin Hews' cheeks, and
his eyes grew brighter again.

"Owston," he said, "you were right. I said that I should
finish with the Buddha, and I shall keep my word. This
is my one great final success," he went on, caressing the
statuette. "There is nothing in the world more beautiful
than this. No single object of gold or porphyry, of silver,
or bronze, or jade, or ivory, to compare with it. Stop!
Your messenger's fee!"

He opened a drawer and flung across a bundle of notes,
held together by a rubber band.

"You needn't mind taking them, Owston," he went on,
almost pleasantly. "A gentleman of fortune who risks
his life has been paid with good gold since the days of
the Crusaders. There was never a thousand pounds better earned. Put it in your pocket."

I am afraid I did not stop to consider the ethical point
of view. After all, I had done my job and risked my life.
I pocketed the money.

"You may hear from Joseph, even though it is for
the last time, as soon as he discovers that he hasn't the
Buddha," I warned him.

"It has cost me something like five thousand pounds,"
Martin Hews said, "to make this room impregnable. It
is impregnable. No man could possibly enter whilst I sit at
this desk."

"But there are two other doors," I pointed out.

He nodded gravely.

"You are thinking of that previous occasion. Quite
right. Now then, about those two other doors. There
is only one that need count. The door into my treasure
house is of solid iron. It opens only from this side, and

it would take half a ton of dynamite to blow it up. As for the second—"

He must have touched a button somewhere, for it rolled slowly open. Upon the threshold stood Huntley, his flat automatic in his hand.

"Quite all right, thank you," his master said, with a nod. "I was only testing the connections."

The man stepped back and the door closed.

"Supposing," Martin Hews went on, "that my man had been overpowered from outside: the first step across the threshold by any one who did not know where to set his foot would land him somewhere very near eternity. I think I am safe here, Major. I am not relying upon man, or man's fidelity. I have made this a mechanical fortress operated by myself. Science, at any rate, cannot play me false."

A smile of placid conceit parted his lips, and I rose to my feet with some alacrity.

"Then, if I may, I will go back to town, sir," I proposed.

"Just as you please," Martin Hews assented. "Joseph may have a try for me, but this is one of my courageous days. I can imagine no more complete joy," he went on gloating, "than to sit here and have my signals work, and for him to come. I know how to deal with him, Major. Sit in my chair whilst I give you a test of it."

"Thank you," I answered hastily. "I would rather not."

"As you will. There are days like this when I want him alone, want all the joy of watching him suffer for myself. There are other days when I am a coward, when my nerves fail me. If I should feel like that to-morrow or the next day, I shall send for you. If Joseph comes, I shall wheel my chair round whilst you fight, and if I see that Joseph is the better man, I shall shoot him in the back.

. . . Send me news when you have any, Major. Mr. Ruben Sams, for instance. Ah, I have not shown you this. Look here. When you get back, you may find Mr. Bloor not so hard to convince."

He stretched a copy of the *Times* out before him and touched a little paragraph with his finger:

Mr. Ruben Sams, the Argentine millionaire, is arriving at Liverpool this morning on the *Orinoco* from Buenos Ayres, and will be staying at the Ritz Hotel.

"Come a little before his time, I fancy," Martin Hews remarked, with a chuckle. "That is why I think that Joseph's star is setting."

CHAPTER XXXVIII

THE papers that evening were flooded with news. There were several very mysterious paragraphs with reference to the reported arrival in London of the celebrated Argentine millionaire, who had already been in the country and engaged in extensive financial operations for about a month, but the whole interest of the general public was focussed upon last night's amazing raid. The leader of the Wolves—the man who was responsible for the organisation and carrying out of that audacious enterprise—was still at liberty. The personality of the man had seized hold of the imagination of the populace. Wherever one went, nothing else was talked about. The limits of speculation and humour were reached in wild surmises. Every review in London that night introduced the famous Chief of the Wolves, and in practically every club and private party the humorists and sensationalists ran riot with their suggestions. A Cabinet Minister's name was freely mentioned, a famous actor was whispered about, one of the chiefs of Scotland Yard was hinted at, a young scion of royalty, with an adventurous turn of mind, was openly suggested. One woman who had been relieved of her diamonds insisted upon it that, notwithstanding his disguise, she recognised by his voice a well-known young man of society, who had whispered a compliment to her even as he had unfastened the catch of her jewels. Fresh rumours multiplied, and to add a touch of drama to the whole thing, before nightfall a reward of five thousand pounds for information leading to the arrest of the leader of the gang was offered through the police by the directors of the Milan Hotel. A great police drive was taking place throughout the whole of the East End of London, not only in the hope of finding the man himself, but also in the hope of acquiring information from some of the more insignificant members of the gang who had not joined in the Great Raid. The marauders who were lying in hospital had the newly printed bills placed by their bedsides. Even those who were in prison were allowed to see them. Five thousand pounds and a free pardon for any one who could give information leading to the arrest of this mysterious potentate of crime! Surely some one would be tempted even to their death! . . .

Towards six o'clock, Bloor came to see me.

"And I thought you a good fellow and a brave man," he groaned, as he took my hand, "but a bit of a simpleton. My God, Major, it's I who was the simpleton. I deserve to be kicked out of the Force. You gave me the chance of my life, and I threw it away."

"You know now, then, that we had Joseph in our hands?"

"I'm just as sure of it as that the real Ruben Sams only landed at Liverpool this morning. Joseph has been playing at a higher game than ordinary jewel robberies. He has taken three or four hundred thousand pounds in cash away from a little group of our financiers who won't believe even now that they weren't dealing with the real man."

"This must be the end of it, anyhow," I remarked. "He can't go on after this."

"Frankly, I don't think he can," Bloor agreed. "He is the most amazing person we've been up against for many years. He left the Milan Hotel at six o'clock this morning. I have just come from searching his rooms. Not a paper, not an address, not a single thing there to help us. Invi-

tations more than you could count, letters of gratitude
for his heroism last night, but not one single thing which
could link him up with any other personality. And to
think," he deplored, a note almost of passionate regret
in that pleasant, even tone of his, "he was my man last
night—the greatest capture of my life. I hadn't the sense
to believe you, Major. It seemed so damnably far-
fetched."

"It can't be helped," I sighed. "We shall get him before
many hours have passed."

"Why do you think so?" he asked eagerly. "You see,
I can't afford to let even an idea of yours pass now,
Major."

"Because," I explained, "I don't believe that under
any circumstances would he leave the country without
going down to Breezeley. He's got an account—an account of hate, I suppose you'd call it—to settle with
Martin Hews."

"It's quite possible," Bloor admitted. "I'll send three
men down there to-night. I must be off now. I've got re-
ports coming in every half-hour. I felt I couldn't rest
until I had owned up to you, Major. I'm sorry—I can't
say more."

"Shake hands on it," I begged, "and have a whisky and
soda."

"The first drink to-day," he replied, with his whimsical
little smile, as I handed him the tumbler. "I've been sitting in sackcloth and ashes."

"Then get out of them now," I advised him. "They're
unhealthy wear. And listen, Bloor, there's something
else. If Ruben Sams of last night was Joseph—and we
pretty well know he was—what about Leopold?"

"I have a man sitting in his rooms waiting for him to
come back from the country, if ever he does come back,"
Bloor confided. "Good night, Major. Better get to bed

early. You had all the scrapping that's good for a man in one day yesterday."

I decided that I was as well in my rooms as anywhere, and I ordered an early dinner there. Afterwards I began to realise my weariness. My sitting-room was warm and comfortable. I threw myself into an easy-chair, and in three minutes I was asleep. . . .

I was awakened by what was undoubtedly a soft tapping at the door. I glanced at my wrist watch and sat up. It was only nine o'clock, so I could not have been asleep for more than twenty minutes. The tapping was repeated. I reached over to the drawer where I kept my automatic, laid it under a newspaper by my side in the chair, and acknowledged the summons.

"Come in," I enjoined.

The door was quietly opened. I looked at my caller for a moment incredulously. I had heard no ring at the bell downstairs, and it seemed impossible that without any form of announcement, a visitor from outside could have reached me so easily. Yet, without a doubt, there he stood —Mr. Leopold, smiling at me deprecatingly as he unwound a thick scarf from his neck, took off a pair of motor glasses, and advanced a little farther into the room. I watched his right hand carefully, but I scarcely imagined that he had come to see me with any malignant intent.

"You will excuse this interruption, Major," he begged humbly. "I hope you do not consider it an intrusion. I have just motored up from the country. Our dear mutual friend was very anxious that I should see you. I am the bearer of a very important message. You permit that I rid myself of some of these things?"

He deposited an enormous ulster, his hat and other impedimenta, upon one of my chairs. The change in him was almost laughable. The somewhat pompous personage of the night before and previous nights existed no longer. His manner was disposed to be cringing.

"Are you alone?" I asked him.

"Absolutely alone," he assured me. "I come in peace, Major. See, I raise my hands. You can search me. I am unarmed."

I believed him, but I saw no reason to run any risks. I crossed the room and passed my hands over his pockets and body. There was no doubt that he was telling the truth. Without a weapon, he was as a child in my hands. I locked the door on the inside, in case he was only an advance guard of more troublesome visitors, and pointed to a chair.

"Necessity," I told him, "is teaching me caution. I can't imagine what you have to say to me that I should want to listen to or take any interest in, but since you are here, sit down and get along with it."

He took an easy-chair and looked meditatively at my whisky decanter. I pushed it towards him, with a glass and syphon, and he promptly helped himself.

"It is unfortunate," he remarked, "that I do not seem to have established myself as *persona grata* with you, Major."

The man's insolence was amazing. I stared at him almost doubting my senses.

"If there is one person," I rejoined, "who has done more than any other to earn my distrust and dislike, it is you. Even last night, during the great raid, you were helping your master."

"Naturally," he admitted, "I am, as you have doubtless opined, a Wolf. Life, however, is purely a matter of self-interest, with you as with myself, I should imagine. You happen to be on one side and I on the other, but we may still be honourable opponents."

I came very near losing my temper then.

"If you want my opinion of you," I said, "it is that you're a damned rascal. That's the first thing I have to say. The second is this. If you want anything from me, you'll open the way to negotiations by telling me what has become of Miss Essiter."

"Ah," he remonstrated, "that is not my affair."

I moved my chair a little closer to his.

"You were the person who planned her abduction," I reminded him. "I rather think that since you are here, and not at my invitation, it will become very necessary for you to tell me, unless you want to be choked where you sit."

He waved me away. I will do him the credit to acknowledge that he did not look the least afraid, although I was strongly inclined to try the primitive methods.

"It is true," he confessed, "that I was concerned in the abduction of Miss Essiter, but you see, Major, we both act under orders. I was acting under orders from my Chief, and you from yours. I had to obey. I am here and in your power. You can throttle me in an hour's time just as well as now. Supposing we let the matter drop for a moment. I suggest that you permit me to disclose the reason for my visit."

There was common sense in what the man said. He would be as much in my power at any time as he was at the present moment.

"Well, get on with it," I conceded.

"I am an ambassador," Mr. Leopold confided. "To tell you the truth, that is rather where I come in. I am often one of our friend's ambassadors when he has affairs on this side of the river. I have approached some very influential people on his account. I might call myself his West End Chief of Staff, just as Abrahams takes my place in the East End. You have never met Abrahams, I think?"

"I have not."

"An unpleasant fellow," Mr. Leopold declared, with a sorrowful little wag of the head. "He has his ways—his methods of persuasion. He obeys his orders. He was a market gardener, a prize-fighter afterwards. A little more physique, and he might have attained to great honours, they say. A slim, insignificant-looking fellow at first sight, but a rat, Major—more a rat than a wolf. A man with a narrow face—personally, I hate a man with a narrow face. I never trust them. Yet Abrahams is useful. He does his work well. He was one of the fortunate few who escaped last night."

"Did you come here to talk about Abrahams?" I demanded impatiently.

"I accept the rebuke," Mr. Leopold replied. "To tell you the truth, the warmth of your room, the excellence of your whisky and soda, tempted me to wander a little from the subject. I am the bearer of a message from our friend."

"From Joseph?"

Leopold shrugged his shoulders.

"Why mention names? He has tried half a dozen. The one that amuses him most is the pseudonym he adopted that night at Claridge's—'Mr. X.' You can understand that during the last month, he has not been too anxious for the name of Mr. Ruben Sams to appear in the newspapers. Shall we call him Mr. X.? He wants to see you."

"Not half as much as I want to see him," I rejoined. "What are you after—the five thousand pounds?"

Leopold shook his head.

"That is a sum which will never be claimed," he prophesied. "I am treating you with complete frankness, Major. I am an ambassador. Joseph wishes to see you."

"Then I wonder he isn't here," I observed. "He seems to find his way in and out of my rooms at will."

"He finds his way in and out of any one's rooms," Leopold declared calmly. "For the moment, however, it is his wish that you visit him. You have an unfortunate friendship with an official of that terrible organisation upon the Embankment, a kindergarten of its sort, without a doubt, but at the same time state-directed and a source of possible inconvenience to a person in our friend's position. Mr. X. felt no certainty that Inspector Bloor might not be spending the evening with you. Hence my visit. Mr. Bloor knows a little too much. He was a long time starting. He is moving rapidly enough now. We were walking a stretched wire last night, Major. Bloor made the mistake of his life when he refused to listen to you in the Grillroom of the Milan. I doubt whether he will ever have another chance."

"Why not?" I demanded.

"Because we are beaten," Leopold said calmly. "It is like the Chief, though, when the end comes, to see it. We have run our course."

"So you have come for that five thousand pounds, after all?"

My visitor looked at me as one might have looked at an ignorant child.

"The person who earns that five thousand pounds," he said, "will spend it in eternity or nowhere. When I say that we are beaten, I mean that we must disband. Mr. X. will leave this country when he chooses and how he chooses. He will live abroad when, where and how he pleases. Five thousand pounds, fifty thousand or half a million will never bring him inside any prison."

"Swank!" I exclaimed contemptuously. "Joseph's day is over, and he knows it."

Leopold patted his stomach gently.

"Answer me this question, Major," he begged. "Why are you occupying these rooms? Why did you begin combing the West End of London with Miss Essiter to keep you company?"

"To find Joseph," I told him, "and I damned well found him."

"And lost Miss Essiter. Never mind that, though. You admit that your object was to find Joseph. Can you lay your hands upon him at the present moment? You cannot. Very well, I am here to take you to him."

"Thank you," I replied. "I am waiting until I can go with a police sergeant and a warrant, and I don't fancy it will be long."

"On the contrary," Leopold assured me, "I think if you do not accept my offer, you and Joseph may never meet in this world."

"By-the-by," I reminded him, "there's a warrant out against Mr. Ruben Sams for swindling. That might possibly bring us together."

"Not a chance. Mr. Ruben Sams has made a brief descent upon the West End. He has done exceedingly well: he has done so well that he has—to put it bluntly—shut up shop. Mr. Ruben Sams has evaporated. There is no such person. From now on, believe me, warrant or no warrant, Mr. Ruben Sams does not exist upon the face of the earth."

I was beginning to get more interested. There might be some definite purpose, after all, in this strange visit.

"Let's get on with this," I suggested. "Put your proposals into plain words before I decide what to do."

"Mr. X. wants to see you," Leopold announced. "I am to offer you a safe conduct."

"And your guarantee?"

"Mr. X.'s word—and the young lady."

"Miss Essiter?" I exclaimed.

He inclined his head gently.

"Since that unfortunate evening at the Blue Skies,"

he said, "the young lady has remained under the protection of my Chief. If it is your wish to get into touch with her he will give you the opportunity. I am to take you to Joseph, and he will make certain propositions to you. If you fail to come to terms, there is no harm done. Your personal safety is guaranteed."

"By you?"

He tapped a cigarette upon the table and lit it.

"You have always misunderstood my Chief," he declared. "He has never been a bloodthirsty man. You have been an annoyance to him. You have been in his power half a dozen times. You still live. You are likely to live. When the tocsin sounds and the fight is on, he fights—he fights like no other man on earth. When the battle can be won by wits, he is one of the last persons to introduce the wrong note."

"What about that poor child Rachel?"

Leopold wagged his head mournfully.

"You speak of other things," he protested. "She was on her way to betray her master. For what other reason did she come to your flat? You know. She was obsessed with jealousy. She came to play the informer. Entirely through her, Joseph was compelled to leave his old headquarters in the East End and blow them up. She was punished according to the law which prevails amongst the Wolves, and I venture to add that it is a just law. If Joseph had said the word, you would have found a dagger in her heart."

I filled my cigarette case, placed it in my pocket, and rose to my feet.

"Well," I announced. "I'm ready. How do we go? Am I to be blindfolded and gagged?"

"Nothing of the sort," Leopold replied, shaking the cigarette ash from his trousers and also preparing for departure. "I have a car waiting in which we can drive to the house where Joseph is living without the least pretence at concealment. You may possibly recognise it. You will certainly be able to find it again without difficulty. All that is demanded of you is that if you should fail to come to terms with my Chief, for twelve hours after your return here you keep silent."

"Just my word?" I asked incredulously.

"Just your word. It is one of Joseph's great traits in life that he has the courage to trust. He loathes melodrama. One might see over the top of a handkerchief; an odour, a keen sense of locality, any trifle might help you to triumph against the ordinary means of drugs or blindfolding. He scorns the obvious tricks. If it were daylight, I should take you just the same. You are going to be brought face to face with the man for whom you have searched night and day, and you will leave him when your conversation is finished as though you were an ordinary caller, but if by any chance it should occur to you to break your parole you would be lying upon your back before to-morrow night, and the stars might wink down at you, but you would not wink back. No threat, you understand," he went on, "no threat at all. It just happens. It has happened to one or two; if my Chief's judgment is right, it won't happen to you. There are men who keep their word as naturally as they breathe. Joseph thinks you are one. If so, you are safe. If he is making a mistake, he may suffer for it, but so most surely will you."

I put on my hat and coat, assisted my guest into his, and descended to the street. An ordinary limousine car, with a chauffeur in plain livery, was waiting. We drove off together, and in unbroken silence I took note of our passage through the familiar thoroughfares.

CHAPTER XXXIX

The streets were emptying except for the night traffic, as we turned up Baker Street, past Grove Road and Lord's Cricket Ground, through Hampstead, Golder's Green, and Finchley, and increased our speed as we came to the open country beyond. When we turned off the main road, about halfway to Hatfield, I asked Leopold a question.

"Much farther?"

"We are almost there," was the well-satisfied response. "You can see the lights of the house amongst the trees."

We turned in through broad gates guarded by twin lodges, drove for a mile along a well-kept, curving avenue, and crossed a park studded with magnificent trees. Always in front of us, the lights were twinkling from a large Georgian mansion which my companion pointed out to me as our destination.

"You are paying a visit," he confided, "to Sir Bruce Pettefar."

"The devil!" I exclaimed. "Is Joseph going in for titles?"

"All that you need to have in your mind for the moment is that you are paying a visit to Sir Bruce Pettefar," Mr. Leopold replied coldly. "We have finished, if you please, with all references to Joseph, Ruben Sams, and such matters. Sir Bruce is an invalid who has lived here for many years. He still has affairs which need attention, however, and I have recently become his secretary."

A very handsome and well-kept estate, so far as one could judge in the faint moonlight. A butler admitted us and welcomed Leopold as though he were one of the household.

"You will excuse the other servants having gone to bed, sir," he begged. "Sir Bruce is a little restless to-night. You will find him in his sitting-room. He told me to take you and the other gentleman to him directly you arrived."

We crossed a large, old-fashioned hall, and the butler knocked upon the door of one of the front rooms. A languid voice bade us enter.

"The gentleman you were expecting, Sir Bruce," he announced, and left us.

So the supreme moment had arrived at last, and I must confess that I entered that room with all the nervous excitement of a schoolboy. I knew from Martin Hews and Bloor, and also from my own observation, of this man's amazing skill in making up and in counterfeiting personalities, but I still for a moment thought that I was confronted by a stranger when I glanced towards the tall man in a well-cut but rather shabby dinner suit, who stood with his back towards a roaring fire, a cigarette in his mouth. His black hair, no longer sprinkled with grey, was brushed smoothly from his brow. His cheeks were hollow to emaciation. A kindly critic would have called his nose aquiline, whereas it was in reality almost hooked. He had a high forehead and the mouth and jaw of a strong character. It was actually not until he smiled that I was able to trace the slightest resemblance to the man whom I had fashioned in my thoughts.

"Well, Major," he greeted me. "Welcome! I thought I could count on you to take the risk. We meet for the first time under our proper personalities. Not a touch of make-up, not a flick of the paintbrush, not a layer of wax, not a wad of stuffing under my clothes. Here I am for what I am—Joseph."

"I didn't come to see you," I told him bluntly. "You are no use to me under my parole, although," I added, looking at him closely, "I am very glad to have seen you as you really are. I shall not forget."

He smiled.

"It will be of very little service to you," he assured me. "If the circumstances were propitious, I should be very glad to have a small wager with you. Within a few hours of your leaving here, I would pass you in the street or sit in the same restaurant with you, or even talk to you, and you would not recognise me. We all have our gifts, you know," he added, with a queer touch of vanity. "I must admit that you are an exceedingly useful man in a scrap. You keep your head better fighting than you do in the amenities of life. I am the greatest master of disguise who ever breathed, either in the criminal world or upon the stage."

I was fuming with impatience.

"I didn't come down here to discuss your accomplishments," I reminded him. "I wish to see Miss Essiter."

"That," he admitted, "is part of the bargain, but you can imagine that I did not take the trouble to send for you simply to afford you an interview with the young lady. I have business with you myself."

"Is Miss Essiter here?" I demanded.

"She is. You see, I do not attempt to deceive you. She has been with me for some time, the companion of those weary hours which I have to spend in my establishment here to keep up this rather troublesome identity—the identity of Sir Bruce Pettefar. Will you be content with my assurance that you will see her before you leave this place?"

"She will leave it with me," I declared.

Joseph sighed gently.

"This British truculence!" he murmured gently. "Do please get this into your head. This is not an encounter; it is a meeting. I doubt whether there is a firearm in the place except a shotgun or two a long way from here. I am Bruce Pettefar, an invalid, who made his money in South Africa and who has owned this property for over eleven years. Compose yourself, and pray do not remain standing."

I sank into an easy-chair. It was curious that, unscrupulous though I knew Joseph to be, and in desperate straits at this particular time, I never dreamed of disbelieving him. The situation was making its appeal also to my not over-acute sense of humour. This was the very pleasant library of an English country gentleman, in which I took my ease. Leopold was perhaps a little out of the picture. Joseph, however, notwithstanding his slightly Jewish type of features, might well have been the host of such an establishment.

"You have courage, Joseph," I acknowledged. "There is a reward of five thousand pounds for your apprehension, and half Scotland Yard, including my friend Bloor, are searching for you."

"Ah, no," he pointed out, "they are searching for Mr. Ruben Sams. I should imagine," he went on, a whimsical smile parting his lips, "that there are a great many people, including a duke, a lord, and various Members of Parliament, who are very anxious to find Mr. Ruben Sams. It was a cleverly worked-out affair, that. I happened to know that Ruben Sams was detained in Buenos Ayres—an affair not to be mentioned in the newspapers, or the shares of a certain company might have gone down. To transform myself into Mr. Ruben Sams, arrived in England according to schedule, wasn't the easiest thing in the world, but I had the good fortune to collect a little

of that money which, in due course, if my noble clients
had not been so impatient, almost greedy, I may say,
would have been paid to the credit of the genuine Argentine millionaire."

"So even Mr. Ruben Sams," I remarked, "made the
game pay?"

"To the tune of between four and five hundred thousand
pounds," Joseph confided. "A useful sum of money, and
very welcome. I was never meant to be a poor man,
Major. I never shall be. I may die at any moment, but
whether I die within the next half-hour, with a smashing
of windows and a spitting of automatics, whether I die
then or in twenty years' time—which, between ourselves,
I rather fancy to be my allotted period—I shall die a
rich man."

"And, in the meantime," I asked, "what is it you want
with me?"

"One thing, and one thing only. I want one half hour's
interview with Martin Hews."

I stared at him, indifferently comprehending.

"What have I to do with that?"

"Everything. Martin Hews has had other mercenaries,
secretaries, whatever you like to call them. He has trusted
none of them. I believe that he trusts you. You have his
ear. Before I disintegrate—for that is what it really
comes to—I wish for half an hour's conversation with the
man who has been my greatest enemy."

"For what purpose?" I enquired.

He made me no answer for several moments. He abandoned his place upon the hearthrug, strolled over to the
sideboard, so thoroughly British with its arrangement of
drinks, helped himself to some whisky with a little splash
from the syphon, lit a cigarette, and threw himself into
as easy-chair quite close to mine.

"I do not offer you refreshments of any sort, my

enemy," he explained, "because I know that you still have that crude and melodramatic idea that poison may lurk in the glass, or drugs in the cigarette."

"That little affair at the Blue Skies—"

"Ah, that of course still rankles. Your experience there has naturally made you over-cautious, but believe me, that was a scientific induction into the spirit of whisky of an anaesthetic for which the hospitals will give me a fortune when I am prepared to part with it. There-fore—"

"I would rather like a whisky and soda," I inter-rupted.

"Leopold, can I trouble you?"

With a little wave of the hand, my host turned towards his Chief of Staff. Leopold mixed me a whisky and soda, and another for himself.

"Well, I was at this point in my discourse," Joseph continued. "For sixteen years, Martin Hews and I have been bitter enemies. The first cause of our quarrel lies behind the curtain. Since then we have come into the open. We have declared ourselves. We have both been—shall I say?—in the same line of business. We have ransacked the world for its treasures and sought to acquire them. I claim for myself—I shall always claim it, if justifica-tion for my life is needed—that we followed the example of those others of our more noted predecessors—Pizzaro of Italy, Cortez of Spain, Drake of England; but there was this difference between Martin Hews and myself: whatever I stole, if you fancy the word, came back again into the markets of the world. What Martin Hews grabbed was for his own greedy longings, his own gloating eyes and his alone—his own selfish joy. Shall I ask you to choose between us? I fought like those others, my pred-ecessors, for what I could win from foreigners and strangers, from the gluttons of trade, from the sneaking pilers-up of millions. I risked my life many a time, my liberty all the time, the chance of being accounted a common thief from beginning to end. And what did Martin Hews risk? Nothing. He set no bold face towards his enemies. He boarded no ship, swung no cutlass. He sat in his chair, with all the devilish devices of science to protect him close at hand. Grudgingly, with stingy fingers, he paid a gang of robbers to fight against mine, to steal where mine would have stolen, to acquire if possible by cunning what my Wolves would have torn with their teeth. Then there came—it was inevitable—Donkin's downfall. There is no one left for us to fight against. My men are fat with gain. I myself am weary. I have credits at the banks of every capital in the world. I have money enough to satisfy a Monte Cristo. I have quitted the field. Martin Hews is welcome to everything else in the world he has the courage to strike for. All that I ask before I leave the whole field open for him is one half-hour's plain and simple speech alone with him. What of that, Major Owston?"

So this was Joseph! Here was the real man, speaking naturally, his cheeks washed of the mummer's adjuncts— the man himself. I looked at him, long and curiously. Somehow or other, I began to understand the extraordinary ascendancy he had gained over his followers. Once in my early military days in one of our textbooks, I had come across an essay on greatness in man, a study of the qualities which make for successful leadership. I could conceive of those qualities in the man who lounged there a few feet away from me, waiting for my answer.

"But where do I come in as regards this interview?" I persisted. "I have been in Martin Hews' employ only a few weeks. I have no influence over him. Why not ask for your interview and have done with it?"

"Because," was the patient reply, "I perhaps know
Martin Hews better than you do. You have been with him,
as you say, only a few weeks, but you are the only man
in life he trusts. Martin Hews, believe me, is living now in
a state of terror. Thanks to you, he has attained his
ambition. With the passing of the one-eyed Buddha into
his possession, he has the greatest collection of treasures
brought together by one man in the world, and he sits
there, shivering and afraid. He knows very well that many
of those treasures have been acquired by bloodshed. Many
of them, cunning as the serpent though he has been, have
passed into his hands illegally. Very few of them indeed
have been bought in the open market. By degrees, year
after year, he has estranged the sympathies of every one
who might have helped him. He is alone now, and he sees
the writing on the wall."

"All this may be true," I conceded, a little impatiently,
"but Martin Hews never pretended to be a philanthropist
any more than you have done. I suppose I am stupid, but
frankly I don't see what you're getting at. Tell me in
plain words what it is you want from me? Do you want
me to go to Martin Hews and persuade him to see you?
He won't do it. I can assure you of that now. I don't
know why, but he is more terrified of you than of any
human being in the world. I should be just as likely to
persuade him to make me a present of the one-eyed
Buddha as to let you willingly cross the threshold."

"There might be a consideration," Joseph murmured,
so softly that his voice scarcely reached me. "You forget
that his niece is here."

For a moment I saw red. I felt all the horror of en-
forced inaction. My word was passed for the period of my
visit and for twelve hours afterwards. Joseph was safe.
For the first time I began to regret that I had come.

"You want me," I said, "to propose to Martin Hews

that he see you for half an hour, in return for which you promise to hand over his niece."

"Precisely."

"As against that," I reflected, "in twelve hours after I leave this place, my parole will be up. There is nothing whatever to prevent my sitting outside your gates until that time and taking Miss Essiter myself."

"Nothing whatever," Joseph assented, with a faint smile, "but when the twelve hours is up both our hands will be free."

I brooded over this for a minute. Perhaps it was the thought of the delay which made me discard my idea.

"You say that Miss Essiter is here under this roof?" I challenged him.

"Naturally," he drawled. "I do not seek for companions to keep them in another part of the world."

I sprang to my feet. Joseph remained still stretched in his chair. I think that it was part of his scheme to keep me in as disturbed a frame of mind as possible.

"Let me remind you," he begged, "that the element of melodrama in our struggle has finished. You have not been trapped into any secret house of dangers. I have told you before that Miss Essiter is here. If you wish for her presence, there is no need to play the Mexican cowboy, or the Sherlock Holmes sleuthhound."

"Very well, then," I decided, "I wish for her presence now. I will give you my answer when I have seen her."

Joseph shrugged his shoulders.

"Leopold," he begged, "perhaps you wouldn't mind ringing the bell."

CHAPTER XL

It all came about so naturally that for the first few seconds I could scarcely believe in its reality. A brief message confided to the butler, and, a moment or so later, Beatrice crossed the threshold and came a little hesitatingly into the room. She showed no signs of ill health or ill treatment, only as her eyes met mine a sudden flame crept into them.

"My dear Beatrice," Joseph announced, rising with lazy courtesy to his feet, "I conceive that it has become my duty to remove a small misunderstanding. You recognise our friend, Major Owston?"

She and I were no longer lay figures in the drama of our meeting. Joseph's careless use of her Christian name had maddened me, and Beatrice had certainly ceased to be the indifferent châtelaine of Breezeley Mansion. I could see her bosom rising and falling underneath her gown. She looked at me with an expression which left me dumbfounded. Some of it might have been due to the unexpectedness of my coming, but it seemed to me that there was also anger in her eyes.

"Yes," she assented coldly, "I recognise Major Owston. What is he doing here?"

"He has been engaged for some time," Joseph explained, "in a quixotic search for you."

"He might have spared himself the trouble," she laughed, with a very distinct undernote of scorn in her tone.

Joseph held out his hands in protest.

"My dear Beatrice," he expostulated, "hear my confession. Major Owston did not desert you on that memorable night at the Blue Skies. He was in my way, and I removed him."

She looked from one to the other of us. Leopold wheeled up a chair, but for the moment she ignored it.

"You removed him?"

"Precisely," he continued smoothly. "You were told, I think, that he joined some friends in a carouse. You read the report of the proceedings in the police court next morning. All wrong, my dear Beatrice. All, believe me, part of one of those little schemes to which I sometimes have to resort, to gain my ends. The idea of that angers you, perhaps, but see how ready I am to put things right when it is possible. Major Owston has devoted all his time since that unfortunate affair to hunting us down; he has neglected all his other duties, he has run greater risks than he knows of. He joined in no carouse that night. His comparative silence in the police court was a very clever move on his part which enabled him, I am sorry to say, to deceive and take advantage of our friend Leopold. Against you, he is blameless. He touched no drink in the club. He was the victim of one of the most wonderful scientific inventions of the day, which, had I chosen to walk the ordinary ways of life, might perhaps have made me famous."

She looked across at me, and I read in her changing expression the turmoil into which Joseph's words had thrown her.

"Is this true?" she asked me passionately.

"It is true that I am blameless except that I ought to have known better than to have accepted Leopold's invitation at all," I answered, looking her in the eyes. "I went into the secretary's office merely to sign the book. The world came to an end with me there in a second. I woke in a police cell. They engineered everything that happened between."

The rush of relief to my heart as I watched her was one of the happiest sensations of my life. I saw something more human shining out of her eyes, something which seemed to bring her nearer to me than ever before.

"But I am ashamed," she acknowledged.

I raised her fingers to my lips. I refused to allow it place, but strive how I would, notwithstanding the joy of this meeting, something of that haunting and terrible fear still lingered in my heart. I had not the courage to put it into words, and she did nothing to help me. Our moment had passed, and I felt that I had failed to take full advantage of it.

"My dear Beatrice," Joseph continued, "I want you to use your influence with Major Owston. I have already told you that Joseph, hand in hand with Mr. Ruben Sams, is on the point of disappearing forever. Before I go, I want one half-hour with your uncle."

She shook her head.

"He would never see you, and besides—"

"Besides what?"

"I don't think it would be good for either of you. You would quarrel."

"On my part, there would be no quarrel, I can assure you," Joseph declared. "There are a few words long overdue between us. They should be spoken. I have come to the conclusion that the only person who has any influence over your uncle is Major Owston. Why should he not persuade him to see me?"

Beatrice shook her head.

"My uncle will never consent to see you," she declared with conviction.

"Why not?"

"He is far too frightened of you, for one thing. His

nerve has been giving way for years. I do not believe that there is any person breathing who could induce my uncle to let you inside the house."

For a single moment I fancied that I saw something of the old dangerous light flash in Joseph's eyes. His manner, however, remained unchanged. He shrugged his shoulders.

"Then, since you will not back me up here, Beatrice," he said, "I will ask you to spare us another ten minutes whilst I finish my business with Major Owston. Where shall we find you?"

"I shall be in the billiard room," she said.

I never could understand why every one obeyed Joseph without hesitation. Beatrice rose to her feet, and, rather avoiding than seeking my eyes, she left the room. The disturbing question remained unasked. That terrible uncertainty still existed. Joseph came back to his place. He stood looking at me grimly and doubtfully.

"The world is no place," he said, his eyes watching my face all the time, "the world is no place nowadays for poor men."

"Isn't it? I seem to have rubbed along in it somehow."

"Uncomfortably, my dear enemy. You were in the direst straits when Martin Hews took you into his employ."

"Quite true," I admitted, "but I had kept something worth having."

"Melodrama again," Joseph sighed. "A soldier of honour! You're warning me off, Owston."

"I'm hoping you're not going to offer me a bribe," I admitted. "It's hard enough as it is to remember my parole."

"I was thinking about it," he acknowledged. "If money does not tempt you, something else might. What about Beatrice?"

Something in his manner of speech, his icy insolence, maddened me. Once more the passion blazed up in my heart, and at that moment, although my word of honour was involved, Joseph was in danger of his life.

"What is she to you that you should dare to dispose of her?" I demanded. "Answer me. I insist upon it. She has been with you alone for ten days."

Again he smiled, but this time there was a measure of contempt in his gesture.

"You poor simpleton!" he scoffed. "I could see what you were thinking; so could she. Beatrice is my sister. Haven't you yet discovered that?"

I am not ashamed to confess that for a few moments the relief almost overwhelmed me. Joseph patted me on the shoulder in unexpectedly human fashion. He himself went to the sideboard and refilled my glass.

"You don't know much about Beatrice," he observed, "or you would realise that you would never have found her alive under the conditions you were thinking of. You had better go and make your peace with her. I can see you're no use to me."

I rose to my feet, too dazed for words. For once Joseph was certainly top dog.

"One moment more, and I shall be done with you," he concluded. "Haven't you realised during the last few weeks, when you were making yourself rather more than troublesome to me, that I could have disposed of you a dozen times? I gave you your chance in Down Street. I should have killed you if you had been with Rachel, simply because you would not have been the sort of man I wanted for Beatrice, but, since then, have you never asked yourself why I did not get rid of you as I have the others? I'll tell you, Owston. Beatrice has had the hell of a life with that satanic old beast, and it is time some one took her away from it. Go and make your peace, if you can. Leopold will show you the way."

Leopold piloted me across the hall.

"You needn't hurry," he whispered in my ear, as he indicated the door. "He won't turn in until three or four o'clock in the morning, and he and I have a great deal to talk about. I'll take you back to town in my car—let you know as soon as I'm ready."

I was too confused to answer him. It seemed to me that with all my soul I was trying to cleanse my brain of the faintest vestige of those thoughts which had been torturing me. I turned the handle of the door, entered, and closed it behind me. Beatrice was seated in an easy-chair by the fire. She looked up startled at my coming. I fancied that she had been crying.

"Beatrice, I am the clumsiest beast!" I exclaimed, bending over her.

The loose black sleeves of her gown fell back as her arm were stretched out towards me, soft and white. Her eyes told me that I was forgiven.

"You are," she admitted, "but you are rather a dear!"

We talked until the fire was nearly burnt out, and then we sat, silent for a time. Finally Beatrice, with a half-scared little laugh, sat up in her chair.

"Henry!" she exclaimed. "Whatever time do you suppose it is? You don't think Mr. Leopold's forgotten all about us, do you?"

I glanced at my watch and was horrified. It was past two o'clock. I opened the door and looked out. The whole place was in darkness.

"It seems to me as though every one had gone to bed," I told Beatrice.

"Come along," she said. "We'll find them."

She took my arm. We visited the library, a smaller

room called the office, the dining room. Not a soul anywhere! Then I opened the front door and looked out. There was no car there.

"Mr. Leopold must have gone away and forgotten you!" Beatrice exclaimed. "I'll have to get one of the servants up. You must sleep here."

But even in the midst of my happiness, a sinister thought crept into my mind. It was not like Joseph to abandon anything he had set his mind upon.

"Beatrice," I ventured fearfully, "you don't suppose he's gone to Breezeley?"

She looked at me, herself terrified for a moment. Then she rang the front-door bell. Its echo resounded through the house. Very soon lights flashed out, and the butler made his appearance, apologising for his *déshabille*.

"Mr. Leopold was to have taken Major Owston back to London with him," Beatrice explained. "I am afraid he must have forgotten all about it."

"I am quite sure he did, miss," the man replied. "Mr. Leopold left with Sir Bruce soon after eleven o'clock."

We looked at one another, and the same fear was reflected in both our faces.

"Harding, is there another car in the garage?" Beatrice asked.

The man shook his head.

"There's nothing at all, as it happens, miss. The Daimler went to London for repairs last night. Sir Bruce took the Rolls himself."

"How does one get away from here?" I enquired. "How far is the railway station, or any place where one can hire a car?"

The man looked disturbed.

"You're not thinking of going away to-night, sir?"

"I must," I insisted.

He was genuinely perplexed.

"The railway station's two and a half miles away, sir," he confided, "and I never heard of any night trains. The only thing I can think of is for you to walk on to the main road and try to get a lift to Finchley. One of the garages might be open there."

"Can't we telephone?" Beatrice suggested, with a sudden inspiration.

"Most unfortunate, miss," the man regretted. "Sir Bruce was trying to telephone himself. It is because he failed to get through that he thought it best to go up to town. We can get no reply from the exchange at all. The instrument is evidently out of order."

Beatrice's mind was swiftly made up.

"Wait for me five minutes," she begged. "I sha'n't be longer. We'll do as Harding suggests—get on to the main road."

"But you're not thinking of leaving, miss, at this hour?" the man protested. "Sir Bruce will be terribly upset. I'll call one of the men. There are some bicycles in the shed, and I dare say I can do something."

Beatrice was already halfway up the stairs. It was obvious that Harding was perfectly honest.

"I think we'd better go ourselves," I explained. "Miss Essiter and I have cause for some uneasiness, and the sooner we're in town the better."

"I'm very sorry, sir. I wish there was something I could do. I'll get a man started off in a quarter of an hour."

I shook my head.

"I don't think it would help," I said.

Beatrice was downstairs in a short walking skirt and thick shoes, even before the time she had said, and we started off on our wild pilgrimage. The walk in the darkness through the park was all the time difficult. We stumbled often against the bent white hoops which protected the side of the road, splashed into puddles, and when we finally reached the gate, very nearly crashed into it. In the lane, the going was easier, and in less than ten minutes after we had reached the main road, an empty van on its way back to London picked us up. We descended at the first garage at Finchley, knocked up the proprietor, and hired a good but slow Rénault car and an unwilling driver. I bribed him into good humour, and we started off on our strange journey. The lights were still lit, all the way to London, but dawn broke as we passed through the City. The shops were beginning to open in the suburbs, and by the time we reached the Tilbury Road, the country began to disclose itself in a grey, streaky light. As we neared our destination, my companion's clasp upon my arm tightened.

"Henry," she whispered, "I am afraid."

"We are doing all that we can, dear," I reminded her. "I was with your uncle this morning. It was he who sent me back to town. He showed me all his devices for self-protection, and it seemed to me that he was, as he said, impregnable. I don't think that even Joseph would be able to get inside the house."

"He could," she confided uneasily. "There is a way. Only we three know of it, though."

"Who is the third?" I asked quietly.

"Minchin."

My heart sank.

"I don't trust Minchin," I muttered.

"I shouldn't," she agreed, "but what could tempt him to play the traitor? He gets five hundred a year and five hundred pounds bonus every year that my uncle is alive and well. Not a penny in his will. Besides, remember he has been with him eleven years, and he has never done anything in the least suspicious, although he has had plenty of opportunities."

I tried to console myself with that, and we relapsed into

a brief silence. Soon we passed the station, and then, for the last time in my life, as sinister and forbidding as ever in the chill morning, the mists rising from the swamp, and the bank of thick fog rolling up from the river, I looked upon the house of my detestation.

CHAPTER XLI

As we drew nearer, our apprehension increased. The whole front of the house seemed to be in darkness except for Martin Hews' library. From every window there the lights were ablaze—a curious, ghastly illumination against the sickly daylight and the blackness of the rest of the house. I stared at it with fascinated eyes. It was Beatrice who first saw the more sinister portent. She gripped my arm suddenly.

"The car!" she exclaimed. "There, in the shadow of the house. Joseph is here!"

The same foreboding was torturing us both, but we avoided putting it into words.

"You can get into the house?" I asked.

She nodded.

"Through the servants' quarters," she confided. "Minchin and I have keys; no one else."

She led me round to the back of the building and paused for several moments before a heavy oak door. Eventually she opened it, and we passed into a stone passage. Turning and twisting, we reached the staircase and climbed to the third storey. Here, a door of sheet-iron led into the front part of the house. Beatrice opened it with her key, after several efforts, and we were in one of the carpeted corridors. She turned the handle of a door at the end and passed swiftly across a very beautiful bedroom towards another door, through the hinges of which came a faint chink of light. We were within a few feet of it when we both stopped short. She gripped my arm and looked at me in horror. It sounded as though some animal in pain was sobbing—little fitful, tremulous cries, yet each one of them linked with a sob.

"I can't stand this," I cried. "Come!"

We heard a cracking sound and a gibing voice—Joseph's—a hoarse laugh, and again the cry. I pushed open the door, and just as though my feet had been rooted to the ground by one of Martin Hews' electric appliances, so I stood there, absolutely without power of movement. It was a sight so extraordinary that the utter loathsomeness of it only really gripped me afterwards. All the furniture had been pushed away between the desk and the door. Joseph, with a long whip in his hand, stood in the middle of an open space, and hobbling round in a circle was an object which for the first second or two I scarcely recognised. Then it all came to me. I saw and I understood. Martin Hews, his wig torn off, as bald as man could be, his clothes disarranged, was lumbering round in grotesque little jumps, whilst Joseph cracked his whip. It was his body, just as we had always seen it, but beneath were the most terrible, the most distorted, strange little legs, about a foot and a half in length, with tiny feet, upon which were blue silk socks about the size of a child's gloves, suspenders and blue silk underclothes scarcely more than six inches long. Realisation came with a sickening wave of horror: it was Martin Hews' secret, entombed by his vanity. He was a monstrosity. His legs were there, dwarfed, more hideous than anything ever displayed by the most abnormal of freaks in a travelling show. Whilst we hesitated upon the threshold, he staggered as though giddy and fell over. He lay upon the floor, and Joseph mocked him.

"Up, my brave little man!" he shouted. "Up, and round the course! Show us how you work your little ninepins. Up you get!"

Crack went the whip again. Martin Hews, his body

writing in pain, made a pitiful effort to struggle to his feet.

"Minchin!" he sobbed out.

Then I saw for the first time that Minchin was also there, lounging in an easy-chair, smoking a pipe—an interested and applauding spectator. He put his head back and laughed.

"Don't cut it too short, Guv'nor," he begged. "Twice more round, eh? Twice—"

He broke off. Turning slowly round, he saw us. Suddenly the numbness left my limbs. I felt like a wild animal, and I dare say I behaved like one. I reached Minchin first. I picked him bodily up, flung him into a corner of the room, and then I went for Joseph. He saw me coming, flicked at me with his whip, a cruel gash which I never felt. I saw his eyes harden, his mouth set. I knew that this moment had been in our lives from the first. If he was armed, he made no effort to draw. He came towards me, and we crashed into one another, well away from the poor sobbing little object upon the floor. It was a fight of a sort, I suppose. I remember nothing of it—nothing until I felt Beatrice's arms around my neck, pulling at me until my hands upon his throat slackened.

"Henry!" she cried. "You've killed him!"

Joseph opened his eyes. He raised himself with the help of his hand.

"Not he," he muttered, with the ugly ghost of his old smile. "I give in, though, Beatrice. Your man is the better —muscularly."

He staggered to his feet and sat on a chair. He must have been in terrible pain, but not even the vestige of a groan escaped him. I looked around. Martin Hews was in his little carriage—I learned afterwards that Beatrice had placed him there—a ghastly, horrible sight still, but with a rug wrapped over him tightly. Minchin had crept stealthily away. Joseph leaned forward.

"That man," he said, pointing to Martin Hews, "has escaped death at my hands because death means no suffering. He will never forget this afternoon. Your mistake, Owston, is in thinking of him as a human being. He is the devil incarnate. He starved my mother to death. He would have starved us, had he not thought we might be useful to him. I came from America to kill him. I stayed to fight him in every way. I prayed that he might not die before I had hurt him the only way he could be hurt—through his vanity, the miserable little toad!"

Martin Hews, in his chair, was gibbering. I could not understand a word he said, but apparently Beatrice did, for she searched the room and brought back his wig. He placed it upon his head, covering himself up a little more closely. Even then he was a creature one would not willingly look at.

"Give me some wine or brandy," Joseph demanded, looking up abruptly from his place. "I have the brains, Owston, and I fancy that I have some skill in fighting, but here I must give you best. You have hurt me badly."

I went to the secret cupboard, poured him out some brandy, and gave it to him. Martin Hews made strange noises. I took him some too. He drank it, and as he drank, he seemed to become a little more his natural self.

"Some more," he insisted, holding out his glass.

He drained his second portion to the last drop, drew a deep sigh, and settled himself more comfortably in his chair. Waving us out of the way, he swung round and paused at his desk. He looked across at us all, and I saw that the brandy had brought him but a passing relief. His head hung down. I expected at every moment to see him fall over from his chair. Nevertheless, he busied himself for some moments, apparently, with some trifling task at his desk, searched for and found a cigarette, lit it, and slipped back amongst his cushions.

"Joseph," he said, "I will return good for evil. I will give you the chance of your lifetime. I will show you something, the envy for which will be a blight upon your life, if you manage to escape the hangman for another year or two. I will show you your failures and my successes. Come!"

We all followed the chair. He turned and waved us back.

"Never in my life have I taken more than one person at a time into my tabernacle," he said. "We go alone, and remember that what I show you, I show you for your misery."

Joseph rose a little languidly to his feet. It seemed to me that he was still dazed.

"You shall see the one-eyed Buddha," Martin Hews went on, "which lay in the vaults of the Milan Hotel when it was supposed to have gone up in smoke. You shall see the Corregio Donkin took from your people. You shall see the bronze which cost two of your men their lives, but it came to me. You shall see the tapestries which Isaacs found whilst your men were sharpening their tools. No, not you," he added, motioning us away. "You have another task. Go back the way you came and ring the bell outside the third door on the left in the courtyard, for to-night is over. I want to know where those others were lurking when Minchin opened the doors. Go!"

His appearance was still terrible, and I hesitated. Beatrice, however drew me away.

"You must obey," she whispered. "It is the only chance with him when he is like this." . . .

From the threshold I watched them. Martin Hews was some minutes producing his keys, but eventually the great door swung open. Just before the two disappeared into the shadows, Martin Hews turned around in his chair and looked at us. Sometimes I have fancied to my last day that look will haunt me. I am convinced that he was trying to send me a message. His lips were parted in something which, if it was not a smile, was at least a travesty of it. It was the wide-open grin of a satanic gargoyle, a leering promise of evil, a foul gesture which the pencil could never reproduce or the mind of man recall. Then he disappeared, and we could see no more—only the carriage, gliding on in ghostlike fashion, and Joseph staggering by its side, supporting himself more than once by clutching at the wall. I heard the click of the other door, and I heard it close. Then we descended and moved across the courtyard in the grey morning light. We passed the first door, and the second—and there was no third. We looked at each other.

"What did your uncle mean?" I demanded.

"I cannot imagine," she answered.

But even at that moment we knew. . . .

The ground beneath our feet shook and rocked. There was first of all a hissing sound, and then the most tremendous explosion I have ever heard. The walls of the north wing, which enclosed the gallery, seemed suddenly to split and crumble and fall outwards. Red flames—great hungry tongues of them—curled and leaped towards the skies. Clouds of smoke shot up and drifted away, darkening the whole of the countryside. The crash of further explosions followed, the sound of falling masonry in every direction. It was my fancy, of course, but in the first moment's silence that ensued after that awful pandemonium, I fancied that I heard a shrill, mocking laugh; I fancied that I could see that strange travesty of a human being, as the time came, turning round in his chair, leering at his companion, oblivious of death for himself, joyful only if he could revel in one spasm of the other's agony. It was fancy, of course, but I could have sworn I heard the laugh ringing out from the centre of that burning chaos. We drew farther away, for the flames were spreading, and the heat was intolerable. The men who came running out from the house and tower could do nothing but gape upwards in amazement. Firemen and police were soon swarming over the place in helpless inactivity. I led Beatrice towards the car. . . .

At the bend in the road before the station, I looked back for the last time. A fresh column of smoke was curling up to the sky. There was the thunder of masonry as another of the jagged walls crashed to the ground. The sky above was lurid, the roar of the flames seemed to scorch our cheeks, even at this distance. I pointed behind. There was something ruthless in this terrible devastation. Beatrice was clinging to me wildly, and my own voice shook.

"It is finished," I told her. "The child has played with his toys for the last time."

There was a great deal of rough justice about Rachel's commentaries when we went to see her at the hospital a few days later. She shuddered with excitement when we told her of Joseph limping along by the side of the carriage, disappearing down the corridor into the chamber of death.

"I don't know that I'm sorry for either of them, though," she decided. "Martin Hews—well, he never ought to have been allowed to grow up—a poor creature like that, eaten up with vanity, all brain and no heart, and getting worse every year. Joseph—well, he was my man once. He was wicked," she went on. "He had a heart of flint. I curse him night and day for what he did to me. He was as cruel as they make 'em, and yet there was always something inside him, pulling the other way.